DRAGONS LUCK

ROBERT ASPRIN

ACE BOOKS, NEW YORK

THE BERKLEY PUBLISHING GROUP
Published by the Penguin Group
Penguin Group (USA) LLC
375 Hudson Street, New York, New York 10014

USA • Canada • UK • Ireland • Australia • New Zealand • India • South Africa • China

penguin.com

A Penguin Random House Company

DRAGONS LUCK

An Ace Book / published by arrangement with Bill Fawcett & Associates

Ace Books are published by The Berkley Publishing Group.
ACE and the "A" design are trademarks of Penguin Group (USA) LLC.

For information, address: The Berkley Publishing Group,
a division of Penguin Group (USA) LLC,
375 Hudson Street, New York, New York 10014.

ISBN: 978-0-425-27252-7

PUBLISHING HISTORY
Ace trade paperback edition / April 2009
Ace mass-market edition / May 2014

PRINTED IN THE UNITED STATES OF AMERICA

10 9 8 7 6 5 4 3 2 1

Cover art by Eric Fortune.
Interior text design by Kristin del Rosario.

DRAGONS LUCK

"Joyous fantasy with continuous action and a creative cast of characters."
—*SFRevu*

"[The] paranormal support cast is three-dimensional . . . The whodunit is [a] fun sort of a paranormal version of Fritz Lang's *M*."
—*Genre Go Round Reviews*

DRAGONS WILD

"*Dragons Wild* is a lot more straightforward urban fantasy, complete with the semi-standard trappings of a secret race of supernatural beings dwelling amongst, and influencing, normal people. But Asprin pulls it off with skill and style, delivering a thoroughly satisfying, energetic story that begs for continuation. In fact, it's actually one of the best things I've ever read from him in terms of entertainment and atmospheric value . . . Is it fun? Oh yes."
—*The Green Man Review*

"Asprin tackles a new kind of comic fantasy, a little more serious and hard-boiled than previous books. Featuring a likable rake and plenty of action and quirky humor, this series opener belongs in most adult and YA fantasy collections."
—*Library Journal*

"Colorful."
—*Publishers Weekly*

"This is the start of what looks like will be a great urban fantasy series that is funky, funny, and fun . . . Robert Asprin has begun another fine myth with his first entry in his wild dragon culture."
—*Midwest Book Review*

"Delightful."
—*Monsters and Critics*

continued . . .

DRAGONS DEAL

by Robert Asprin and Jody Lynn Nye

The MYTH Series

by Robert Asprin

ANOTHER FINE MYTH
MYTH CONCEPTIONS
MYTH DIRECTIONS
HIT OR MYTH
MYTH-ING PERSONS
LITTLE MYTH MARKER
M.Y.T.H. INC. LINK
MYTH-NOMERS AND
IM-PERVECTIONS
M.Y.T.H. INC. IN ACTION
SWEET MYTH-TERY OF LIFE
MYTH-ION IMPROBABLE
SOMETHING M.Y.T.H. INC.

by Robert Asprin and Jody Lynn Nye

MYTH ALLIANCES
MYTH-TAKEN IDENTITY
MYTH-TOLD TALES
CLASS DIS-MYTHED
MYTH-GOTTEN GAINS
MYTH-CHIEF
MYTH-FORTUNES

by Jody Lynn Nye

ROBERT ASPRIN'S
MYTH-QUOTED

The DRAGONS WILD Series

by Robert Asprin

DRAGONS WILD
DRAGONS LUCK

by Robert Asprin and Jody Lynn Nye

DRAGONS DEAL

by Jody Lynn Nye

ROBERT ASPRIN'S DRAGONS RUN

The PHULE'S COMPANY Series

by Robert Asprin

PHULE'S COMPANY
PHULE'S PARADISE

by Robert Asprin and Peter J. Heck

A PHULE AND HIS MONEY
PHULE ME TWICE
NO PHULE LIKE AN OLD PHULE
PHULE'S ERRAND

DRAGONS LUCK

Prologue

George was impressed, though, he suspected, not as much as he was supposed to be.

Southern California wasn't his normal hunting ground, and every time he visited it, he found he liked it less and less. He kept being reminded of something he had once heard said about the area: Once you took away all the tinsel and glitz, what you had left was tinsel and glitz.

He found all the faddishness of what restaurant or club was in, much less what designer clothes one wore or food one ate, to be depressingly shallow and frantic. In his own private protest, he had long since consciously decided not to play their reindeer games.

He was an out-of-towner and an outsider, and made no effort to hide the fact. His suit was off-the-rack and not custom-tailored, and his shoes were comfortable and durable rather than one of the flimsy, short-lived imported fashions.

In one sense, this was appropriate, as George was himself an unimposing man. Anyone passing him on the street in the Midwest or the Northeast would barely notice him, much less remember him a half dozen steps later. In the youth-and-beauty-oriented culture of Southern California, he was as invisible as a homeless person, noticed, if at all, with distaste.

Even his rental car was an economy-sized Ford, readily sneered at by the valet at the trendy restaurant he pulled up at. At least, he assumed it was trendy. The girl at the car-rental counter had recognized it readily enough when he asked for directions.

None of this bothered George in the slightest. It was expected and, in some ways, gratifying. Anonymity was a plus, if not a necessity, in his chosen profession. What was more, he was sure enough of himself and what he could do that he did not feel the need for outside admiration or reassurance.

The hostess sized him up and dismissed him with one glance before asking if he had a reservation in a voice that assumed he didn't.

"I'm here to meet with Flynn," he said with deliberate casualness.

It was entertaining to watch the transformation that came over the hostess at the mention of Flynn's name. Her bored, skeptical expression changed in an instant to a beaming smile of welcome. With a smooth glide she came out from behind her reservation stand to escort George personally to Flynn's table.

Yes. People knew who Flynn was. Even George knew who he was, though they had never met or spoken before he was contacted for his recent assignment.

There was a noticeable break in the deal-making conversations throughout the room as the combatants realized where George was being led and paused in their negotiations to appraise him.

Yes. Everyone knew who Flynn was. What amused George was the knowledge that while everyone knew that Flynn was, perhaps, the most sought-after agent in the country, very few knew what he really was. George knew. Flynn was a dragon.

Though not a dragon himself, George was more than familiar with what they were: descendants of a shape-shifting, size-changing race that first resisted, then blended with the humans when that species rose to prominence. Centuries of mixing with and interbreeding with humans had thinned the blood and weakened their powers, but their basic characteristics remained the same. They were long-lived, resistant to disease or injury, and highly charismatic. They were also selfish, greedy, power-hungry, and utterly ruthless regarding any perceived threat to their amassed fortunes or power bases.

George knew all this because he was not human himself, and had made it his life's work to hunt dragons . . . for pay, of course.

Flynn rose to greet him as George was led to the table. He was tallish, with dark, wavy hair, gleaming white teeth, and what could only be called a California tan. Impeccably dressed, he could have been the poster boy for a "Beautiful California" ad campaign.

"George," he said, flashing his teeth and extending a hand. "So good of you to join me."

George ignored the hand as he seated himself.

"I was under the impression that I didn't have much choice in the matter," he said, flatly.

"I simply felt that, considering the substantial fee you charge, I deserve a face-to-face debriefing." Flynn smiled. "Not just a few written pages in a report."

"There was also something said about withholding the balance of my fee until we met," George said.

"That was an unfortunate misimpression," Flynn said. "The balance of your fee has already been deposited in the designated account."

George calmed down but was still not completely mollified.

"Well, there's also the matter of this breaking my rule against meeting my clients face-to-face."

Flynn shook his head.

"I understand. It's the whole 'man of mystery' thing where no one knows your face," he said. "Well, I'm certainly not going to share your description with anyone. The whole trust thing should be a two-way street."

"You're talking 'trust' to someone who hunts dragons for a living," George said with a smirk. "Maybe we know different dragons."

"I see your point," Flynn admitted. "Very well, then perhaps the knowledge that the deposit to your account included a sizable bonus for your inconvenience will help mollify your discomfort. Fifty percent, if I recall correctly."

It did, and George caught himself smiling. He quickly reminded himself that the dragon he was dealing with was successful mostly because of his ability to use glamour . . . the power to charm others into doing just about anything and have them grateful in the process.

"It helps," he said, carefully. "I'm still not wild about this, but what's done is done. Shall we order?"

He picked up the menu and started to peruse it.

"I think you'll find the cuisine here a pleasant change from your normal fare," Flynn said with a smile.

"We'll see," George returned. "Remember, I'm fresh from spending several months in New Orleans. They have one or two good restaurants there . . . and some of the best service I've ever encountered."

The two men carefully stuck to minor cocktail-party chit-chat until after the meal had been consumed and the dishes cleared away.

"So," Flynn began, sipping at his coffee, "shall we get down to your debriefing? I'm very interested in hearing your observations firsthand."

"Well, I assume you've already read my report," George said.

"Yes, but take it from the top as if I hadn't," Flynn answered. "I want it fresh from your own memories."

George took a moment to collect his thoughts, then began.

"Griffen McCandles and his sister, Valerie, are the orphaned offspring of two half-blood dragon parents. He is just coming to the age when his secondary powers, if any, should emerge. You hired me to track McCandles and test him to see if he would be any kind of a threat to you.

"I found him shortly after his uncle Malcolm informed him of his heritage. Apparently both he and his sister had been kept in the dark about even the existence of dragons until that point. His immediate reaction was to go to his sister, both to pass the information on to her and to seek her counsel.

"At that time, they were approached and offered refuge in New Orleans by Mose and his gambling cabal. It's common knowledge in that area now that Griffen is being groomed to take control of Mose's operation.

"Over the period of a couple of months, I both watched Griffen's development and arranged a few minor tests of my own. He is a fast learner . . . disturbingly fast.

"When I finally confronted him, he proved to be a formidable opponent. Though he had only been aware of his dragon heritage for a few months, he demonstrated a surprising familiarity with his new powers, which include animal control, shape-shifting, and fire-breathing.

"As I said in my report, while he is still developing, I feel you should take him seriously as a potential threat and monitor both his development and activities."

With that, George leaned back and picked up his own coffee, waiting for the inevitable questions.

"Very concise," Flynn said. "But without much detail. You really feel that he's a serious threat to me?"

"Actually, what I said was that you should take him seriously as a *potential* threat," George corrected. "As near as I can ascertain, for the time being he's content to sit in his holdings in New Orleans and run his gambling concern. I don't really see him coming after you unless you provoke him in some way."

"But, if provoked, you see him as a serious threat?" Flynn pressed.

George sighed.

"He's still very young and unfamiliar with either his powers or the current pecking order of dragons," he said. "As I mentioned, however, he's showing amazing growth for the short time he's been consciously working at it."

"Could you give me an example?"

"Well, I've already mentioned the development of his secondary powers," George said. "What I feel is more significant is how he is using them and interfacing with others. There has been a sudden growth spurt of people joining his gambling operation, mostly for the chance to work with Griffen. It's said that he tangled with some of the local drug gangs and not only survived, but backed them off. Melinda sent one of her sons in to try to seduce his sister, Valerie, but they saw through his glamour and sent him packing."

"So Melinda is taking an interest in him as well," Flynn said, thoughtfully.

"Only peripherally," George said. "I think her main interest was in his sister. The point is, they stopped him cold. Not bad for a pair of effectively untrained dragons."

"I see." Flynn nodded. "Anything else?"

"More rumors than anything confirmed," George said. "It was being bantered about in hushed tones that he's somehow formed an alliance with the spirit of a deceased voodoo queen. That's something I've never heard of another dragon doing. I've also heard that he's somehow in touch with some of the Eastern dragons."

"The Eastern dragons," Flynn said, suddenly attentive. "What sort of connection does he have there?"

"Nothing definite," George said. "He has a girlfriend who followed him down from college and supposedly is somehow tied in to the Easterns. It's my guess that they're curious and keeping an eye on him . . . rather like you are."

"All that in a few months," Flynn said. "And you don't see him as an immediate threat to me?"

George hesitated.

"Basically, I don't see him as having any motivation to come after you," he said, slowly. "Perhaps if you would share with me what your specific concern is, I could appraise the situation more accurately."

It was Flynn's turn to be silent for several moments.

"You claim to know dragons," he said at last. "In your research, have you come across anything regarding a prophecy?"

George blinked, then shrugged.

"Just some old tale about there arising a near-full-blood dragon who would unite the various dragon factions into one powerful force. Is that the one you're thinking of?"

"Something like that." Flynn waved. "I just find myself wondering if some of the appeal that young Griffen is experiencing is from other dragons wondering if he's the one from the prophecy."

"I doubt it," George said. "Almost every culture has some variation of a savior legend, someone who will either appear or return to put things right. While it's reassuring, I don't think there are any who take it seriously."

"You're probably right," Flynn said, rising and putting out his hand. "Well, I certainly appreciate your taking the time to humor my request for a personal debriefing. It's been most informative."

George rose and shook the offered hand without thinking.

"As you said, you paid for it," he said. "Just because he isn't an immediate threat, though, I still think you should take young Griffen seriously. He is formidable, and that is a word I don't use often or lightly."

"Oh, I'm taking him seriously," Flynn said with a smile. "So seriously, in fact, that I'm putting several things on hold to fly down to New Orleans to see to him myself."

George stared at him.

"If you were going to do that, why did you bother hiring me?" he said.

"Until I heard your report, I wasn't sure he was worth my while," Flynn said with an easy shrug. "Now I'm convinced that he needs to be checked out and tested further by me personally to see if he should be recruited or killed."

While George had a long-standing hatred of dragons, he realized that he was developing a specific dislike for this one in particular.

One

It was getting to be late September in the French Quarter, which meant the weather was cooling off enough that it wasn't necessary to run the air conditioner full-time. This was a break from both the muggy, sweat-inducing heat every time one set foot outdoors, and from the sky-high electric bills.

Griffen McCandles couldn't sleep, so he eased out of bed to wander out into the living room, being careful not to wake the sleeping form burrowed into the pillows next to him.

Fox Lisa and he were occasional lovers with no rules or restrictions on each other. The problem was they were simply on different schedules that only occasionally overlapped. She had her day job waitressing at G. W. Finn's, while his own duties overseeing the gambling operations, as well as his own personal preferences, made him a night owl.

She had called him about hooking up after work, and while he had willingly complied, now that she had dozed off, he was wide-awake.

There was no light on in the living room, which was unusual, as he normally kept at least one lamp on to help him navigate his way to the john without tripping over something or banging his knees. Still, it wasn't unheard of. The French Quarter, with its power surges and antique wiring, tended to eat lightbulbs like candy.

As he was groping his way toward a light switch, he suddenly became aware that there was someone sitting on his sofa in the dark. His heart nearly stopped as he realized he had been caught completely vulnerable.

"Do not be concerned, Griffen McCandles. You know who I am."

Forcing his heart rate down to somewhere near normal, he switched on the light and turned to greet his visitor.

"Hello, Rose," he said. "I wasn't expecting you, to say the least."

The young black woman with the long, waist-length hair smiled at him in return.

"I apologize for visiting your home unannounced, but at some times it is more difficult than others to make contact, and I needed to speak with you."

Rose was a ghost, a voodoo queen who had been dead for eight years. Shortly after he arrived in New Orleans, she had approached him on Jackson Square one night to ask his intentions toward the supernatural community in town. She had also given him a necklace of small black and red beads that he wore constantly, and had helped him out of some awkward, potentially dangerous situations.

"You know," she continued, "you should really have some wards set on this place . . . on your sister's, too. It was entirely too easy for me to enter. If you ask Jerome, he should be able to help you with that."

"May I offer you something to drink?" Griffen said, then realized how silly the thought was.

"That won't be necessary." Rose smiled. "But thank you for the thought."

"So, what can I do for you?"

"Strangely, that is exactly why I wanted to speak to you," Rose said. "I have a favor to ask of you."

"Name it," Griffen said, then regretted his words.

He really didn't know what he could offer a ghost in the way of help, and wasn't sure he wanted to know. Then again, was it possible to say no?

Rose raised her eyebrows.

"You may wish to consider carefully before agreeing," she said. "It is not something I would ask slightly, nor something you should agree to hastily."

"Okay. What's the favor?" Griffen said, grateful for the out.

"Every thirteen years there is a gathering of supernatural and spiritual beings," Rose said. "A conclave, if you will. The location rotates through various host cities. There is one happening this year over the Halloween weekend, and New Orleans has been chosen to host it."

"So what's the favor?" Griffen frowned. "Do you want me to be a speaker or something? If so, I don't really think I'm qualified. Mose would be a better choice. If you'd like me to, I could ask him."

"I actually had a more active role in mind," Rose said, carefully. "If you are agreeable, it is my wish that you serve as moderator for the conclave."

"Moderator?" Griffen echoed. "I'm even less qualified for that than to be a speaker. I don't know any of these people . . . or types."

"That's what makes you the perfect choice," Rose said. "You have no affiliation or alliance with any of the groups attending. More important, you're a dragon. Dragons don't usually attend these events, so everyone will be a little scared of you. It will help keep everyone in line."

"Keep them in line?" Griffen said with a frown. "What sort of beings are going to be attending this conclave?"

"Think of them as normal conventioneers in town for the weekend," Rose said. "You certainly have enough experience dealing with that from your time in the Quarter."

"So does everyone else who lives here," Griffen countered. "What do you need me for?"

"How do normal conventioneers act?" the voodoo queen pressed.

"Well, usually they wander through the Quarter, drink too much, make passes at the locals and each other, and sometimes wander down the wrong streets at night and get mugged or into a fight," Griffen recited. "The pattern doesn't change that much whether they're sailors or librarians."

"Now imagine that same behavior at a supernatural conclave." Rose smiled.

Griffen did, and didn't like the image he got.

"I see your point," he said. "But seriously, Rose, I wouldn't know what to do or where to begin."

"I can help you with that as the event approaches," Rose said. "This conclave is important . . . potentially crucial for the future of everyone involved. The important thing is that you agree to help."

"But . . ."

"You do agree, don't you?"

"Well, yes, but . . ."

The bedroom door opened, and Fox Lisa emerged blinking into the light.

"What's up, lover?" she said, yawning into a fist. "I thought I heard voices."

"It's just . . ." Griffen began, then realized that Rose had disappeared.

"Unexpected visitor?" Lisa said, peering around the room. "Hell, invite her in. You know I don't mind."

"I . . . I don't think that would be a good idea," Griffen said, wondering how much he should explain, if at all.

"Lighten up, lover," Fox Lisa said with a bawdy wink. "I keep telling you you've got to get into the spirit of the thing."

Griffen was totally unable to explain why he found that so hysterically funny.

Two

"**You** did what?!"

The outburst took Griffen aback. He was sitting in Mose's, as he so often found himself when seeking Mose's advice. It had occurred to Griffen previously that, outside of card games, he had rarely seen Mose out of the older man's home. Whether Mose was simply more comfortable in his own surroundings, or he just didn't like to get out in the Quarter, Griffen couldn't be sure. Regardless, his usually stoic guide seemed unduly stressed.

"I agreed to Rose's request. What else could I do considering the help she has given me?" Griffen said.

"Look, son, I know your sense of honor has swelled up a whole lot more than most of the people your age. But you've never struck me as this stupid," Mose said.

Griffen looked at his mentor in confusion. He had never found Mose this unbalanced, not to mention harsh. A part of himself winced over his teacher's roughness, the rest of him hit the other end of the scales. He wanted to retaliate.

"I don't see how agreeing to an ally's need is stupid, Mose," he said.

Mose seemed to draw himself inward, centering.

"Sorry . . . sorry. Wrong phrasing, Griffen. You caught me by surprise is all. That doesn't happen much when you reach my age."

Griffen watched as Mose's eyes momentarily fogged, as if

he were looking at memories and times long since past. Griffen had grudgingly learned that a dragon's outward appearance had little to do with his actual age. His friend Jerome had been the first to show that to him—a man he knew as another face around campus who had turned out to be much, much older than Griffen.

Still, Mose was such a timeless figure in so many ways, that this momentary display of emotions further set Griffen aback. The older dragon suddenly seemed . . . tired.

"I don't get it, Mose," Griffen said. "What is so startling about this all?"

"Well, to start off, I would never have expected Rose coming to you, or anybody for that matter, with such a request," said Mose.

Griffen hadn't thought about that yet. Rose was in many ways an enigma to him. He had no experience with voodoo queens or ghosts, and found the combination of the two a little disconcerting. He leaned forward, obviously curious about Mose's take on things. The other man shook his head, expression and tone growing more calm and controlled by the moment as he centered himself.

"Well, it's not an everyday request from just anybody. Don't get me wrong, Rose was a fine woman while alive. And I've heard nothing but good things about her since she has crossed to the other side. Still, I don't pretend to understand her motivations. In this, or in anything."

"Well, make some guesses. What do your instincts tell you?" Griffen asked.

"The big one is that these kind of meetings tend to get real cliquey real quick. In years past, Rose would be representative if not head of the local voodoo community. Now she's switched groups. She represents the spirits and ghosts and wandering souls, and maybe there will be some confusion about just whose interests she is most concerned with."

"That's not all, is it?"

For once Mose showed his emotions fully, half-rising out of his chair and his face flushing. This alone let Griffen know how much the matter was taxing him.

"Of course not! You don't have any idea what goes on at this type of thing! You are far too young, far too new on the scene, to take on such a responsibility. Dragons don't usually take part in these conclaves, and when it gets out that you're not only attending, but helping to run it as well, you're gonna have everybody and their kid brother watchin' to see how you do. Anything goes wrong, you could end up holdin' the bag. At the very least, it would be an embarrassment and a loss of face. At worst . . . I just don't know."

Griffen paused for a moment, keeping himself calm before responding. The comment about his youth, as well as his ignorance, got him more riled up then he would ever have expected.

"So, what do I have to expect?" Griffen said, keeping his voice controlled and outwardly calm.

He had half expected a full rundown right then. Mose had been his most valuable source of information since he had fallen into a world full of dragons and strangeness. What he didn't expect was for Mose to look away, seemingly embarrassed. Again, the older man took a deep breath, calming himself before speaking and obviously hiding his embarrassment.

"To be honest, Griffen, I don't know. Never in my long years did I attend such a conclave, much less moderate one. Dragons don't 'lower' themselves to such meetings as a rule. In my case, it just never came up."

"What do you mean? How could it not come up?" Griffen said.

"You seem so competent, sometimes I forget how new to all this you are. You were raised as human, which frankly isn't the way most dragons do things. Anyway, you have the human fallacy of thinking all supernaturals are connected. It just isn't so. Most dragons don't even see the other things out there in the shadows, much less deal with them. Especially lower dragons . . . like myself."

Now it was Griffen's turn to look away in embarrassment. He had been told about his blood and Valerie's being somehow more concentrated than most dragons', but it so rarely came up. Even after all that had been forced upon him, some days he still didn't believe he was a dragon. Some days he still wondered if he was simply insane.

"What can you tell me?" Griffen asked.

"Nothing," Mose said, voice suddenly hard. "Griffen, you are a strong, confident man far beyond your years. You have made your decision. The timing being what it is, it behooves me to leave it to you. On this, you are on your own."

"What do you mean?" Griffen said, confused and feeling the first hints of panic.

"I mean this is your baby now. I don't know enough. Anything I could say might just mislead you. I won't just be another obstacle for what will prove a very difficult task."

With that, Mose stood. Griffen was still staring, confused and at a loss for words, as the older dragon walked past the younger. He briefly clasped Griffen on the shoulder, then headed out the door, leaving his own apartment, leaving Griffen alone.

Through all the confusion, Griffen's main thoughts were centered on the simple question. What had he gotten himself into?

Three

Griffen strolled down Bourbon Street. His destination was the Irish pub up on Toulouse, but he never missed the chance to do a little people-watching. It was amazing what could be seen just glancing into the open doors and windows of the French Quarter bars as one walked along. By the time he had turned down Toulouse, he had already seen a small fight, several lovely eyefuls dancing on bar tops, and two of the silver cowboy street performers rolling something he doubted was tobacco. Ordinary sights by now, but always worth a glance.

The last thing he expected to see was two dragons, arguing.

It was a little hotel bar a block away from the Irish pub. Griffen had never been in there, as its upscale atmosphere and fairly yuppie clientele had never held any attraction for him. This time was different, as just a glance brought him to a stop.

It was the first time he had looked at strangers and known, on some level, that they were dragons. They sat at one of the small tables, talking with the exaggerated hand movements of a heated debate. He wasn't even sure why he knew what he knew. Whether it was their posture, eyes, movement, he just didn't know. But his instincts were sure.

Physically, the two couldn't be more different. The first was a huge man, his suit not quite tailored enough to hide the roughness of his frame. Griffen had never actually seen anyone who truly didn't have a neck. It was as if he were a barrel someone had stuck a bucket head onto.

The other was tall, slim, well built, and seemed polished compared to the rough man next to him. Somehow he seemed more real than the other. His tan was rich, as if he had never spent a day without seeing sunshine. His jaw was square with an easy smile, his hair wavy with just a hint of tousled wildness. The first man wasn't smiling; he seemed to be just baring his teeth and forcing his words through them.

The two stopped whatever they had been discussing in hushed tones as the rough man's eyes fell on Griffen, still standing out on the street. He hushed the other, who turned and didn't hesitate to beckon Griffen in. There was no reason for Griffen to refuse the invitation, but still he approached warily. Despite the man's warm smile, his eyes were a bit too keen. As if he was seeing every detail, analyzing each in turn.

"Mr. McCandles, welcome," the polished man said, nodding, no question in his voice.

"This is him?" said the other man. He was either uncaring or unable to hide his surprise.

The other's eyes flicked briefly, not actually rolling, but the slight change in expression spoke volumes. There was very little respect here. The rough man noticed and seemed to hunch in on himself, head receding a bit more into his shoulders, eyes narrowing. He reached out a hand and took Griffen's, applying much more pressure than was needed for a handshake.

"Skinny, ain'tcha? You ever do something that doesn't involve sitting on a bar stool?"

His voice was surprisingly soft, but hostile. He was obviously trying for a reaction, and Griffen didn't care to give it to him that easily.

When the other man spoke, he had an earthy, mellow self-confidence. He offered his hand to Griffen instead of simply taking it as the other one had. They shook, and the grip was comfortable and unforced.

"Mr. McCandles," he said, "or may I call you Griffen? This is Stewart Waters. And I'm Flynn."

"Earl, actually," Waters said, his smile making it clear he was aware the correction would irritate Flynn.

"Only if I have to sign checks; otherwise, Flynn suffices."

"You a ball fan, McCandles? 'Course not, otherwise you'd be askin' for my autograph already," Waters said.

Griffen tried to remember where he had heard the name. A player? Semipro or pro? Second-string somewhere probably . . .

"Mostly I just follow college," Griffen said, politeness waning quickly. "Once players start worrying about the paycheck, they start to get dull."

"Dull! Why, you little twig . . ."

Griffen blinked once. "I'm sorry, I thought you were a dragon. Do you really think I need to show my muscles?"

Flynn's smile widened at the corners, and his eyes seemed to catch the light as they gleamed. Griffen hadn't seen admiration often in another dragon's eyes. Apparently the speed of the response, as well as its phrasing, impressed Flynn. Waters simply stared blankly, trying to figure it out.

"You'll have to excuse Waters. Low blood, but lower intelligence. It was just what we were discussing," Flynn said.

"This parasite says I have to retire next year, when I haven't even gotten started. Do I look like I can't play anymore?" Waters asked.

"No, you look perfectly fit," Griffen answered.

"And that is just the problem. You haven't aged. You've

got just enough blood in you that you could keep knocking heads into your sixties, and every sports commentator in the country will be screaming about steroids and drugs and by that time, probably, cloning. You can't keep playing a game for twenty- and thirty-year-olds without gaining the wrong type of notoriety," Flynn said.

"That's what I got into this for. You promised me fame!" Waters said.

"I promised you a chance at fame, which you blew by being a hothead. And I told you the conditions were that after ten years, you retired and went and wrote cookbooks or something. Or, God forbid, coached."

"You stupid vampire. You made a fortune off of me, and I got screwed."

Flynn stiffened, perhaps because of the insult. His tone grew sharp.

"Compared to most clients, you gave me pennies. And I should ruin you for flying down to New Orleans with some cockamamie scheme of trading yourself to the Saints. Idiot."

"At least I seek fame, instead of just money. Is it true you take IVs of melted gold to get you going in the morning?" Waters shot back, flushing angrily.

"Oh no, I just swim in it, à la Scrooge McDuck," Flynn said.

Griffen laughed at Flynn's easy volley, and Waters grew more sullen. Flynn winked at the young dragon, even though he didn't look much older than midthirties himself. Griffen doubted his age matched his face.

"Pull up a chair, Griffen. No reason for you to stand there."

Flynn pushed a chair toward Griffen. A drink was already waiting, and as Griffen reached into his wallet, Flynn waved him off, putting a few bills on the bar. The Quarter had bro-

ken Griffen of refusing free drinks, but still the gesture surprised him from an utter stranger.

Waters put a hand on the back of the chair, knuckles
grazing Griffen's back.

"No, don't pull up a chair. I'm not done talking with my
agent about extending my ball contract."

"Not a chance, Waters," Flynn said. "You don't have anything to offer me."

"You mean besides the money from the contract?" Griffen
said.

The other two dragons exchanged a glance, for the first
time having a meeting of minds. Waters burst into a chor-
tling laugh that set Griffen's teeth on edge. Flynn's smile
became a smirk, but he still shot a bit of a glare at the
other.

"Stow it, Stew. He's new."

"New nothing—he's a baby! This is the kid who scared
Stoner? Big tough government dragon!"

"Thanks for the drink. Glad I could give you a few laughs
in exchange," Griffen said, starting to rise.

Waters rose, too.

"Where you going, baby?" he said.

Flynn glanced at the other two dragons.

"Sit down, Griffen, for a moment," he said. "Waters is an
ass, but I didn't mean any harm. See, for the most part, the
big dragons in this country know each other. Not quite a
good old boys' network, more everyone keeping track of everyone else. Now, Waters isn't a big dragon, not even tops in
his industry, but you qualify, or will. So it was a bit of a shock
you didn't know me," Flynn explained.

"Meaning you are a big dragon?" said Griffen, not taking
his chair again and not taking his eyes off Waters.

"I'd say yes if I weren't so damn modest."

Flynn winked, and Griffen found himself smiling again.

But lost it quickly as Waters cracked his knuckles loudly, vying for attention.

"He's agent for every major dragon in entertainment. Sports, movies, news, stage, even books," Waters said.

"Though I'll be damned if I see much money from the last. They do all come to me," Flynn said.

"And give you ten percent?" Griffen said.

"Sometimes as much as forty on a few cases. It's amazing what some people will sign," Flynn said.

Griffen cocked his head, looking at Waters.

"And your beef with me seems to be?"

"No beef, just figured I'd get a little of that fame I been wanting. I smash your face in, maybe I can sign on with Stoner after I dump this scum sucker," Waters said.

He took a step toward Griffen. Though he didn't show scales, his skin seemed to darken, harden. It was as if his dark skin were turning to brick, or stone, but it still moved and rippled like flesh.

Griffen cocked his head the other way.

"I don't think that's a good idea," Griffen said.

A soft growling tugged at the attention of the three dragons.

Two dogs, medium-sized, glared up at Waters. A moment ago they had been asleep in the bar. Now their ears were back and teeth bared. The larger one's shoulder blades began to tense.

"You think I can't pound down a dog?" Waters sneered.

The smaller dog barked, a surprisingly loud bark. It drew the attention of the people in the bar and out on the street. One of whom began walking toward the entrance.

"Griffen," Maestro said. "Was expecting you up the street for pool. Is there a problem?"

That last phrase was said with a bit of edge. His hands were in plain sight, but Griffen had heard a few stories in the past few months. Dogs Waters could handle. This, maybe not.

The bartender looked over.

"Maestro, how the hell have you been?" he asked, and quickly assessed the situation. "Right, what's going on here? Maestro, you need a hand?"

"Just what I was asking my good friend Griffen here," Maestro said.

Waters looked from the men to the dogs to Griffen. Flynn chuckled slightly. Griffen had noticed that he had watched him the entire time. There seemed to be another gleam of admiration in his eyes, but also something more . . . calculating.

"What did I say about the wrong kind of notoriety?" Flynn said.

"Fuck you, Flynn," said Waters.

Everyone watched as the large man left the bar, stopping to glare at Maestro as he stepped to the side. Maestro only smiled slightly, and asked, "Did you use to play sports?"

That did it. He was gone, and Griffen really wanted to know how Maestro knew the perfect thing to say. Flynn laughed, loud. Griffen turned a speculative eye to the other dragon, and he shrugged.

"Some guys just aren't worth fifteen percent. I'm half-tempted to try and get him a TV hosting gig on Antarctic Public Broadcasting. But I hate to waste a favor."

"You really can pull that kind of strings?"

Maestro looked at the two of them and walked over to chat with the bartender. Griffen signaled over his head, buying the man a drink, then sat back down with Flynn.

"Inside my bailiwick. I don't pay much attention outside of the entertainment business, of course, but that's enough for one dragon."

"So," Griffen said, suddenly suspicious, "what are you doing in town?"

"Ha! Sharp question. I could, of course, have sent some paper-pusher to ride herd on the boy wonder. But I'm about to start preproduction on a major picture down here, so I'm checking out the location. Multitasking, you know?"

"Okay, and what is your interest in me?" Griffen asked.

"Who says I have an interest? I do very thorough research before I come to a new location. Research besides shooting locations and local talent agencies."

"So you knew me because you looked into the local dragons?" Griffen said skeptically.

"Oh, hell, you are quick. I rarely come on location even when I'm the one trying to put things together from scratch. Don't have to anymore. But New Orleans with Halloween coming up, a young dragon who's making the most interesting ripples? Curiosity compelled, I came and poked my nose in."

Distrust made Griffen pause and think those comments over carefully. He didn't like being under the microscope, but Flynn's honesty was refreshing. He just couldn't seem to help liking the man.

"You seem more startled than expected. Look, I'm sorry about the idiot, but I can't be responsible for every stupid thing he thinks up. Surely this can't be the first time a dragon surprised you with a face-to-face?" Flynn asked.

"True, but that doesn't help me feel at ease. The last was Stoner."

"Ah, well, damn. Doesn't that just take the wind out of my sails? Tell you what. Going to be around for another month at least now that I'm immersed in this damn deal. We'll probably run into each other. If you need anything, though, here's my card."

He pulled out a small, embossed business card and slipped it over to Griffen and looked him over again closely. Griffen sensed that he wanted to say more, but Flynn just shook his head and stood up.

"No pressure now. There really is no need." Flynn nodded to Griffen and headed out the door.

Outside, once beyond sight of the bar, Flynn smiled to

himself. An honest smile, the kind that brings to mind cats and canaries.

"Just the right mix of truth and lies," he said to himself, and strolled down toward Bourbon.

Four

Valerie sat in her apartment, staring into a mirror. It wasn't something she did often. Vanity wasn't one of her main drives. In fact, the only mirror in the place was in the tiny bathroom. She shifted uncomfortably, leaned on the edge of the sink, and stared into her own eyes.

A soft knock at her door was still loud enough to startle her out of her reverie. Val bent at the sink and splashed a little water in her face. Another quick glance in the mirror showed her face calm, if a little too serious. Nodding to herself, she went to the front door and opened it.

"May I come in?" Mai asked.

The smaller woman poked her head into Val's apartment, looking around. Val shrugged a bit, unsure what she was looking for. Griffen had never mentioned Mai to Val while they were in college, but since meeting in New Orleans, she and Mai were fast becoming friends.

In fact, Mai had seemed to go out of her way to befriend Valerie, to open up with her more than she seemed to with Griffen. It had given Valerie something she didn't really realize she was missing: a girlfriend, someone she could let her hair down with and trade dirty jokes and warm comfort. Val had come to appreciate Mai's perspective and knowledge. Even with that, she had to admit she still didn't really understand Mai.

"Sure thing," Val said.

Val opened the door and waved Mai inside. After she closed the door, she noticed Mai still looking around. Well, if you don't know, ask.

"What are you looking for?"

"Nothing, privacy mostly. I never knew Valkyries were such slobs."

Mai grinned as she said it and waved a small hand at scattered clothing over Val's couch and a small pile of take-out containers on the table. Val rolled her eyes. She knew that she was nowhere near as messy as some. Mai, though, seemed to keep herself, and her surroundings, bordering on immaculate. Sometimes Val just wanted to throttle her.

"Sorry, we can't all have wrought-iron shafts shoved up our rears, Flower Drum. At least I can eat without the area being declared a disaster zone," Val teased.

Though if truth be known, the two together was a disaster worse than the sum of its parts. Valerie and Mai attacking a full dinner could give waiters heart attacks the Quarter over.

"You just don't know how to enjoy your food properly. Amazing, considering how big you are."

Val grinned at the familiar banter, but there was a slight flash in her eye. One hand idly touched her stomach. Mai noticed it, and her expression softened and went a touch more serious.

"Relax, it's not showing yet," Mai said.

"Wh- What do you mean?"

"Oh, please, Valerie. You've been out of sorts, far too serious, and there are other signs."

"Everyone has been out of sorts and serious lately. Silly, isn't it? I mean, after all, no one's tried to kill any of us in a few weeks. Things should be springtime and light."

"Yes. Silly," said Mai.

The two stared at each other. Val, tall and strong. Mai, small and delicate. Mai's expression was absolutely unreadable, as blank and lovely as a doll's. Val tried, but something leaked past. A touch of spark in her eyes, as if daring Mai, or the world, to react first.

"Is it Nathaniel's?" Mai inquired, face still unreadable.

Val's face broke in a mixture of surprise, sadness, and, above all, relief. She sank into a chair, holding her face in her hands. Not crying, but showing signs close to exhaustion. Mai approached slowly, almost cautiously, and wrapped her arms around Val, hugging her.

"Yes," Val said, then more angrily, "Yes! That son of a bitch."

"Literally, from the rumors I've heard from Melinda."

Mai tried a gentle smile, but Val was still angry as she looked up. Weeks later, and she was still furious at the dragon, Nathaniel, who had come to New Orleans specifically for the purpose of trapping her. Using seduction and magic to affect her will and defenses.

"Was it the glamour? Normally I'm safe, careful. Did that bastard magic me into forgetting myself?" Val asked, and pulled herself away from Mai.

Letting her arms drop to her sides, Mai took a step back. She thought for a few moments and gave a bare nod.

"Most likely. The glamour probably added to the excitement, the rush, and we know your judgment was affected."

"Then he wanted this to happen."

"No . . . well . . . maybe, but I doubt it. He wanted you, wanted to bed you. He pushed with his glamour for that. That is what you got caught up in. To think much past that might be his mother's style, but as calculating and manipulative as he can be, he tends to focus on the short-term goal."

Val stood and started to pace the room. She seemed so full of bound energy that it was surprising the small apartment could contain her. Mai took a seat, giving her more room and watching her.

"How did you know?" Val said.

"Besides the personality changes? Well, one big clue, it's the French Quarter. You've stopped drinking," Mai said.

"Then others have noticed."

"Val, you have a bad habit of making statements of things that should be questions. No, I don't think anyone else has noticed. One, most of them don't know what to look for. Two, everyone has been wrapped up in their own business."

"But not you?"

Mai shrugged and clasped her hands in her lap.

"For the most part, I've been feeling a little lost. As much as I enjoy the area, and the company, I haven't really heard anything from back home lately. Not even a request for updates. My days are my own and really beginning to drag."

"Must not be easy, being a spy," Val said.

Val's tone was sarcastic, but some of the teasing was creeping back in.

"I prefer to think of myself as a double agent, or at least a double entendre. I mean how much of a spy can I be when I told Griffen that's why I'm here?" Mai said.

"One of the reasons you are here, and you didn't really tell him much of that."

"Hey, if I'm bored, maybe I should get a job like you! Need another relief bartender?"

"Nice change of subject, but with the fortune-cookie mystique, you could probably make more as a fortune-teller."

Val grinned, and Mai smiled secretively. With dramatic motions, Mai draped the back of one hand over her forehead and held the other out toward Val, fingers spread. Val tensed as the motions were aimed at her stomach.

"The wise one sees all and knows all. What lurks in your secret heart! Hear her words and tremble," Mai said.

"Get on with it."

"Don't tell Griffen."

Val stopped in her tracks and stared at Mai.

"I have to tell him. He's my brother, and the last thing he needs after he starts to get everything under control is me surprising him with this."

"Exactly; right now he's struggling. He has just started to gain proper confidence, and already burdens are being heaped onto him. This could be the very thing that overwhelms him completely," Mai said.

"If I don't tell him, it leaves him in danger. If Nathaniel comes back because of this, Griffen won't have any time to prepare."

"Why would Nathaniel come back? Even if he planned this, which I doubt, how could he know? You will worry Griffen for nothing, put his already taxed nerves even more on edge."

"But . . ."

Val couldn't say it. Keeping a secret like that from her brother would be nearly impossible. They were too close, and the strain on her would be great.

"I know it will be hard," Mai said, and frowned. "But if you tell him, he will want to protect you. He will charge off to find Nathaniel, charge right into Melinda's territory. This way you protect him, not the other way around."

Valerie sank into a chair again and stared at Mai. Her mind whirled, but a part of her knew that Mai was exactly right. Between protecting her big brother and being honest with him, protection came first. She nodded.

"It's for the best," Mai said, and got up to hug Val again. "Trust me."

After a moment's silence, Mai spoke again.

"So, are you going to keep it?"

Val sighed, then shook her head.

"I don't know," she said. "I'm still thinking about that one."

Five

Waiting in front of Tower Records, carrying a copy of the *Times-Picayune* as he had been instructed, Flynn spent his time surveying the passing crowd. Mostly they were obvious out-of-towners, suited conventioneers, and a smattering of tourists in shorts and T-shirts. Here and there were locals, including service-industry types in their tuxedo shirts and black pants, and costumed street performers, all getting ready to give their best try at moving funds from the pockets of visitors into their own. All in all, it reminded Flynn vaguely of Disneyland only without the rides.

Mostly, he was idly curious if he could spot his hired muscle before they contacted him. In the past, when he had hired rough-off artists, they fell into one of two categories. Either they were well dressed and soft-spoken with dead eyes that looked at you without seeing a person, or obvious muscle flexers, who swaggered with the knowledge that just their appearance was intimidating. For the present job, Flynn was hoping for the cold, calculating type. He had a feeling that swaggering bullyboys wouldn't get too far with the McCandles lad.

One of the rolling boom boxes was coming slowly up the street, a dark sedan with the sound system cranked up to the point where it assaulted the pedestrians like a strong wind. A strong, noisy wind. Flynn eyed it with distaste. It was playing rap music. Of course. Not for the first time he found himself wondering why those who liked rap music felt obliged to share it with everyone in a four-block radius, while those whose taste ran to classical music were content to listen to it through the earphones of a Walkman or iPod.

To his surprise, the mobile noise pollution pulled over to the curb next to him and stopped. The passenger-side window rolled down, exposing the face of a young black man, late teens or early twenties.

"You Flynn?" The question was half-shouted over the music.

Flynn realized with dismay that this was the contact he was waiting for. For a moment, he was tempted to deny his identity and walk away. Then, with a mental shrug, he decided to go ahead with it. When in Rome.

He nodded his agreement.

"Get in the back and let's talk."

Opening the door to the backseat, Flynn wondered how they were supposed to talk over the racket the sound system was making. To his surprise, the driver, a thin black man even younger than the one who had first addressed him, turned the music off without being asked even before they pulled away from the curb.

"Hear tell you're lookin' to put the hurt on someone," the passenger-side rider said.

"There's someone I want made an example of," Flynn said, carefully. "Hospitalized or dead. Doesn't make any difference to me. If things are the same here as other places in the country, hospitalized costs more."

That was standard for rough-off work. Just hospitalizing someone meant the musclemen had to know what they were doing. It also left the victim alive to identify them and possibly press charges. In short, it usually cost more to have someone's arm broken than it did to have them killed.

"Either way, it'll cost," said the passenger.

"Cash," added the driver.

"I know," Flynn said. "I've got the money with me."

There was a moment's silence.

" 'Course, we could just stick a gun in your face and take the money," the passenger said, casually. "Save ourselves a bit of work."

Flynn heaved a mental sigh and let his glamour flow out.

"Just to keep things simple, let's pretend we've all done things like this before," he said with a smile. "Now I do a lot of work away from my home base. Over the years, I've developed a method for finding . . . shall we say, special help when I'm in a strange town. Back home, part of what I do is to provide certain of my clients with various types of illegal substances. If I need help, what I do is call home to my regular supplier. He in turn contacts one of the handlers in the area I'm in and arranges a meet, which is why we're talking now."

He leaned back in his seat.

"If anything goes wrong at that meet, both my supplier and his local contact will be upset because they're getting a piece of the action. The local man is particularly upset because he's guaranteed the people I'm meeting, and if they get cute, he ends up looking bad. Maybe with a new enemy he doesn't want."

He paused for a moment for that to sink in before continuing.

"It might interest you to know that our local contact is impressed enough with my supplier that he offered to provide the needed help for free. I turned him down because I believe in paying people top dollar when they do me a favor. Just remember, though, whatever price we agree on is definitely going to mean more money for you than if I had taken him up on his offer. Now then, shall we get down to talking business?"

Again, there was a moment of silence.

"The price depends on the job," the passenger said at last, a little sulkily. "We'd have to charge extra to go after someone here in the Quarter. The cops don't like it 'cause it scares the tourists."

"I expected that," Flynn said. "I am thinking about the Quarter, but the target's a local. It could be explained as a grudge fight instead of random violence."

"That still could be a problem," the passenger said, gaining confidence as the negotiations progressed. "That ups the chance that he knows us or that we might be seen by someone who knows us. Seems like everybody knows everybody down here."

"Maybe," Flynn said. "But he's only been down here a couple of months. He's probably not as well connected as the longtime residents."

"We'll see," the passenger said, judiciously. "This guy got a name?"

"He's a young kid, early twenties, just out of college," Flynn said. "Like I said, he only moved down here a few months ago. Name of McCandles."

In a sudden move, the driver pulled over to the curb and stopped the vehicle.

The passenger turned in his seat to stare directly at Flynn.

"McCandles?" he said. "Are you talkin' about *Griffen* McCandles?"

"That's right," Flynn said. "Why? Do you know him?"

"Get out of my car."

The statement was made with such finality that Flynn was startled.

"I don't understand," he said. "What's the problem?"

"The problem is that either you don't know who you're talkin' about, or you're some kind of special dumb," the passenger said, shaking his head. "Well, we ain't dumb, and there's no way we're goin' after Griffen McCandles. That man is protected big-time . . . and I don't just mean the cops. Word is he has supernatural help. If TeeBo knew who you had in mind, there's no way he would have even had us talk to you. Now get out of my car, and I mean *now*. You want to go after Griffen McCandles, I don't even want to be seen talkin' to you. Now *get out*."

Standing on the sidewalk again, Flynn watched the car drive off. If the McCandles boy had built that much of a reputation in just a few months, then maybe George wasn't exaggerating when he described the young dragon as "formidable."

One thing was certain, though. If Flynn was going to continue with his plan, he couldn't rely on local contacts. He'd have to try another tactic. Maybe import someone.

Six

It was the silence that first caught Griffen's attention. A bar is never completely quiet, a French Quarter bar least of all. The Irish pub was no different. Still, a sudden drop in the constant background noise caught and held his attention.

He couldn't immediately track the source of the change. People were still chatting. The music, never Irish, still played. A couple pretended to shoot pool on the back table between their flirting. All this flashed before his attention, then he looked down. Looked down, and saw the dogs.

There were three of them. A high number for the pub, but he had seen worse. Griffen had gotten used to the fact that dog owners in the Quarter tended to take their animals *everywhere*. Sometimes, when a particularly yappy bunch came in, it annoyed the hell out of him. Usually not, though. The sounds of puppies at play had become "normal" to him. Part of the background noise that made a happy bar.

These three had been doing their part. Running from patron to patron, looking for attention. Wrestling with each other over a bone one of the chefs had brought for them when she got off shift. It had been the sudden stop in their antics that had caught Griffen's attention. All three now sat in a line in front of one of the entrances. Sat, and stared.

That was enough to bring Griffen fully on guard. Even though no one else seemed to be paying attention. Griffen turned slightly away from the bar, freeing his legs in case he needed to move quickly. He only relaxed slightly as the door opened, and Slim walked in. He didn't turn back to the bar.

Slim was a tall, thin man whose skin always looked darker because of the pristine white suit he always wore. He was one of the Quarter's street performers. A living statue, with red, white, and blue stripes on his tie and the band of his tall, white top hat. He was also one of the few humans gifted with the ability to control animals.

As soon as he was in the bar, the dogs pounced. Griffen had experienced similar reactions, and expected Slim to calm them as he tended to. Instead, Slim plopped down onto the barroom floor and spent several minutes scratching and rolling with the excited beasts. The dogs' owners glanced down to see who was riling up their pets, then went back to their drinks with wry smiles.

The play stopped so abruptly that another lull rolled through the bar. If Griffen hadn't been watching closely, he would have missed the slight change in Slim's expression completely. One moment the man had been covered in tail-wagging dogs, the next he was alone. Each canine went back to its owner's side and lay down, as calm as it had been excited. All from what appeared to Griffen as an instant's concentration. Slim's brow barely furrowed.

Slim stood up and brushed off his suit. He nodded to the bartender, who didn't seem to mind that the dogs had gotten the first greeting. Then he picked up the large, white bucket that he used to collect his tips and headed toward Griffen.

"Can I have some words with you, Mr. Griffen?" Slim said, nodding to one of the tables set a bit apart from the bar.

Griffen had to admit to himself that Slim's entrance had impressed him. Particularly the subtlety, the complete lack of interest anyone had shown. Griffen's own animal control was a skill he was still developing. Being a dragon seemed to give him a boost in strength and power, but his control was still shaky. Slim was a natural.

"Sure, Slim."

Griffen gathered up his drink and went over to the table as Slim reached into his bucket for a few ones to buy his own drink.

"Tell me something, Slim," the younger man said, as the entertainer joined him. "How come nobody bats an eyelash when you do something like that?"

Slim looked over at one of the sleeping dogs, which twitched lightly in its sleep. It seemed to calm under the man's attention.

"Well, hell, this here's the French Quarter. 'Sides, everyone does know ol' Slim has a way with chillen and animals."

"Then why don't you use your talents in your act? Bring a dog or bird or something into the bit, and the tourists will eat it up."

"Why don't you do some fire-breathin' in Jackson Square? Tourists will eat it up."

Griffen was taken aback by the sudden harshness in the man's tone. He reminded himself Slim had threatened him before. That he was, in his own way, a dangerous man. Even with his own powers to protect him, Griffen felt somewhat vulnerable.

"Some things ain't given to us to make the tourists laugh. Or to fill the pockets, ya hear?" Slim went on.

"Sorry, Slim, I didn't mean any offense," Griffen said.

"Well . . . no, guess you didn't, Mr. Griffen. Sorry, it's a sore spot. Not everyone thinks the same way 'mongst folks like me. I remember this here fine gal in New York did just that. Lovely girl, worked with pigeons, but didn't hold that 'gainst her none. 'Course she also had squirrels. Picked pockets and the like. Gots into all sorts of trouble . . ."

Griffen let him trail off. It was the first time Slim had really shared anything personal with him. Slim seemed to shake himself, coming back from whatever memory he had drifted into.

"Anyways, touchy subject. Specially since it always comes up at the big meets. 'Spose I been bracin' myself for when the fightin' starts, ya know?"

"You mean at the conclave?" Griffen asked.

"Yep. Damn near forgots what I was lookin' for you for. Got some stuff for you."

Slim reached into his bucket again and pulled out a black folder. Griffen took it from him and looked inside. The contents looked no different than what one might receive at any convention: a map of the Quarter, a hotel map with meeting rooms marked off, a list of helpful phone numbers.

"I been helpin' Rose out. Doin' the stuff that it's helpful to be fully corporeal for. All the attendees gets a folder like this. We'll work up an itinerary as the guest list gets finalized."

"I didn't know you were attending, much less helping to organize things," Griffen said.

"Well now, the other animal-control people is attendin' this year. Since this is my home, falls to me to help things go smooth. 'Course, I sure hope I don't end up stuck bein' the main spokesman. We is too damned independent. I don't want to be the one holdin' the bag."

"Can't say I blame you," said Griffen.

He felt a good amount of the irony from that statement. It looked more and more like he was going to end up the main bag holder.

"Slim, you mentioned a guest list. I'd really appreciate if someone would tell me who, and what, exactly is coming to this thing."

"Rose didn't tell you?!" Slim said, face more than a little shocked. "Well, damn. Guess I understand since things ain't too solid yet. Keep in mind this might change as invites get accepted and declined."

"Invitation only, right?" Griffen said.

"Uh . . . mostly. Always a surprise or two at these things, ya know?"

Slim leaned back and started to count off on his fingers.

"First comes us animal types. So you can figure the shifters, too. All sorts: chimera, werewolves, no tellin' what mix yet."

Griffen thought inwardly, *Shamans and werewolves, oh my.*

"The local voodoo people will show. They ain't helpin' out like they should, though. Don't rightly know why. Figure a handful of other human magic users, wicca and the sorts. Again, no idea what mix exactly. Then, 'course, Rose and a few from the other side."

"Vampires?" Griffen asked, intrigued.

After all, if there were going to be ghosts and werewolves, who knows?

"Didn't get invited. Too much trouble. The emotion ones depress or piss off everyone. Other sorts . . . well, after Rice and the like, you just don't want to meet the types of vamps that New Orleans might attract."

"You're probably right. Is that it?" Griffen said.

"Pretty much. Bigwigs aren't showin'. Likes the . . . well, like the dragons. Oh, somethin' different. First year the fey kids are gettin' in."

Griffen blinked.

"The what?!" he asked.

"Yeah, they been tryin' for a long time to get a spot in the meets. Call 'em changelings. Supposed to be what the fey leave behind when they snatch a human kid. Bunch of bull ya ask me, but the kids gots some power."

"Then why haven't they been included before?"

"Mostly 'cause they are weird. Even by our standards. Even push Quarter standards, you listen to some of the rumors. Only reason they get a shot this year is because the conclave is here. Never met one myself, of course, but that's what I hear."

Slim finished his drink and stood abruptly, straightening his suit again.

"That's all I got for now. I'll call you sometime to talk 'bout the itinerary."

"You sure about that list?" Griffen pressed.

"Pretty sure. But remember, always a surprise or two."

Slim walked toward the door and had it halfway open when he stopped, looking down at his empty hand. He had left his bucket back at the table. Before he even turned, one of the three dogs stood up and was dragging it to him in its teeth. He scritched the dog affectionately and winked to Griffen before leaving.

If anyone found it odd, no one commented. Or even looked up from their conversations. Which left Griffen stuck on one very important question.

What could be too odd for the French Quarter?

Seven

Griffen really didn't want to talk to Detective Harrison. If nothing else, he wasn't sure what to say to the man.

"By the way, Detective, there will be a bunch of weird, supernatural types hitting town over the Halloween weekend. You might want to keep an eye out for them, but don't lean on them too hard."

That would raise some questions Griffen would just as soon have left unasked.

Still, the vice detective had done him some favors in the past, mostly because he hated feds operating on his turf even more than he hated protected gambling operations. Knowing there was potential trouble coming down the pipeline and not alerting the policeman would be a poor way to pay him back.

Griffen decided against calling Harrison on his cell phone for fear it would make the whole thing too official for comfort. Instead, he would try to meet with the detective casually, making it appear to be a chance run-in.

To that end, he put the word out through his various watchers in the Quarter to alert him when Harrison was spotted in the area but not actively working.

He thought this would buy him a bit of time to figure out what he was going to say, but the call came back almost immediately, letting him know that Harrison was eating at Yo Mama's.

Sometimes he wished his network of watchers was a little less efficient.

Padre, one of his favorite bartenders, was behind the bar when he rolled in. Catching his glance, the man jerked his head slightly toward one of the back booths, then rolled his eyes in mock exasperation. Not knowing quite what to make of the signal that had been passed to him, Griffen made his way toward the indicated booth. It didn't take him long to figure out what Padre had been trying to tell him.

Harrison, as always looking more like an overweight biker than a cop, was sprawled loosely in the last booth, a half-full bottle of beer in front of him.

"Well, look who's here," the detective drawled. "My friend the Grifter . . . or should I say Mr. McCandles. Pull in, son. Let me buy you a round or two."

Harrison waved at Padre as Griffen settled into the seat across from him. The young dragon certainly didn't need to use his enhanced powers of observation to realize that Harrison was more than slightly tight.

"So, what can I do for you?" Harrison said, his words a little slurred. "The only time I see or hear from you is when you want a favor. Nobody wants to drink with a cop except other cops."

"Are you okay, Detective?" Griffen said, genuinely concerned. "You seem a little out of it. Is anything wrong?"

"Wrong?" Harrison said, louder than was necessary. "How could anything be wrong? I'm a cop with the NOPD. We've got the world by the short and curlies. Ask anyone. Better yet, read the newspaper. Everybody loves us."

Padre brought over the round of drinks. As he set Griffen's Irish in front of him, he caught his gaze again and widened his eyes slightly in mock exasperation. Griffen understood completely and sympathized. Dealing with drunks was an unpleasant but nightly occurrence for anyone working in the

Quarter. Dealing with a drunken cop in your bar, however, was a no-win scenario for any bartender.

"I was just curious," Griffen said, pointedly ignoring the detective's condition. "We've got the Halloween weekend rolling up on us. Is that a problem for you and yours? Do you have to lay on extra help or what?"

Harrison made a rude noise, blowing a short raspberry through his lips.

"Hell. It's no big problem," he said. "It's like any other weekend. Just a bit more crowded, and the crazies are wearing costumes is all. Tourists getting drunk and messing with each other and the locals, same as always."

"Well, they do keep the Quarter green," Griffen said, trying to make light of the situation. "Tourism is one of our biggest industries down here."

"Tourists," Harrison said, like the word tasted bad. "Why do they call it tourist season if we can't shoot 'em?"

"Oh, come on," Griffen said. "They aren't all that bad. In fact, most of them are pretty decent and well behaved."

"Niggers, fags, and dope addicts! That's all the French Quarter is!"

The intrusion on their discussion came from a suit at the far end of the bar. The speaker was obviously drunk and loudly lecturing his companions, who were trying vainly to quiet him down. They were obviously conventioneers, still wearing their name badges on their lapels.

Most of the late-night crowd, heavily local, pointedly ignored him. They had all heard it before.

Harrison, however, leaned out into the aisle and stared at the offending party, blinking his eyes as he tried to focus.

"Right on cue," he said. "I may have to bend that boy a little."

"No big deal," Griffen said, hastily. "Padre's got it under control."

There was an unspoken rule in the Quarter: Let the bartender handle any altercations unless he or she specifically called for help. Even as Griffen tried to calm Harrison down, Padre came down the bar toward the trio, leaned close, and said something softly to them. Even though he couldn't hear the words, Griffen had heard the routine often enough to know it by heart.

"Excuse me, gentlemen. I'm afraid you'll either have to lower your voices, or I'll have to ask you to leave."

"Don't worry, Mr. McCandles," Harrison said, regaining his upright posture. "If it comes down to it, you won't have to testify. That would be a hoot, wouldn't it? A cop calling a professional gambler as a character witness."

Griffen started to protest, but the situation erupted again.

"Don't tell me to quiet down!" the drunk was declaring, shaking off the restraining hands of his friends. *"And if you lay a hand on me, I'll sue your ass and this bar for everything they got! You want me out of here? You're gonna have to call a cop!"*

Harrison was out of the booth and walking up to the man before Griffen could say anything more.

"You want a cop, mister?" he said flashing his badge. "You got one. Let's step outside."

The drunk gaped at the detective.

"Bullshit! You don't look like no cop I've ever seen!" He turned his attention to Padre again. *"Who's this? Your boyfriend?"*

Moving fast for his bulk, Harrison took the drunk backward off his bar stool and onto the floor. He had a fist cocked and ready to go, then he hesitated and took a deep breath.

Still gripping the drunk with one hand, the detective hauled him erect and set him on his feet.

"We want our *visitors* to have a good time when they're down here," he hissed, "so we'll just call this a misunderstanding."

He glanced at the man's two companions.

"Take him back to the hotel and don't let me see him on the streets until he's slept it off."

He shoved the drunk into the arms of his friends, who gathered him in and hustled him out the door.

Harrison watched them go, still breathing hard, then walked unsteadily to the door and stood staring after them. A few beats later, he stepped out onto the street and strode off in the direction the men had taken.

"What in the world was eating Harrison?" Griffen said, when the bartender came to the booth to clear away the empty beer bottles.

"He's been suspended," Padre said. "Got a reprimand for roughing up a couple frat boys."

"What?"

"Yeah. They were slapping one of the kids that tap-dance for tips around. Calling him names and asking if he gave blow jobs. Harrison stepped in and put a stop to it. Next thing you know one of their daddies is suing the city and the police department for undue force." Padre gave a sigh. "Harrison ended up holding the bag on the whole thing. It hasn't improved his opinion of tourists, to say the least."

Griffen reflected on the situation as Padre moved off. He knew from his own experience that tourists could be a pain. Most of them were okay, but there were some that seemed bound and determined to start trouble. He was just glad that it was the police's job to ride herd on them.

Then it occurred to him that in a few weeks, he would be trying to perform the same function for the conclave. He stopped being glad.

It also occurred to him that Harrison was not a good person to talk to about the conclave that was hitting town.

Eight

The shooter had been sitting in a window seat in Harry's Corner for nearly two hours, quietly nursing one beer after another as he watched the street outside. In actuality, he was watching the gateway to the apartment complex that was kitty-corner to the corner bar.

He was from out of town, Biloxi specifically, but had visited New Orleans and the Quarter often enough to have a fair grasp of its layout. He was a little surprised, however, that he had been brought in for this job instead of whoever it was that hired him using local talent. Still, the money was good, and it looked like an easy, fast in-and-out job.

Suddenly, he came out of his reverie. The target was just emerging from the complex gateway. As the shooter watched, the target—just a kid, really—checked to be sure the gate had locked behind him, then set off down the sidewalk with a long-legged, rapid stride, passing right by the bar where the shooter was watching, but on the other side of the street.

Trying to keep his movements unhurried, the shooter gathered up the paper shopping bag from the floor next to his feet and left, leaving a half-full beer behind him. The bartender and the other customers barely registered his departure.

He held the distance he was following his prey at about half a block as the youth headed off across Jackson Square. Now that he was moving, the shooter's normal patience fell into place. He would keep following the target until they reached a deserted stretch of street, then he would make his move. All he needed was a space where there were no pedestrians within twenty or thirty feet . . . and no cops, of course. At that distance, at night, witnesses were notoriously unreliable, if they decided to involve themselves at all. Within fifteen or twenty minutes, he could be back in his car and on his way to the expressway. Another half hour, and he would be out of the state.

He could follow all night, waiting for his opportunity, or, if it was necessary, make his move along this very stretch as the youth returned to his apartment. He hoped for a better setup, but this would do in a pinch.

He was pleasantly surprised when, after the target had crossed the Square, the youth turned left toward the river rather than turning right toward Bourbon Street and the profusion of bars and nightclubs. Maybe the kid was out to take a walk along the river. If so, the job could be over much quicker than he had anticipated.

Picking up his stride slightly to narrow the gap, the shooter hefted the bag he was carrying. Inside it was his favorite weapon, a double-barreled shotgun cut down until it was barely ten inches long overall. No way to check ballistics on a shotgun, and he rarely needed to use the second barrel.

The target crossed the street, heading for the river. The shooter hesitated for a moment, making a quick sweep visually to see if there were any police cars in the immediate area, then followed. As he started up the inclined driveway, he was suddenly aware of footsteps approaching him from behind. Before he could turn, he felt something hard being pressed against his side.

"Just keep walkin', mister," came a voice from behind him. "Hang a left up here into the parkin' lot."

The shooter was struck by the irony of the situation. Here

he was about to do a job on someone, and it seemed he was getting mugged.

"This is far enough," came the voice again. "Put the bag down, then step away from it and turn around. Keep your hands where we can see them."

It seemed whoever he was dealing with was versed in police procedure. Probably from the other side. It also occurred to him that he was now in the exact situation he had been planning on catching his target in. A deserted stretch of space with no witnesses.

He followed the instructions and turned slowly. There were two of them, both young and male. Both black. One of them was openly holding a nine-millimeter semiautomatic pistol.

"If this is about money," the shooter said, calmly, "I can—"

"Shut up!" said the pistol holder. "Check the bag."

His partner picked up the paper bag, hefted it, and looked inside.

"Shotgun," he said. "Cut-down."

"Uh-huh," the pistol man said, not taking his eyes off the shooter. "You working alone or with a partner?"

"Alone," the shooter said, then immediately wondered if he should have lied.

"Well," said the pistol man, "it seems we have us a bit of a problem . . . or, at least, you do."

"What's going on here? Patches? Is that you?"

The target, no longer headed for the river, was walking up to the group.

"Oh . . . Hi, Mr. Griffen," said the pistol man, suddenly looking a bit embarrassed.

"Hi yourself, Patches," the target said mockingly. "Mind telling me what you're doing here?"

"Well, I . . . we . . . we spotted this guy following you

and thought we'd check him out," the young gunman said. "He's got a shotgun in that bag there."

"I know he was following me," the target said. "That's why I was leading him up to the Moonwalk. The question is, what are *you* doing here? This isn't your normal neighborhood."

"Well . . . Okay. We were watching out for you."

"Any particular reason?" the target pressed.

"We heard that someone had a contract out on you," the gunman said. "My brother, TeeBo, said we should keep an eye on you and step in if anything went down."

"He couldn't just give me a call and warn me?"

"We weren't sure if it was true or not," the youth named Patches said. "Besides, this way, if we did you a favor, he thought maybe you'd think you owed us a favor sometime."

The whole scene had a vaguely surreal feel for the shooter. Not only had he walked into some kind of a trap—or double trap—it seemed the others had all but forgotten about him as they continued their conversation.

"Well, you tell TeeBo that I appreciate the gesture, but I don't think I want to owe him a favor over this." The target was smiling. "Sometime, maybe. But not now and not over this. Put the gun away and give him back his bag."

"If you say so, Mr. Griffen."

The gunman's pistol disappeared, and he nodded to his partner, who tossed the paper bag at the shooter's feet.

"Um . . . mind if we stick around for this?" Patches said. "We won't do nothin', but I'd kinda like to see this. I know TeeBo will want to hear about it."

"Suit yourself." The target shrugged. "But you'd better move a little farther away. If this guy uses a shotgun, he probably doesn't shoot that straight."

The two black youths eased a few steps to the side, and the target turned his attention to the shooter.

"Well?" he said. "Anytime you're ready."

The shooter stared at him for a moment, then, moving slowly, he bent over and took the shotgun out of the bag. Without going near the triggers, he broke the weapon open, removed the shells, and threw them away.

"If you don't mind, I think I'll pass on this one," he said. "All this is more than I bargained for, and I've got a bad feeling I'm way out of my league here. All I want now is to walk away from the whole thing."

"That's acceptable." The target nodded. "Just go back and tell whoever hired you that if he sends anyone else, I won't be as generous."

He turned his back on the shooter.

"C'mon, Patches," he said. "At least let me buy you two a drink."

The shooter watched the three young men walk away and decided then and there that this had been his last job.

Nine

As usual, the crowd was light in the late afternoon at the Irish pub. The bartender was idly browsing through the newspaper and didn't even look up, much less wave, when the man who had been playing the video poker machine finished his beer and wandered out the side door.

In the seemingly random pecking order of the bar-centered social life in the Quarter, the video poker players, sometimes referred to as video crackheads, were pretty much the bottom of the food chain. They rarely if ever interacted with any of the regulars or even the bartenders, except to get another beer or to break a twenty from the latter. Instead, they would sit glued to their chosen machines for hours, staring at the screen as they sipped their drinks and pumped more money in as needed. In a bar that was heavy on conversation and pool, this put them well under the radar. One rarely noticed their coming or going, or even their presence while they were there.

This made the role ideal for the man who had just exited the pub. Unlike most, he worked at being unnoticed. In fact, the last time he had been in town, he made a point of hanging at this specific bar and establishing himself as one of those invisible video poker players. It was the perfect guise in which he could watch and listen yet not be seen. Even now, he doubted the bartender knew or remembered his name.

Of course, being a shape-shifter helped.

Reflecting on that, the man smiled to himself. For all their self-trumpeted powers of size changing and shape-shifting, the big bad dragons barely scratched the surface of the possibilities of those skills. Young McCandles might be excused because he was still new to the game, but the older, more experienced dragons didn't have that alibi. Their pro-longed ignorance was yet another example of dragon arro-gance. If you had enough power, why bother learning finesse?

Sure, big flashy changes were impressive, like shifting your form into an animal, especially a mythical one. But the same skills could be used to perform smaller, less noticeable changes that were much more useful in one's workaday life.

Changing one's hair color or length or the color or shade of one's complexion was easy, but effective. So was adding or subtracting twenty years to one's age. Changing gender was a bit more challenging, especially since it usually meant chang-ing one's garments as well, but it could be done.

One of the man's favorite changes was one he was using with his current disguise. Making one leg slightly longer than the other changed his walk and the whole way he moved and held his body. In this disguise, planted in front of a video poker machine, the man had been in the pub at the same time as young McCandles and not been recognized, even though the youth had every reason to remember him. Even the much-lauded dragon powers of observation were useless unless one chose to apply them.

The man's thoughts were interrupted when his cell phone rang. Glancing at the caller ID, he winced. He had been ex-pecting this call sooner or later, but still dreaded it.

Looking quickly up and down the street to be sure there was no one within hearing, he leaned against a wall in the shade and opened the phone.

"Talk to me," he said in his traditional greeting.

"George!" came an agitated female voice. "Where the hell are you?"

"Hello to you, too, Debbie," he said, making a face at his reflection in a window. "I'm fine, thank you. How about yourself?"

In actuality, his name wasn't really George. Though he was known by that title to those who employed him, his closely guarded secret was that he was only one of a team. The entire team was referred to as "the George" because of its purpose . . . to hunt dragons for pay. As one of the team's main field agents, however, he found that even the team was referring to him more and more as "George." That was one of the annoyances of working with a team. He was about to have to deal with another one of those downsides.

"Cut the crap, George," came the voice of his distant teammate. "We haven't heard from you for over a week. What are you doing?"

"I'm taking a little self-prescribed vacation," George said. "I figure with the bonuses we got from my last job, I could afford some time off."

There was a pause at the other end of the conversation.

"I suppose that's right," Debbie said with grudging acceptance. "You could have called in and told us, at least."

"Yeah, sure." George laughed. "And get told there was a new hot assignment that was too good to pass on. No, thanks. I'll do it my way. If that's not acceptable, you can always fire me."

"Very funny," his teammate said. "Okay. You're on vacation. Where are you, anyway?"

Now it was George's turn to hesitate.

"George," came the voice, stern now. "Please tell me you're not back in New Orleans."

George searched for an adequate answer, but none came to mind.

"Goddamn it, George!" his teammate exploded. "You can't—"

"Listen, Debbie," George interrupted. "I only . . ."

"No, *you* listen!" she shot back. "You know the rules."

"I should," he snarled. "I wrote most of them."

"Then you also know why the rules are there in the first place," Debbie said, coldly. "What we're doing is dangerous without adding complications. These are dragons we're playing with, for God's sake. We only get so many passes at the table before the luck changes. That's why we only work on assignment and for a healthy fee. That makes it business and keeps them from hunting for us on a personal basis. We can't get involved emotionally!"

"I know, I know." George sighed. "You're right. It's just . . ." He hesitated again.

"Talk to me, George," Debbie said, using his own catch-phrase, but her voice softened a bit. "What's really going on there? Are you going soft on this McCandles kid?"

"I don't know," George said. "He may develop into a real pain in the butt, but right now he's okay. Maybe it's because he was raised not knowing about dragons and hasn't settled into the role yet. Still, he's dragon."

"Okay. So what is it?"

"It's Flynn," George said, his thoughts suddenly coming into focus. "He really got under my skin the way he insisted on a face-to-face meeting. He's everything I hate about dragons raised to a higher power. Now he's down here trying to work a number on young McCandles using the information we dug up for him. I just want to keep an eye on things as an uninvolved observer."

"Uninvolved observer. Right. Just be sure you keep it that way." Debbie hesitated. "Want any of the team down there for backup?"

"No. I'll handle this myself," George said, glad for the offered support. "That way, if anything blows, it won't splash on anyone else."

"In theory, anyway," his teammate said. "One thing you should be aware of, though. You may have some extra company.

There's a report here from one of our watchers that says Melinda's daughter Lizzy is on her way down there if she isn't there already."

"Lizzy? That psycho?" George was genuinely startled. "What's she coming down here for?"

"Unknown," Debbie said. "As far was we can tell, her own family doesn't know she's headed for the Big Easy. Just watch your back, okay?"

George found himself looking up and down the street again as he signed off. Lizzy! This just kept getting better.

Ten

Flynn was tired of waiting.

He had given the McCandles boy his hotel and room number on the back of his business card when they first met, but the youth had yet to contact him. After several days of hanging around the hotel, Flynn said to hell with it and went out searching.

Having studied George's report, he felt that Griffen should not be too difficult to locate. First of all, he knew the apartment complex where the young dragon and his sister lived. Flynn decided against approaching him there, however. First, it would alert McCandles as to how much information Flynn already had on him. Second, he wanted to hold off meeting the sister until he had a better fix on Griffen himself.

That left the young McCandles's usual haunts.

When he ate out, it was often at either the Café Du Monde or at Yo Mama's Bar and Grill on St. Peter Street. His favorite watering hole was an Irish pub a few blocks off Bourbon Street.

Flynn decided to try the pub first.

It wasn't hard to find, but it was nearly deserted in the late-afternoon sunshine. The bartender was reading a newspaper, and a couple of middle-aged women were sitting at the bar deep in a quiet conversation.

Remembering that Griffen was mostly a nocturnal person, Flynn decided to try again later.

He killed time over an early dinner at a small restaurant on Decatur Street, then swung by the Café Du Monde, pausing to listen to the music of the street entertainers on Jackson Square. He did enjoy the French Quarter when he visited, though it was a marked change from his normal habits to be able to walk wherever you wanted to go. In Southern California, one drove everywhere, including to fetch the mail or visit your neighbors.

It was full dark when he reached the Irish pub again, and this time his patience was rewarded. Griffen McCandles was sitting at the far side of the bar, apparently engrossed in a small notepad he had on the bar before him. The youth glanced up as Flynn walked in, and smiled in recognition, waving for the man to join him at the bar.

"Mr. Flynn," he said. "It's good to see you. I've been wanting to ask you about a couple of things."

"You could have called me," Flynn said. "And it's just 'Flynn.' Not 'Mr. Flynn.'"

"I would have, but I didn't know which hotel you were staying in," Griffen said, signaling the bartender for a round.

Flynn tried not to stare at him.

"It was on the back of the card I gave you when we first met," he said, trying to keep his voice casual. "The name of my hotel and the room number."

"Really?" Griffen said. "I didn't notice. Oh well, we're here now. May I buy you a drink?"

Flynn had to fight to keep from shaking his head. Of all the reasons he had thought of as to why Griffen hadn't called, it never occurred to him that Griffen hadn't bothered to look at his business card. In Flynn's world of show business and power meetings, communication was as natural as breathing. It seemed that things were run a bit differently here.

"That explains a few things," he said. "I was starting to feel a bit neglected as a visitor."

"I'm sorry," Griffen said, hastily. "I really don't know what protocol is in these situations. I'm still pretty new to this whole dragon thing."

"No harm done," Flynn said casually as he gave the bartender his drink order. "You've probably got a lot on your mind."

"You can say that again." Griffen grimaced, taking a sip of his drink. "Besides, I didn't know how sincere you were when you offered to advise me. The big-league dragons I've run into so far haven't been exactly helpful."

"Who all have you dealt with so far?" Flynn said, though he already knew the answer.

"Well, I've had a couple of conversations with Stoner that were less than pleasant," Griffen said. "And my sister had a run-in with a guy named Nathaniel, who's supposed to be the son of someone named Melinda."

Flynn made a face.

"Not exactly glowing examples of dragons," he said. "Let's just say we're not all like that. And if you're asking, yes, I was sincere about my offer to help you."

He smiled warmly. This was going even better than he had hoped. For all George's warnings, young McCandles was as naive and trusting as a puppy.

"I sure appreciate this," Griffen was saying. "I keep feeling I've gotten in way over my head with this whole conclave thing."

"Conclave?" Flynn frowned.

"Yeah. There's some kind of conclave of supernatural people that's due to hit town just before Halloween," Griffen said. "I've gotten roped into helping with it as a moderator."

"They're still having that conclave?" Flynn smirked. "Take my advice and don't sweat it."

"Really?" Griffen blinked. "I thought ..."

"Look, Griffen," Flynn said, glancing over to be sure the bartender was out of hearing. "The ones attending the conclave are a bunch of supernatural wannabes. As a dragon, you're the real thing. That's why dragons usually don't even bother showing up. Mostly, they'll be afraid of your sitting in because they know they're not in your league. Be polite, but there's no need to show them much respect. Just slap them down fast if anyone starts to get out of line, and they'll follow your lead."

"If you say so," Griffen said slowly, reaching for his notebook.

Flynn suppressed a smile as he watched the young dragon scribble a few notes. If young McCandles followed his advice, there would be few happy people at the conclave . . . including Griffen.

Eleven

The French Quarter had always seemed centered around its vice. Actually, it centered around enjoyment, which is only vice to some. Still, especially from the outside looking in, music and food seemed merely runners-up to the grand vice of alcohol.

That being said, between the police coverage and the well-experienced bartenders, serious problems were few and far between. Exceptions hardly counted, such as big occasions like Mardi Gras and Spring Break, where the majority of the drinkers just didn't have enough experience. During the average nonstop party that was New Orleans, difficult cases tended to be very low-key.

There was always the one who needed a cab home. The occasional person curled up in a doorway who might be homeless or might just be a tourist past his limit. A few locals staggering the handful of blocks from their favorite bar to their homes, with a few stops along the way. Rarely an angry drunk, much less a fight, that the bartenders hadn't handled a dozen times before.

Of course there were always exceptions.

The bar was one step up from the daiquiri shops and beer dispensers that littered Bourbon Street. Very little local trade, and all of that young and slumming. A little hole with too much neon and attractive girls selling body shots to tourists. And, as seemed to be the pattern with such places, a little bar in the back, the music muffled, where a single bartender could keep the serious drinkers cut off from the herd.

Only a single occupant occupied the back bar. She had been sitting there for the last two hours, drinking. For the last half hour, she had been ranting. Sometimes to herself, sometimes to the bartender. Sometimes to the empty bar stool next to her. Only generous tipping and a sense of self-preservation on the bartender's part had kept her from being asked to leave.

Anyone in earshot would have known that her name was Lizzy. She had a tendency to refer to herself in the third person.

"What the hell is Lizzy drinking!?" she said, slamming her half-full glass on the countertop.

The bartender winced. She had already broken one glass that way tonight. Though, miraculously, she hadn't cut herself.

"Raspberry vodka, straight," the bartender said.

"Well, I don't want it. It's boring me. Make me a . . ."

Her eyes flicked about as if searching. The television in the corner caught her eye, an advertisement for a new truck. Despite no apparent alcohol in the ad, she shot a finger up as if it had just sparked an idea.

"A mojito!"

"Sorry, Lizzy, we don't make those here."

Lizzy glared at the bartender, whose name she couldn't remember, or even remember if she asked. Several nasty responses, both verbal and extremely physical, flashed through her mind. Most of those would have caused her the trouble of moving on to another bar though, so she bit her tongue hard. She tasted just a drop of blood.

"Fine! Just make me something interesting. And hard."

The bartender nodded and turned to the rows of bottles behind him. She caught just a bit of relief on his face in the mirror, and briefly contemplated shoving a toothpick into one of his lower vertebrae. Her gaze slipped from his reflection to her own, and for a moment she got caught up in contemplation of her own image.

She knew she was pretty. She had made sure of it. Not conventional beauty, but eye-catching, stunning in her own way. Petite, barely over five feet tall, body almost too thin. The lines of her body were sharp, almost harsh angles that accentuated modest and subtle curves and made her seem somehow . . . dangerous. Beautiful, in the way of a well-made stiletto.

She ran a hand through her hair, a rich brown, with just a flash of red in the highlights. She smiled slightly to herself, knowing how many human women would kill for a hairdo like hers. Hair back in sweeping lines that accentuated those of her face. Just a few strands and waves out of place, giving it that windblown look. Expensive, if she had gotten it at the spa. Hard to manage through conventional means. Though just a bit out-of-date.

Then her eyes fell upon her own staring back in the mirror, and she looked away. Lizzy, properly named Elizabeth, remembered with some wry distaste that she had never been allowed to think of herself as just human.

"You know why Lizzy is in town?" she asked the bartender as he set down her drink.

"You told me some." He nodded.

"Well, I'll tell you again," she growled.

She sipped her drink and looked at it curiously, not recognizing some of the mixed flavors. For the moment she was too bored with trying to set herself apart to bother with the third-person nonsense. Besides, once in a while it got her thinking that Lizzy really was another person. And that was not a good thing.

"Nathaniel was always a mama's boy," said Lizzy.

"Who's Nathaniel?" the bartender asked.

"My brother, you nit! Now shut up and listen. That's what bartenders are supposed to be for."

She smiled openly and a little nastily as she watched him control his face. Maybe most drunken tourists would have missed the little tics and signs of strain. And though he nodded and looked attentive, for the next few moments she remained silent, slipping into her own thoughts.

Thoughts of her brothers, especially Nathaniel. Thoughts of Melinda. It wasn't easy having one of the country's more powerful dragons as a mother. Suck-up Nathaniel, currying favor, doing everything Mommy asked. Like that was a way to win love.

"Damn it, I was her favorite!" she said.

The bartender jumped.

"I *am* her favorite," she said.

Lizzy sipped more of her drink and dipped her finger in it, starting to draw pictures on the bar top.

"Oldest daughter, almost oldest child. Way too many sons running about. Everyone knows I'm next in line. I'm heir. Mother to daughter, that's Melinda's way. Nathaniel will never ever, ever stop that. Even if I have to drop Mama's little boy in the ocean."

"I don't think your mother would appreciate that."

"Shows what you know, little monkey. Mother loves competition, especially among the boys, but I'm above that. Any day she's gonna get back to grooming me for the top spot . . ."

Any day, like in the old days. Before things started getting . . . different. She knew Melinda was only biding her time. They were dragons, time was what they had most of all. All those other rumors . . . they were just wrong . . . stupid.

"And now little Nathan has gone and found himself a tartlet! Thinks to give Mother a new daughter. Mother can't have any more daughters. She can't! I won't allow it! I'll find her, and when I do . . ."

She drifted off again, lapsing into silence.

"Two days . . . been here two days, and haven't seen hide nor hair of anyone more interesting than a drunken monkey.

I mean, really, what kind of dragon would come to this waste-land? One who is testing the limits of a regenerating liver? There is nothing to do here, nothing to see, and no power! It makes no sense!"

"Dragon?" the bartender asked.

Elizabeth looked up at the bartender suddenly, and he backed up two steps automatically. Her eyes flashed, and in the conflicting neon they seemed . . . fractured. Like a smashed mirror, different colors butting against each other without blending, the most vivid of those a violent purple that seemed almost to glow.

Lizzy had never learned to control her eyes. Especially in one of her moods. Melinda always used to say, somewhat coldly, that she had her father's eyes.

"This was a good drink," she said, still glaring at the bar-tender. "Nice mix of flavors. So I won't drag you out back for a little light entertainment. Take care now."

She stood and dropped a few bills on the bar without looking at them. She started to weave her way through the crowd, making her way back to Bourbon Street. A few feet from the door, she stopped in her tracks and stared outside.

Flynn was walking down the street.

"Him?! Here?! What the fu—"

She jumped midword. One of the men on the dance floor, seeing a seemingly drunken girl wavering on her feet, had stepped up and placed both hands firmly on her rump. His surprise squeeze had sent her nearly half a foot into the air.

She whirled on him so quick that he didn't have time to move back. With one hand she grabbed his wrist, fingers iron-strong and grip just shy of painful. The other hand reached out and slapped his backside, gripping just as firmly as he had. It was his turn to jump, but his eyes quickly went excited and smoldering, and a cocky grin started to spread on his face.

His grin faded, and his eyes started to widen, whites

beginning to show. Lizzy slid against him, hands still in place, looking to the world like nothing other then a girl cuddling up to a likely guy. No one could see the claws that had replaced the tips of her fingers, or the blood that soaked into the black material of his pants.

She stretched up on her tiptoes to purr into his ear.

"The word for today . . ." She paused, and her tongue flicked lightly over his ear. It was forked. ". . . is manners."

With that, she sank back down slightly, then brought her head smacking upward against his. He crumpled, and she left him on the dance floor as those around suddenly noticed a problem and rushed to help.

By the time she had slipped onto the street, there was no sign of Flynn. She cursed and set out to search.

Twelve

The cell phone rang. Despite the fact only half a dozen people alive in the world had the number, George had had a bit too much fun programming the ring tones lately. Especially after the last call he had received, "Murder by Numbers"—it had just been too much to resist.

"Hello, Debbie," he said.

"Whoever invented caller ID really needs to die," the woman on the other end said sourly.

"You write me a contract on him, and I'll be happy to oblige you," George said.

"Interoffice bribery is against your regulations."

"I thought we were beginning flirtation. Wouldn't do that for just anyone, you know."

"Also against regulations. Now stow it. We, well, *you* have got problems, George."

"I always have problems."

"And I bet you bring each and every one down on yourself," Debbie said.

George looked at the time. It was a little past midnight, and he had been planning on an early night. The hotel room he was staying in had next to no luxuries. It did have a coffeepot, though, and something in his teammate's tone sent him over to it.

"So what did I do now?" he asked. "Everyone over there

falling apart because ol' George isn't there to beat down the big scaly baddies?"

"There is no need to be snooty. You've trained some excellent hunters on staff, and those of us in auxiliary service have never needed *you* to hold our hands."

"No flirtation, no bribery, no hand-holding. God, when did this bureaucracy turn into no fun at all?"

"Again, stow it. I got a call from your latest client today."

George held the phone away for a few moments and reined himself in. The first things he thought about saying were counterproductive.

"If that supercilious bastard wants a refund, you can kindly inform our 'client' that he, too, can be turned into a set of matched luggage."

"Hmm, do we have a record of his preferred dragon form on record? He doesn't strike me as a type to stick to the traditional scales and leather motif. Anyway, he asked for just that, but it was by way of an opening gambit. Claimed that since McCandles is unharmed and still breathing, you owe him another pass."

"To which you replied that our contracts specify one pass, and he did not pay for a guaranteed kill, only a direct confrontation," said George.

"Yes, I did, so he tried renegotiating for a direct-kill contract, at a discount of course," Debbie said.

George watched drips fall into the coffeepot. Idly he put his thumb against the hot plate. The sting of it gave him a reason for groaning.

"That's it, we never deal with anyone from California. Ever, ever again. Make a bylaw."

"We'd get busted for discrimination. Besides, good money out of that part of the country. Come on, George. Focus a bit, won't you? Vacation or not, you are slacking," Debbie said.

He had been focusing. Obviously, Flynn was unsatisfied with his own attempts to "test" young McCandles and wanted some serious pressure put on. Or maybe Griffen was just getting under Flynn's skin enough that he was ready for murder. That thought alone made George like the kid a little.

Mostly, though, George was thinking about his little "vacation" here. He had intended to cause Flynn some trouble, and so far hadn't done much but monitor. That and a bit of indirect contact with McCandles, just for kicks. Maybe it was time to take things up a step.

"And what did you tell him, Debbie?"

"That you were on another assignment. He, like most of our clients, doesn't know he is dealing with a team of hunters, so he didn't ask for another agent. I did give him a referral to another hitter. A human, solo act but good contacts, someone we wouldn't mind seeing disappear from the face of the earth."

"Any chance of dropping a dragon?" George asked. Human or not, he was always keeping his ears open for new talent.

"Unlikely; if Flynn goes that way, it will be mostly a scare tactic. Though a few shots from the right type of rifle will put the kid in the hospital. From your report, he hasn't learned regeneration yet."

"I haven't seen any sign of it, and it seems more his sister's kind of talent anyway."

George paused, thinking things through for a moment.

"Debbie, I need a favor."

"No."

"Debbie, this is me. I need you to track this hitter you referred Flynn to. If he comes to New Orleans, I want to know, and I want to know everything else about his movements when he is here."

"George, this is a noncontract. You have no business using company resources because you have decided to keep a pet. He's a dragon, George! A scaly, power-hungry, arrogant beast. You've hated them for as long as I have."

"Yes, and I'm telling you Flynn is worse. The kid on his own, he's no threat. He might even be okay. If Flynn gets his hands on him, then it will be a real mess. If Flynn drops him, well, it won't be so bad, but do you really want the reputation spread that a human could do a job we couldn't?"

"That's not—"

"You know that's the way Flynn will spin it," George said.

There was a long pause. Long enough that George poured himself half a cup from the still-brewing coffee, just to keep from saying more. A few drops steamed and sizzled on the hotplate.

"Okay, but we keep this quiet. You might be all right with breaking the rules, but I'm more in the trenches when it comes to office politics. And, George, no markers if you take the hitter. No cards."

"Why?" George asked.

"Because Flynn was also prying into your other assignment. Apparently 'someone' left a Knight of Swords on his door."

"Hmm . . ."

"No. No card, George. You are not hunting this man. Don't poke the bear more than you need to, at least not till we have paper on him."

George sighed.

"You are right. If I interfere, and I haven't decided I will yet, I will keep it anonymous."

"Good . . . thank you. I'll keep you informed."

The phone went dead. George sipped his coffee. He had a minor tinge of guilt. He really shouldn't have lied to her. But at the very least he had already decided to interfere.

He'd have to think about a card.

Thirteen

Griffen was brooding. He had holed up with a whiskey on the very end of the "family side" of the Irish pub bar. Which meant that other than when the bartender and the occasional person headed to the men's john, he was left alone with his thoughts.

Those thoughts were all about the conclave. He had started to feel more and more overwhelmed, a surge of near panic pushing him out of his apartment late afternoon. He just couldn't seem to get his head straight and was feeling antsy and nervous. Eventually, he had stopped by the A&P and picked up a new notebook and a pen. His plan was to sit at the bar and write out what he knew, and some of his own thoughts. Mostly he was hoping to pin down some thoughts in words he could organize and examine to get his own head straight.

That notebook was depressingly empty. He had filled up a whole two pages with the various groups supposed to be involved and the little he knew of each thanks to Slim and Flynn. Then he had drawn a blank. His own thoughts were too chaotic to get a toehold on. And he had begun to realize he only had the smallest clue of what actual issues were going to be discussed.

What was worse, he didn't quite know what a "moderator" was supposed to do. Was it his job to settle debates? Or just hold the peace? How far was he supposed to go to keep order? Much more, how far was he willing to go? Maybe it was just his mood and Irish, but he was beginning to feel even more lost than he had when he first found out about dragons.

He was so wrapped up that he didn't notice Jerome till he was pulling up the stool next to him. Griffen looked up, eyes not quite tracking, then did a double take and smiled. He reached out and shook Jerome's hand.

"Hey, Jerome, haven't seen you around for a couple of days. How are you doing?"

"Same old, same old, Grifter. You?"

"Still trying to get my damn head around things. If the others in charge of this conclave are even a third as disorganized as my head right now, it's going to be a real mess."

"Are they keeping you in the dark on purpose?" Jerome asked.

"Possibly. Been thinking just that. I've been wondering if maybe I shouldn't put word out among our network to keep an eye on the delegates. I mean, if I don't know what to expect, the more viewpoints the better. We might even have to think about considering security."

"Oh, that's a great idea," Jerome said.

His tone was a bit sharp, and, to Griffen's ear, bitter. Griffen looked over at his friend seriously for the first time. He hadn't noticed the rings around Jerome's eyes before, the haggard touches to his features. Jerome looked strained. Angry.

"Problem, Jerome?"

"Look, we got some of the best watchers, shills, dealers, and the rest I ever did meet. Our operation is tops, but it's not designed for that sort of work. We don't have much in the way of thugs, and what we do have is tied up on the regular games."

Griffen closed his notebook and took a sip of his Irish.

"You're right." He nodded to Jerome. "I hadn't thought of things that way."

"Yeah . . . I noticed."

If anything, the tone was sharper this time.

"Okay, Jerome, you are right, I admit it. Still you're pissed. What am I missing?"

"Damn it, Griffen, what aren't you missing? When was the last time you asked, or even thought, about the operation you are supposed to be running? Your head's been so wrapped up in this conclave that the only time you think of us is when you need us for it."

"Whoa, whoa. You haven't come to me with anything either."

Jerome's hands clenched for a moment, as if he wanted to do something but was restraining himself. He nodded.

"Sure, boss, sure. I ain't brought much to your attention. When you first started, I had to, but then you started asking for regular reports and things got covered when you asked. Then Rose comes along and . . . hell, there hasn't been anything I couldn't handle on my own, so I let you work through things. But, still, you've gots a job to do. It ain't a nine-to-five like some people, but it's what pays your rent and puts food on your table and whiskey in your glass all the same."

Griffen didn't hip-shoot that. Though a part of him wanted to say it was a job he never asked for, but that was a small, small part that he was immediately ashamed of. Jerome and Mose had done a lot for him, did a lot for him. He wasn't all too sure he'd still be alive if not for them. He certainly wouldn't have been living comfortably in his new favorite place on earth.

"Again, you're right," Griffen said finally.

"Go on, I'm listening." Jerome took a sip from his drink, and it was clear to Griffen he was finally working to control his voice.

"I've been getting tunnel vision. And I'm sorry for that. I won't say I'm totally to blame, but next time you have my permission to give me a kick in the ass if you have business I need to be attending to."

"Want to make that an order, boss?"

Jerome smiled, and Griffen found himself returning it. Despite the frustration both felt, they were friends.

"An order for the next butt-kicking sure. Not an order for all time," Griffen said.

"Damn, guess I'll have to make the most of it."

Jerome clapped Griffen on the back, and some of the tension eased from his face. Griffen hadn't really realized how much this had been on Jerome's mind, and with that realization came a need to understand more. As tempting as it was to let things slide and go back to their drinks, Griffen pressed on.

"You aren't happy that I agreed to Rose's favor, are you?" Griffen said.

"Not without knowing a lot more, no. That was risky and foolish, and you of all people should know better. Besides, I've got to ask myself, where is our end? What do you or your people get out of sticking your nose in a mess of folks that we haven't ever dealt with in the past?" Jerome asked.

"Just because you haven't dealt with them doesn't mean we won't have to someday," Griffen said.

"Sooner rather than later now that you are on their radar."

"Now that I've been thinking on it, dragon or no dragon, I think if I wasn't already on some of their radars, Rose wouldn't have come to me. One thing I hope to gain out of this whole mess is to find out how the rest of the world responds to dragons, and me specifically."

Now it was Jerome's turn to stop and think.

"Well now, I can't say that's not something worth learning. But it seems an awful little reward for what could be an awful lot of trouble."

"Maybe you're right a third time. Has Mose been feeling the same way?" Griffen asked.

"Hell if I know." Jerome lost what good cheer he had

gained. "He's been worse than you. I go to him with something, and he says 'run it past Griffen' or 'that should be
Griffen's baby.' Between the two of you, I've been the one left
trying to hold things together. And I'm too small a fish, or I
wouldn't have backed you for the frickin' job."

"Nice to be appreciated," Griffen said.

"Yeah, well, if you want to make it up to me, you'll go
brace Mose on it. I want to know the lay of the land before
we get hit with anything too big to handle."

Griffen sighed and nodded. He had already planned to go
see Mose soon. Now he had better questions.

Conclave pushed aside for the moment, Griffen's head was
beginning to clear.

Fourteen

Mai was bored.

She was sitting in her apartment, staring out the window into her semiprivate courtyard. Her apartment was opulent, one of the higher-end condos in the Quarter. Fully furnished, secure, in the heart of the action. It even came with off-the-street parking, which she wasn't using because she rarely enjoyed driving. She enjoyed being driven.

Her gaze kept drifting to the phone. She should call someone, check on . . . things. Yet every time she picked the phone up, she would stare at it for a few moments and invariably put it down. She knew what answers she would hear. Positive responses. Positive, but predictable. There just didn't seem to be any point.

She stared out the window.

She just couldn't help herself. She was simply used to a more active lifestyle than she was finding in the Quarter. Oh, the nightlife was good, and the shopping okay, but she didn't know what to do with herself. Mai had always thought of herself as a big-city girl, and in so many ways the Quarter and those in it had a small-town mentality. Oh, there was a city wrapped around it, but it was just another city, nothing special.

Looking back on things, she realized she had started to grow listless and that the boredom had been creeping up on her for quite some time. Back before Griffen had known about being a dragon even. Michigan had just not been her style, though she had gone for more day trips than Griffen would ever realize. Her family's money had made a jaunt to New York or even farther no problem. Sometimes those trips had just been for fun, sometimes to report in.

That was the real kicker. Back then she had felt more active, more involved with her little espionage role. Her family might have seen it as a lesser post for a somewhat difficult girl-child, but she had seen potential in Griffen even then. She had had a lot of fun plotting and planning for possible contingencies. Now that her plans were set in motion, she was in waiting mode. So much had to simmer and stew, so much had yet to come to a head.

The other dragons of the East, young and old, were moving into position. She didn't have to do anything, not at the moment. No prod necessary, no strings to pull. Of course she was pleased that things were going so well, but it left her with little to occupy her mind or time.

And Griffen . . . So different now, so new. She found herself drawn to his new confidence, his new power. Attracted to the man he had become and the potential he had yet to tap. At the same time, she missed the boy. The naive young dragon who hadn't a clue about the world. No ambition, no cares. Easy.

For little stretches of time, she could wrap herself up in him. In enjoying the Quarter as he saw it. Helping and guiding him as he learned what it was to be a dragon. Pulling subtle strings, showing him choice bits and pieces of a much larger world. That was even more fun than what they shared in bed. Though Fox Lisa had proved a surprising and interesting diversion.

She had no intention of rushing Griffen's progress. He already seemed to be growing so fast; any faster, and it might upset everything. He was drawing enough attention as it was. Besides, despite her current boredom, Mai was nothing if not patient.

He was just so wrapped up in this conclave of his. That was her one regret so far. She would have steered him away from this whole mess if she could have. Not only did it keep him distracted and growing more distant, but she had no way to predict or try to control the influences he would encounter once it got under way.

Like so many dragons, she barely bothered with other supernatural creatures. They weren't in her class, within her sphere of influence. Oh, she had dabbled when she was younger. Her family often tended to disregard her, so she made it a habit to track others who were disregarded. She even remembered the boyfriend she brought home one day who claimed to be a tengu. Her parents really gave her hell for that one. Though she had never been quite clear if they were more upset that he wasn't a dragon or that he was Japanese.

What would Griffen meet? Who would he be drawn to? What would be drawn to him? How could she make it all work for her?

She left the phone and window behind. It was about time she got off her ass and got back to work.

A short walk took her from her place to Griffen's. He had given her a key to his security gate a while ago. A move that Val had seemed to disapprove of at the time. Not to mention Jerome. Mai was afraid she might have to do something about that weakblood soon.

Of course, Griffen didn't know she had taken the liberty of making up a key for his apartment. Nor did she really feel any need to tell him. No sense bothering him with little details.

From the look of things, both he and Val were out. Mai knew that Val was scheduled to work that day, but Griffen's habits were more unreliable. Just to be safe, she knocked at his door. When no answer came, she slipped inside. She always moved with natural grace, but when she wanted to move silently, cats would die from sheer jealousy.

She had only a little hope of finding what she was looking for. She had no idea how long it would be till Griffen returned, and didn't want him to know that she had rifled his apartment. Still, a quick look though his drawers and desk should be safe enough. She started to move toward his bedroom.

And stopped when she saw exactly what she was looking for, haphazardly dropped on his couch. Right next to his TV remote and a DVD case for some movie she had never heard of. She rolled her eyes and picked up the little notebook Griffen had been carrying around for a few days. If she wanted to know what Griffen was encountering in this damn conclave, she would find out the easy way. His own private notes.

She sat on the arm of his couch, careful not to disturb anything, and flipped through the notebook. Her lips pursed, and her foot twitched idly, as if her toes tapped to some unheard music. She was a bit disappointed by how little Griffen seemed to know. She couldn't help but feel he was setting himself up for a big fall.

Then she flipped the page, and her eyes widened in surprise. She ran a finger over the words at the top, a great bold heading underlined several times. She tapped a manicured nail against the heading.

Flynn's Thoughts

She scanned the page, a list of advice and suggestions that she knew at once weren't Griffen's own thoughts. Nor the comments of anyone in his immediate circle. Mai read the page twice and looked back at the heading.

"Flynn," she whispered to herself.

Very carefully she put the notebook back exactly as she had found it. Despite the apparent lack of care it had been set

down with, Mai took no chances. She left as silently as she
had entered, locking the door behind her. Her lips began to
slip into a smile, one that slowly spread as she walked back to
her apartment. Her eyes lit up with a spark of anticipation
that they hadn't held in months.

Once back in her apartment, she picked up her phone.
This time there was no hesitation, no thoughtful stare. She
dialed a special number, one Griffen would never be told
about. Just as he would never see this side of her. Not if she
had anything to say about it.

There was no greeting when the phone picked up on the
other end. Just silence, empty and waiting. Mai smiled just a
bit more.

"I need a full check on a Western dragon. Flynn, Earl.
Primary focus, current whereabouts and activities. Include
rumor," Mai said.

"One hour," a flat, monotone voice answered. The phone
went dead.

Mai put it back in its receiver and sat. She didn't spare a
glance for the window behind her. She could wait, she was
very good at waiting. And suddenly, she was no longer bored.

Fifteen

The Quarter is always transient. People come for weeks, for years, for an hour while passing through. It rarely matters, because the outside world hardly seems to exist when one is in the Quarter. Time is at a standstill. So much so that some come for a weekend, never leave, and hardly remember that they were supposed to.

For those coming to New Orleans, there are a host of different types of accommodations. Hotels, motels, full resorts. Even apartments that are sublet. Some locals flee the city during big events, whether it is a football bowl or Mardi Gras. And when a room with a balcony can bring in a thousand dollars a night on Bourbon Street, more than one local property owner has used the tourist dollar to fund their own vacation to far-off locations.

Even when no specific event is going on, one can always find a room. A quick Internet search, a check of the classifieds, and it is little trouble finding a nice apartment for the night. In some ways it is far more convenient than trying to find a hotel room. As time goes by, hotels ask more questions, keep better records, and grow more suspicious about checking an ID than an average Joe who just wants cash up front. Subletting an apartment for the weekend was often easier than finding a place to live for a year.

The assassin sat alone in such an apartment.

He was a big man, well muscled and tough-looking. A bald head first made him seem menacing, but, if anyone had thought to take a second glance, it made him seem neat. His clothes, black and loose, were immaculate. His hands were covered in skintight black-leather gloves. Nearly as thin as surgical gloves, but much less conspicuous. His eyebrows had a light sheen, and it would have taken a keen eye indeed to realize they had been lightly coated with Vaseline.

No matter how advanced investigation techniques became, you had to find a sample for DNA to be recognized. Hair follicles were easier to find than skin cells. And there were ways of dealing with skin cells.

The assassin glanced out of the apartment window. It was early yet, barely six, and he could just barely make out the sign of the target's favorite pub. An Irish joint from the sign, but he had no plans to approach closer than he was now. The contract had come with surprisingly good information on the target's activities, but it had also come with a time limit. Two days was almost no time for a true professional hit, and if the money hadn't been as extraordinary as the intel, he would never have taken the job.

According to the intel, the target, one Griffen McCandles, tended to drink late and often. Quite regularly, he didn't leave till closing, around two to four in the morning. A perfect time, minimizing threats and potential witnesses and casualties. This area was far too heavily patrolled for the assassin's liking during the day and evening, but early morning the police presence should be reasonably lax.

The assassin almost smiled. In some ways this town was the worst and best environment for this kind of hit. Getting away with most scenarios would be difficult, but afterward . . .

A crowd to fade into, a city of roads to get lost on, and the chances of making the newspaper slim to none. Griffen McCandles would be reported as a surprisingly violent mugging, if he was reported at all. The police would know the truth, but no one would want the newspapers to frighten the tourists. Any investigation's hands would be tied as a result, not that he was particularly worried about local cops.

If the target didn't come to the pub tonight, tomorrow night the assassin would have to move to Plan B. The target's home. Not only wasn't there as accessible a vantage point, but it would make escape much more difficult. He would have to take the shot just as the target passed through the security gate. The timing would be bad, but it was worth it.

If the intel was wrong entirely, he would have to trace things back to the client himself. That would be much more work, with no payment for the hit. Still, one had a reputation to maintain.

Early or not, the assassin began his preparations. He had already cleaned and prepared himself at another site. The outfit was brand-new—well, actually bought years ago elsewhere and put aside, like all of his other "work clothes." Easily disposed of if necessary, and a white shirt and a pair of blue shorts would make him into an entirely different person if he needed to strip. He pulled out his rifle, which he knew enough. Fired in a private range enough times to break it in. Also easily disposed of. He could leave it on-site or on the target's body, and it would still give no help in tracking him down.

Just to be safe he broke it down, cleaned it, and reassembled it, setting it on a small table by the window. No balcony in this place. With a balcony, people tended to look up. Without one, they almost never did.

With that he settled in to wait, watching the street via a mirror aimed toward the window. It was enough to watch by, and he was good at waiting. A few hours without moving, a single shot, and he would be much richer. Well, two shots, both to the head. For some reason the contract insisted. As if one would not be enough? The assassin pondered this to pass the time.

"You present a real quandary for me," a voice said behind him.

What the assassin did not do was jerk around in surprise. He was astonished he hadn't heard anyone enter; he was 90 percent sure that was impossible. Impossible or not, if the speaker had wanted him dead, he would be dead. He was 99 percent sure of that.

He turned slowly and took in the plain-looking man before him, holding a pair of semiautomatic pistols. The grip on the pistols, and the cold gaze, identified him as another professional. Though his dress was far too stylish and noticeable. There was a low table between the two professionals.

"What sort of quandary?" the assassin asked.

"I have decided to thwart your client. You are my best opportunity, or at least preventing your hit is. And I see before me a professional of such quality that I know I can't talk or bribe you out of a contract taken."

"You talk too much, and I see no quandary. You should have shot me."

George sighed, and the barrel of one pistol wavered a fraction of an inch. The assassin noted this but did not yet see how to turn it to his advantage.

"Yes, you are a professional, but I am a bit of an artist, you see. I haven't hunted a . . . person of your quality in quite some time. I find taking such an easy shot distasteful," said George.

"Then you are in the wrong line of work."

"This is not my line of work. I am on vacation. Slumming as it were. Don't take this the wrong way. I am well and truly impressed by you without seeing you take shot one, but I am used to much more dangerous opponents."

The assassin said nothing. The eyes told it all. This man's eyes said that he was relating simple truth. The assassin was mildly curious what sort of "opponents" he was used to, but didn't care much. He was in this work for the money, not the sport.

George sighed again, and again the pistol dipped a moment. His left hand. His right must be dominant. The assassin was watching for any more weaknesses when the man surprised him.

George leaned forward, and tossed his left-hand weapon across the table halfway between the two. The right-hand weapon never wavered. The assassin kept his eyes on that gun, never once glancing to the one on the table.

"I have decided to be sporting. That is your weapon. I will leave this room, but not the building. You will not leave the building, not alive. Not unless you kill me first, understand?"

"And if I decide not to play your game?"

"Feel free to try to change the rules, but it is simple. You will not leave, or get your hit, until I am dead."

The assassin had a quick mind and was good at percentages. He took this offer, this game, at face value. But he had no intention of following the other man's lead.

"Why should I trust that weapon? Toss me the empty and keep the full so you can kill me with your conscience clear?"

He knew the answer, knew that this sportsman before him wouldn't do such a thing. He mentally counted to ten and fought to keep his breathing regular. He wanted to hold his breath, hoping this ploy would work.

It did.

"Very well, take the other," George said.

Carefully, oh so carefully, George moved toward the table. He reached down, blindly, keeping his piece trained on the assassin. Only when he had the other gun in his hand did he glance down. Just for an instant, his right-hand pistol drooped.

The assassin moved in that instant, kicking the table up, jarring George's hands. A blade, long and sharp, was in the assassin's hand. It cut through the tendons of George's right wrist, as a hard blow struck his left.

Blood sprayed.

The assassin kept moving, using his momentum to drive George's left wrist into the wall. The right-hand gun fell, the left hung loosely in George's pinned hand.

The blade slashed across George's stomach, then up and in.

The assassin held his opponent on the blade, not releasing the limp hand still holding a weapon. The stomach blow was a killing one, but a slow death. The assassin needed information.

"How did you find me? Who are you?"

He twisted the blade, George groaned. The smell of blood and worse filled the room.

"Ah! Ahn . . . oh! I say, you are good. Better than me if truth be told," George said through pain-bared teeth.

Which seemed obvious to the assassin given their current situation.

"Answer!" said the assassin.

"Yo . . . Ah! Your contacts and middlemen aren't nearly as professional as you. What with your rush job I managed to track down the person handling your booking. But to be fair, I had advance warning on who to look for."

The assassin twisted the blade again, and George arched against the wall, closing his eyes, momentarily groaning. He seemed too coherent to the assassin; it unnerved him.

"Pity, really, I did try to play as fair as I could," George said.

The assassin knew his business. Still, he only noticed that George's right wrist had stopped bleeding an instant before the fist cracked against his jaw.

The assassin lost contact with his foe for a moment, then George simply vanished.

The cold weight of a pistol barrel dug into the back of the

assassin's skull. A blow to the back of his knees sent him kneeling to the floor.

"So much for sportsmanship," George said.

The blade the assassin had left in George's sternum sliced along his throat. His last thought, almost idle, was to wonder why George hadn't shot him, now or earlier.

Too noisy.

Sixteen

Even though the Voodoo Museum was only a half block off Bourbon Street, very few tourists found it. It was far enough north of the main concentration of bars and souvenir shops that one did not come across it in a normal prowl down Bourbon Street, and even if one had a map and was looking for it, its frontage was nondescript enough that it was easy to overlook.

Most of the Quarter locals at least knew of its existence. If nothing else, it was only a half block from the Clover Grill, a favorite twenty-four-hour greasy spoon that people migrated toward when they needed a break from gumbo and red beans and rice, and felt the need for a plain old hamburger or maybe some waffles.

Griffen had passed the place dozens of times but had never ventured in. Now, pausing at the doorway, he found himself wishing he had yielded to his curiosity at least once. As it was, he knew little to nothing about voodoo, and so felt woefully unprepared for the upcoming meeting. Still, it seemed there was no avoiding it.

Taking a deep breath, he pushed through the door.

The room he entered looked to be a small living room and was sparsely decorated with a few paintings and a wooden rack holding various flyers and promotions for swamp tours. A young black man was sitting behind a wooden table reading a book and glanced up as Griffen entered.

"Are you here to make an appointment or just to view the exhibit?" he said, reaching for the cigar box that apparently served as his cash register.

"I was told that Estella wanted to see me," Griffen said.

"Ah, yes." The man nodded. "You would be Mr. McCandles. Go right back. Estella is expecting you."

He indicated a curtained archway to his right, then rose and locked the main entrance, flipping over the CLOSED sign as he did so. He saw Griffen's concerned look and smiled.

"Merely for privacy, I assure you," he said.

Griffen was not completely assured but ducked through the curtained archway.

He found himself in a series of small rooms, again suggesting what was originally a residence rather than designed for commercial use. There were several glass cases scattered about, displaying what he guessed were magical items, and one corner seemed to be set up as some sort of altar.

"Back here, Mr. McCandles."

He followed the voice and found himself in a small study. There were several chairs arranged in a half circle in front of a crudely carved wooden table covered by a colorful cloth, behind which sat a tall, slim woman.

"It was good of you to come, Mr. McCandles," the woman said, rising and extending a hand. "My name is Estella. I wanted a chance to speak with you privately before the conclave."

"Thank you for inviting me," Griffen said, formally. "I've been looking forward to meeting you."

He took one of the chairs facing her, which was surprisingly comfortable. In fact, the entire room was quite cozy, and Griffen found himself relaxing despite his earlier misgivings.

"I understand there have been some complaints that my group is not doing its part in preparing for the conclave," Estella said, watching him closely.

"I've heard a few comments to that effect myself," Griffen said, "though I heard it expressed more as disappointment than as complaints."

"So it's other people making those comments, not you," Estella pressed.

"I can assure you, it's not coming from me." Griffen smiled. "If nothing else, I don't know enough about what should or shouldn't be done to prepare for the conclave to try to complain or criticize anyone."

Estella blinked at this easy admission of his ignorance.

"I guess that brings me to my next question," she said. "What makes you feel you're qualified to moderate the conclave?"

"That's even easier." Griffen smiled. "I don't. Think I'm qualified, that is. As a matter of fact, one of the things I wanted to tell you was that if you or your group object to my sitting in as moderator, I'll gladly step down."

Estella frowned.

"You make it sound like you don't want the job."

"Not only do I not want it," Griffen said with a grimace, "I can't imagine why anyone would want it. There's too much that can go wrong with very little upside."

"Of course, there's the status," Estella said, carefully. "Then, too, it would be an ideal position for someone, say, who wanted to gain more influence over the various groups. Maybe even controlling influence."

Griffen shook his head wearily.

"I've already had this conversation once with Slim," he said. "I have absolutely no interest in organizing or gaining control of other groups. I have a gambling operation I'm trying to run. That's it. I wouldn't know what to do with any of these groups even if I were given control."

"Are you sure you're a dragon?" Estella said with a faint smile.

"As sure as I am of anything these days," Griffen replied.

"Well, you sure don't sound like one," she said. "At least not like any dragon I've heard of. So if you don't want to moderate the conclave, why are you doing it?"

"I was asked," Griffen said. "Frankly, I couldn't think of a way to say no."

"And just who was it that asked you?"

"I don't think it's a big secret." Griffen shrugged. "Rose asked me. Or maybe I should say her spirit."

Estella leaned back in her chair.

"That's what I heard," she said. "If you don't mind, could you describe her for me?"

"Well, she's black, looks to be in her midthirties. Her hair is very thick, and she wears it long . . . halfway down her back. About six inches shorter than I am, and I noticed her hands have very long fingers."

He hesitated, trying to put words to the picture in his mind, but Estella waved him to silence.

"That's her, all right," she said. "I was just having a little trouble believing it is all."

"Why?" Griffen said, taken aback. "I thought that communicating with the spirits of the dead was one of the main beliefs of your group."

"It is," Estella said. "I just can't figure out why she's approaching you . . . without even a ritual . . . when I haven't seen or heard from her since she died. I mean, I am the one who took over the temple and have been running it ever since."

"I . . . I really don't know," Griffen said, a bit shaken. "If you'd like, I'll ask her the next time she contacts me. Unfortunately, she seems to pick her own time and places. I've never been able to figure out how to initiate contact."

"It's no big thing," Estella said. "It made me curious is all. I guess that answers the questions I had. You can count on the support of me and mine at the conclave. Oh, and, Mr. McCandles?"

Griffen cocked his head at her.

"Don't be too quick to discount the usefulness of any of these groups. We may not be hotshot dragons, but we're not exactly powerless, either."

"Wait a minute," Griffen said quickly. "I didn't mean to speak poorly of your group or any of the others who will be at the conclave. When I said I wasn't interested in trying to influence or control them, I only meant that I couldn't see any way they would be of help to my gambling operation."

"I'm just saying you should withhold judgment." Estella smiled. "We just might surprise you."

Seventeen

Early morning in the Quarter. The quiet time, the dead time. Garbage trucks had already been by to pick up the refuse of the night before. Most of the bars were closed, most of the music lowered to a dull murmur. Few tourists who came to New Orleans had the stamina to last the night. Locals drifting home from after-work downtime. Homeless, too tired to bother asking the occasional passersby for spare change. And a bare handful of people heading out to more conventional nine-to-five jobs. That was all that stirred at such an hour.

Val often found herself awake at this hour. Sometimes she just woke early and couldn't get back to sleep. Today though, she hadn't yet been to bed, and although she was a bit groggy, she felt way too wired to even think about sleeping. She had to be at work in three hours and, after a debate with herself, decided she'd rather push through her shift tired than try to grab an hour nap and then drag herself out of bed again.

Which left the problem of what to do with herself for the interim. If she hoped to make it through the dull stretch of afternoon bartending, she had better keep her energy up now. If she sank into the couch and flipped on the TV, chances were she'd crash and crash hard. She changed into loose sweats and running shoes and headed out the door. A run, a hot shower, and lots of coffee would see her through just fine.

It was a ghost town outside, which actually appealed to Val. There was no such thing as a "city that never sleeps" despite what ends up on tourism brochures. There wasn't even anyone abroad who knew her well enough to wave to her, a rarity in the Quarter. She started running as soon as she was out of the apartment complex's security gate.

Exercise had always been a good escape for Val. As her legs and arms began to pump, she found comfort in her own strength. The movements were automatic, muscle memory from years of training and working out. Her endorphins kicked in, and her physical body began to burn and buzz on its own natural high. While her body focused on the simple, her mind could run over the complex, as she slipped inside her own head more and more and let the outside world drift away.

Lately, she had been noticing how her body was changing. She was growing stronger, faster, without much increase in her exercise regime. In fact, she was having to push herself harder and longer just to get the same kind of tired exhilaration she used to get. The harder she worked, the stronger she grew, and the stronger she grew, the harder she had to work. She was beginning to wonder what limits there were to a dragon's strength.

She crossed Decatur, the only street with any kind of car traffic at this hour, and headed up the large concrete stairs and over to the Moonwalk. The stairs still burned, aches and little tendrils of pain going up her legs. She smiled to herself and tried to remember how the old saying went. Pain lets you know you're alive?

There were a few other joggers on the Moonwalk. A couple whom Val had seen on other mornings nodded to her in passing. No breath was wasted on greetings. These were people serious about their fitness. No one jogged in New Orleans because it was the fashionable thing to do.

The Moonwalk itself stretched pretty much the entire length of the Quarter. Val knew she would go back and forth across it several times before she was ready to quit. She put herself into a comfortable pace, keeping her heart rate up but nowhere near her top speed. This was no sprint. Still, she passed anyone going the same direction as she.

Would she have noticed any of that if Griffen hadn't come to her after their uncle Malcolm had told him about dragons? She had always been strong, fast, and very good when it came to anything physical. She should be; she worked hard enough at it. If Griffen hadn't shown up, if he hadn't brought her into his problems, she would probably have gone her whole life without getting this introspective.

Val wasn't quite sure why that thought scared her so.

Most of the time she still didn't think of herself as a dragon. Griffen seemed so preoccupied with extending his abilities. Animal control, charisma; hell, she was surprised he hadn't started trying to use dragon fire to make toast in the mornings. Then she reminded herself wryly that he didn't cook.

Val hadn't experienced any of that. Other then the rare times when she had swelled in size, her signs of dragonhood were subtler. Like the speed, and her body's growing strength. Maybe it was just that she was younger and less developed, but she didn't really feel the need, or the ability, to control a stray dog or blow smoke rings through the air.

Were there varieties of power? Different dragons with different areas of expertise? When Mose spoke, he seemed to be saying that for the most part any dragon with pure enough blood could do what Griffen was doing. Val and Griffen shared the same blood, so why did she feel she would be different?

Feelings, now that was something she didn't often think about. Feelings were a big part of what had gotten her more and more curious about dragons and their various traits and abilities. For a while now, her gut had been telling her something was wrong, something was about to break. No . . . not her gut. It was like a weight on her heart. A sharp, heavy pang.

Val shook her head and tossed the thought aside. She was just imagining trouble, convincing herself of problems. After all, something bad was always coming. Especially with this new life as a dragon that her brother had brought her into.

And where did this baby fit in her new life? *Did* it fit in? She still didn't know how she felt. How she should feel.

She checked her watch and was a bit surprised that she had already been at it for more than an hour. She felt just as energized as before, barely even out of breath. Which was good—she shouldn't have any problem getting through work—but it did sort of confirm everything she had been pondering while running. Sighing slightly, she turned off the path and started to head back to the steps, back to Decatur, then back to what she had now taken to calling home.

If she hadn't been tired, hadn't been deep in thought, she might have noticed the car on the other side of Decatur. It had registered out of the corner of her eye as being parked. She never noticed that the engine was on.

She had just stepped off the curb when it came at her.

Tires squealed. The car seemed to leap into motion, like a pouncing tiger. It cut across the two lanes of traffic, causing another car to slam on its brakes to avoid a collision, and straight at her. She had just enough time to catch sight of the small woman behind the wheel as she jumped to avoid it.

The woman was smiling, teeth white and gleaming in the morning light. That smile scared Val more than the speeding car.

If she had jumped back onto the sidewalk, Val would have been crushed. The car leaped the curb at a sharp angle, the driver clearly anticipating such a natural reaction. Val's mind was as quick as her body; she leaped forward, onto the street. The car tried to jerk back, but it was too late. The driver couldn't fight the momentum. The car swerved back onto Decatur, fishtailed, then took off, leaving Val half-crouched in the middle of the street.

She straightened carefully, fully alert now to any other threat. Her pulse pounded, her breathing was suddenly rough and erratic. The driver of the car that had braked was out of his door and headed toward her. She shot him a glare that stopped him cold, well out of arm's reach.

"Are you all right?" he asked.

"No, but I'm not hurt," she answered.

More help started to arrive, people who had seen the attempted hit-and-run. The whole affair had taken seconds. Val tried to shrug them off, to get away as easily as possible before she ended up having to fill out a police report. She was too busy worrying about what this all meant to be bothered with such nonsense.

Especially since, for a split second before the car launched at her, that weight on her heart, that tiny bit of warning she had been trying to pass off as imagination, had throbbed. It had all happened too fast to be a merely human reaction, but she knew.

She knew she had started to move just before the car did.

Eighteen

Tuesday night and nothing to do.

Griffen sat alone in the Irish pub. It was rare, the pub being so empty. Especially at night. Yet here it was, 10:00 p.m. and he and the bartender were the only occupants. They had both agreed on a Hammer horror-movie fest on one of the movie channels, but then had slipped into silence. It wasn't an uncomfortable silence, but still Griffen was searching his mind for a topic, any topic, that could get a decent conversation rolling.

He was saved when the door opened and Flynn strolled in. Griffen noticed with some amusement that Flynn never seemed to dress down. All his clothes were of high quality and, if not tailored for him, of a very good cut. Even at his most casual, his shirts tended to be silk. Griffen waved him over and, relieved to have some company, bought his first drink.

Then silence descended again.

Griffen bristled as Flynn turned his attention to the TV. He hadn't run into the other dragon often, and still had many questions for him. Especially after his meeting with Estella. It had raised questions not only about the groups at the conclave, but about dragons as well. At least, how dragons seemed to be perceived by others.

It wasn't till Flynn caught his eye and tossed a glance at the bartender that Griffen caught on. When things were busy and noisy, there wasn't much problem talking about things that you might not want overheard. In a dead-silent bar, there was no way they could talk dragons or ghosts or shifters without drawing too many questions.

Well, almost no way; this was the Quarter after all. Ghosts and voodoo were common enough. Still, Flynn wasn't a part of the local scene, so maybe he didn't realize that. Griffen shrugged inwardly and thought up an easy solution.

"Hey, Flynn, how about a game of pool?" he said.

Flynn turned his attention to the tables and frowned a bit. Seeing his obvious hesitation, Griffen was afraid the silence would win. Flynn looked almost disdainful of the idea.

"Well . . . how about we make things interesting?" Flynn said.

The bartender stepped up to them.

"Legally, I can't allow any betting in the bar," the bartender said. Then he looked around at the emptiness and shrugged, smiling easily. "So keep your money in your pockets and settle up outside, and if anyone comes in, keep your traps shut."

Griffen nodded his thanks and walked over to the back table. A bit of etiquette he had picked up since coming down to New Orleans. At least in a bar like this one, with two pool tables. If both tables were open, and you chose to shoot on the table closest to the bar, it was an invite for the bartender and anyone sitting there to feel free to watch and comment. If you went to the far table, people, bartenders especially, tended to give you your privacy.

Flynn walked over, still seeming reluctant, and started looking through the bar cues for the one that seemed most true. Griffen started to rack.

"Five thousand a game good stakes?" Flynn asked.

Griffen paused with a ball in his hand. He felt like shaking his head to clear his ears, sure he'd heard wrong, and looked up to find Flynn smiling broadly.

"If you don't feel the pinch, what's the point of playing?" Flynn said. "Five thousand isn't much, but it's enough that losing stings."

"More than stings," Griffen said, suddenly a lot more wary.

"I did say we should make it interesting. If you lose, put it down on your taxes as consultant fees."

Griffen realized that this was more than to make the game worthwhile. Flynn seemed to be testing him, gauging just how much his advice was worth to Griffen. Of course . . . he just might win.

"Well . . . all right, but I'm using my stick."

"Fair enough. I would if I had packed one."

Flynn selected a stick and began to chalk it while Griffen unlocked one of the small lockers the bar kept for the pool players and began to assemble his cue. A good stick versus bar wood was always an advantage, but Griffen had never seen Flynn shoot and had to assume he was good. Five-thousand-dollars-a-game good.

"Straight or French Quarter League rules?" Flynn asked, surprising Griffen again.

"You know the local league rules?"

"But of course; the ball and hand is a very interesting twist for a position player. You didn't think this was my first trip to New Orleans, did you?"

"Straight, please," Griffen said. He had just begun to pick up the league rules and wasn't confident enough yet to risk it.

"Drop the 'please.' You really need to learn to throw your weight around more," Flynn said. "Especially if you hope to keep control of this conclave."

"Still not sure how much control a moderator has or is supposed to have."

"It's always better to be in control. And it's always easier to start from a position of control and power than to try to scramble for one when you need it."

"Yeah but—"

Griffen got cut off as Flynn lined his cue up and broke.

The eight went in the pocket.

Griffen stood there, stunned.

"Another?" Flynn said, exuding confidence while keeping his voice bland and innocent.

Griffen had seen eights sink on the break before. It took both skill and luck, and was something he had never pulled off before. It wasn't usually repeatable. Usually.

"See," Flynn said, "now I'm working from a position of power. It makes you hesitate because you aren't sure just how much power. If you come on strong, others toe the line. Especially if they are already nervous about dealing with a dragon."

Griffen nodded and began to rack again.

"And what's to keep them from seeing you as a bully?" Griffen said.

"Why should you care? Beyond it doesn't matter how they see you. If bullying is what it takes to get the job done, why look for a weaker tool?"

Griffen didn't have an answer but didn't like the question. Flynn broke again, this time nothing fell, and Griffen stepped up to the table.

"Why would the other groups out there be so worried about a dragon trying to take them over?" Griffen said.

"They are afraid. Fear makes them stupid. They know dragons could rule if we chose to, and don't think to ask why we should bother," Flynn said.

"You really see them as that much less?"

Griffen had a three-ball run, then missed. Flynn stepped up to the table.

"Why wouldn't I? Shifters, spooks, spell slingers. They don't have anything we don't have, and none of them have our power or variety."

"But within their own sphere aren't they stronger? Can you take all the different animal forms a chimera can?" Griffen said.

Flynn had a four-ball run, but miscued when Griffen asked that question.

"No, but then I never really got into shape-shifting. I like myself as I am."

"What about the fairies, the changelings? I haven't heard about what they can and can't do."

"They are letting those nuts in this year? I didn't know their standards had gotten that lax. Those aren't fairies, not really. Oh, they claim they are part of them, but have no proof. In fact, I've never seen or heard of any real evidence there are fairies," Flynn said.

Griffen was down to the eight, but the shot was lousy. A bank into the side pocket was his best bet. He missed.

"Okay, the changelings, then. What can they do?"

"Well . . . okay, you've got me on that one. From what I've heard on rumor, they have a wide range of powers, but each one has its own unique gifts and styles. Only no one has any proof on whether the stuff is real or some form of hypnosis or illusion. You know the old legends of fairy gold turning to trash in the morning? Same deal. The effects don't often seem to last."

"Often?"

"Again, there are rumors of more, but nothing I would put any credit into. Plus everything I've heard says they only have limited control over their powers. Kind of flighty and undisciplined. Shouldn't be too much trouble for you."

Griffen watched as Flynn put ball after ball away. Including—eventually—the eight. Griffen winced and felt his bank account shrink by another big hunk.

"Another?" Flynn asked.

"Double or nothing?" Griffen said, voice strained.

"Now, why would I let you off the hook that easy? Then you wouldn't learn anything."

Flynn grinned, and Griffen found himself racking again. Flynn broke, and again nothing fell. Griffen began to shoot.

"Okay, since my 'consultant fees' are mounting up. I've been a little worried about security. I can only be in so many places at once. What if something goes wrong?"

"You've got a crew, don't you?"

Griffen winced again, thinking back to his talk with Jerome.

"Let's just say they are busy elsewhere."

"Hmm . . . remember what I said about throwing your weight around? If you are the head dragon, you need to act like it."

Griffen had run the table. He was aiming on a fairly easy shot on the eight.

"Didn't I hear a rumor about you and some drug dealers?" Flynn asked.

Griffen miscued, and came close to scratching.

Flynn smiled and stepped back up to the table.

"Only a brief incident," Griffen said. "Why?"

"Well, seems in this town they would be ideal. Good for thug work. Let's face it—expendable. And not likely to talk about any weirdness they might see, not to anyone who matters and will listen anyway."

"I really don't think I want to end up owing anything to that lot."

"So make it a cash deal up front, no favors or anything," Flynn said.

"Well . . . if things got desperate . . . maybe," Griffen said dubiously.

Flynn scratched with two balls left on the table.

"Damn!" he said.

Griffen took the cue and very carefully lined up his shot.

He looked at Flynn to see if he was going to speak, then checked his shot again. Much to his relief, he made it.

"Only other option would be some type of tag or mental tracer. An amulet or coded ID badges or something like that," Flynn said, and began to put his stick back.

"Don't you want another game?" Griffen said.

"Nope. Always quit while you're ahead, kid. 'Thus endeth the lesson.'"

Griffen watched Flynn leave the bar. He couldn't bring himself to be too angry. Back in school he had pulled similar stunts when playing cards.

He never realized just how it felt.

Nineteen

"**You** sure are limber."

Val jumped. She had been sitting out in the courtyard of her apartment complex, thinking of not very much in particular. It was sunset, fading slowly to night. For once her shift at work had been busy, and she had been enjoying the solitude and a little downtime. Only when she had sat down, no one had been in the complex but her.

She looked around, and a figure slipped out from behind a tree. It was a small woman, slim and attractive. She flowed as she moved, every step natural and smooth, a kind of roll to her hips that would have made Val feel awkward. Then she smiled, and even in the dim light Val recognized that grin.

"You!"

Val stood quickly as she recognized the woman who had tried to run her over. This was the first time she had seen her when the woman wasn't behind the wheel of a moving vehicle. She looked dangerous, deadly. Something about her made Val's heart beat a little faster. Perhaps it was those eyes.

They were broken, it was the only word Val had for them. Like stained glass smashed and crushed together. Shining as if backlit and filled with malevolence. Eyes that swept up and down her, appraising, judging, . . . hating.

"Wow, you are bigger than I thought. A real cow."

"Why, you little pips—" Val started.

"Little, honey—the Statue of Liberty is 'little' compared to you."

Val was throwing a punch before she had even thought about it, long legs rushing her forward as her fist drove for the woman's nose.

The hit never landed. She moved so fast Val couldn't track. It was like trying to punch a single raindrop. The woman crouched, Val's swing whizzing over her head. She straightened then, and gave a little push to Val's elbow that twisted the momentum of her missed punch and whirled her about, wrenching her shoulder.

"Who knew my brother had such a thing for livestock?" Lizzy said, looking Val over from behind.

Val started to turn back to Lizzy, only to jump again. The smaller woman had moved forward, and now was pressed against Val's back. Her hand was very firmly squeezing Val's ass.

"Mmm. Tender, though. Bet you'd taste good with a little seasoning," Lizzy said.

Val growled and swung back around, trying to bring her hand down like a hammer onto Lizzy's head. Lizzy stepped to the side and, with a fluid, circular motion, gripped Val's wrist and added to her momentum, driving Val's own fist into her thigh.

Val yelped with pain as her muscles spasmed, leg almost buckling on her.

Lizzy laughed like it was the funniest thing she had ever seen, and her laughter matched her eyes. It was broken, lilting up and down the scales randomly. She actually clasped her hands over her belly as if trying to contain it.

"Oh oh ha! All that strength and only the bittiest little training. I thought this was going to be fun!"

Her face instantly shifted from mirth to anger, as if a light switch had been thrown.

"You . . . SIT!"

The short woman jabbed two fingers into Val's breastbone, and the force of the blow was staggering. Val found herself stumbling backward, only to crash into one of the chairs. She sat there, stunned, gasping for breath.

"Do you have any idea what you've put me through!?"

"What—" Val gasped.

"Shut it! I'm rantin' here! Girl doesn't know when to listen to her betters, does she? Stupid cow."

Lizzy began to pace back and forth, gesturing wildly as she spoke. She only looked at Val occasionally, and seemed to be talking to an audience, or to herself, or some combination thereof.

"Came all the way down here. Used up all my emergency cash. Couldn't use the credit cards. Oh no, of course not, Mumsy watches those accounts, doesn't she? Likes to know where her favorite little girl is. All because you and my idiot brother think you can replace me. You can't! You won't!"

"What brother?" Val snapped, regaining some of her composure.

"It doesn't shut up, does it!"

Lizzy looked back at Val, and her eyes flashed. They seemed almost to swirl.

"Nathaniel, you stupid. Who else have you been bumping headboards with? Wait, no, don't answer that. I so very much don't want to know. Ugh. And it took me days to find you. Days! What kind of person lives in New Orleans and never walks down Bourbon Street?"

"Shows what you know. Most locals don't bother with it," Val said.

Lizzy went still. A moment ago she had been all motion, now she could have been a statue. Her gaze bored into Valerie.

Then, slowly at first, she began to change. She stretched, expanded, till she was as tall as Valerie. Even her clothes seemed to change with her, though Val was pretty sure that was just their cut.

She changed again, milky white scales spreading over her skin. They flowed like water. Iridescent, catching the light and tossing it back like moonstone. Her tongue flicked out, long and forked.

Then again. And in a moment Valerie was looking at an exact copy of herself.

"I can be anything I want. You are already dead, but if you piss me off, I'll use your own form to rape your brother. So shut it."

Val quivered with rage, and the armrests of the chair snapped in her hands. Lizzy nodded and smiled at the display, and shifted back into her own form.

"No one knows I'm here. No one is gonna know. They don't let Lizzy have her fun, especially not if she plans on breaking her brother's toys," Lizzy said.

Val surged toward her again, swelling in size as she went. Lizzy seemed shocked by the motion, perhaps thinking Val properly cowed. Either way, Val's fist cracked into her stomach, a fist nearly the size of a football.

"I am no one's toy," said Val.

Lizzy fell, and Val was on her. She struck her twice more before Lizzy began to block. Val managed to grab one of her wrists, and slammed her hand into her face, going down on one knee and trying to pin her smaller opponent.

Then Lizzy smiled, blood running from her smashed nose.

"Oh, good, you can be fun!"

Lizzy shrank. So suddenly and rapidly that she slipped free from Val and slipped behind her in an instant. With Val having gained size and Lizzy losing it, she was now less then half as big as Val. She grinned and slammed her foot into the small of Val's back, sending her flying through the air.

Val twisted in midair, instincts panicking, and cradled her stomach as she fell.

Lizzy stood still as rock again, nostrils flaring.

"No."

Val didn't have time to react as Lizzy jumped at her. She grabbed Val by the hair and by the throat and smashed her head back into the ground. Val's vision blurred, and she found herself staring up into Lizzy's eyes.

"Let me see . . ." Lizzy said, glaring downward.

Her eyes widened and her nostrils flared again. She jumped back from Val and held her fist up to her mouth, looking like a shocked little girl.

"I'm gonna be an auntie?!" she said, her tone a mix of shock and confusion.

Val staggered to her feet.

"I don't know what you are talking about," Val said.

"Sure you don't. Only person I ever saw that worried 'bout their stomach in a fight was Mum when she had Thor on board."

Lizzy rushed at her, and Val braced herself, ready to fend off another attack. The last thing she expected was to be hugged about the waist and lifted into the air. Lizzy swung her back and forth, dancing from foot to foot.

"Yeeehee, I've never been an aunt!" Lizzy said.

And just like that she again dropped Val, who landed heavily on her rear. Val could only sit blinking as she watched the other woman's face go through a dozen emotions in an eyeblink. From joy to confusion to black anger.

"Oh, this is so . . . I don't know what . . . I should kill you both . . . but . . . I . . ."

Lizzy seemed lost in thought. Val reacted; she grabbed up a nearby flowerpot and stood, slamming it into the side of Lizzy's head. It smashed against her skull.

Lizzy blinked, still standing and seemingly unfazed as dirt and broken pottery fell from her hair. Val noticed that her nose had healed.

"You know, if you are going to fight other dragons, you need to learn how to make the right kind of claws," Lizzy said, voice suddenly completely calm.

She reached out and slapped Val, not as hard as she had been hit before, but there was a splash of blood. Val stepped back, hand flying to her cheek. Three short tears marred it.

Lizzy lifted a hand that was now tipped in talons, like a hawk's. But each bladed claw seemed rough. Val couldn't get a good look as they shifted away, back to dainty fingers and manicured nails. Lizzy sucked the blood from her fingers absentmindedly, as if she didn't realize what she was doing.

"This changes things, but I don't know how yet. When I decide, you'll be the first to know," Lizzy said.

Val didn't know what to do. She was still so angry, but she wasn't stupid. She had no idea what she could do to faze, much less stop, this madwoman. Lizzy walked past her, heading toward the door out of the complex.

"Oh yeah," Lizzy said without looking back. "No one can know I'm here. Tell anyone—anyone!—and you'll force my hand."

She actually waved as she left. Val just kept staring, hand still held to her cut cheek.

She had never thought of the possibility of an insane dragon.

Twenty

Flynn was very pleased.

So far, everything had gone just as anticipated. In fact, things seemed to have been going a bit smoother than he planned. He had half worried he would have to have Mose removed before Griffen would open up to him. Only to find that the boy's current mentor had been distancing himself.

As far as Flynn was concerned, he had set Griffen's course perfectly. The chances were good he would self-destruct. Especially if he actually believed Flynn's ideas and tried to do something as foolish as ally himself with the local drug dealers. Humans, no matter how tough they were with other humans, were just not equipped to monitor a supernatural conclave.

Even if Griffen didn't self-destruct, he should lose control of his friends and supporters. He was too young, too inexperienced to wield power without being a bully. What a quaint term, "bully." As if the world were some child's sandbox. If Griffen survived, he would soon be looking for a new home. And Flynn would be ready to extend an invitation to California, complete with job offer. Now that he had set the lad on a path to power.

Hell, after that little pool game, Griffen was paying for his hotel and travel expenses.

Flynn figured he didn't really need to stay in New Orleans any longer. Oh, he could do more damage, or finesse things a bit more. Still, Griffen had his card, if the young idiot remembered where he'd put it. He could always call for more sage advice. It was about time Flynn packed up and let nature take its course.

There was a knock at his hotel door.

Flynn looked suspiciously toward the door. Someone wanted something? Just when he had been on the verge of packing his suitcase? Flynn had been at this game far too long to believe in coincidence.

Of course, he never could refuse a good game. He let his curiosity guide him and opened the door.

"Hello, Earl," Mai said.

Flynn took a step back, surprised despite himself. He had, of course, heard that McCandles had contacts with a representative of the Eastern dragons, but Mai? She smiled, a bit demurely, and stepped into the room. She brushed against his arm as she passed, and the scent of jasmine clung to her skin.

"I should have known," Flynn said, frowning.

"Oh, now, you make it sound like a bad thing I am here."

"It probably is. Still, let's go through the motions, shall we?"

"Let's."

The two eyed each other for a moment, and Flynn shut the door. There was a tension here; there always had been with Mai. He always thought that it must be the same type of sensation two chess masters felt when they played. Well . . . one chess master, and one very promising amateur.

He had no doubts which one he was.

"You are staring," Mai said with another small smile.

"Ah, yes—the motion. Well, you do look very good, Mai."

"Thank you," she said.

She did, too. She was in a dark red dress cut to make one think of a kimono without actually being one. It hung off one shoulder and revealed a lovely expanse of skin. One side was split nearly to the hip, letting her shapely leg slip into the light now and again.

"It's been a long time," Flynn said.

"Yes, it has. Shall I say it first, or should you say it?" asked Mai, smile sliding from demure and starting to resemble a smirk.

"Together, I think," Flynn said.

"On three."

"One," said Flynn.

"Two," said Mai.

"Three. What is your interest in Griffen McCandles?" they said together, in perfect unison.

Flynn laughed, a rich, honest laugh. Mai pretended to blush, but her eyes glinted. He knew she was enjoying this as much as he. She walked over to the little table in the room and sat down, crossing her legs and letting her skirt slide loose to the thigh.

"I asked you first," she said, and stuck out her tongue like a child.

"Of course you did."

Flynn shook his head and took the other chair. He steepled his fingers, and the two watched each other, silence stretching into minutes. They both knew the game very well, and old rules stated that whoever talked first, lost.

"Of course," Mai said, as if reading his thoughts, "I have made a career out of breaking old rules."

"Yes, you have. Whereas I have made them work for me. To answer the question that you did not ask first"—Flynn paused to stick his tongue out at her, then winked—"the boy shows potential. I would like to harness that potential."

"Of course you would. And I would like to see him harness his potential," Mai said.

"What, with nothing in return?" Flynn asked.

"Well, he is fun in bed."

"Marry me, Mai," Flynn said.

For the first time Mai's expression dipped to a frown. Flynn smiled, knowing he had scored a point; it paid to deviate from the script now and again.

"We have been down that road. Not a chance, Earl."

"You know I hate to be called that," he said.

"Of course," she said.

"We would have been absolutely terrible for each other."

"Perhaps. You will never find out now will you? That is what you get for courting my father, when you should have been courting me."

She stood and smoothed her skirt into place. Flynn remained seated, though he knew he could prolong the meeting if he stood. If he would meet her halfway.

"I thought you should know—now that I know you're in the game, I will undo whatever it is you have set in motion," Mai said.

"If you can. I always could check your moves in the past." Flynn nodded to her.

"But, as you said, it has been a long time."

Mai began to move to the door, then paused. When she turned, her smile was back on her face. She reached down her décolletage, and drew out a small envelope.

"Oh yes, this was taped to your door. Sorry if I peeked."

She handed it to him, smiled once more, and left before he could open it. He shook his head, looking at the door. Well, the game was now worth staying around for at least. He opened the envelope.

The contents were even more surprising than Mai's presence.

A Knight of Swords tarot card.

He half growled to himself and chucked it in the wastepaper basket. He wasn't irritated by the card so much, but by the puzzle. Had the minx really found it? Or worse, had she brought it herself?

Could Mai know he'd hired George?

Twenty-one

Val didn't know what to do.

It had taken a day for the cuts on her face to heal to thin pink lines. It had been a day where she had avoided everyone. A day when she looked inside, tried to figure out what she should do. What she could do.

Her first reaction was to protect her brother. The thoughts that followed that were more convoluted. Which protected Griffen more? Telling him about the threat of Lizzy or heeding her warning? And somewhere in the darker parts of Val's mind, she wondered if she was really protecting him at all or if she was just afraid.

That thought she pushed quickly away. What filled her wasn't fear, it was anger. Every time she thought about that fight, brief though it might have been, her hands tightened into fists and her jaw clenched. If only she knew where Lizzy was. If only she had reason to believe that this time there was a chance that things would be different.

She had spent a lot of time in the last day staring into her mirror. Watching the cuts on her face. It seemed that they almost healed as she watched, the speed of her flesh knitting just slightly slower than the eye could follow. As if she could watch for just a second more and actually see the change. But she always blinked eventually, and when she looked back . . . well, who could be sure?

So much for not believing in being a dragon. As if a brawl

with a shape-changing psycho bitch hadn't been enough for her. Something inside Val shifted suddenly. Her worldview, and self-image, changing ever so slightly.

They looked little more than scratches now, those cuts from those odd claws. She was tired of hiding. She needed to move, to walk, to center herself. Valerie hit the streets.

She didn't think about where she was walking. She just walked, still sorting through her own thoughts and emotions. However, unlike her jog a few days ago, when she had tuned the world out, she only let part of herself sink inside now. She seemed almost hyperaware of the people she passed, instincts judging each for level of threat, and rational mind backing up the judgments with a second glance.

She was just so angry. Furious. On the brink of true rage, and the sad thing was that her anger wasn't aimed toward Lizzy. She was angry at herself. Valerie always thought of herself as so strong, so confident. She had devoted a good chunk of her life to being as fit and competent as she could be. It wasn't the fact that she lost that bothered her. It was how badly she lost, how little she had fazed Lizzy. She should have done something more, hurt her more.

Valerie needed to recenter.

She realized just where she was a few doors away from her destination. She hesitated for only a moment, then decided to trust her feet, trust her instincts. She walked up to one of the security doors that marked the entrances to the French Quarter apartment buildings and rang the top buzzer.

It was a few minutes before Gris-gris opened the door and looked at Valerie in surprise. She hadn't even thought of what time it was, and didn't now. She had her hands on his collar and her mouth against his before he could even say hello.

He still hadn't had a chance to speak as they moved inside, the security door closing behind them.

* * *

Uncounted hours later, Valerie lay atop Gris-gris. She idly nuzzled at the hinge of his jaw and shifted her weight subtly, back and forth. Testing his . . . stamina.

Gris-gris moaned softly and ran his fingers down her long spine, tips of them playing against her tailbone.

"You don't quit, do ya?" he said

"Mnn, probably not," she said, and bit lightly into his shoulder.

Other small marks, from harder bites, decorated his dark skin. Still moving idly, languorous, she slipped to his side, one leg curled around his. She couldn't help gently licking at one of the half-moon-shaped marks.

Gris-gris reached down and gently cupped her chin, drawing her face to his. She was taller than him, but curled against him as she was, her eyes were level with his. Both pairs were slightly unfocused, heavy, but his also held a touch of concern.

"So, ready to tell me what was wrong?"

"You saying something was wrong for you?" she all but growled, surprised at her own tone.

"Meant before," Gris-gris said. "When you came to my door."

"I don't know what you're talking about," she said.

She took her chin out of his hand firmly and rested her cheek on his chest. She didn't feel like looking into his eyes anymore.

"Come on, Val. You never been like this before. All the times we've been together, you've been together. This is the first time I've seen you so . . . needful. Not just hungry. You needed to feel good, and you needed to get and keep control."

"Are you complaining?" Val said.

"You know I'm not."

"Then, hush. Just like a guy to ruin things with the wrong kind of pillow talk."

She really didn't want to go there. Especially since he was right. As soon as they were in his apartment, she had taken control and kept it. Not just control of the situation, but control of herself. She had almost hurt him with her strength when they first began.

What he'd missed was how much good it had done her. Controlling herself while abandoning herself, it had been a difficult balance, but it had given her what she needed. She felt herself again. Despite never having used quite these means to "center" herself before.

Gris-gris smiled.

"Well, damn, never heard that one before," he said.

His hands slid to her hips, and, with gentle pressure, he rolled her over. She felt the line of his body press against her back, and craned her neck to look back at him. A gentle but firm bite on the back of her neck stopped her, and his arms wrapped around her, hands beginning to wander.

"Nnn . . . what do you think you are doing?" Valerie said, shifting against him.

"Shut'n up, ma'am," he said. "But if you can't talk with me, you might want to figure out who you can."

Valerie started to answer, and it turned to a gasp. Gris-gris chuckled a satisfied, masculine chuckle. Then it was quite some time later before either was in a mood for thinking again.

Still, he had raised an interesting thought.

Twenty-two

More and more Valerie had been living off her own money. Ever since she started her bartending, she had paid for her own food and drinks and clothing and entertainment. She was actually damn proud of that. Before New Orleans, her lifestyle had been mostly supported by her uncle, just as Griffen's had been.

Now the only thing she wasn't paying for was the rent, which she could have managed if she switched from part-time to full-time. Of course it was nice not to have to worry about it, and she might end up working more anyway just to fill the time. Still, it was a good feeling to be self-sufficient.

It also meant she often lost track of just how much money Mose's gambling operation had to be bringing in. Walking up to his home again, a private residence tucked away from the hustle and bustle of the Quarter streets, Val found herself wondering if Griffen had bothered to check into the figures of his new "business" partners.

Especially since Mose owned his place, the place they were staying, and who knows how many others. Not to mention seeming to employ Jerome full-time, and the shills, dealers, and others in the gambling ring to whom these were essentially part-time jobs. For an operation on the gray side of legal, or worse, it was amazing how profitable it all had to be.

Val pushed that thought aside. It wasn't why she was here. In fact, she had been very careful to mostly stay out of the gambling side of Griffen's new life. To her, Mose was a source of information on what it was to be a dragon. That was more than complicated enough for her tastes.

She had Gris-gris to thank for the idea. Mose was someone she could talk to. Not about everything, maybe. She didn't trust anyone fully. Even her brother couldn't be trusted sometimes. Like when it came to his not making a fool of himself. But when it came to dragon business, Mose was the top contact on a very short list. She had only waited for the last of the marks on her face to fade before approaching him.

She used the key she had been provided to open the street-level gate and started to Mose's front entrance. Inside, she could hear the murmur of voices. The closer she got, the more she recognized Mose's calm, quiet voice. The second voice was Jerome's, and he was anything but calm.

"Damn it, Mose! I deserve some answers. I've earned that much," Jerome said.

"That you have, son; that you have. But you don't need them."

"The hell I don't. Oh, maybe I can do my job without 'em, but that doesn't mean I don't need them."

"Jerome, I'm not ready to . . ."

Mose drifted off and Val, who was still several feet from the door, could hear him sigh.

"You might as well come in, Valerie. It's not locked," Mose said.

She realized sheepishly that if she could hear him sigh, he could hear her walk. Though how he knew just who it was she couldn't be sure. She walked the rest of the way to his door and let herself in.

"I'm sorry, Mose, I didn't mean to—" she started.

"Didn't think you meant to eavesdrop, Valerie. Way we were talking, it would have been hard not to overhear. Though I'd take it as a courtesy if you'd give a shout at the front gate if you aren't expected," Mose said.

"Fair enough."

Valerie took one of the vacant chairs, which left Mose, Jerome, and her all looking at each other. Mose seemed a bit tired to her, but it was Jerome who really caught her eye. His face was drawn, darkened rings under his eyes, and his posture was wire tight. If she hadn't known any better, she would have thought she was looking at a man right on the edge of his resources.

She gave serious thought to excusing herself, not really wanting to intrude. Still, anything that would affect these two would affect her and her brother. She couldn't just up and leave without knowing what it was. Not to mention the things she wanted to talk over.

"So, is this about Griffen?" Val asked bluntly.

It was Jerome who answered her.

"Yes . . . no . . . damn it, I don't really know. That was what I was trying to figure out," he said.

"Jerome has some questions about my stepping back from the management of our affairs," Mose said.

"I thought you had already talked to Griffen about that," Valerie said.

Jerome focused more on her. His eyes filled with questions. Valerie latched on to the most obvious one and shrugged.

"There isn't much we don't share when we talk, Jerome. It's part of being brother and sister," she said.

She tried very hard not to think of what a hypocrite that made her. Hiding not only her scuffle with Lizzy, but, more important, her pregnancy.

"My sisters and me don't talk like that. Still, no big deal. Yeah, we did talk, and he's gotten better at switching his interests between the games and this conclave of his. I got no gripe with him," Jerome said.

Valerie hadn't even known that Jerome had siblings. She hadn't asked much about his family. Or Mose's for that matter. She did ponder for a minute on just how little she knew about people she had to trust.

"So what's the problem?" she asked.

"I got no gripe with him, except he's put off talking to Mose for too long." Jerome turned his attention back to Mose. "I need to know, Mose, why you are backing off now of all times. I thought when we brought Griffen down here, you'd still be doing the job till he's really learned the ropes. Five, ten years at least."

"Are you saying my brother can't handle the job?" Val said.

The other two jumped a little at her tone. Well, Jerome jumped, and he was already a little twitchy today. As far as Mose, the wrinkles around his eyes tightened a bit, and that was enough of a cue for Val. She had learned a while ago how male dragons seemed to react to a good dose of ire from a female.

"No, he isn't saying that," Mose said. "In fact, we have both been surprised by just how quick Griffen has picked things up. But Jerome, he thinks like a dragon, and dragons think in long spans. Griffen hasn't been at the job long enough to have experienced all of the surprises that can pop up."

"Like a meeting of supernatural crazies hitting town just when the balance of power is being shifted from an older dragon to a younger," Jerome said.

"Jerome!" Mose said sharply. "I make my decisions for my own reasons, and I don't have to explain them. *I've* earned that much. The only person I might owe an explanation to is Griffen, when he asks for it. It will be up to him, as your new boss, to decide if he should share."

"But—" Jerome said.

"You're tired, you shouldn't have come here after a long, hard night. Come on back later when we can talk about it calmly," Mose said.

Jerome slumped in his chair, holding his head in his hands. For a long moment, Valerie was afraid he would break down, but she wasn't sure in what fashion. He seemed to shudder, and when he looked up, he seemed much calmer. Much more like the Jerome she was used to.

He got up and left without another word. Mose tracked his every movement, and Valerie thought she saw a glisten in his eye. He blinked, and it was gone, but he let his posture slip as he eased back in his chair.

"Damn, I hates bein' so hard on the boy."

"Then why were you?" Valerie asked.

"Because he is stubborn as a mule sometimes, Ms. Valerie. And as the joke goes, you got to be kind, you got to be gentle, but first . . . you have got to get their attention," Mose said.

Mose reached out for a decanter and glass set on a side table, but his hands were shaking. It was the first time those hands had looked old to Valerie. Old, callused, hard worked. Without a thought, she rose and went over to the table to pour him a drink. Mose took it.

"Thank you kindly. Now, our little melodrama aside, what can I do for you today?" Mose said.

Valerie sighed and poured herself a drink as well. She went back and folded herself into the chair, pulling her legs up under her. Well, it was now or never.

"Mose, do dragons get . . . feelings?" Val started.

"Like what sort?" he said, and she caught the bit of wariness to his tone.

"Doom, danger, impending peril. The sort of gut reactions that most people pass off."

"Ah . . . sometimes. Like you said, most people just pass off such hunches; part of being a dragon is not ignoring one's instincts. Sometimes, of course, it's just collywobbles . . ."

Again, she noticed his hesitation.

"And other times?" Val said.

"You said it was gut reactions. Tell me, was it really your gut?" Mose said.

Val blinked at him.

"No, my heart."

Mose nodded to himself, as if she had confirmed what he had been thinking.

"Time to talk the stuff of legends again. It is said that, very rarely, a dragon learns to see beyond what is. Well, not see, feel. The old phrase was 'a heart free from time' though the translation may have suffered as years have passed," Mose said.

"Are you saying I'm sensing the future?"

"Not really, it's more picking up on pain that is to come. Pain of the heart, of grief, not of the body. Don't think you are going to get some 'spidey-sense' or any such nonsense," Mose said.

"My grief, or others'?"

"Good question. I haven't the foggiest. And I don't really know if any of this is true, or applies to you. Still might just be collywobbles."

Val thought, not so much of what he was saying but of what she wanted to say next. Somehow, it just didn't feel safe, or smart, to bring up the subject of Lizzy.

Not directly anyway.

"I want to learn how to fight," Val said.

Now it was Mose's turn to blink at her.

"What do you mean? I had assumed with all your working out you would have had a decent fill of martial arts."

"That's not quite what I mean. I want to know how to fight . . . as a dragon."

"No, you don't," Mose said.

Val reined in her temper and merely gave him a questioning look.

"Look . . . I mean it. Dragons fighting dragons, if that's

what you mean, just isn't done. It takes so much effort, or special skills, to seriously hurt each other. Too much collateral damage. Those old legends said two dragons at war would crumble mountains, and I am not sure that was a metaphor."

"And what if I don't have a choice, and find myself without the skill I need?" Val said, and her voice caught ever so slightly.

Mose slumped back in his chair again and narrowed his eyes.

"Are you talking theoretically?" he said.

"I . . ."

He held up a finger.

"No games."

"No . . . probably not," Val said.

Mose turned his gaze from her and stared out his window. His eyes were much too far away for him to simply be looking at the courtyard outside.

"I have to think on that one, Valerie. I'm . . . not a fighter, haven't been since I was a kid. Let me think on if I can in good conscience help you find what you are looking for. Much less whether I can give it to you, or find someone who can," Mose said.

Valerie started to speak, then thought better of it. She followed Jerome's course and left without another word.

She could still see Mose staring out his window as she approached the gate to the street. He didn't seem to be seeing her.

Twenty-three

The Mystic Den was one of the most closely guarded secrets in the Quarter. Many of the people who lived and worked in the Quarter did not even know of its existence.

It was the lobby bar for the Royal Sonesta Hotel, one of the largest and most expensive hotels in the Quarter. Even though the hotel itself fronted on Bourbon Street, there was no street entrance to the Mystic Den, so it was overlooked by those who prowled and barhopped their way along that famous tourist attraction. You could only get into it by going through the hotel lobby or via a corridor at the back of the Desire Oyster Bar.

The bar itself was quiet and furnished with deep, comfortable chairs and sofas, a far cry from Griffen's normal haunt at the Irish pub. That was one of the reasons he had chosen this location for his meeting with Slim. It was getting to a point where too many people knew to look for him at the Irish pub.

In honor of the occasion, Slim had forsaken his trademark white suit and striped top hat for a pair of loose-fitting slacks and a sports shirt. Without his street entertainer's costume, he blended right in with the sparse afternoon crowd in the den.

"I dunno, Griffen," he was saying. "Seems to me like you're makin' too big a thing out of the whole security problem."

Courtesy of their meetings over the last several weeks regarding the conclave, Slim had reached a level of comfort where he now addressed Griffen by his first name rather than as "Mr. McCandles." Unfortunately, this also meant he was comfortable criticizing Griffen's plans.

"I always thought extra security was a good thing," Griffen said. "The only way you know you don't have enough security is when things start going wrong. I'd rather not see that happen."

"Maybe," Slim said. "But too much obvious security can send a bad message, too. Looks like you're expecting trouble. Even worse, it looks like you don't trust the attendees."

Griffen grimaced.

"I *am* expecting trouble, and I *don't* trust the attendees."

"Of course," Slim said. "But you can't let it show. Man, you're a dragon. You're supposed to be confident and in control. You don't want to look like you're tryin' to bully people around."

"I thought I had that covered," Griffen said. "That's why I was suggesting we go to outside help. If I use any of my own crew, it'd look like I'm having the dragons team up on the rest of the conclave."

"Outside help?" Slim said. "TeeBo and Patches and their thugs?"

"I know," Griffen said with a sigh. "I'd really just as soon not owe a favor to them or any other drug dealer. I don't see many other options, though."

"I wouldn't even think of that as an option," Slim grunted. "Their solution to anything is to shoot it. I really don't think that's what you want."

"Okay. You're right," Griffen said, spreading his hands in surrender. "I didn't like the thought either. That's why I haven't contacted them. It's just that the conclave is less than a week away, and I still don't have a clear fix on what I'll have to deal with."

"I'm not sure of that myself," Slim said. "But I wouldn't count too much on that week."

"Excuse me?" Griffen said.

"You don't work as much with regular tourists and conventioneers as I do," the street entertainer explained. "A lot of folks, if they're planning on attending a convention or even a football game down here, like to come in a few days early to see the sights and party down. Wouldn't surprise me none if some of the conclave attendees popped up in town ahead of time."

Griffen covered his eyes with one hand as if his head was throbbing.

"This just gets better," he said. "How am I supposed to try to keep people out of trouble if I don't even know who they are? Or should I say, what they are?"

"Well, first of all, I don't think you should feel any kind of responsibility for anyone who wanders into town early," Slim said in a strange voice. "And I don't think you'll have that much trouble spotting folks with the conclave even if they aren't wearing suits or name badges."

Griffen glanced at him sharply, but the street entertainer simply nodded toward the bar's lobby entrance.

Following Slim's gaze, Griffen saw a mixed gaggle of what looked like teenagers boiling through the door, followed by one young man who looked to be in his late twenties. It had every appearance of a high-school outing complete with a harried chaperone.

It would have been, at best, a mildly annoying distraction . . . except the group seemed to be headed directly toward the table where Slim and Griffen were sitting.

"What on earth . . . ?" Griffen murmured, but didn't get a chance to finish.

The crowd lurched to a halt in front of their table, forming up into a rough half circle. On closer examination, there were only about a half dozen of them, but their youthful energy and eager faces made it seem that there were a lot more of them.

Suddenly nervous and self-conscious, the group began to fidget, glancing back and forth between Griffen and their chaperone.

"Mr. McCandles?" that individual said, stepping forward.

Griffen stared at him for a moment, then nodded.

He wasn't sure what was going on, but he suddenly felt like a featured stop on a guided tour. To say the least, he wasn't wild about the sensation.

"We just wanted to take this chance to meet you before the conclave started and to express our thanks for letting us attend."

"And you are . . . ?" Griffen said, deliberately not rising or offering a hand for a handshake.

"Oh! We're the fey . . . or the changelings, if you prefer," the leader said, hastily. "This is our first time to attend one of these things."

Strangely enough, Griffen had already figured that one out himself.

"Actually," he said with a small smile, "I was fishing for a name."

"Of course. I'm sorry." The leader was momentarily flustered. "My name is Tink."

He started to extend a hand, then withdrew it and bowed stiffly.

"Tink?" Griffen said, raising an eyebrow.

The leader flushed slightly.

"Well, my given name was Archibald, but everyone knows me as 'Tink.'"

"All right . . . Tink," Griffen said carefully. "While your thanks are appreciated, I'm afraid they're misplaced. Even though I've agreed to moderate the conclave, I've had no say as to who is or is not invited. In fact, of all the groups I've been told are attending, I probably know the least about yours."

"Are you really a dragon?"

This came from a coltish, small-breasted young lady in short shorts and a *Lord of the Rings* T-shirt.

Griffen stared at her with his best poker deadpan until she dropped her eyes and took a step back.

"You'll have to forgive us," Tink said, interceding. "We're all excited about the conclave, and, frankly, most of us have never seen, much less met, a dragon. I hope you aren't offended."

"No offense taken," Griffen lied. "And, for the record, yes, I am a dragon. Now if I might ask a question, how did you find me?"

"Oh, that's one of the things we're good at. Finding things and people," chimed in a boy with features so smooth he might have been mistaken for a girl. "That and hiding."

"I see," Griffen said. "Any other powers I should know about . . . if you don't mind my asking?"

The group exchanged glances.

"The thing is," Tink said, "there are various powers we have. Not everyone has the same powers, though. If you'd like, we could give you a demonstration."

Griffen suppressed the image that flashed though his mind.

"That really won't be necessary," he said hastily.

He reached for his drink, more to give himself something to do with his hands with so many people staring at him, then stopped. His usual light amber glass of Irish whiskey was now clear. Tentatively, he raised it to his nose and sniffed.

"It's gin," declared a girl with short black hair and a nose ring. "That's one of my powers."

"Impressive," Griffen said carefully. "Unfortunately, I only drink Irish whiskey. Would you mind changing it back?"

The girl suddenly looked uncomfortable.

"Um . . . I can't do that," she said. "I can only change liquids one way. I don't know how to do reversals."

"I see," Griffen said, successfully suppressing a smile.

"Let us buy you a fresh drink," Tink said, frantically signaling the bartender, who had been watching the proceedings with vast amusement.

The assemblage waited in silence while the bartender brought Griffen's new drink over and was paid by Tink, who waved off any change.

"Well, we'll run along now and quit bothering you," he said, gathering up his charges with his eyes. "I can see you're busy. We just wanted to say hello and thanks. Maybe if we get a chance, I can fill you in a little on the fey . . . if you're interested, that is."

The pack moved off, already chattering back and forth among themselves before they reached the door.

"So what kind of security do you figure you'll need for them?" Slim asked with a grin.

"I'll admit they aren't what I expected," Griffen replied. "I didn't know what to expect, but that wasn't it. I just wonder if they'll have any problems getting those kids into any of the bars or clubs."

"They've probably doctored their IDs," Slim said, "but don't let their looks fool you. It's the fey blood in them. I'll bet there wasn't one in that group who's under fifty."

Twenty-four

Long after the Irish pub had closed for the night, Mai found herself walking by the shuttered doors. Toulouse, two blocks off Bourbon, was absolutely deserted at this hour. Still, she expected company.

He came around the corner a block away and started to head toward her. She knew he could have appeared at any time; he could have surprised her. Instead, he wanted her to see him coming. It seemed he wanted her to feel safe. Which was unnecessary—if she cared about feeling safe, she wouldn't have caught his attention.

He limped ever so slightly, one leg just a bit shorter than the other. His face was unremarkable, his body perhaps a bit under average in size and build. His clothes were cheap, just a bit dirty, and of muted colors. As he stepped up to her, she couldn't help but smirk. His eyes narrowed as he caught her expression.

"You think you are clever, don't you?"

"Of course I do, George," Mai said.

George straightened and before Mai's eyes he became a different person. Taller, stronger, more handsome. His face had just a touch of Spanish overtones. Even his hair was more styled now.

"Is this the real you?" Mai asked.

"Does it matter?" George said.

"No, I suppose not."

"How did you find me out?"

"What, that you were stalking Griffen as a videocrack addict? You are good, one of the best shape-shifters I've ever seen. But not the best. You don't smell like most playing those machines. Your eyes track things a little too closely. And even though they are a different color now—yes, I noticed—they have the same kind of predator glint."

George reached into his pocket and pulled out a long Knight of Swords tarot card. Mai had slipped it to him just after the vampires had made their appearance at the pub. She knew that it would be enough to bring him to her.

"And how many of these did you slip others you suspected were me before you hit pay dirt?" he asked.

"Does it matter?" she answered with his own words.

"Yes, too many of these floating around might jeopardize me, as innocuous as they are."

Mai seethed a bit inside. Yet if that was what it took to get the ball rolling, she could admit a failure. This once.

"Fine. Only one. A homeless man. He stared at me blankly, then yelled at me for not giving him money. Still, I thought it might be you not wanting to admit I had caught you," Mai said.

"And what put you on guard for me?"

"Now, do you really expect me to tell all my tricks?" Mai said.

"What do you want, dragon?!"

George spat the last word like a curse, and Mai cocked her head slightly. She pursed her lips, tasting her words before she let them out.

"In the old legends, Saint George the dragon slayer was fighting a European menace. What do you have against a dragon of the East?"

"A dragon is a dragon. Where it comes from doesn't matter to me."

"How narrow-minded of you," Mai said.

"And how like a dragon for you to say so. Grabbing the arrogant high horse and trying to control the conversation, and everything else. If it quacks like a duck . . . I ask you again, who or what tipped you off to my presence? You wouldn't have found me if you hadn't been looking."

Mai smiled and began to walk toward Bourbon Street. George followed a pace behind. In this form he walked with a bit of a jaunty gait. Looking just a little like a cock rooster, as if he were looking for action.

"Funny, those vampires showing up tonight," Mai said.

"Not as funny as you pretending to stumble so your little friend would not catch you slipping me the card," George said.

Mai ignored his grin, and his gibe.

"Who tipped them off as to where to find their 'moderator,' do you think?" she asked.

"I figure it had to have been fairly anonymous. Other than a quick tip over the phone, they should have been given at least a description of him, if not a picture," he said.

"Very astute of you, but it doesn't answer my question," Mai said.

"And you did not answer mine . . ."

George trailed off as he saw her smile widen. *I can't believe I'm having to drop him this many tips,* she thought. *This is the terror of little dragons everywhere?* She had to remember his skills leaned toward hunting and toying, not intrigue.

"Flynn hates vampires," he said.

"Sort of puts him above suspicion, doesn't it? Besides, who else is in town who might have done something to make me watchful for your presence?"

"Damn it, I knew I shouldn't have left that card."

George stopped and folded his arms over his chest. Mai leaned against one of the Quarter's faux gas lamps. She kept her expression frozen, letting him come to his own conclusions.

"He really gets up my nose, that one does. Typical dragon, using even someone he hates because he can," George said.

"Just because he has said he disliked vampires in the past, you think that means anything? Even if he was being honest, it would be much to his liking to put two enemies against each other," Mai said.

"Which is, of course, exactly what you are trying to do," George spat back.

Mai shrugged and waited.

"Very well," George said finally. "If Flynn wants to play with vampires, it shouldn't be too hard to get him stumbling over his own toys. But I'm doing this because it will irritate the overgrown set of matched luggage."

Mai bowed her head without taking her eyes off his.

"It never entered my mind that you might be doing it for me."

"Good. You won't see me in the Irish pub again. Do not look for me elsewhere."

"Why? Rumor had it you never hunted someone you didn't have a contract on."

"Unless I deem them a threat. Besides, so far I'm not truly hunting Flynn. But let us keep that between you and me."

"Of course. If you'll answer me one question."

George paused again, considering.

"Depends on the question," he said.

"I watched you in the pub, when you thought you were invisible. If a dragon is a dragon, why do your eyes seem to show you to be warming up to Griffen?"

He hesitated a beat too long, and Mai knew his answer would be a lie.

"All part of the disguise. I never assume no one is watching."

With that he turned and, in an eyeblink, a large dog was running off into the night. Mai watched him go, extending her senses to the utmost to make as sure as possible that he didn't circle around to follow her. When she could no longer perceive him even distantly, she started back to her apartment.

"Well, that's him aimed properly, then," she said to herself.

About a block away she paused and clenched her fists as a wave of frustration passed through her.

"And one day, I'll figure out how the damned chimeras don't ruin their clothes in a shift. All the bloody designer outfits I've shredded over the years . . . gah!"

Mai stomped the minor frustration off, and by the time she reached her apartment she was once again basking in a job well-done.

Twenty-five

Griffen had picked up a tail.

Thankfully, this time it wasn't of the green, scaly variety. That had only happened a few times, and always unexpectedly. Being followed, however, that was becoming far too common for his liking. Since moving to New Orleans, he had been followed by everything from federal agents to a cockroach. Not that he was entirely sure there was a great gap between the two.

This was different, though. Even when Homeland Security had been keeping an eye on him thanks to the interference of a dragon named Stoner, Griffen had been able to identify his watchers with only a bit of effort. This time, try as he might, he had yet to catch a glimpse of whoever, or whatever, was following him. He just knew they were there. It was as if he could feel eyes always on him.

Whoever his tail was, they were disturbingly good.

He had first noticed it early that afternoon. He had gone out a little early to check his public mailbox on Royal Street. There hadn't been anything interesting, and when he came out, he first picked up the "watched" sensation. Looking around, he saw no people paying him attention nor any cockroaches or big shaggy dogs.

Griffen was learning more and more to listen to his instincts and senses. Though he grew increasingly sure he was being watched, he didn't really feel any sense of threat. To play it safe, instead of going home as he planned, he swung down to Decatur Street to check out the DVD releases at Tower Books.

His new stalker followed, Griffen was sure of that, but again he couldn't catch sight of them. He picked up a few DVDs he had been wanting anyway and thought about some of Padre's advice concerning tails. One line particularly came to mind—change your routine. So where Griffen normally would have taken a right on Chartres and gone down to his place, he went left and popped into a two-story bookstore that he was fond of.

Griffen thought maybe if anyone followed him in, he could catch them in the stacks. He waited and listened, but no one came in. Not once did the bell over the door chime. And still he felt someone was watching, as if someone were right behind him, breathing down his neck.

A bit nervous now, he touched the beads around his neck, the ones given to him by Rose. He was beginning to wonder if she, or one of her ghostly friends, was the cause for all this. But he had never felt her as a presence before. Always when they interacted, she was just there, seeming solid and alive.

Without really thinking about it, Griffen pulled a small book off the shelf and went to the counter. He hated leaving a place without buying something, and he wanted to maintain an illusion of a fairly normal round of shopping. Just in case his pursuer hadn't yet realized that Griffen had noticed them.

By now Griffen was more than a little edgy. He really didn't like the constant attention and intrusions that he had been forced to accept since learning of dragons. Keeping his route different from his usual, he headed over to Royal. He picked up his pace, hoping to force his watcher to do the same. Then he abruptly ducked into Pirates Alley, a narrow walkway leading to Jackson Square.

He stopped dead, hoping to catch whoever was behind

him as they rounded the corner. His back almost against the wall, keeping himself shielded from Royal Street as much as possible, he waited, sure that he would at least get a glimpse of them.

And waited. Senses stretched to the utmost. Ears and eyes fixed intently, trying to take in everything in front of him.

. . . And waited some more.

Griffen's shoulders slumped. Nothing, nobody. Not even a bug or cat or anything. He started to scold himself in his thoughts, sure now that he had just imagined the whole affair.

"Aren't you going to do anything interesting?" a voice said, from a half foot behind him.

Griffen whirled at the sound. Later, when his heart wasn't pounding away in his throat, he was sure he would be embarrassed by just how high he'd jumped. He had been so utterly intent on the street in front of him that he hadn't heard anyone approaching him.

Of course, looking at him, he wasn't entirely sure he would have heard anyway. It was one of the changelings. The young boy who even in daylight was androgynous enough to be mistaken for a girl. He blinked at Griffen with an oddly mixed expression, curiosity and disappointment.

"You've been following me?" Griffen said.

"All day! I figured a dragon would do something better than shop for movies and books. Don't you do anything interesting?" the changeling said.

"Well, the Quarter doesn't really start to liven up till sundown . . ." Griffen started, cutting off when he realized he was defending himself to a stalker. "You shouldn't have snuck up on me, sc . . . startled me half to death."

"You really shouldn't admit to being scared. Some of us, we are scared all the time, but we don't admit it. That just gets you targeted."

Griffen looked at the young man, who seemed no more

than fourteen. Slim had mentioned that the changelings were older than they looked, but that comment clinched it. Even in a lilting prepubescent voice, it betrayed experience and even wisdom a fourteen-year-old would never have.

"Look . . . I don't think I got your name when we first met."

"Because Tink didn't do the formal introductions. We are fey stock, for cryin' out loud, and everyone got so excited about meeting a dragon that we skipped the basics. It's why I thought I'd come find you myself, see if you lived up to the fuss."

Griffen noticed he still hadn't told him his name.

"Missed the mark, did I?" Griffen said.

"No, didn't mean anything like that, Mr. McCandles," he said hastily. "We are only here 'cause of you; a dragon makes us feel safe. Feel important. Besides, you picked up on me following you. Most wouldn't."

"How did you manage to trail me so well?" Griffen said.

"Oh, I can see a little farther than my eyes is all. You felt my gaze even though I was a good four blocks away all the time. Have to say, your tactics are pretty good. Even most of the shape-shifters would have been caught."

Now the changeling sounded full of admiration. Griffen was beginning to realize that balanced emotions were not going to be this bunch's hallmark.

"Though your taste in movies stinks. Picking up Stooges when they had Marx Brothers? Really."

"I already have all the Marx Brothers. Stooges were lower on my list," Griffen said.

"Well, that's all right, then. But if anyone puts out Ritz Brothers on DVD, I'm going to have to start looking into some heavy-duty curses. Some things are better left dead."

Griffen shook his head and decided this conversation needed a radical switch.

"Shouldn't you be with Tink? Where is he?"

"Oh, umm . . . let me check."

Before Griffen could answer the young-seeming man's eyes went cloudy. Not unfocused, but actual clouds seemed to roll over them, a thin layer of fog appearing to hover just a centimeter over the eyes themselves. Condensation started to form on the ends of his lashes.

"Damn . . . he is heading toward your Irish pub that you didn't meet us at last time. From his expression, he's looking for me through you. I think I'm going to go hide now."

"No, you don't," Griffen said firmly.

The changeling's eyes snapped back into focus, the fog dissipating. He blinked, and small drops flew from his lashes, looking a bit like tears on his cheeks. It was so slight a physical sign that Griffen could doubt he had even seen it and knew anyone who wasn't looking for something magical would just overlook it. It was something very outside his experience, both from before and after he had started to learn of dragons. He was beginning to be impressed by the changelings.

"Fine, if we hurry we can get there before him. Guess I could use a drink."

With that, the changeling walked past him and turned toward Toulouse. Having made a decision, he moved without hesitation, practically bouncing along at a pace that Griffen had to hurry a bit to keep up with. Griffen shook his head again and hurried.

Sure enough, they beat Tink to the bar, though Griffen wasn't sure how. Then again, he wasn't sure how the fogged-over vision of the changeling with him really worked. The two sidled up to the mostly empty bar, and the bartender stared at them.

"Sorry, Griffen," the bartender said. "Friend or yours or no, I got to card him."

The changeling was already holding out an ID.

"Every friggin' time," he muttered.

The bartender looked over the card carefully, even running his nail over the seams and texture, then shrugged and went to pour their drinks. While he was a bit out of earshot, the changeling leaned over to Griffen.

"It's not the ID that's the problem, it's replacing them every ten years or so. No one would buy the right birth date, and unlike some, I don't have enough glamour to do up a fake on the spot."

It was then that Tink came in, surrounded by the rest of the changelings. He stopped in the door, the rest gathering tightly around him like a flock of nervous geese, and his expression wasn't happy. He moved forward again, glaring at Griffen's companion.

"Hey, big man," the changeling said as he approached. "You forgot to do intros last time."

Tink stopped again, and his expression surprised Griffen. He looked startled, even embarrassed. It was very much the look of someone who had just had an obvious oversight pointed out to him. Griffen hadn't expected it to be a big deal.

"That's no call for going off and bothering our host." Tink tried, but Griffen didn't think his heart was in it.

"You didna' say I couldna'," the changeling said.

Griffen didn't have enough experience with accents, but the one the boy suddenly adopted sounded an odd blend of Scottish and Irish. Again, it drew Tink up short and made Griffen wonder if there was more going on here. Was it a quote from somewhere perhaps?

"True enough," Tink said. "Mr. McCandles. If I may introduce you to my companions as they are currently called. This is Nyx, Robin, Hobb, and Tammy."

He pointed out each in turn. Nyx was the young woman with the piercings who had changed Griffen's drink. Robin and Hobb had to be a couple from the way they seemed to always be holding hands. Tammy was the coltish, attractive young girl Griffen had noticed earlier. She shot a sour look at Tink and stepped toward Griffen, taking a bit of a breath to swell her modest chest.

"That's Tamlin, Mr. Dragon," she said.

"Tammy suits you so much better," Nyx said.

Tammy, which Griffen had to admit was a better name for the young blonde, shot the other a dirty look and took a step back to rejoin the group.

"And that is 'Griffen' please," Griffen said, still wincing over "Mr. Dragon."

"And he skipped me over, punishment for bothering you, Mr. McCandles."

That was from the changeling who had been following Griffen. Sure enough, Tink had skipped him over. Again, Griffen wasn't sure why. As the changeling took a sip of his drink and held out a hand, he had a bit of a smirk.

"They call me Drake," he said.

Griffen shook his hand.

"I notice you all say that is how you are called. May I ask why?" Griffen said.

Tink took a seat at the bar, leaving Griffen between him and Drake, with the rest all milling about on their feet. He signaled the bartender and ordered for himself. He had to wave twice to get the man's attention. On an afternoon shift with the bar still nearly empty. Griffen had already noticed the bartender and the other few patrons weren't paying any attention to them. By now, he just assumed it was the changelings' influence.

Once Tink had his drink, he explained.

"It's tradition and magic. Never give out your true name, or secret name. Most changelings pick or find or are given a name that they use in public. Many ritually discover a secret name as well, which they adopt as their 'true name,' ignoring whatever their human parents saddled them with. A lot of us grab our names from mythology, or popular media," Tink said.

"So why can't I be Tamlin?" Tammy put in.

"Because he was a man, and, by most reports, human. And Tammy just fits too damn well," Tink said.

"You said 'human parents'? From the little I've been told, you don't think you come from humans?" Griffen asked.

"Not really. The current belief is that we are left behind by the fey for reasons known only to them. Mostly it's believed we are half-human half-fey, products of seduction or worse. Since no one's reported seeing a fey in ages, it's kinda hard to confirm, but changelings keep popping up. Usually to parents with next to no magical background," Tink said.

"Hence shunning the birth name and taking on new names?" Griffen said.

"Not quite," Drake put in. "See, that fits in this day with the current trend of rebellious angsty teenagers. Most of us are from a generation that still respects parents. Parents who could never understand, or deal with, a magical child. Think of it as adopted children who found out the parents who raised them aren't really theirs. All sorts of mixed reactions depending on the child. Still doesn't change all the history and love that takes place in the sixteen or so years it takes a parent to change a baby into an adult."

"And then there are a few, very few, who are found by other changelings and taught what they are from early on," Tink said. "Myself included, which is why I feel responsibility to do the same for others and took on my current role."

"The rest of us had to find our way, to find others like us."

That was from Hobb. The young man squeezed the girl's, Robin's, hand and smiled affectionately. Griffen had to smile, too.

"Okay, so what about actual full-blown fairies, then?" he said.

"What about full-blown dragons?" Tink said. Then he shrugged and went on. "Depends who you ask. Historians tend to put it all down to a few tribes in Ireland who disappeared when the Romans were smashing the crap out of the Celts. But the way they tell it, they were just primitive nature-worshipping humans who hid in the woods real well. Which is about as satisfying and truthful as saying all dragons are big ravening lizards hungry for virgin flesh."

"So a kernel of truth hiding something a whole lot deeper?" Griffen said.

"That's what we figure; otherwise, where did we come from? But a lot of that is faith. We don't know. There never have been lines of changelings. No history passed down from father to son. And no big, winged sprite popping up and saying 'Hey kids, where the hell have you been?' It's one of the reasons we get so clingy, with ourselves and each other."

Tink looked up from his drink.

"Sorry, Mr. McCandles, we shouldn't be bending your ear," he said.

"No, no, I'm fascinated. I want to know as much as possible about every group attending," Griffen assured him. "And remember, 'Mr. McCandles' isn't necessary. Just Griffen."

"Sure thing. Anyway, we should be going. See you at the opening ceremonies."

Tink stood and gathered up the others. Drake was the last to follow, finishing his drink and stopping just briefly for a parting comment to Griffen.

"Interesting choice at the bookstore by the way," Drake said.

As soon as the changelings had left, the bartender noticed that Griffen's drink was empty. Of course it had been empty for some time, but Griffen made no comment as he got it refilled. He did reach down to his bags and pull out the book

he had hastily purchased earlier. He laughed softly to himself.

"Figures," he said.

A copy of *A Midsummer Night's Dream.*

Twenty-six

Forget the one about the rabbi and a priest. If there wasn't a joke that starts, "Two fairies walk into a bar," there should have been.

That was the thought that went through Griffen's head when the doors to the Irish pub swung open and two of the changelings came in. So he was failing to suppress a smile when they approached him, which was probably not the best of facial expressions. The younger of the two practically bounced up and down, a foolish grin spreading over her face. Again, he was reminded of a pack of puppies, and was glad that this time there were only the two.

The younger-appearing one, who was all smiles and giddy energy at being greeted with a smile, was called Robin. She was probably the most attractive of the bunch, though she looked young for her seeming age. Almost too young for Griffen's tastes, but she did have a certain allure about her. Another bad joke popped into his head, something about making the puppy's tail wag.

Sometimes Griffen just couldn't help himself.

The other one had introduced himself as Hobb. He was one of the more sedate and inward-directed in the group. He still smiled broadly at Griffen, but where Robin threw her arms around Griffen and hugged him before he could react, Hobb seemed hesitant even to shake his hand. Nervous, like he was afraid of being burned.

Robin and Hobb very much had that couple feeling. Though from the way Robin was squeezing Griffen and pressing her slender curves against him, he had to assume it was an open couple. Especially since Hobb showed no sign of jealousy at all. Actually, except for the smiles, Griffen found himself having a hard time reading the changelings. As if their emotions and thoughts were different from his experience, subtly . . . alien.

"Pull up a couple of chairs," Griffen said, prying Robin off him.

He half suspected she'd jump in his lap if a chair wasn't available.

"It's good to see you here again, Mr. McCandles," Hobb said.

The young man pulled up a couple of spare chairs and held one out for Robin. She hopped into it and leaned back to give him a kiss on the cheek. He smiled, and the smile wasn't puppyish at all, before taking his own seat. Definitely the couple vibe, Griffen thought again.

"How many times do I have to tell people? You can call me Griffen," Griffen said.

"I knew a gryphon once," Robin said.

"Oh?"

"Yeah, but he was just a chick. Wings had barely grown in at all," she said.

Griffen stared at the fairly spacey young woman. It didn't help that her voice was soft and childlike, too. It was a Marilyn Monroe–esque voice. For the life of him Griffen didn't know how to respond to such a comment.

Hobb noticed and chuckled to himself. He put a hand on Robin's shoulder.

"I told you, a baby gryphon is called a cub, not a chick," he said.

"But they hatch from eggs!" she protested.

"Then how come no one has ever heard of a gryphon omelet?" Griffen asked.

Forget sanity. He could banter with the best of them. The two changelings grinned at him sunnily.

" 'Cause a mama gryphon is a real menace, of course," Hobb said.

"But you should open a restaurant and cook up some. Griffen's omelets," Robin said.

"Oh, please. I'm busy enough." Griffen rolled his eyes, and the girl exploded into giggles.

A couple of drunk tourists sitting a few seats away looked up. One of them, a large man with too much belly, pulled himself out of his seat and began to stagger over their way. Griffen was tracking him carefully, and also noticed that the fat guy had caught Hobb's attention. Robin seemed oblivious.

"Shure have a pretty laugsh there," the drunk slurred.

Robin looked up and sighed, rolling her eyes.

"Not now!" she said sharply.

"Oh, come on, babycakesh. How 'bout a kish?"

"You really hit that one hard, that's the hammiest line I've heard in a long time," Hobb said.

Griffen half expected the drunk to turn to Hobb and try to start a fight. That seemed to be the usual pattern with such incidents. Instead, he seemed totally fixated on Robin.

"Oh, fine!" she said.

Griffen was curious now. He watched as the young changeling pressed two fingers to her lips, then pressed them to the drunk's lips. He clumsily kissed her fingertips, and a hand started to reach out for her wrist. Only to stop in mid-motion as his eyes went glassy.

"Look at your friend," Robin said.

He did, lips still pressed to her fingers. She leaned up and whispered in his ear, voice soft and sultry.

"Isn't he haaandsome," she said.

The man nodded, and pulled himself away from Robin. The three watched as he staggered over to his friend and sat back down. Griffen was about to ask what that was all about when he got his answer.

"What did you say to me!" the other drunk said.

"Come 'ere. You knowsh you wantsh it," the drunk who had harassed Robin said.

The second drunk was on his feet and backing hastily toward the door. The whole bar was now watching as his friend pursued him, pursing his lips for a kiss. The doors slammed behind them, and the bartender started laughing. Even for the Quarter, that was a good one.

Robin turned back to Griffen, all smiles again.

"Sorry, Mr. Griffen. Talking to a real live dragon is sooo exciting. So I leak a little."

Griffen held back his first response, and his second. He was trying to phrase his third when she reached out and slapped him on the shoulder.

"Magic, silly! I do attraction magic too well, and sometimes it backfires."

She glanced over at the door, where the two had departed, and shrugged.

"It'll wear off. Normally it takes more work, unless a spark is already there. Closet case," she said.

Griffen shook his head.

"And you, Hobb? You were one of those who didn't jump on the chance to show off when we first met."

"Uh . . . my skills aren't really of the public show-and-tell variety," he said, and seemed to draw inward.

"Hobbykins isn't really a people person. We didn't really come here looking for you, it's just that Bourbon Street was too hustle and bustle for him," Robin said.

"Bourbon Street is too hustle and bustle for me. Don't worry about it," Griffen said.

Hobb looked at him gratefully and straightened up again. Griffen decided it would be a good time to ask something that had been weighing on his mind.

"I've been wondering, what do you hope to get out of this conclave? I mean, I sort of understood what you as a group expect, but personally. What does it do for you?" Griffen asked.

"For me . . . I have reason to want to explore some of the human magic users. Especially the healers. This is a good place to make contacts," Hobb said.

"And I just want to meet everyone I can! I hear those garou are just too studly for words."

Griffen and Hobb exchanged a glance. Robin put an elbow into both of their ribs.

"Hey, you two. A fae has to be true to her nature! Men!!" she said.

Hobb laughed and swiveled her around for a kiss. Griffen smiled and discreetly turned back to his drink. After a few moments, the girl's small hand reached out and smacked him on the back of the head.

"And that hurt!" she said, rubbing the elbow she had put into his side.

"One of the perks of being a dragon. Tough skin," Griffen said.

He was beginning to warm to the changelings. At least to these two. Though they were a little too much in your face for his liking, they had more variety than most of the other groups he had encountered. He liked the bit of randomness.

He could do with the one being a bit less physical, though. Tough skin or not, she'd almost made him spill his drink.

"Okay, Griffen," Hobb said, "I have been with this one long enough to know when she is getting too loopy for her own good. Time to tuck her in before she starts yet another bar brawl."

"Oh, you are no fun! Just 'cause you claim to be a lover not a fighter—" Robin started.

"Well, isn't that the pot calling the kettle black?" Hobb interrupted.

"Ooo, I can beat you up any day!" Robin said, and swung at him, almost dumping herself out of her chair.

He caught her and steadied her, with what Griffen noticed was much practice.

"Come on, dear. We've got a big week ahead of us."

He gently pulled her to her feet, and despite her protests, she didn't fight him too hard. Griffen had to shake his head and smile.

"Good night, you two."

"Good night, Griffen," Hobb said.

"It's not a good night if I'm only going home with one of you." Robin pouted but winked at Griffen.

For all her talk, it was clear she didn't mean it. It was actually a nice change for him. He waved as the two walked out the door, and took the opportunity to hit the sandbox.

When he came out again, the bartender was waiting by his seat.

"Hey, Griffen, should your two friends be headed toward Rampart?"

"Not that I know of, why?"

" 'Cause they stopped on the corner and looked both ways like they were confused. Thought you might want to go make sure they weren't lost. Play wingman maybe."

"Thanks, I appreciate it. I'll be back soon."

Griffen headed out the door and started toward Rampart. It wasn't after midnight yet, so he didn't worry too much, but the bartender was right. It was best to check. If it hadn't been a busy night, the bartender would probably have done it himself.

Griffen heard the shouts from a block away.

"Get the fuck away from her!" Hobb shouted.

"Stop!" screamed Robin.

Griffen was running.

Robin was down on the ground, a hand cupped to her face. Two black kids, both taller than the two changelings, were closing on Hobb. One held Robin's purse.

Griffen was still a half a block away when one of the muggers hit Hobb in the nose. Blood sprayed, spattering both of them. The other fisted him somewhere in the torso. Hobb raised an arm to ward them off, but he clearly had no fighting experience. Another hit to the head sent him down to the pavement.

One of the muggers seemed to be reaching for something at his waistband.

"Stop! Police!" Griffen shouted.

The muggers didn't look up. They just turned and ran.

Griffen almost chased after them but stopped instead next to the fallen couple. He started to reach down to help Hobb up.

He half jumped back when the changeling screamed like a trapped animal and scrabbled away from him.

"Hobb . . . Hobb! It's me, Griffen."

"Mr. Griffen, stop," Robin said. She was on her feet. Her cheek seemed to already be swelling.

Griffen stopped, holding his hands out to his sides.

"It's okay, Hobb. I'm not going to hurt you," Griffen said.

Hobb got shakily to his feet, blood was running down from his nose. More blood than Griffen would have expected. It covered his shirt.

"That's pretty much the opposite of what he was worried about," Robin said. "Hobb was born cursed . . . It's the blood, you see."

Griffen stared from one to the other, not comprehending. Hobb sniffed, and pulled out a wad of napkins from his pocket. He started to plug up his nose.

His eyes were very sad. Griffen would have expected fear or anger. Not that.

"Those muggers," Hobb said. "They won't be waking up happy . . . or maybe at all."

Griffen began to remember something important. Something he had forgotten when dealing with these boisterous changelings.

Every fairy tale has its dark side.

Twenty-seven

It had started simply enough. Things seemed to these days, then grew out of control. Griffen and Mai had been enjoying a friendly chat with Maestro on the "family side" of the bar at the Irish pub. The conversation had been light, mostly a criticism of the current coach of the Saints, and hopes that next season would be better.

"They still have a shot this year of course," Maestro was saying.

There was a glint to his eye that had Griffen pretty sure he was just playing devil's advocate. More and more he was liking the company at the Irish pub. Maestro was a perfect example. Always ready to talk movies or sports with his fellow Michigander, and very good about not prying into personal areas. Griffen rose to the bait.

"They haven't won a game yet," he said.

"Didn't they win one or two at least?" Mai put in.

"Those were preseason games," Griffen said.

"But the season is still early. Never know what's going to happen," Maestro said.

"Still . . . it just isn't the same as college football," Griffen put in.

The doors of the pub opened, and a noticeable lull fell on the place. That wasn't a common occurrence at the Irish pub. Everyone noticed newcomers, especially strangers, but usually there wasn't much in the way of reaction. Tourists did find their way off Bourbon Street now and again after all.

This group was different. Griffen had never seen five people look more out of place. It wasn't anything about their appearance. Each was dressed in fairly upscale business attire, except one woman in a clingy dress of a deep burgundy red. They seemed a little pale perhaps, their eyes a bit sunken, as if they had just woken up. That wasn't the problem, though. In the Quarter, where a good number of people didn't wake till after noon and rarely if ever saw the sunlight, those sorts of qualities went largely unnoticed.

They just didn't belong, and he was hard-pressed to think of anywhere they might belong. A funeral parlor perhaps. Griffen didn't know what he was looking at, but he was sure he didn't like it.

A cloud hung over them, he decided. Griffen had never seen a person, much less a group, who better fit the old expression. It was like an aura of dampness surrounded them, not malicious or volatile. More like a wet blanket, heavy and suffocating.

All around the bar, conversations died off. Smiles slipped from faces. A few of the moodier drunks hunched over a bit more into their beers. One of the video poker machine addicts spilled his drink. In a few moments, over half the bar was silent and either casting sidelong glances at the group or staring openly.

What Griffen noticed most, though, was that they waited until they had at least that much attention before moving into the bar enough even for the door to close behind them. They had stood there for those few moments, almost posing, then they'd advanced toward a few empty seats at the front of the bar. Those people sitting on the edges of the gap seemed to edge away unconsciously, one even scooting his stool a few inches to the side.

"What can I get you?" the bartender asked.

"Wine, white," said one who looked just a bit more pallid and clammy than the rest.

The others nodded, and the woman in the burgundy dress took a step forward and leaned against the bar, displaying her not-inconsiderable cleavage.

"And a man," she said.

The bartender, a French Quarter veteran, began to pour the drinks with only a brief glance at the woman's charms. That glance was actually closer to a glare, and his tone was a bit hard as he set out the drinks.

"We dispense alcohol, not people. If you really think this is that kind of bar, maybe we should put these in plastic," he said.

The first man who spoke grabbed the woman's elbow and pulled her back away from the bar. He moved to sit in one of the empty stools and shot her a brief warning glance. Griffen thought he felt the "cloud" of the group thicken somehow.

"Please forgive Vera; she misspoke."

"Like hell I did, Lowell," Vera growled behind him.

"We are looking for a Griffen McCandles. We were told he drinks here often," Lowell said.

That confirmed what Griffen had been afraid of. Even sitting across the room from the group, that one spat of infighting had given him the hunch that these must be more conclave delegates. Even though it had already officially started, he had been warned that a few more might trickle in.

Of course, that left the question of what they were. A different type of changeling? They certainly didn't have the . . . enthusiasm that the others he met had. That snap would have fit right in with some of the shifters he had met. Griffen was about to rise and go meet them when someone put a restraining hand on his arm.

Surprisingly it was Maestro. Even more surprising, to Griffen, was the bartender's reaction.

"Who's that, then?" he said.

The man, Lowell, reared back. There was no other word for it; his head jerked back and his body followed, like a cobra about to spread its hood. The others in his group, including Vera, began to spread out a little.

"I understood that he is here almost nightly, and well-known among the regulars," Lowell said.

"You sure you got the right bar? I don't know of any Gregory Candles at this place," said the bartender.

"Not Gregory, Griffen," Lowell said, blood starting to rush to his pale cheeks.

"They actually name guys Gordon anymore? Poor man. That'll be $32.50 for the drinks, by the way," the bartender said, and moved away to another customer.

Lowell stared at the bartender's back, mouth hanging open and gaping like a fish. All around the bar, people went back to their conversations, some of them with smirks on their faces. Griffen, now warned off, didn't stare any more, or obviously less, than anyone else in the bar.

"Back to what you were saying, I sure do miss the spirit back in college ball. Not just the fans, the players. Those kids were hungry," Maestro said.

"That's one word for it." Griffen nodded, as he kept one ear fixed on the group across the bar.

"Oh, good job, Lowell. That was just marvelous work," Vera was saying.

"Shut up," another said to the woman.

They began to square off.

"Both of you shut up," Lowell said.

The man looked down immediately, Vera took a few more moments and glared resentfully at Lowell. Griffen was making a quick study of the group dynamics. Something about them kept tugging at his memory, but he just couldn't put his finger on what. He was pretty sure they weren't shifters, at least not any type he could name. Some sort of human magic user he hadn't met? Sure didn't have the feel of the voodoo or wicca.

"If you think you can do better," Lowell said, "be my guest."

From the way Vera smiled, Griffen knew that was absolutely the wrong thing for Lowell to say. She was a person who always thought she could do better.

"Excuse me!" she called out.

Her voice was loud enough to cut through the conversation and bar music. More than that, though, her own personal cloud changed. The air seemed to thicken, choking and hot. Hotter and harsher than the aura that had surrounded the group. In fact, the others around Vera seemed to back away from her slightly, wrapping themselves in their overall damp aura as a form of protection. It wasn't the air as much as the atmosphere, the . . . vibes. Griffen began to wonder if they were some form of psychic.

To make the tension more acute, there was a . . . hole in the sensations above Vera herself. It was as if she were an oasis, a spot of light in the darkness. That more than her voice dragged the attention of most of the bar back to her. There were a few men, whom Griffen knew had been having hard times, who stared at her like men in a desert who had just stumbled upon a glass of water.

When she was sure she had the bar's attention she smiled, and the air thickened more. The sensation was unbearable to Griffen, and he had to wonder why no one else seemed to notice that something was wrong. Only Mai held an expression that indicated she was aware of being manipulated and not liking it one bit.

"Thank you," she said. "Now, please, if anyone could point me to Griffen McCandles, I would be very thankful. We merely have business to discuss with him."

A man spoke, one of those who had looked at Vera most intently. He and Griffen had only met in passing, but Griffen had heard that he had recently lost his wife. She had been a crack addict, and after her third time in rehab, he had lost her. Under the weight of whatever Vera was doing, his eyes glistened with unshed tears.

"Did you say Griffen McCandles?" he asked.

"Yes, I did indeed," Vera purred.

Griffen braced himself for the end of the charade.

"Sure I know Griffen McCandles," the man said, and took a long pull on his beer. "Man owes me two hundred dollars. I heard he had skipped town."

Vera deflated, slumping, the smile falling from her face. With the change, the aura through the room changed, crashing back into a damp depression like that the group had when they first walked in. Only more intense. Griffen almost spoke out to stop the wave that passed over his bar.

"Vera," Lowell snapped. "Enough, this won't do us any good. We will simply meet with McCandles elsewhere."

He reached out and took her elbow again. On contact, the overpowering feeling in the bar faded, receding back to the cloud hovering just over the small group. Not a few people gave unconscious shudders of relief, or knocked back drinks just a bit faster than they usually did.

Lowell pulled out his wallet and put a fifty on the bar. The bartender spared him another glance. He had kept an eye on the situation but hadn't seemed to get captivated by Vera as some had.

"If Mr. McCandles should"—Lowell glanced at the man who had answered Vera—"return to town, please do tell him we came looking."

"Sure thing, but you'll be leaving now," the bartender said.

Lowell nodded and hustled Vera out the door; the others followed, pale shadows.

"Fucking vampires," Mai whispered so low only Griffen heard her.

Griffen jerked his eyes to hers, and she nodded. Suddenly a lot clicked into place for him. At least about the group. He had been told there were vampires who fed off depression and emotions and could influence and create those emotions. He never thought it would be anything like that, though.

" 'Scuse me, lover," Mai said. "Sandbox break. Always feel the need to splash a little water over my face after something like that."

Griffen nodded, and she stood and walked over to the ladies' room. He couldn't remember ever seeing Mai that frazzled. She even stumbled and had to catch herself on one of the video poker machines. The player reached out to steady her, but she waved him off and went into the bathroom.

Vampires. They weren't supposed to be at the conclave, and now he understood why. Griffen had seen some odd things lately, but nothing that had felt so . . . wrong. What sort of defense was there for most people against something they didn't even realize was happening?

For that matter he still didn't quite understand how the bar had reacted.

"Didn't expect you to seem so surprised, McCandles. Not after being in the Quarter a few months," Maestro said.

"What do you mean?" Griffen said.

"Hell, a group of outsiders come in looking for someone that they can't even spot in a crowd? You think they are going to get an answer? The circle forms with the horns out, I know you've been told that," Maestro said.

"Yeah, but I hadn't seen it like this. I mean, that guy doesn't know me from Adam," Griffen said.

"He's seen you, here and often enough. He ain't ever seen them before. That's all it takes down here," Maestro said, then with a bit of a smile; "Of course, wouldn't hurt to buy him a drink in thanks."

Twenty-eight

Mose was tired.

He was tired more often lately. He hardly ever went out anymore. Even then, it was usually just for a stroll or a brief chat with old friends. He had fewer old friends around, and those he did have . . . Well, he had been in the area too long. They had gotten older; he had started old and stayed that way forever. Or so it seemed to them.

And that age? Mostly only showed on the face and hands. His body was still strong enough that he sure didn't worry about his safety when he did go out. Sometimes he even left his gate ajar. Not often, he wasn't often that stupid. Just if he got into a mood. In case someone should try something. A bit of exercise and entertainment. Oh yes, his body was fit, just tired.

There was no doubt about it, he thought wryly, his ass was dragon.

He did keep active though, in his way. It was just that as time went on, he had learned to conserve his energy. These days he had taken up drawing again. He didn't think he had much talent, but a dragon's eye and a few centuries of off-and-on practice can do wonders.

He was sitting outside, enjoying the late-afternoon sun, a tall glass of lemonade beside him and a small drawing note-book in his hand. He felt like one of those old men he used to laugh at when he was younger. Except old men in his day didn't draw,. They worked, hard. They played chess. Sometimes they whittled.

He heard the gate open and looked up to see Griffen coming in. The boy was one of the most powerful young dragons he had ever met. Stronger and more varied now as an amateur than Mose had been during his heyday.

Yet he walked toward him hesitantly, almost sheepishly. His whole body language was unsure. Mose had Jerome's reports that outside, when dealing with others, Griffen was more confident. With his friends he was comfortable. When he had to, he stood as a leader, as a dragon among men. It was only with Mose, and from reports perhaps with Flynn, that he became more meek, nearly subservient.

All the more reason for Mose to back away.

"I started to use my key, but it was unlatched," Griffen said.

"I like to let the sounds of the street drift in now and again," Mose said blandly.

"Mind if I pull up a chair?"

"Not a'tall."

Griffen dragged over the other outdoor chair Mose had for company. Mose would have offered him some lemonade, but it would have meant sending him in for a glass. Too much like sending him off like a servant for the conversation Mose suspected they were about to have.

The two sat in silence for some time. It was a comfortable enough silence, the sounds of the city a soft susurrus around them. Mose felt Griffen's eagerness but wouldn't rush him. He never rushed.

"Mose . . . you know why I'm here."

"Yes, I reckon I do, but you are going to have to spell it out."

"I know, but I'm going to have to do it the long way."

Mose nodded and eased back a little more comfortably. He smiled slightly. That was the way he would have done it.

"When I came down here, I had my doubts. Beyond my doubts about myself, I didn't know what good I could do you. Or why anyone would want to pass over something they'd worked a lifetime for to someone they had never met. The idea that my heritage makes me somewhat more powerful than you doesn't make a whole lot of sense. You were plenty powerful enough for this group; so is Jerome."

"Jerome isn't as strong as I am, Griffen. He knows it. Besides, you can take this group further than I could. It is good people, with good potential. They should be more than just New Orleans grifters."

"Still, others could have led them."

"You're right, I have known dragons who fit the bill, ones I had more direct experience with."

"So why me?"

"Hmm . . . mind if I go the long way myself?" Mose asked.

"I made sure I didn't have anything else planned tonight," Griffen said.

"Shouldn't take that long, but us old men, we like to tell stories now and again."

Mose took a sip of his lemonade as he organized his thoughts.

"Not too long ago, before you were born, there was an election year, and the local authorities really decided to clamp down on the 'unsavory' types around here. They went around busting every grifter, bum, con, whore, and lowlife they could find. This was when I was still an employee of this fine organization, not its boss. Before I classed the place up some. And I got picked up doing three-card monte."

Mose checked Griffen's reaction; he seemed perfectly content to listen, even though he clearly didn't see where this was going.

"People got crammed into cages built for a third of what got shoved in, and it was days before anyone even thought to start draggin' people up to get judged. Now, me, I didn't mind. A few others who worked in our ring got nabbed, too, so I wasn't alone. Others weren't so lucky."

"You met Jerome, didn't you?"

"You're quick, now shut up. No going and ruining a fella's story by cutting in."

Griffen smiled and nodded.

"You kinda ruined the punch line, but yep, there was this snot-nosed little urchin, skinny as a snake, and all alone. But that didn't faze him. Watched that lad go from person to person, looking them over, and moving on. He would chat with a few for a moment, move on again. Never approached anyone likely to rough him up just 'cause he was in arm's reach. By the end of the first day he had four guys, myself included, lookin' out for him with nothing expected back. Just 'cause we were the sort to look out for thems that needed it. When they let us out, he looked over the judge, and said, 'He's all right,' and I knew to trust it."

Mose shook his head and chuckled.

"He's lost some of his openness with it, learned to keep a button on his lip, not tell everything he sees. But I tell you, Griffen, he may not be as powerful as me, but I never did meet a better judge of character."

"And he was up in Ann Arbor feeling me out for more than a year," Griffen said.

"Hell, no, he had you sussed out after the first night. He spent a year getting you ready in case we had the opportunity to pull you down here. Trust is hard to build."

"But, Mose, that doesn't tell me why you are backing out now. I still need your advice, but when I thought you were just pushing me away I wasn't worried. Now Jerome tells me you are pulling yourself more and more out of the loop, and Valerie confirmed it. So what gives?"

"Griffen, you don't need my advice. In fact, I probably set you back every time I give it. Oh, I help you in the short term, but you have got to stand on your own feet sooner rather than later."

"So by holding back you are what, forcing me to grow?"

"Something like that, or I would if you weren't running off to find a replacement for me. You need to be figuring things out yourself, not letting other dragons run you."

"Flynn helped when you wouldn't."

"I choose my own replacements. I chose you!"

Mose stopped and calmed himself. Yelling at him was counterproductive. Even though Griffen got on the defensive about Flynn, it was a good thing. Defensive was better than meek.

"Griffen, you are destined to be a great force in this world. A force of nature practically. If you get it in your head that you need some mentor figure, it will be years before you learn otherwise."

Griffen got up and paced. Mose watched him, saw that he wasn't satisfied with these answers. He didn't want to go the last step, but he owed it to Griffen. Still, to get through to him fully, Mose would have to be blunt.

"Griffen, I'm dying," Mose said.

Griffen stopped and stared.

"We dragons age funny, but something you'll hear from all the old-timers is that you feel when your clock is running down. Maybe it's just in our head, maybe it's a self-fulfilling prophecy. But on my clock the ticks are getting slower, and there is no way to wind it back up again."

"How long?"

"I don't know, but I've been feeling it for a while now."

"I . . . I don't know enough to ask if you are sure. You wouldn't say it if you weren't sure."

Mose considered his next comment for the longest time yet, rolling it around in his head, tasting it on his tongue.

"Griffen, I know you think well of me, but you have to remember, low blood or not, I am a dragon," Mose said.

"And?"

"And dragons can be some of the most selfish bastards you ever did run into when it suits us. You ask why am I backing off. Would you really want to spend your last few years chained to a job, an office? Even as nice an office as this?"

Mose waved to his courtyard, to his house. He picked up his glass and lifted it to the sky.

"So, I think you don't need me, and I haven't figured out what I need. So you must forgive an old, selfish dragon and let me try to find the peace I may. Knowing that what I have poured my life into is in good hands."

Griffen started to say something, and Mose cut him off.

"And, I'd appreciate it if you told Jerome something else, or nothing. He and the others here, they will make a big fuss. I don't want a big fuss. I'm telling you 'cause you need, and deserve, to know. And 'cause I've grown to love you in a real short time, son. But when I do slip away, one way or the other, I want to go quiet. I say, live big, and leave them remembering your living, not your dying."

"That's a lot to bear, Mose."

"You've got the shoulders to do it, lad. Jerome saw it, and I've seen it. Stop doubting yourself."

"Well . . . all I can promise is that I'll try."

Griffen started to leave, but stopped as Mose stood up. He walked over to Griffen, and wrapped his arms around him tight. Griffen stood stiffly for a moment, then hugged the older dragon back.

"You'll do more than try," Mose said, and smacked Griffen on the back.

Griffen nodded and left, locking the gate behind him. Mose smiled and went back into his house. Inside, he picked up his phone and dialed a number he hadn't touched in years.

"Hello?"

"Hello, Danielle," Mose said.

"Papa!"

"I just wanted to say, it looks like pretty soon I'll be coming for a visit. Time to see my grandchildren and all."

"Oh, that's wonderful. Will you be staying long?"

Mose looked out into the sky.

"Might be I will," he said, "just might be."

Twenty-nine

Sometimes, Griffen felt his life had just gotten too . . . complex.

The day had started normal enough, for the French Quarter anyway. The sun was bright. The tourists were out keeping the lifeblood of the area pumping and green. A quick stop by the Royal Mail had shown a surprise package in, a backordered series of books he had forgotten buying. So far, the day had been nothing but pleasant. He found his spirits high, his troubles somehow distant.

Such a state of mind is not meant to last.

Valerie had gotten him hooked on splurging on beignets and coffee at Café Du Monde when his mood was high. At their prices it couldn't really be thought of as a splurge. Yet something about the atmosphere and sugary confections always made Griffen feel slightly decadent. More so, than he imagined, than any of the five-star restaurants in the Quarter would. Though to be honest, he had yet to be truly tempted by the outrageous prices when the area was filled with inexpensive two- and three-star places that would knock anyone's taste buds for a loop.

After a lazy time of people-watching, Griffen went to walk off the meal. He decided to avoid tourist-heavy streets like Royal and Bourbon, preferring today to enjoy the buildings more than the scenery. He paused by a window of a tiny antique shop on Chartres, looking over a variety of old pocket watches and knickknacks. The sorts of things that were fun to peer at but he would never find reason to purchase.

He was aware of eyes watching him, and suddenly the mood of the day shattered.

At first he thought it was the shopkeeper inside, checking to see if he was a gawker or a viable customer. The feeling came from behind, though, eyes heavy on the back of his neck. Griffen had never asked if this were part of being a dragon. Most people claimed to be able to feel someone watching them. Dragon powers or no, he trusted his instinct.

Griffen felt his meal, just moments ago a pleasant warming, now a heavy wetness in his stomach. His pulse was elevated so suddenly and quickly that he knew it was something more than the average pickpocket or hustler. He did his best to suppress his nervousness, trying to be cautious. He glanced at the window in front of him instead of through it, trying to catch anyone's reflection. Nothing. Next he glanced out of the corner of his eyes. Nothing. Finally, he turned around fully.

Nothing.

Now his worry started to grow to fear. Usually by now the feeling of being watched should have faded. If anything, it had intensified since he had turned. Nervous but resolved not to show it, he rested his hand on his pocket, taking a loose grip on the folding knife nestled inside. Usually nothing more than something to open boxes or peel fruit with, its cool weight gave him some minor comfort.

Griffen tried to focus on the feeling, trying to give more attention to his instincts. He extended his sense out, reaching for a greater feel of his environment. Suddenly, a wave of curiosity crashed over him. Curiosity, mixed with daring. It was such a shock to his system that he actually took a step back and rested one hand on the wall. That wave of emotion had not been his own.

Now Griffen truly did not know what to do. The intensity of his misgivings was soaring, and his own fear rose with it. Never before had he felt someone else's emotion, and this had been so intense that, for a moment, he didn't know what feelings inside were actually his. He—yes, he was almost sure those were his emotions—mostly wanted to retreat. To run away and get another person's opinion on just what might be going on.

That option was taken away as the source of the attention on him appeared. A great, shaggy beast of a dog stepped out from behind a parked car. The gray of the car almost exactly matched the dog's fur, complete with random brown streaks that could have been dirt, rust, or natural coloration. The animal was just shy of being the size of a Great Dane, and had easily watched Griffen through the windows of its cover.

Griffen was suddenly caught by a conflict of his instincts and his logic. Logically, he started to relax. The odd sensations, from being watched to the burst of feelings, could all be an extension of his animal control. He really didn't understand what he did, or could do, yet.

His instincts, though, those screamed to stay on guard. He puzzled over this, brow furrowing as his pulse continued to race. Something was wrong. Why was the dog approaching him? Where had it come from? Stray cats were common in the Quarter, stray dogs rare, especially one that big.

"Good boy, you just stay there, boy," Griffen said coaxingly, while reaching out to make the command more than words.

He had learned through Jerome and Mose that dogs were one of the easiest things to control. They wanted to please. Just a little push . . .

The dog ignored him. Continued to walk until he was right next to Griffen. Tentatively, Griffen reached out with his hand, though not the one on the knife, while pushing harder with his will.

"Now listen here, there's a good dog . . ."

He stopped, hand still a good six inches from the dog. It had lifted its head, and their eyes locked. There was a spark of intelligence that no dog should hold in its eyes. The unexpected shock froze Griffen for a moment.

A moment was all it took. An unpleasant warmth slid down Griffen's leg. The dog, most definitely male, had decided to treat him as it might a lamppost.

"You!" Griffen started, but the dog had already lowered its leg and bolted.

After another stunned second, Griffen shouted again and took off after the dog. The head start and four legs quickly outdistanced Griffen, and the dog turned down Wilkinson, a side street that only stretched a block and was rarely busy. Griffen kept chasing, enraged. His sock squished.

What Griffen found when he turned the corner was a scene from a horror movie. Not one of the modern hack-and-slash travesties, a classic. At some point, the canine monster must have stepped in a puddle. Along the sidewalk were paw prints. First distorted from running. Then just distorted. Then they were human.

Griffen froze, rage freezing to ice. There was no one on the street, and the prints only went for a few more feet. Griffen didn't even think about continuing his pursuit. It could too easily be a trap. He backed up, carefully, returned to Chartres. His mind was full of new ideas.

The main one was simple though frighteningly close to overwhelming. He was going to have to get used real quick to there being more than dragons and ghosts in New Orleans.

Another thought took longer to fully form. In fact it only hit him halfway to the apartment complex, where he planned to change, and maybe burn, his pants. The footprints hadn't been of a bare human foot. They were prints of shoes. That alone sent his mind tumbling into confusion. It went against everything that should be logical.

More to the point, though, the dog had most definitely been male. The shoe prints had most definitely been those of high heels.

Cross-dressing shape-shifters—only in the French Quarter.

Thirty

Despite an increasingly hectic life, Griffen had made it a point to get out a bit early and stop in during Val's work shift at least once or twice a week. If she was actually busy, he would wave and pass on by. More often than not, though, she had, at most, two customers who couldn't bother giving her the time of day. Then he would step in, chat, catch up on gossip. It was a way of staying connected with his sister, and that was very important to him.

Today was a normal shift, which was to say, pretty much empty. Val sat at the end of the bar, reading a novel. Occasionally she would glance up at the one customer—a boring-looking man sipping at a coffee and reading the local paper. When she saw Griffen, her face lit up, and she waved him on in, obviously glad for the relief.

"Hey, Big Brother. Long time, no see!"

Griffen sat in a chair a few feet down from the customer and rolled his eyes at his little sister.

"You saw me last night," Griffen said.

"That was this morning, and you had Mai on your arm and more than a few whiskeys in you, so I don't think you qualified as seeing much of anything."

"Oh, come now, you were just getting in yourself and complaining about needing to crash before work," he said.

Val put a drink out for him.

"And again back to Mai on your arm. Damn, am I glad that place has thick walls and ceilings," she said.

"We didn't do anything . . . well, not anything too athletic," Griffen said.

"Ugh! Please spare me the sordid details of your nocturnal habits. I'm going to start leaving the stereo on when I go to bed. Loud!"

"Better than your spending four nights a week sleeping somewhere else. Who is it this week?" Griffen said.

"I am sure I don't know what you are talking about. That will be four fifty for your cocktail, sir."

Griffen grinned at himself; as soon as she slipped into bartender mode, he knew he had won this round. Of course, the first time he forgot to tip, she had changed the locks on his apartment door. He made sure to put an extra couple of dollars on the bar.

"So how is life as a French Quarter bartender?" Griffen asked.

"Oh, the usual. I picked up a German tourist who keeps calling me Brunhild and trying to pinch my ass. And I hear that Mitch down in that little dive on Conti got fired . . . again. Pretty boring on the gossip fare."

"Well, here's one for your pot, then. There is supposed to be a convention of Bible thumpers in next week," Griffen said.

"Good God, no, isn't that the same weekend we are getting in a bunch of porno types from California?"

"In theory, no, they are just low-budget filmmakers, but that's the rumor. Expect some real clashes," Griffen said.

"Pardon me," she said.

Val walked over to one of the wooden beams running from floor to ceiling in the bar. She quietly put her hands on both sides of it, and knocked her head firmly several times. Dust fell from the ceiling.

"I take it you finally managed to get a night shift?" Griffen said, sipping his drink and trying very hard not to laugh.

"Next Saturday."

"Kind of what I had figured."

Valerie glared and picked up his empty glass.

"Jack and Coke, right?" she said, a glint in her eye.

Griffen put the money on the bar for his next drink before she even poured, and left it up to her. She slumped her shoulders slightly and poured him his usual Irish.

"So, how about with you. What life-threatening madness encroaches on your life this hour?" Val said.

"Well, most recently . . ."

"Excuse me, sir, could you pass the sugar?" the sole customer at the bar asked.

"Sure."

Griffen absentmindedly passed the sugar to the man. Then did a double take. Between being asked and passing the sugar, the man had changed into someone else.

George smiled blandly at him.

"Thank you. And perhaps the cream?" George said.

"You!"

Val was coming around the bar as she said it. In her hand was the blackjack kept for emergency use only by the bartenders. Griffen was on his feet, moving to intercept, and knew it wouldn't do any good.

George's stool was empty.

"Teleporter," he said from behind the bar, "remember? I thought you dragons were supposed to be quick."

Val swiveled toward him, but now Griffen was firmly in the way. Unless she wanted to climb over him, George was reasonably safe. At least, from her.

"What are you doing here?" Griffen said.

"You know, I rather like it on this side of the bar. There is a sense of power. I can see why you would be drawn to it, Ms. McCandles," George said.

"Please come over here so I can wring your damn neck," Val said.

Griffen waved her off.

"Again, 'George,' what are you . . . ?"

"Oh, relax, the both of you. I'm on vacation. I always loved this city during Halloween. Just think of this as a courtesy, so you know I'm not here to cause you trouble."

"And we are supposed to believe you why?" Valerie said.

"Hmm, does this help?"

George vanished and materialized back on his bar stool. He nonchalantly folded up his newspaper and crossed his hands over his lap. Then he looked Valerie square in the eye and lifted his chin.

"Feel free to hit me if it will make you feel better. I think we've already proved that it won't do much in the way of permanent damage."

Valerie thought for a moment, then lowered the blackjack to her side. She walked back around to the other side of the bar. Which left Griffen standing there feeling silly. He sat back down in his seat.

"Well, if we are playing things this way, can I buy you something other than coffee?" Griffen asked.

Valerie banged something noisily behind the bar. Griffen flinched.

"No, thank you, alcohol doesn't affect me the same way it affects you. Caffeine actually works better," George said.

"You are both getting on my nerves. If you've nothing else to say other than 'Hi, I'm not here to try and kill you,' then I think you can leave," Val said.

George nodded slightly and began to stand up. Only to reach into his pocket. Valerie set her hand on the bar, the blackjack still clenched in her fist.

Slowly, carefully, he pulled out a small plain card with nothing but a phone number on it.

"Actually, I also came specifically here to apologize to you. I was hunting Griffen when you got yourself involved. Still, if I had been a gentleman, I would have backed off and waited till you were otherwise occupied," George said.

"Nice to know you would have waited till I was distracted, then tried to kill my brother," Valerie said.

Griffen really felt he should get involved. Do something to derail this train wreck. Self-preservation, however, said otherwise. He kept his mouth shut. Forget George; all he would do would be to try to kill him. His sister would destroy him.

"Hmm, interesting perspective," George said. "In any case, I would make amends."

"How?" Val asked.

"By asking you on a date," he said.

"What!?" Griffen blurted before thinking about it.

Val swung the blackjack menacingly at both of them.

"Did you set this up for some dumb reason, Big Brother?" she asked.

"Why would I?!" Griffen said.

"Calm down both of you. This was my own idea, and a wild one at that," George said.

"Which brings up the question, why on God's green earth would I go on a date with you? Much less as some apology to me?" Val asked.

"Why, because there is this lovely masked ball that I'm sure you are dying to attend."

"What masked ball?" she asked.

"Why, the traditional one at the end of the conclave. Where I'm sure you'll want to keep an eye on your brother surrounded by people in costume who might have a grudge," George said.

There was a long moment of silence. Valerie stepped toward George and snatched the card from the table. He was just starting to smile when the blackjack swung up and sent him flying backward.

Griffen very carefully kept his eyes on the blackjack as Val turned to him.

"What?" she said. "He said I could and didn't say there was a time limit."

"Actually, I pretty much saw that one coming. Feel better?" Griffen said.

"Much," Val said.

George picked himself up off the floor and brushed himself off. His jaw showed no real sign of just having been crushed by a sap. Still, he made no move to approach the bar again.

"Well then, you have my number. I suppose it's time to find a less hostile drinking establishment," he said.

With that, he shifted, leaving Griffen and Valerie looking at a very large, shaggy dog. The dog opened its mouth, tongue lolling, bowed its head to the two, and bolted out of the bar.

"So," Valerie said, turning her full attention to Griffen, "what masked ball?"

Griffen's attention was still on the door. His mind focused on the dog that had been George. A very familiar dog.

"Honestly, this is the first I've heard of it. Besides, I'm still trying to figure out what George was doing in heels," he said, absently.

Val looked at her brother.

"What?!"

"It would be so easy!" Lizzy said to herself.

She stood on a third-story balcony, watching the Quarter. Well, no, that wasn't quite right. She was watching the French Quarter as it could be.

From here she could see it all. She could see the security gate that led to the complex that the McCandleses shared. She could look down the street. See the road where Valerie would turn to go to work. The road she could come back down if she went to the A&P. The path Griffen would stagger back down when he got worried about following the same roads and took the alternate path he always took.

Then she could see Valerie on the road. Not that she was there. It was an "already happened" Valerie. Valerie as Lizzy had watched her jogging early this very morning. Lizzy watched as she ran through people, who of course couldn't see her. Didn't feel as Valerie ghosted through them in Lizzy's sight. Valerie wasn't there; she was only in Lizzy's eyes, because she was in Lizzy's memory.

Then Valerie shifted slightly, her jogging outfit actually changing from gray to blue as Lizzy pictured a Valerie that could be. All of a sudden a figure lurched out of nowhere. Big, massive, vaguely hound-shaped. It bit into Val's thigh and Lizzy could hear the bone crack. She could taste the blood as suddenly she was not just on the balcony, but down in the image. She was the beast, and she heard Valerie scream as Lizzy's large, jagged teeth next sank into her throat.

Or perhaps . . .

Next Lizzy saw Valerie as she was when she came home from the grocery. Not carrying many bags, not needing much. A few sodas, maybe something she could heat up for the night. Or something odd. A jar of pickles, a bunch of bananas, caramel popcorn. Things Valerie wanted because already her body was craving things for the baby.

Wait till it grew a little more, Lizzy thought. Some of the things a dragon mommy craved could get really interesting.

A shot rang out, and Lizzy felt the butt of the rifle strike her shoulder. The first blow took Valerie in the head, and there was no blood. Skin too thick. But it distracted her, held her. The next blow took her in the belly, then another, then another. Six shots into the stomach, and no more Auntie Lizzy.

Lizzy gasped and threw the phantom rifle from her. That last thought, it had been sad. So sad. Tears were streaming down her face. She couldn't remember the last time she'd cried because she had been sad.

Maybe instead . . .

Now Lizzy saw Griffen. She had watched him many times in the last few days. Mostly she watched him when he was with her, Valerie, the one Lizzy hated. He seemed so weak, so young. She hadn't really seen anything in him that she hated. Not like her brothers at all. She didn't really want to hurt him . . . but she could.

She saw him now, as if he were walking home after a night's few drinks. Staggering just a bit, which was impressive for a dragon. It must have been a long night.

Lizzy steps out of the shadows into the light of the small bookstore. It always left a light on the street at night. She wears a dress so tight she might as well just have shifted her skin to a different color. She breathes deep and steps toward him, swaying.

He blinks, but reaches for her. How could he not? She smiles, and kisses him. Now her tongue is in his mouth, and the skin in the mouth, it's not so tough. It would be nothing to just . . . push . . . into something soft and weak.

Mai grabs her from behind. Lizzy has heard of Mai, seen her a few times since she has been stalking Valerie. But never tangled with her. Now she feels a grip strong as marble and looks into eyes as cold as a spider's.

Lizzy gasped again and threw herself away from the balcony, against the brick wall of the building. Her heart was racing. Even in her own head, Mai had been something Lizzy didn't want to face.

Lizzy looked out on the street and had to blink twice, hard. There she was, Valerie, and not just in Lizzy's head. Real, solid, walking as if she owned the world. She walked into her apartment complex, the gates shutting securely behind her. Not enough to keep Lizzy out, but she felt as if they were taunting her.

Lizzy snarled.

"Why?" she said. "Why can't I just beat her? Why do I care? Someone tell Lizzy!"

She whirled to the girl cowering in the corner of the balcony. Out of sight from the world. She had been there when Lizzy had fallen from the roof onto the convenient balcony. Lizzy had swatted her down, then turned her attention to the street.

She could smell the girl's terror. She was so afraid of Lizzy that she hadn't screamed once.

"Well? Nothing to say? Lizzy is better than her! Prettier. Stronger. Maybe not smarter . . . but what are smarts these days?"

She stalked toward the girl, her voice seemingly filling the world. Or was that just her own ears? No one had once looked up from the street at her. She couldn't have been that loud. Or was she concealing again? Not that it mattered.

"Maybe you think you are smart, you are pretty. You are, for a human. You have nice hair," Lizzy said.

The girl curled up a little tighter. Lizzy smiled cruelly, but she did like the straight black hair. Maybe she should go back to that color sometime?

"Do you have family? Answer Lizzy, or I will be very upset."

The girl nodded mutely.

"Brothers?"

She nodded again.

"And when one of them brought someone home, a girl. What did you feel? Fear? Anger? What?!"

Lizzy did her best to make her expression soft. It didn't take much. There was a yearning inside. A need to know, to understand.

The girl looked her in her many-colored, fractured eyes. Lizzy noticed her eyes were kind of a soft watery brown. Like a deer's.

"I . . . I was . . . happy for them," the girl said in a voice so soft Lizzy could barely hear.

Lizzy's blood went cold. Her smile faded, and her eyes narrowed. The girl burst into tears.

For some reason that made her smile.

"Oh, poor little girl. You must not be right in the head. No wonder Lizzy startles you so. Don't worry. Lizzy will put you to bed. And when you wake up, remember this was all a dream."

She moved forward quickly, struck the girl just enough to knock her out. Lizzy picked her up and carried her inside the apartment.

"I don't know why I am talking to silly puppets like you," Lizzy said to the girl in her arms. "I need someone who has a chance of understanding."

She peeled the girl out of her clothes. Looked at her for a moment, and decided that yes, she was pretty. Then tucked her snugly into her bed and pulled a nearby stuffed animal from the dresser and put it next to her head.

Lizzy watched her sleeping for a moment. Reached out and stroked the lovely hair once. Thought about killing her and left to get a drink.

There had to be someone in this town she could talk to.

Thirty-one

Of all the fears and worries Griffen had regarding the conclave, there was one he had not figured on at all. He had no experience at public speaking.

The requirement surfaced suddenly when it was casually mentioned to him that, as moderator, he would be expected to give the welcoming speech at the opening of the conclave. He felt uneasy when this was first mentioned, and by the time the official beginning of the event grew closer, this had escalated into a full-blown panic.

Back in college, he had signed up for one speech class, mostly because it presented an opportunity for him to get closer to a certain young lady who had caught his eye. As it turned out, she was already living with someone else, but by the time he had learned this, he had actually attended several classes and absorbed some of the rudiments of speaking to an audience.

After trying to seek advice and pointers from some of his current colleagues and discovering that living as a gambler or hustler in New Orleans gave them even less experience with public speaking than he had, he found himself desperately trying to recall those few lessons he had treated so lightly in school.

"Try to start with a joke. It establishes a rapport with the audience . . ."

"Don't fidget with your hands. If possible, work without note cards. Note cards encourage you to fidget . . ."

"Don't touch the podium. If you're nervous, you'll latch on to it with a death grip and never let go . . ."

All these and more were echoing in his mind as he surveyed the crowd of conclave attendees assembling for the opening. The watchwords did little to ease his nervousness, so he did what he always did in times of stress. He studied the people.

It had been decided that the opening would be conducted as a social gathering or cocktail party rather than with auditorium seating. Theoretically, this would encourage the attendees to mingle rather than bunch up in groups. It wasn't working.

Instead of sitting in small groups, they were standing in small groups, speaking only with those they arrived with and ignoring or glancing covertly at the other similar groups. An uncomfortable number were simply standing silently and watching Griffen.

The changelings were actually sitting on the floor in a group near the front, whispering quietly among themselves while smiling eagerly at Griffen. There was a notable open space between them and any of the other attendees.

Estella was standing against the wall farthest from the door with a half dozen people Griffen assumed were from her voodoo temple. When she met his eyes, she gave a faint smile and a small nod of recognition and encouragement.

Slim was standing with two other people off to the left of the podium. They seemed to be saying very little, spending most of their energies watching the other attendees. Griffen remembered that the street entertainer had mentioned when they first met that his circle of associates was neither very large nor particularly organized.

The ones that Griffen knew the least about and had next

to no time to meet or speak with were the shape-shifters. They seemed to be divided into two groups, or was it three? One small group lurked in the corner of the room and seemed to watch everyone at once. Another small bunch of four or five stood in the exact center of the room, eyes intent on Griffen. The final collection was a loose semicircle surrounding the center bunch, keeping at least two feet separate from them. They talked with each other, occasionally glancing at the center group or leaning toward it as if to listen to anything going on. They struck Griffen as nervous for some reason.

He also realized, even broken up as they seemed to be, the shifters were easily the largest group. Lump them all together, and they seemed to take up a good quarter of the bodies present.

Griffen was suddenly aware that no one had entered the room for several minutes and that an increasing percentage of the crowd was watching him expectantly. Postponing the inevitable was no longer an option, so, steeling himself, he stepped up to the podium.

"Good evening," he said, managing not to wince at the magnified sound of his voice from the public-address system. "I'd like to welcome you all to the conclave. My name is Griffen McCandles, and I've been asked to serve as moderator for the event. This is the first time I've done this, so if anyone objects or feels they can do it better, I will be happy to surrender the position to them."

He smiled at the crowd. They stared back at him. So much for opening with a joke.

"As this is a comparatively small gathering, we have dispensed with the notion of name tags or badges. It is hoped that by the end of the conclave, you will all know each other at least on sight. The lack of badges will also help keep you from being targeted as out-of-towners if you choose to explore the Quarter when not actively involved in the conclave."

This actually drew a small ripple of laughter, even though Griffen had not intended the comment as a joke.

"As far as exploring the Quarter goes, we have arranged for discounts at both the Voodoo Museum and the Haunted History Tour if any of you are interested. Just mention to the money taker that you are with the conclave, and they'll charge you the lower price. If, however, you choose to strike out on your own, there are a few cautionary notes I'd like to pass along."

Griffen paused for a second. He had worked on keeping this part lighthearted, but he was afraid it still sounded threatening.

"The French Quarter is a major tourist attraction, and people who work here are used to tourists and conventioneers. They will do their best to make your visit enjoyable, hoping that you'll come back again. You should keep in mind, however, that it is a living community, not an amusement park, and that many of the locals from the Quarter and surrounding areas are economically depressed. In plain talk, that means we have a number of pickpockets, muggers, hustlers, and other predators who will be watching for opportunities to separate you from your money in ways that are often illegal and occasionally dangerous.

"We would therefore suggest that you try to travel in groups or at least with one or two other people from the conclave. When possible, stay on the river side of Bourbon Street, particularly late at night, unless you have a native guide to help you steer clear of the more dangerous areas and bars."

Griffen paused and glanced around the room.

"Of course, it cannot be ignored that this particular group has abilities and powers not found in your average batch of tourists. Now, everybody who comes to New Orleans likes to kick back and let go a bit, even more than they do on normal vacations. While we want you to have fun, I'd like to remind you all that many of your fellow attendees, myself included, live here on a permanent basis. If you feel compelled or required to use your powers during your stay, we'd ask that you try to do it as inconspicuously as possible. Otherwise, it could potentially cause problems for us down the road."

He deliberately did not look at the changelings as he spoke, but from the corner of his eye he could see Robin and Hobb shift uncomfortably.

"But enough of that," he said, smiling. "There are many open discussions and demonstrations scheduled over the next several days. Of course, attendance is not required, but I know that I, for one, am looking forward to many of them."

And not looking forward to others, he thought, but didn't verbalize that part.

"On Saturday night there will be a Masquerade Party and Dance. Costumes are not required, but if you wish to . . ."

He broke off as a small disturbance rippled through the audience, causing people to turn and look toward the door. Following their gaze, he saw that a small group had just entered and was standing just inside. As quick as he noted this, he recognized two of the people who had been looking for him at the Irish pub. Lowell and Vera. The vampires had just dropped in to the conclave.

After pausing for a moment, apparently to be sure he had the room's attention, Lowell detached himself from the group and approached the podium. His eyes narrowed slightly as he recognized Griffen from the bar, then he gave a small shrug and a smirk.

"Mr. Griffen McCandles?" he said. "So glad to meet you . . . at last. My name is Lowell."

Griffen noticed that as Lowell spoke, he half turned so

that he was addressing the room as much as the moderator.

"Yes, Mr. Lowell," Griffen said with a smile. "Is there something I can help you with?"

"As a matter of fact, I was hoping to get permission from you for me and my group to attend the conclave." Lowell hesitated for effect. "In case you were not aware, my colleagues and I are vampires."

That got a reaction from some of the assemblage, particularly the changelings. Griffen was gratified to realize that, for a change, he was not the least-knowledgeable person in the room.

"I'm afraid you're laboring under a misconception," he said. "This is not my conclave. I've merely been asked to moderate the event, and as such have nothing to do with the invitation list."

"That's what we heard," the vampire said. "Still, since it seems the proceedings have already begun, we felt it was only polite to approach you as the moderator. It seems our group was somehow overlooked when the invitations were issued."

"Yes. I heard about that," Griffen said. "Something about vampire arrogance and how it was a disrupting presence for the conclave."

Lowell threw back his head and gave a short bark of laughter.

"Forgive me," he said, not sounding at all apologetic. "You must, however, acknowledge the irony of the situation. A dragon . . . near pure blood if I've heard correctly . . . lecturing vampires on arrogance."

"I keep hearing about that." Griffen smiled. "Perhaps if you knew more dragons, you'd realize that we aren't all alike. Stereotyping groups is an easy rap, and often erroneous."

"My point precisely," Lowell said, pouncing on the opening. "I think you'll find the same thing applies to vampires. Originally, we weren't even planning on attending."

"What made you change your mind?" Griffen asked, his curiosity piqued.

"Why, you, of course." The vampire seemed genuinely surprised by the question. "At first we thought this gathering would not be worth our time, but then we heard that a dragon would be participating . . . even if only as a moderator. That made us rethink our entire position. If a dragon feels this conclave is worth his time, then perhaps we should reexamine our own thoughts and biases and attend . . . even if uninvited."

"That raises an interesting point," Griffen said. "I thought that one of the limitations on your movements was that you could not enter a place uninvited."

"Please, Mr. McCandles," Lowell said. "That concept is allegorical. It was meant to assure readers that evil . . . meaning us . . . could not affect them unless they welcomed it. You see, that is just one of the misconceptions that we might be able to dispel by attending the conclave. I'm sure we share equally false assumptions about some of the other groups who have gathered here."

Griffen hesitated. He was still not wild about the vampires' presence at the conclave. Still, what Lowell said made a certain amount of sense.

"Unfortunately, we're still faced with the original problem," he said, stalling. "It's not my place to decide who may or may not participate."

"Perhaps we could poll the other attendees," the vampire said. "If our presence will upset too many of the invited participants, we'll leave."

"That's a possibility," Griffen said. "Before we do, however, I'll have to ask you to stop using glamour on the group or at least tone it down a bit. We do want this polling to be fair, don't we?"

Lowell looked startled.

"Yes. Of course," he said. "My apologies. Sometimes one

relies so much on a power one literally forgets one is using it. I'm sure you have the same problem from time to time."

It was decided to allow the vampires to participate in the conclave.

Thirty-two

As soon as the matter of the vampires was dealt with, Griffen gave the podium over to Slim. Theoretically, Slim was supposed to give a rundown on the events to come and a brief outline of what was to be discussed. In practice, almost as soon as Griffen had stepped down, people had started to file out. Griffen wasn't sure he liked the thought that everyone seemed to have attended the ceremony to get a look at him.

First out the door were the groups of shape-shifters. The ones lurking in the corner departed first. The changelings kept looking back and forth between Slim and the other attendees. They were gawking openly, no two of them looking in the same direction. Randomly, Drake stood up and started to follow the shifters out the door. Tink took that as a cue and followed, gathering up the others as he went.

The vampires were the next to go, followed by Estella and her group. Actually, they followed directly, and Estella stopped at the door and made some pass with her hands that Griffen didn't recognize. Only then did she step through and leave the hall.

Griffen realized he hadn't seen Rose that night and was a bit surprised. Actually, mostly he wanted to go have a word with the shifters. It was high time he met them and found out a little bit about what they expected from the conclave. Without at least that much information, Griffen had no idea how to prepare for them.

Unfortunately, Slim was walking toward him with the two he had been standing with earlier.

"Griffen, like ya to meet two of those attendin' from my side o' the tracks. This here is Johansson. He's from Vegas. The other is Margie, down from Wyoming."

Griffen shook their hands and blinked a bit. Johansson was a small, round man with a red complexion that made him look permanently flushed. Margie was thinner than Slim, and almost as tall. Her face was hard and serious, as if she had never smiled.

"Not what you expected?" Margie said.

"No, I hadn't realized that there would be so few of you. Or that you would come from so far," Griffen said.

"There aren't that few of us, but most don't care about dealings with others. Margie and I come from hubs, like Slim, so have to keep an eye on the world at large," Johansson said.

Griffen was hard-pressed to try to figure out what Las Vegas, New Orleans, and Wyoming had in common. Or why they would be called hubs. For once, he was saved having to ask.

"You seem distracted. We can talk later," Margie said, and abruptly turned and walked to the door.

Slim and Johansson shared a look.

"Well, she's hardly ever wrong. What's on your mind, Griffen?" Slim asked.

"I didn't want to be rude, but I was hoping to talk with some of the shape-shifters tonight," Griffen said.

Again, there was a look. Johansson shrugged and walked toward the door, leaving Slim and Griffen alone in the big room.

"Shouldn' be a problem. The talk is they is stayin' in this hotel. Most of the lower ones will still be hanging around. Go check the lobby bar," Slim said.

Griffen noticed a bit of an edge in his voice that hadn't been there before.

"I didn't mean to step on your toes, or ruffle your friends."

"Not friends, just like-minded folk. And you didn't. Just don't expect me to come share a drink with you and them."

Then Griffen was completely alone as Slim walked out. More than ever, Griffen wanted to talk with the shape-shifters. If only to find out why Slim's attitude had changed so abruptly. He felt woefully underqualified for this job.

Sure enough, the lobby bar was full. It was an open bar, with several low, comfortable chairs strewn away from the bar itself. Someone had moved the chairs together in a great amoeba-like configuration for the sake of conversation. Griffen stopped and saw a repeat of what he had seen during his speech.

There were essentially two rings of chairs. An inner ring held only five chairs, one of which was empty. Sitting in the other four were the group of shifters who had stood in the center of the room earlier.

Then, a foot or so away, was a much looser and wider ring of chairs. Here sat the other shifters, again talking among themselves, but at the same time keeping an eye on those in the center. It was as if they didn't want to miss anything said but didn't feel comfortable interfering.

As Griffen approached, most eyes turned his way. Particularly those of the inner circle. No one said anything or so much as gestured. But the vacant chair was plain enough. Without asking, Griffen walked over and took a seat in it.

There was an excited murmuring behind and around him from the outer ring. Those four he was now sitting with merely nodded to him. A small gesture of welcome, or of acceptance.

One man nodded a bit more deeply than the others. He was a fragile-looking man, with short black hair that Griffen noticed seemed very soft. He was dressed elegantly, though a bit too flashy. By Quarter standards they were gay men's fashions.

"Mr. McCandles, I am Jay. It has been decided that I will do most of the speaking for the shape-shifters you see here," he said.

"A pleasure," Griffen replied.

He noticed that the group he had seen lurking in the corner was not present. He asked the obvious question.

"What about the other group I saw?" he said.

The four shared a glance. Griffen was getting a bit tired of that.

"I do not speak for them. How much do you know about shape-shifters?" Jay asked.

"Not much at all. To my knowledge I've only met one other."

"You have met others. But you speak of the chimera you battled."

"Yes, but what do you mean by 'others'?"

Griffen didn't wonder how he knew about his fight with George. Though he couldn't be sure whether he was getting more used to supernatural sources of information or to the French Quarter rumor mill.

"You and your sister have the power, to some extent at least. You see, that is one of the difficulties faced by choosing who and how many speak for us in such a gathering as this."

As Jay spoke, Griffen noticed that his accent and speech were very refined, cultured. His movements and gestures were short, seemingly abrupt, but he also seemed to have an uncommon grace. Except for an occasional odd tilt of the head, he was what Griffen thought of as a well-bred gentleman.

"We shifters share nothing in common except our ability. Even more than the animal-control types, those you see here have different ranges, origins, even blood. But we are lumped together because our primary attribute is to change form. Even though by that definition alone, you would be one of us."

Griffen started to fear this was going the same place his initial conversations with Slim had gone. And began to reassure Jay that he wasn't interested in controlling a group of supernaturals.

"I have no intention of——" he started.

"No, that was not meant to insult your pride or to insinuate that you wanted leverage over us. I was merely explaining how unfair things were. We have sitting behind you a werewolf, a woman who can become a wolf. But she has no other form, just the one wolf. Next to her is a man who can only change his hands, but he can change them into practically anything. What do they have in common?"

Griffen fought the urge to look behind him at the people pointed out. Somehow he thought it would be rude to stare at those sitting in the outer ring of chairs.

"Not much," Griffen admitted.

"Exactly. And the personalities and motives change from person to person as well. Some shifters spend ninety percent of their time in animal form, and the human world is only a passing nuisance to them. This causes all sorts of difficulties. Even ignoring putting them in the same room as those whose sole talent is the bending of animals to their will."

Ah, so that was why he had been picking up some tension from Slim toward the shape-shifters and back again.

"So, unless it is some personal matter, we only discuss at the conclave what affects all shifters, regardless of type. That is why we are here," Jay said.

That made a certain type of sense to Griffen. A personal gripe or issue could be brought up by anyone. But having a set spokesmen at the outset for dealing with the larger matters, the ones that affected everyone, would prevent confusion.

"So, why you?" Griffen asked.

"Ah, natural ranking. We four are the most powerful shifters attending. And though I am not the most powerful"—— Jay paused to nod to a wild-looking man whose eyes were constantly flicking from face to face—"it is agreed I speak best and fairly. In my day job I am a judge, so I also have knowledge of human laws."

"Good to know, but what makes one shifter more powerful than another?"

"Variety. How many forms? What are his limitations? Does he have to maintain mass? Side benefits and powers like being able to shift objects, such as one's clothes. I believe your chimera not only had multiple unrelated forms, but also had other tricks, including protection from fire. He might even be more than he claims. This really sets him fairly high compared to the young lady who howls at full moons and may fear silver bullets."

"Does that really . . . ?"

"I do not know. I have never tried shooting her," Jay said.

Griffen shook off the thought and instead focused on something that was nagging him.

"Okay, but how can you speak for them if you don't speak with them? Standing and sitting segregated seems awful cliquey to me."

Jay blinked, obviously taken aback. Several of the others stirred, and the wild-looking man chuckled, before saying, in a voice like gravel, "We don't do it to them, they do it to themselves."

"Quite," Jay said. "We have had no fights for dominance or any of that nonsense. Any of them could have taken the empty chair, but they hold themselves back in mixed admiration and fear. Even if they could have brought up the courage to step forward, most of them would ask 'May I join you?' and would have taken a 'No' without hesitation. The fact that you sat without asking marks you as one of the elite, even though they are setting the standards of the elite."

Griffen looked back now, at the faces of all those listening to the conversation. They were right, each one held that nervous admiration of a . . . well, of a fan. These four were the equivalent of shifter rock stars, at least as far as the conclave was concerned.

"Okay, so what about that other group I saw?" Griffen said.

"Actually, they were locals. You'll probably have some trouble with them. They call themselves 'loup garou,' the French, or, I am told, Cajun word for werewolf. They are quite powerful as far as variety. They have complete control, not just man to wolf but all stages in between, including a monstrous form to make a Hollywood effects man slit his wrists for being a dismal failure. Very pack-oriented, but in-dependent, too. They only showed up to make it clear that what any of us says does not apply to them. Arrogant thugs," Jay said.

Much as when he had first met the changelings, Griffen felt overwhelmed. Too many new concepts too quickly. He was going to need some time to think of some better ques-tions, but at least now he had a small grip on who, and what, he was dealing with.

"One last question, if you don't mind me asking. What 'variety' are you?" Griffen said.

"That in some circles is a very rude question, Moderator," Jay said, smiling coldly.

"I did say 'if you don't mind.'"

"True, and I don't. There is no name for me. I do birds."

"What birds?"

"Any birds, size, shape, color, even sex. It makes no differ-ence. I am limited to that, but within my bailiwick have no limitations. If it has feathers, I can manage it with a bit of work."

"If you don't mind my saying, you don't look much like any bird I have seen," Griffen said.

Jay smiled and ran a hand through his hair. He pulled the

short strands up enough that Griffen could see they weren't strands at all. They were very soft, downy black feathers. So fine he would never have been able to tell.

"You just haven't seen one that has evolved enough."

Thirty-three

One of Griffen's oddities since leaving college life behind in Michigan and beginning a dragon's life down in New Orleans was that he simply did not own an alarm clock. It was a trivial thing, something he rarely noticed and never commented upon. His sleep schedule was open, and if he ever needed to set an alarm, there was always his cell phone.

In fact, the cell phone was often his wake-up call, whether he set it or not. The loud buzz of an incoming call was the first thing he heard on any given morning. It never failed to annoy him.

This morning was no exception. The phone yanked Griffen out of a deep sleep, the kind of truly black nothingness that comes before the real dreams start. He jerked upright with a gasp, lunging for the phone. The bedside table still showed faint gouges from similar surprise wakings, but Griffen was learning to control his reflexes.

He popped open the lid of his phone and saw just why he felt so startled and groggy all at once. He had gotten a generous four hours of sleep.

"Mr. McCandles, we gots some big problems down here."

"Slim . . ."

Griffen recognized the voice through the haze of sleep and shook his head, trying to clear it more. Not quite tracking, he said the first thing that came into his head.

"Isn't it time you started calling me Griffen?"

"Well . . . let's just wait till after this here meet is done with. Might feel different 'bout that by then. We got problems," Slim said.

Griffen was already up and getting dressed.

"It's nine in the morning, Slim," Griffen said, voice slightly muffled as he pulled on his shirt.

"Sorry 'bout that, but not every attendee is quite as nocturnal as you. Be glad it ain't a normal convention, or you'd have to get here every day by now."

"Right. I'll try to remember to be more thankful that these aren't 'normal' conventioneers."

Despite his sarcasm, a wry smile pulled at his lips. As troublesome as it might be, at least his life wasn't boring. He hurried out the door, cell phone still pressed to his ear.

"Fill me in while I'm on my way," Griffen said, heading out the security gate and onto the street.

"Sure thing, but not the Sonesta. The problem is in the garous' hotel room."

Griffen quickly changed his course, taking a right at the first street he came to.

"The Best Western? Up on Rampart right?"

"Right, which may or may not be a helpfulness. Anyways, I'm headin' up there myself, so you might beat me. Just head on up to the room. They is waitin'," said Slim.

"Okay, but you still haven't told me just what is going on."

Rampart was only a few blocks away, but a few blocks on hurried feet without proper sleep or anything resembling breakfast seemed to drag on forever. Griffen kept his strides long and fast, but didn't run. He had learned the hard way that running through the Quarter was great fodder for the local rumor mills.

The last time he had just been trying to pick up a snack at the A&P during a commercial break. By nightfall he had gotten a full barrage of everything from jokes about his taking up jogging to whispers that he had been running from someone. He didn't even want to think about what would spring up if he ran and looked worried at the same time.

Slim clicked his tongue. "I don't quite have all the details. Got a panic call from one of the lesser wolves. They all sharin' a couple of adjoining rooms there and he heard a snarl and sounds of a fight in the john."

"Is that all?" Griffen asked.

"Well . . . he opened the door and said their leader had been attacked. By some 'thing' he said," Slim added.

"Umm? 'Thing'?"

"Yeah, here's where it gets garbled. Couldn't put together 'nough words for me to have a clue what he found in there."

Griffen started to slow his pace to a normal walking speed.

"Slim, that doesn't exactly sound like an emergency. By the time we get there, whatever fight happened will be well over."

"Yep, you right 'bout that. Fact it was over when the kid opened the door. He just too far out of his depth not to yelp for help," Slim said.

Griffen again noticed a bit of the disdain in Slim's tone that he and the other animal-control people had for the shape-shifters. He didn't have the time and patience just then to question it again.

"So why are we running over there?" Griffen said.

He didn't say, tempting though it was, why the hell did you wake me?

" 'Cause, the critter is still there."

Griffen stumbled over the uneven sidewalk and almost fell. He stared at his phone for a moment.

"Right . . ." Griffen said, petty objections instantly fading. "Be there in five minutes."

He closed his phone and took off at a faster pace. He would deal with the rumor mill later.

* * *

The Best Western was not by any means a high-end hotel by New Orleans standards. However, it was fairly cheap, clean, and could officially boast being inside the Quarter, even though it was on the very edge. Needless to say, Griffen didn't have any problems just walking in and heading up to the third floor. In fact, he hadn't even seen anyone behind the counter.

Slim had beaten him after all, and stood in the hall outside the room with one of the younger shape-shifters Griffen had seen at the conclave. He had never heard the young man speak. Like most of the lesser members attending, he deferred to his particular leader.

Slim was talking to him.

"Now, you stay out here like I tol' you. No one, and I mean no one, comes in till me or Moderator McCandles says so."

The young man simply nodded and crossed his arms over his chest. He looked tough, on guard, enough that Griffen had little worry that anyone would try to push past him. Still, Griffen could see the relief in his eyes. It was obvious he didn't want to go back into the room, and Slim had come up with a good way to save face from outside.

Slim winked at Griffen and walked over to him. His expression made it clear that he caught the kid's relief, too.

"You ready to face the unknown, Moderator?" Slim said nodding to the door.

"Doesn't look like I have much of a choice," Griffen observed.

"Good. 'Cause I can'ts wait to see what gots the pup all riled like."

Slim grinned and opened the door. Griffen had no problem with letting him go in first. The bathroom door was open, but from the entranceway Griffen couldn't see inside. He did hear the young wolf whimper slightly as he passed.

Griffen carefully closed the hall door before moving forward.

Before he took another step, a wave of stench rolled over him with almost physical force. It made him think of stagnant water and a men's urinal that hadn't been cleaned in years. He didn't know for sure, but assuming garou had more acute senses of smell than most people, he understood more why one wouldn't want to come back in the room after getting out.

Then he could see into the bathroom, and he couldn't stop himself from staring.

Slim, standing next to him and staring just as openly, said it best.

"Sheee-iiit."

The figure in the bathroom was big, a good seven feet if it stood up straight, but it was hunched over, its posture apelike. It seemed to be made completely of plant matter. A swirling mass of bark and vines and moss mimicked skin. Grasslike hair spread in a lawn halfway down its back. Each piece of vegetation seeming to writhe of its own accord. It was constantly in motion even while hulking there. Algae spread over its chest bubbled slightly as it breathed.

Griffen couldn't help noticing it had mushrooms growing between its toes.

"What is it?" Griffen asked

"I don' have a single clue. Somethin' local, I think. Heard 'bout somethin' similar. A spirit of the swamps," Slim said.

"Somehow I don't think spirit fits. Anything that smells that bad has to be mostly corporeal," Griffen said, trying to fight off shock with humor.

Slim half started to smile. Then the street entertainer saw the body crumpled next to the toilet. It was the garou leader, his clothes ripped and a large green splotch marring the top of his head. He wasn't moving.

Slim rushed forward.

The creature straightened, head brushing the ceiling and leaving a green smear. It swelled up menacingly.

Griffen put a hand on Slim's shoulder and stopped him.

"Ease down, Slim," he said, keeping his eyes locked on the imposing figure.

"Are you nuts? Look how bad that monster beat him. The man might be dead," Slim said.

"Funny you caring, Slim, but look again. The clothes are ripped only at the seams. I think our friend here is only responsible for the clout to the head. I take it an unconscious shifter reverts back to their natural form?" Griffen said.

"Some yes, some no. The garou and werewolves are said to," Slim said grudgingly.

"I think he saw . . . this, and panicked. Started to shift, not thinking about what it might do to his outfit, and the creature reacted, just as it was about to react to your rush."

Griffen finally released Slim's shoulder. He hadn't taken his eyes off the apparition in front of him. It had no eyes, but there were two dark blue flowers on what was passing for its head. Griffen got the distinct impression that they were watching him, appraising him.

Slim's glance at Griffen was awfully appraising, too.

"Damn, I heard dragons was fast thinkers," Slim said.

Griffen would have responded, but the creature settled down and went back to its more relaxed slump. A deep gurgling built from somewhere inside. After a moment, Griffen realized that in a harsh, bubbling way it was beginning to speak.

"Moderator . . . good," it said slowly.

"Think he means you is a good moderator, or that it's good the moderator is here?" Slim asked.

"Both," the creature answered.

Slim started, obviously having not expected an answer. Griffen could swear the fronds on the "spirit's" face were twisting, smiling. It was disturbing and comforting all at once.

"Waited," it said.

Griffen pulled up all his courage and took a step forward.

"Waited for what? Why?" Griffen said.

"For you . . . witness. Must be fair."

It moved slowly, a complicated procedure involving all of its seemingly separate plants. Both Griffen and Slim had to hold themselves back from reacting as it bent over the fallen garou. Griffen watched closely, waiting for any sign of violence. No matter how unknown or dangerous the thing might be, he wasn't going to let it harm an unconscious man if he could help it.

After a few moments it stood again. In its massive hand, it held the garou's wallet. Griffen stared as it pulled out several large bills, then dropped the billfold next to the unconscious body. It held the bills to its chest, and they were sucked one by one into the ooze, disappearing into the depths.

Griffen couldn't hide the shock in his voice as pieces clicked together.

"He owed you money!?" Griffen said.

Massive shoulders shrugged like trees bending together in the wind.

"It's New Orleans," it said in its ponderous voice.

Slim choked back a laugh. Griffen felt more like groaning. He rubbed his palm over his eyes and his fingers against his temples. He was really going to have to think about finding some way to improve security. This could have gone much worse.

"Look, as thankful as I am that you aren't some slaughtering monster, you can't leave by the front door. Even on Rampart it would get talked about," Griffen said.

The creature nodded, and again Griffen was almost sure it was smiling. He watched as it leaned over the sink, bent forward, and slowly slid into the drain. Pieces that Griffen were sure would be too large flowed together with slurping, sucking noises. Something about the process strained Griffen's eyes till he had to look away. By the time he had blinked and looked back, the creature was gone, an industrial-strength ring around the sink and a few marks on floor and ceiling the only thing left to show that it had ever been there.

Those signs, and a shape-shifter on the floor who promptly lifted up his head, apparently not so unconscious after all.

"Is she gone?" he asked.

"She?!" Slim and Griffen exclaimed together.

This time Slim didn't try to hold back his laughter. Griffen fought down the urge to throw up his hands as he marched out of the room. Before leaving, he instructed the young shifter to find a mop and clean up.

He could just see this bunch leaving things for the hotel's maid staff.

Thirty-four

Mai had been thinking. Of course, she was always think-ing, but a particular train of thought had captivated her at-tention. She had been thinking about faces.

Faces. She presented so many different ones to different people. Lover and confidante, unnoticed power, old enemy. She was all of these and more, depending on the situation, and the people involved. That was part of the great game that she truly loved. The many different and varied roles one had to play. Some false, some second nature, some true na-ture.

Some more honest than others.

There was one face, one role, that she had been slacking off on lately, an unexpected role that she had slipped into without realizing, one that she found fitted her better than she would ever have guessed. As soon as she realized how little she had played it lately, she knew it was time to take it up again. Decision made, she made her plans and found her-self at Valerie's apartment door early one afternoon.

It was time to be a friend.

She flung the door open dramatically, standing straight and tall and looking as authoritative as possible. Knowing that if the door was unlocked Valerie was in, and probably doing nothing more than watching TV on her couch. Sure enough, Val looked up from the couch, startled by the en-trance.

"Get up. We are going shopping," Mai declared.

She knew that statement to Val was even more random and surprising than her sudden entrance. Sure enough, the other dragon gave her head a shake and stuck one finger in her ear as if to clear it.

"Say that again slow."

Mai grinned, letting herself relax.

"I mean it. You are turning into a lump. All you seem to do lately is work, work out, worry about your brother, and pretend nothing is going on in your own life."

Val smiled a bit, shock wearing off, and ticked Mai's list off on her own fingers.

"Seems like a full docket to me," she said.

"Shows what you know. I'm bored and thus declare a day of shopping, bonding, and associated madness. Come along nicely, and no one gets hurt."

"So, you are bored, and I get dragged along for the ride."

Mai faked a gasp.

"You impugn my intentions? This is all for you. Suck it up, girl, and I'll bring along Daddy's credit card to salve your wounds."

Val smiled more. Mai enjoyed bantering with Val; they both knew it meant both more and less than it seemed to.

"Daddy, huh?" Val said.

"Well . . . someone's daddy certainly. You know I must protect my sources."

"Spy."

"Lump."

Val threw her hands up in surrender and got to her feet. Mai stepped into the apartment and let the door close behind her.

"Go get dressed and off we go," Mai said.

Val looked down at herself, and Mai could practically hear the old discussion popping up. Not that there was anything wrong with that. It was a familiar and fun one. Mai simply would never understand Val's sense of fashion, or lack thereof. For such an attractive woman, she seemed to do her best to hide it. Even alone in her apartment, Mai would never be caught dead in sweats. Sweats that didn't even match.

"I am dressed, Short Stack."

"No, Gigantia, you are clothed. Not the same thing."

Val rolled her eyes and stomped melodramatically off to her room to change. Mai had to hand it to her, when she wanted to stomp, she stomped. Mai eased into an easy chair to wait, a small smile on her face.

A friend! Who would have thought it?

Two hours and half a dozen shops later, the two and a small mountain of bags were in a small boutique on Royal looking at hats. It didn't matter that neither one ever wore hats, or that hats in general were very much out of style for anyone who looked under forty. Practicality had little to do with a shopping day.

Usually most of the bags would have been Mai's, but there was something infectious about Mai when she really got going. Plus, since she was mildly irritated by Val's reluctance to spend on herself, she often snatched items that Val liked and paid for them while the other was still in the changing room. Or slipped the clerk her card, so that when Val's pride demanded she "pay her own way" she would find it already covered. Even friends could get caught up in power games.

Mostly, though, this was giving them time to catch up and talk. Mai started on safe topics, Val's work mainly. Then steered the conversation slowly to where she was interested. At the moment, while fingering a feathered monstrosity she couldn't imagine anyone would actually put on her head, she was telling Val how Griffen had managed to get caught up with both her and Fox Lisa.

"Really?" Val said, laughing. "Strip pai gow?"

"Yeah, and he didn't see it coming. Can't believe you haven't heard that one before," Mai said.

"Well, you never told me, and I don't spend much time with Lisa."

"And Griffen?"

"Brothers!" Val rolled her eyes. "He's all about sticking his overprotective nose in my love life. But as soon as I turn it around, he gets embarrassed and shrugs me off. Big baby."

Mai chuckled, but her eyes narrowed a bit, and her tone went just a touch sly.

"So . . . about your love life."

"What about it?" Val said, expression faltering.

"Oh, so you can shrug it off, too? Maybe it's not a brother trait after all but a McCandles one."

Val looked at her surroundings. Most of the shops they had visited were big on personal attention, pampering that usually wasn't found in these mall-filled consumer days. Unfortunately, that meant there was a shopgirl pretending not to eavesdrop a few feet away. Mai watched her gather up her bags.

"Come on. If we are going to dish, I'm going to need something hot and bad for me," Val said.

"Sounds like your love life, all right," Mai said.

Val glared at her, a very unfriendly look, and Mai waved to the shopkeeper as they headed back out to the street. Mai followed, though she had pretty much figured they were headed to Café Du Monde and Val's favorite sweet vices.

"I wasn't shrugging it off," Val said.

Mai fell into step next to her and a little behind. She glanced at Val and cocked her head.

"If you say so."

"What I meant was that there isn't anything to discuss. Cold turkey," Val said.

"Mmm, from what I hear it wasn't too long ago you were

seen knocking on Gris-gris's door. And that sounded like anything but cold."

Mai had to stop and turn around. Val had stopped in her tracks. Mai shrugged.

"It's the Quarter. Word gets around."

"Heard from who, Mai?" Val said.

"Not Gris-gris, if that's what you mean. Doubt he told anyone who didn't ask him directly. It was third-person by the time it got to me. Remember"—Mai darkened her expression and her tone—"the Lucky Dog vendors see all."

Val shook her head and started walking again. Mai had expected at least a laugh from her but didn't push it. After half a block of silence, Val spoke up.

"So what did it sound like, then?"

"What?"

"If not cold turkey, then . . ."

"Oh. Aggressive. That was the word I liked best. 'Aggressive,' " Mai said.

She could practically see Val rolling the word over her tongue, testing it out.

"Yeah, that sounds about right," Val said finally.

"And since then?"

Mai watched Val weigh exactly how much to say. Val simply didn't have enough practice at disguising her true feelings, and Mai had practiced reading people longer than Val had been alive. Though Mai wouldn't kid herself; she knew her friend had more powerful blood. Still, experience beats power.

"Nothing . . . Well, not much. I sort of got invited to this masked ball," Val said.

Mai grinned, that sounded promising.

"By who?"

"George."

This time Mai stopped in her tracks, and for all her inscrutable behavior, felt her jaw drop. Val kept walking, and

Mai realized belatedly that her friend had dropped that bombshell with expert precision. By the time she caught up, Val's grin was wide enough to make the cat with a canary blush through his fur.

"Bitch," Mai muttered.

"Yep. You had it coming," Val said.

"How could I not hear about this?"

"You don't know everything that is going on in the world? Gasp, shock, better turn in your junior decoder ring. You're a has-been."

Mai thought sourly that Val was definitely enjoying this far too much. Also, that her gibes were hitting a bit too close to home. Her face gave away too much, and she saw Val back-pedal a bit mentally.

"Relax. The only ones there were Griffen, George, and me. I doubted that George would be blabbing it about, and Griffen . . ."

"Has had his head up his ass lately," Mai said.

"Well, up the conclave anyway, which smells about the same."

By now the two had crossed Jackson Square and were set-tling into chairs at the café. Unlike the shops, Café Du Monde was a wonderful place to talk semiprivately. The wait-ers were quick, and cash was collected as soon as the food arrived, and then they vanished to serve others and never ap-peared till it was time to clear dishes.

Mai was a coffee girl, Val hot chocolate. That said much about them. They both had an order of beignets, with an extra order to split.

"Okay, so talk to me, girlfriend. Why would you date George after he nearly killed your brother?"

Mai had to remind herself that other than rumor and the story of Griffen's confrontation with the dragon hunter, she was not supposed to know George. Certainly not on any per-sonal or professional level.

"Mainly I think he did it to get on Griffen's nerves. I won't flatter myself to think he really is doing it because he is interested in me or apologetic over bashing my head in at our last meeting."

"Especially not after you emptied a shotgun into him," Mai said innocently.

"Exactly."

Val smiled slyly and sipped her hot chocolate. Maybe, Mai thought, she wasn't so amateurish in controlling her expression after all.

"Of course, you stated why he might want to ask you along to the dance, not why you would accept," Mai said, just as innocently.

"I have my reasons," Val said.

Here was the real crux. Mai had been noticing changes in Val that could not be explained by her pregnancy. At least not in such early stages. Though it might cost what little she'd gained, she felt she had to press on.

"Reasons you don't want to share, even with me. Come on, Big Butt. You've been stressing over something for a while now. Something that has you working out three times as hard as you ever have since I met you. Isn't it about time you shared with someone?"

Mai waited on pins and needles. She had spent her arrow and had no idea whether it would hit its mark. As inconsequential as this conversation might be, she felt more exhilarated than she had in months.

"I was attacked," Val said quietly.

Bull's-eye.

Mai silently ran over possibilities in her mind.

"If you had simply been mugged, it wouldn't have mattered. You would have wiped the floor with them. What do you mean, attacked?"

"Tell me, Mai. You obviously knew Nathaniel. Did . . . does he have any sisters?"

Pieces fell together with a *clack*. Mai didn't like how they added up.

"A few, only one of whom I can think of who might do you harm."

"Lizzy?"

Mai's train of thought reached an exploding bridge of a conclusion. She almost shuddered thinking of Lizzy meeting Val. As composed as she was, she couldn't help her reactions.

"God, you are lucky to be alive," Mai said.

Val looked at her for a long moment, and whatever she saw seemed to reassure her. She nodded, and bit into another beignet.

"So," Val said, "you see why I might want to accept the acquaintance of a professional dragon hunter."

It was a statement, not a question. Still, Mai found herself trapped between two roles, two faces. She knew what she would do as a manipulator and what she would do as a friend. They were not the same course of action. And the conflict, as deep and sharp a conflict as she had felt in years, had only one resolution.

She had to try to be a friend.

"So call him, dummy," Mai said, and hoped Val wouldn't hear her reluctance.

"What do you mean?" Val said.

"Surely he gave you a way to contact him. You aren't the type to let a man, any man, defend you. Why the hell aren't you on the horn with him asking for advice. Tips. Training?"

Val looked at Mai for another long moment. Without responding, she reached down and pulled out her cell phone. A few numbers later, she was speaking into it.

"George?" Val said.

Mai focused on her ears, extending her senses in a way that few nondragons could.

"Ms. McCandles," George said on the other end. "Called to make arrangements?"

"Perhaps, but not for the date. We need to meet, George. Someplace big, someplace open. Someplace without witnesses," Val said.

There was a long pause on the other end of the phone.

"Is this a challenge? A fight?" George said.

"Something like that, only we should both walk away after. If you want a date, Georgey boy, you are going to damn well earn one," Val said.

Mai could just make out George's low chuckle on the other end of the line.

"Oh, really. Very well. I will call you back with a time and place. And soon, because you have intrigued me, Ms. Mc-Candles."

"Valerie," Val said, as automatically as her brother would have said "Griffen," "and good. I will expect your call."

Valerie closed the phone, and when her eyes met Mai's, they were filled with uncertainty. Uncertainty that grew when she saw a bit of answering insecurity in Mai's eyes.

"What? That seemed right," Val said.

"It was," Mai answered. "I am just realizing. With everything going on . . . I am going to have to secure my own invitation to this damn ball."

Thirty-five

"**How** could you be so stupid?"

Flynn dug his fingers into his thigh, pain helping control his temper. It was that or crush the flimsy cell phone in his hand, and he didn't have the time or energy to replace it. Years of practice meant he did not start to grow scales or claws or anything similar, yet the impulse was close.

"I'm sorry, sir," a thin, contrite voice said on the other end.

"Do you have any idea what that will cost me in the long run? That no-talent hack could have been president one day! And you let him sign on with another firm," Flynn said.

"But, sir, you said he wasn't important. That your project there was far more valuable, and I should just handle it as best I could."

"I had assumed your best wasn't quite so inadequate. Why did I ever let your mother talk me into hiring you?" Flynn said.

"Because it was the only way you could get her to sign a nudity clause in her contract, sir, and you owed the studio head."

"Yes, well, her career has been over for a year. So your career is over now. I'm calling security next to make sure you clean out your desk without any fuss."

Flynn disconnected, cutting off any further protests from the lackey on the other end. If he admitted the truth to himself, he should never have let the kid handle such a job. He just hadn't thought the actor in question bright enough to jump on his current absence. Still, he had to set an example. Besides, he was still disappointed over the low box-office returns off his mother.

"Hey, Flynn, mind if I join you?"

He looked up, surprised to see Griffen McCandles leaning over the railing that surrounded the tables at the Café Du Monde. He smiled, openly to Griffen, inwardly to himself. The folly back at the office aside, the deal he was working on certainly did have the potential to be great. More important, since Mai's little encounter, it was proving to be more and more intriguing.

It was a good thing, to be able to enjoy one's work.

"Sure, Griffen, come on over and order something. Excuse me, though, while I finish up a little business."

Griffen nodded and moved around the railing and into the café proper. Flynn dialed his office number, and the extension to on-site security. If the son was anything like his mother, he would throw a temper tantrum before leaving.

"This is Flynn," he said, as the line was picked up. "I've fired Bradley . . . Yes, that's the one. Let him make some fuss, draw some attention, then put him out on his ass . . . Yes, that's right, he's the example of the year . . . Good. I'll call back for a report later."

He hung up and noticed Griffen looking at him a little oddly. He didn't think the young dragon could pick up on his tension, his anger over the whole issue. Minor though it was. After a few quick thoughts, he decided to probe the issue.

"Never fired anyone?" Flynn asked.

"Not directly, no; when I first got started, I set some policy. Made people make a choice, but there weren't any big issues with the organization itself. Just some of those connected on the periphery," Griffen said.

"Well, sometimes it's necessary. Particularly if someone messes up badly."

"What, no second chances?"

Flynn picked up his coffee and sipped, letting the bitterness roll over his tongue. He was more in the mood for that than the too-sweet beignets so popular here.

"Sometimes, depends on whether you judge a second chance will do any good. Sometimes you've got to know when to cut your losses. More important, you have to remember, as head of an organization, that punishing one person harshly helps keep many more from repeating their mistakes. Or committing worse ones."

Griffen's own drink and a plate of beignets came, and he reached for the confection first. Flynn watched him carefully as he bit into the corner, and a small cloud of powdered sugar rose. He seemed thoughtful, even moody. Or was Flynn projecting his own feelings on him?

"Tell me more about this policy you set and why you set it. Was it for your good or your people's?" Flynn asked.

"I'd like to think both. I think you've heard something about the aftermath, but I decided my people either dealt drugs or worked for me. Not both. I didn't want such a dangerous and messy business ruining the lives of those around me."

"Sounds like a good decision though made more from a moral ground than thinking of the business itself."

"Pretty much. Same reason I'm sorry to say I can't take your advice on using the local druggies as security. It's just too much like going back on my own word."

Flynn nearly bit his tongue and had to keep from spitting out his coffee.

"What? After trying to help, you throw it back at me?"

"No, no, it's nothing like that. It's just—"

"It's that bitch Mai, isn't it?"

Flynn regretted the outburst as soon as he said it. Yes, he

had been heavy-handed with some of his advice to Griffen, but never casually. This was the first move he had made that had not been at all premeditated. He saw Griffen lean back, his eyes narrowing.

"No . . . in fact Mai has never mentioned you at all. Where do you know her from?"

Of course, Mai wouldn't mention him directly. She would use a cat's-paw, if she were involved with this aspect of the game at all. Flynn cursed silently but didn't let a moment's hesitation show as he gave Griffen lies in the form of half-truths.

"I know her family, and her since she was little. She has never liked me, or liked my ways, I might say."

"What ways would those be?"

"Mai has never been good at full honesty, at openness. Her nature is much more subtle."

True, Flynn thought, *every word of it.* Not telling him anything, or even coming close to answering his question, but it should be enough.

"Well, I can't debate that. I don't really know how much she hides."

"Well, if I may . . . just how old do you think she is?" Flynn said.

"Good point. I knew her in school, but that's also where I met Jerome. And I know he is a lot older than he pretended."

"Griffen, maybe I'm speaking out of turn, but it's my feeling you should know what you can about your allies. As far as I know, Mai is older than Jerome."

"Still, Flynn, I just don't think dealing with the local gangs is the way to go. They just don't seem prepared to do anything but shoot at people."

Flynn shrugged and kept the relief off his face. Two steps back, one forward. He rolled with Griffen's change of subject.

"What about my other idea, some form of tracking?"

"It sounds good . . . but how would I pull it off? Somehow I don't think I can convince them to walk around with transmitters in their pockets."

Flynn cocked his head and reached out. His fingers brushed a set of small black and red beads woven around Griffen's neck.

"The person who made these should be able to make similar. For one good at such crafting, it should be child's play."

"Really?"

Griffen took the beads off and ran them through his fingers. Flynn nodded and kept his smile easy and warm.

"Look, Griffen, forgive me for snapping. Tough day at the office, even though I'm not there. Actually, I kind of miss being there."

"I do appreciate the time and advice, Flynn, it's just I have to follow my own gut, too."

"Sure you do, that's what makes you a dragon. No harm, no foul."

Griffen nodded and put the necklace back on. He reached for his wallet, but Flynn waved him off. Soon he was watching the young man walk off across the square.

He picked up his cell phone. Still seething, and needing someone to vent his anger on.

"Security? Flynn. I've changed my mind. If he throws a tantrum, shoot him!"

Thirty-six

Griffen had no idea what to expect from his first "official" discussion meeting at the conclave.

He had some assumptions, and some minor information from Slim and others about what would go on. What he really didn't understand was what his part was to be in the whole mess. He was so new to things supernatural that he didn't feel qualified to give an opinion on the simplest of matters. He certainly didn't think he was a good judge or arbitrator of other people's problems. Griffen hoped that things would go smoothly enough during this first meeting that he could more or less keep his head down.

The topic, as he understood it, was loosely categorized as information technologies. He was sure things would wander a bit around the topic, but the crux of the discussion was to be geared toward a single issue. Someone had proposed that a database be set up listing all known willing supernatural entities and their general locations and territories.

It seemed simple enough, a source of information on who was where and who was near enough to call on for help in times of crisis. Still, Griffen had a growing suspicion in his gut that things would be anything but easy.

The room itself was like conference rooms everywhere. A long table, chairs, pitchers of water, and glasses. Though there were only a few chairs at the table itself. Behind each seat at the table were several chairs, and as people started filing in, Griffen saw what he expected would become a familiar pattern.

The speakers, for lack of a better word, sat at the table. Their groups and advisors sat behind them. Already there was whispering going on as a speaker would lean back to consult the others. Though there were no rules against anyone speaking their mind, it seemed the majority would speak through their leaders.

Griffen had purposefully not sat at the head of the table but closer to the middle of it. If he was going to do any good at all, he figured he would have to be in the thick of things. This was not about power games. At least, not yet.

When it was all said and done, sitting at the table were Griffen, Estella, Slim, Jay, Lowell, Tink, and three people Griffen hadn't met yet. One he knew from sight was the leader of the garou, who was sitting directly opposite Jay and the other shifters. He went by the name of Kane. The other two Slim had mentioned were representing more-scattered and less-represented groups.

One, a stout woman with laughter lines around her eyes, was a wiccan named Gada. She was speaking largely for the collected human religious types other than the voodoo. The last was the one who had proposed the database. Griffen wasn't sure what to make of him, but he claimed to be an alchemist.

The meeting had started with the proposal. That in itself was excruciating. The alchemist, named Nick, tended to stutter and repeat himself. He listed point by point the benefits of such information, then played devil's advocate and brought up every point against it he could think of. Then he brought up points to dismiss the negative ones and debated himself.

"Dis so stupid." Kane put in finally.

Griffen had been told that the garou were "local" more or less. Now he believed it. Kane's accent was somewhere between Cajun and the Bronx. He had to have some family that lived in the Irish Channel. His vocabulary was good, his sense of grammar atrocious.

"He has the right to speak," Slim said.

"For 'ow long? Dis here discussion was only s'posed ta be for a hour or two. He's liable ta take dat all up hi'self."

"I—I—I was o-o-only trying to present a f-f-fair and co-co-complete argument," Nick said.

"Well, to be fair, perhaps it's time we let the table discuss it. I think you have made your pitch," Gada said.

"Incessantly," said Kane, leaning back in his chair and putting his feet up on the table.

For some reason he glared at Griffen. There was a certain insolence about Kane. As if he would push for no reason other than to see who would push back. Griffen saw no reason at this point to give him the satisfaction.

"Sure can't see it bein' a big deal. Never hurts to have too much info or too many contacts," Slim said, starting off the discussion proper.

Gada and Lowell both nodded, Jay and Estella seemed hesitant. Kane sat upright again and slapped his palm down on the table.

"You gonna put our lives up on da Internet? Der still people who hunt supernaturals. All supernaturals. Not just dragons," he said.

The blatant dig aside, he seemed to have a point.

"I agree," Tink said. "I've run into persecution before, and even hunters. This is not a safe world."

"It's exactly because it's not a safe world that we need a way to stay in touch," Lowell said.

"I'm not sure I like how you would touch us," Tink said with an easy smile.

There were chuckles from the audience, and a stirring among the vampires. One firm rule during these meetings: no powers. That was the only part of Griffen's job description he was sure on, and he kept a close eye, or whatever, on the vampires' auras of power.

"I am not sure I would trust even others on the list with the whole list," Jay said. "After all, the only people you can truly count on in a crisis are those you know, and know you can trust. There are many predators among us."

"And as a predator I say dis stinks. You are settin' yo'self up for some big troubles," Kane said.

Estella spoke up, and there was something about her voice that caught people's attention. It wasn't any power, other than that of her personality. She was used to speaking to, and commanding, a crowd. It was a preacher's voice.

"How many are lost, or never found? How many of us have lived alone, unprotected? My faith keeps me strong because I have others who can share it with me, but others aren't so lucky," she said.

Slim nodded.

"My folk are all loners," he said, "but even we gets together now and again. The three here, we know pretty damn near all the others in the country. But if somethin' happens to one of us, that goes right in the ol' crapper."

"And there are so many types of wicca and the pantheists and so many others. We are not as tight-knit a group as the vodoun. Such a list would help our sisters and brothers connect across the continent," Gada said.

Kane smiled, and Griffen noticed his teeth were far sharper than they should have been. His jaw seemed a bit too long, too. Not really a muzzle, but certainly big enough to hold all those pointy dentures.

"It figures de *humans* wan' keep tabs on their betters. So they 'ave someone to holler at when tings get tough."

"Excuse me, who are you calling human?" Lowell said.

"Oh, sorry. I no blame you. Vampire see chance at an easy meal, vampire gonna support it. Is your nature, no?" Kane suggested.

Griffen was still mulling over the use of the word "human," but from people's reactions, Kane had struck a nerve. He decided to step in.

"As I understand it, anyone's being on the list would be voluntary. This really is a nonissue. If you want the help of the list, sign up. If not, don't. Each to his own," Griffen said.

There was a long silence as people thought that over. Kane, eyes glinting, seemed unwilling to give up the fight so easily. Yet, he was the first to nod.

"Yo' right 'bout that. Dis is silly discussion. Let da humans 'ave their list."

"Actually, it's not that silly a discussion. I for one want to know what type of security would be installed. After all, it needs to be as safe as possible, without blocking out the people who need it. This is supposed to be a discussion on information technology. Even if you don't use the database, might as well make it as safe and good as possible," Griffen said.

"That I can agree on," Jay said. "I, for one, don't intend to give anyone my whereabouts, especially over the Internet. Yet I've a few ideas that might help make such a system work for others."

"Well, sho'," Kane said, "I reckon I gots some ideas my own self."

And with that the conversation was off on a much more productive route. Griffen leaned back in his chair, proud of himself and how he had handled it. But still there was that bit about the "humans" that he just couldn't quite let go.

They had been into it for about forty minutes when there was a knock at the door. Someone close by, after checking with the group, opened it to find one of the hotel bellmen holding a large package.

"Sorry to interrupt, but this delivery came in for your conference. Catering, I think. It was sent to this meeting room, and specifically to an . . ." He checked the label. "Al Shifters."

Griffen exchanged a look with Jay. He knew he hadn't ordered any catering, but a delivery for Al Shifters? All shifters?

"Does it say who it's from?" Griffen asked.

"No, sir, it came anonymously, which is why I thought I'd bring it in direct instead of phoning in. Just in case, you know?"

"Yeah, it's appreciated. Thanks," Griffen said. "Just leave it on the table."

The bellman put it down, and received a tip from Griffen before departing. As the doors closed, Griffen reached for the package. Only to find Jay way ahead of him.

"After all, for the meeting at least the shifters are my responsibility."

He opened the package.

Inside was a cake.

Specifically a cake from the Three Dogs Bakery. Specializing in gourmet treats for cats and dogs. It looked like chocolate, but Griffen suspected it was some substitute intended for dogs' stomachs. Carob probably.

Kane was growling, as were several other shifters. Though one leaned forward, and Griffen could see his nose twitching.

"Mmm, that smells good."

Lowell laughed, as did several others around the table. The vampires in particular all seemed to be smirking.

"Dis yo' idea of a joke!?" Kane snarled. "You send dis cake, yes or no?"

"No, no, of course not. Still it is rather funny," Lowell said.

"If no you, then who? I tink it one of yo' vamps."

"That's ridiculous! Why would we?"

" 'Cause you vamps always lookin' ta make trouble."

"By teasing a bunch of animals. Please, why would we bother?"

"Animals!"

Griffen stood up.

"Gentleman, please! Mr. Kane, there is nothing that says Lowell or anyone else sent this . . . cake. Besides, it was obviously just someone's idea of a joke, nothing to get this upset over."

"How would you feel if I sent you a set of gator-skin bags?"

Griffen stopped to think about that one.

"Would you include a nice card?" he said innocently.

Kane stared at him, then broke out laughing. He thumped the table hard enough the cake jumped.

"Oh, dragon boy has sense of humor, yes indeed. I may likes you after all."

"Well, I'm glad that's settled," Lowell said.

He reached for his water glass and took a sip, only to spray it over the table in an ugly spit take. Kane started laughing harder, only to be joined by the changelings. Nyx, who had messed with the contents of Griffen's drink when they first met, said through her laughter, "What's the matter? Can't handle your holy water?"

Most of the table was laughing now, and though it was at Lowell's expense, the tense mood had broken. Lowell even managed a weak smile as he grabbed up a napkin and wiped his mouth.

"Not an allegory this time?" Griffen said.

"Oh, it is. It is. But the minx changed my water to vinegar!" Lowell said.

That set off another round of laughter. All and all, Griffen figured the first meeting could have gone a lot worse.

Thankfully, everyone decided to tactfully ignore the few shape-shifters who did divvy up the cake.

Thirty-seven

Griffen found himself mildly amused that such a loose assemblage of people would adhere to an orderly schedule. He realized that it would be next to impossible to run a conclave such as this without one. A schedule was what seemed to separate the conclave from a drinking party and gripe fest. Griffen wasn't entirely sure he wouldn't have preferred the latter.

The meetings scheduled were more open-discussion forums. No decisions were made. Instead it was more on the order of agreements, treaties, and arrangements. All largely on a personal level. This was no governing body, there was no enforcement arm of the conclave keeping a check to make sure agreements were honored.

It was simply that anyone who broke their word would have a mass of witnesses against them, and their word would never be honored again. That and being denied entry to any future conclave kept people from violating their oaths, or more often than not kept them from giving oaths in the first place. Griffen was beginning to realize how important one's word and honor could be in supernatural circles.

Then there were the demos. A few of these would be away from the hotels. One in particular that had caught Griffen's eye was a voodoo demonstration by Estella at her home. That was a couple of days into the conclave, though. Today was something that also intrigued him but apparently didn't need any special location. The hotel would do just fine.

The room chosen for most of the demos was about half the size of the one in which the opening ceremonies had taken place. For the most part, this was Griffen's first look at the business of conventions, and he had to admit he was impressed. The room the hotel provided met all the requirements. A small elevated stage had been assembled in no time flat on one end. In front of it were rows of folding chairs, padded and more comfortable than Griffen would have expected. Next to the stage their was a door leading to a small adjoining room, which they were using as a combination green room and changing room.

Changing . . . that brought to mind another feature Griffen liked about the room. Locks on the inside, and no windows.

"I have to admit I am fascinated by this demo, but don't really understand why it's being put on," Griffen said.

He was sitting in the front row, though at the end of the row, not center stage. Jay, the spokesmen for the shifters sat next to him, and next to Jay were two of the other upper-level shape changers. They were half-turned to watch the door as people filed in. As usual, people tended to clump into groups, with at least a few seats left empty between each group. However, Griffen noted that each of the groups attending the conclave had at least some members at this demonstration.

"In this crowd, there are always many reasons for anything. As you may have noted," Jay said.

Griffen couldn't help but nod. It seemed to him that no one in the supernatural communities seemed to do anything for simple motivations.

"But really, a demonstration on shape-shifting?" Griffen said.

"On different types of shape-shifting. Thus we educate not only the non-shape-shifters present, but broaden the horizons of the more limited shifters. If it weren't for meetings such as these, some of those present would be lucky to meet even a handful of other shifters in their entire lifetimes. Despite the concentration here, we are not all that common," Jay said.

"Not the most important."

This was said by the gravelly-voiced shifter Griffen had noted that Jay and the others seemed to defer to. Griffen hadn't spoken much to him, just enough to catch that he was calling himself "Tail" despite the fact that he didn't seem to have a tail. Griffen checked.

In fact, he looked much like someone he would expect to find sleeping under a bench in Jackson Square. Yet Jay instantly lowered his eyes, and his tone went respectful.

"What is?" Jay asked.

"Competition."

Jay and the other shifter nodded and turned back to Griffen.

"I'm not sure I agree that the competition aspect is the most important, but it certainly is prevalent," he said.

"What do you mean?" Griffen inquired.

"Well, all those serving in this demonstration are volunteers. Which means at very least they have to be confident enough to show off in front of a crowd of strangers. Show off is what they do, and most of those expect to have the most impressive tricks. Truly remarkable demonstrations win the renown of the rest of the shifter communities."

Griffen couldn't help smiling.

"Are there prizes? Trophies? Best of show?"

"Sometimes." Jay smiled back.

The other shifter nodded, and through his matted beard Griffen saw his lips twist into what had to be a smile.

"Got me an apprentice years back from one of these. No

one knew where he came from, but, boy, could he work it," Tail said.

"All the participants are in the other room right now waiting for their big moments. You can bet the tension level is fierce. That's why I am allowing my colleague to take the honor of presenting. I've enough pressure with all the damnable meetings."

As if on cue, the door to the adjoining room opened and in walked the last of the shape-shifter leaders. He was a good head and a half shorter than Griffen, so that he looked small even on the elevated stage. His bald head glistened from perspiration, and he licked his lips nervously as he stepped up to a podium located in the corner of the stage.

"Right, I'm sure you are all anxious to get started, but we decided to wait fifteen minutes past the scheduled time to let stragglers trickle in before we lock the doors."

He paused while a few people waiting by the main doors closed and locked them. He pulled out a set of note cards and started to riffle through them.

"Right, before we get started. Please keep all questions to the end or, better yet, save them for conversation later. Just make sure to keep an eye on any norms about if you are talking in the bar. Along those lines, no photography, no video. Violators will, of course, be disemboweled."

A low ripple of laughter spread through the room. Griffen joined in, though a little bitterly. He tried not to dwell on how flat his jokes had fallen the other night.

"Okay, then, on with the show."

The presenter cleared his throat and glued his eyes on his cards as he began to recite in a slow monotone. Griffen could see why the shifters had chosen Jay to talk during the meetings.

"There are, of course, as many different ways of shifting as there are types of shifters. Some are born with their gifts, some cursed, some find means through spells and science. It all comes down to variety, which is of course what shape-shifting is all about."

The door to the adjoining room opened again and two people walked onto the stage. One, a young man in a bath-robe. The other, a tough-looking man dressed in black jeans and a leather vest whom Griffen had seen standing with the loup garou.

"Take, for example, the 'werewolf' of legend. Here we have two very different varieties of wolf-based shifter. Gustov here is of the more common variety: He finds changing his skin easier under the light of a full moon and nearly impossible when the moon is dark. The moon is nearly full this time of month, so even in day he can assume his other form."

Griffen watched frankly amazed as the young man some-what nervously removed his bathrobe, carefully draping it so that at no time were his privates exposed to the audience. There were a few catcalls, but not many, and those that came were friendly.

Then, with a sheepish smile, Gustov lifted the robe in front of him. He held it open, blocking off everything from the eyes down, then dropped it. By the time it hit the floor, a large gray wolf stood where he had been.

The presenter only briefly glanced up from his cards.

"Notice the seamlessness of the change. None of the pain and agony Hollywood has become prone to showing in their special-effects pictures. Gustov is lucky, as there are indeed those who cannot change without pain, just as there are those who experience transcendent ecstasy as their bodies reconfig-ure. Kevin here, being what is commonly dubbed the loup garou, can change forms just as quickly but, by slowing and controlling the change, can take more than wolf form."

Again, Griffen was astounded. His own encounters with such things had been brief and often so surprising that he didn't notice the change till after it happened. He watched Kevin grow his nails and teeth to claws and fangs, then back again, then shift to wolf in an eyeblink. Then, with a small quiver, his form surged and there on the podium was a six-foot monster that combined all the best, or worst, attributes of man and wolf.

Many in the audience gasped, though not any of the group leaders. Griffen, conscious of the fact that several eyes seemed to flick to him on occasion, had assumed a poker face. Difficult though it was to maintain.

"Startling, isn't it?" said the presenter. It was clear he had expected this reaction and put it on his note cards. "Not quite like anything Hollywood has come up with. Of course, part of that is because each garou tailors their form to what works best for them. This is Kevin's wolf, and there will be none other exactly like it."

Jay muttered next to Griffen.

"Unless it's a good doppelganger or mimic."

"What was that?" Griffen said.

"Oh, nothing. These are good basics, but it's such a broad topic. Putting together an hour demonstration cuts off a lot of possibilities, you know," Jay said.

Meanwhile, both of those onstage had become human-shaped again, Gustov hastily scooping up his bathrobe. Kevin was still fully dressed.

"How'd he do that without ripping his clothes?" someone called out. Griffen looked around and saw that it was one of the members of Estella's church.

"What did I say about questions?" the presenter said, irritated.

There was a bit of a murmur from the crowd. The presenter looked a bit desperately at Jay and his fellow shifters, and received nods from them. He shrugged.

"Right, just this once, but after this, no more interruption."

The crowd settled again.

"To keep it simple, clothes are a specialty skill. Some

actually change the clothes themselves, some . . . well, let's just say the clothes go somewhere else till they are needed again. Now, this is important: Most shifters who don't have to strip or rip through their clothes when they change don't know how they do it. They don't need to, they just do it, and since it is a rare thing, it isn't really studied or understood. No one else in today's demonstration can manage the trick, so if you have the plums, buy him a drink and ask. Just keep in mind the parable of the centipede that questioned its own feet, okay?"

The two headed off the stage, and another figure came out of the door. She was easily one of the most beautiful women Griffen had ever seen. Tall and thin, curved enough that the one-size-fits-all bathrobe seemed strained top and bottom. Her long black hair fell straight to the small of her back.

She paused at the edge of the stage, making sure she had the crowd's attention, and let the robe fall away. She strode nude onto the center of the stage.

The presenter stared openly for a few moments, till she caught his eye and quirked an eyebrow at him. He flushed and almost dropped his cards trying to find his place again.

"Uhhh, um . . . yes. Variety is important. Some of the most subtle tricks are also the hardest. For example, changing one's hair and skin color."

The woman closed her eyes and seemed to tense. At first it was gradual, her dark hair lightened, then reddened, then began to gleam. Her skin became tan, then brown, then black. Then she smiled and began to walk across the stage like a model walking a catwalk, and her skin began to swirl.

Multicolor whirls no natural skin tone could hold started to move across her skin. Blues and greens and purples blended and flowed and moved over her. Her hair was filled with metallic and jewel tones that seemed to flash into existence, then fade back.

Then the pigments of her skin become shapes. As if a film projector was using her as a screen, what started as unnatural colors became flapping songbirds in a rainbow of colors. All alive and realistic, like the world's greatest tattoo. An animated tattoo.

The audience burst into applause.

"Of course, some tricks aren't subtle at all," the presenter said.

The woman threw her head back and, in midstride, she burst apart. Griffen was half-out of his chair, thinking something had gone horribly wrong. His jaw dropped as he realized the woman had become the birds, a hundred of them flapping about. A cyclone of color that seemed to dip, as if bowing, then flew off the stage and back out the door.

The audience was stunned silent by the showmanship of it all.

The presenter shook his head, clearly having been overwhelmed, too. And he had been expecting it.

"Keep in mind," he said, "that even in the multiple forms her mass had not changed. This, among other things, keeps her from ranking among the highest shape-shifters."

Griffen eased back down in his chair but leaned over to whisper to Jay.

"That may be so, but I don't understand why someone with that kind of confidence hasn't pulled up a chair with you four."

"Maybe she wants to be invited," Jay said thoughtfully.

Tail, the wild-haired shifter next to him, laughed in his gravelly voice.

"Invite her to sit? Ha! I'm inviting her to dinner."

Apparently, despite the showstopping number, she was not the last on the docket for this demonstration. The presentation went on.

"Last but not least, one should keep in mind how broad the term 'shape-shifter' really is. There are many who are classified in other groups who have the means to change their form."

For a panicky moment Griffen thought he, as a dragon, was going to be called on to perform. Thankfully, the door opened one more time and out stepped the changeling girl Tammy. She cast a brief, but heated, glance over her shoulder. Griffen was good at reading faces, and knew jealousy when he saw it. Tammy was feeling like a follow-up act.

She seemed to have decided to forgo the bathrobe.

She stalked onto the stage, clearly trying for a model strut, but she didn't have the attitude. Her fey-enhanced youth made her look almost like a child, or at least girl barely out of puberty. Especially compared to the woman who had just vacated the stage. Still, she had a raw appeal that made Griffen feel a little guilty. Very much the gamine.

"Tammy here is one of our new changeling attendees. As this has been their first time attending, she has volunteered to show off some of her shifting abilities."

Tammy stood with her feet together and threw her arms up into the air, arching her back and throwing her head back. With an audible creak, she seemed slowly to lengthen, her limbs especially growing spindly and long. Her skin went a dark nutty brown, and began to roughen. Green shoots started to extend from her fingers.

Tammy stood as a small cherry tree, barely seven feet high. Her roots spread over the stage, a light smattering of soft petals drifting from her branches.

There was a brief bit of applause. This was not as startling as the demonstration before, but it was something different. The cherry blossoms reddened, as if she were blushing.

Griffen heard a low growling from Tail. He looked over curious, to see the man reach into one of his pockets and pull out a small stone. Before Griffen could react, the stone had been hurled toward the stage. Right at one of the leafy branches.

The stone passed through the branch and struck the wall behind.

What had been a tree before was instantly Tammy again.

Though her limbs were a little longer, her skin a little woody in color, she was still very much human shape. There was an angry burst of conversation from the other shape-shifters in the audience.

"Fifteen percent shifting, eighty-five percent fairy glamour. When the other participants agreed to only use shifting, even if they had other abilities," Tail said.

There was a hiss from one of the shifters, a boo from another. Tammy, now fully her old self and quite naked and exposed in front of the audience, burst into tears. She ran off the stage and out of the room as the presenter tried to calm everyone down.

Griffen couldn't help but feel sorry for her. He joined the presenter on stage, using his position as moderator to send everyone away. Competition aside, this was supposed to have been a friendly demonstration. And after the garou's specialty trick with his clothes, picking on the changeling for her glamour seemed . . . petty.

Thirty-eight

Taking advantage of an open period in his schedule, Griffen tried to hook up with Slim to double-check the arrangements for the next day's activities. Though the street entertainer had no official standing in the running of the conclave, he had proved to be a great help at seeing to the myriad of details that went into running an event, as well as serving as a liaison with the local groups.

The problem was, he wasn't always that easy to find.

He was one of those that tended to keep his cell phone turned off except when he was making a call, which made that avenue of communication iffy at best. What was worse, he didn't have any particular movement or behavior patterns, making his whereabouts unpredictable. While he would occasionally hang out with the other animal-control people at the conclave, for the most part he was a loner, seeming to prefer his own company.

One place there was always a chance of finding someone from the conclave was the hotel lobby bar. While the attendees were mostly into exploring the wilds of the Quarter and the locals tended to duck out to drink at their habitual watering holes, the lobby bar was convenient for a quick drink or conversation.

Poking his head in, Griffen did a quick scan of who all were there. Not seeing Slim, he started to leave, then took another look.

Sitting alone at a corner table was Tammy. The change-ling was hunched over her drink, staring down into it while she idly played with the swizzle stick. While, like the other fey kids, she was normally high-energy and exuberant, just then she wasn't looking happy at all.

Looking at her, Griffen wavered for a moment, then heaved a sigh. Pausing at the bar to gather up a drink of his own, he approached her table.

"Mind if I join you?" he said.

The changeling looked at him blankly, then gave a little shrug.

"I don't know why you'd want to talk to me, but sure. Pull up a chair."

Griffen studied her covertly as he sank into the indicated seat. He always thought of her as "the coltish one," and the image still held. While she wasn't all that tall, there was a lean, all-legs look about her that made one wonder what she would be like when she grew up, yet also left one feeling they were glad to have met her at this stage in her development. The look was accented by her outfit. She was wearing short shorts, which made her legs seem even longer, and a bare-midriff T-shirt that accented the soft flatness of her stomach. Topped by a long, slender neck and a pixie mop of blond hair, she was not unattractive at all.

He caught himself and forced his mind back to the issue at hand.

"Are you okay, Tammy?" he said. "It's not really any of my business, but you seem a little down."

The changeling gave a sigh.

"I really screwed things up with that demo," she said, not meeting his eyes. "All the others are really pissed at me. They say I've made our whole group look bad at our first conclave. I don't know. Maybe they're right."

She took a long pull on her drink, giving Griffen a chance to grope for something to say.

"I don't think anyone has come off as well as they would like to, including me," he said. "Except, maybe watzername, the tattoo and bird lady. She would be a tough act to follow for anyone."

"Tell me about it," Tammy said with a bitter laugh. "I was only going to do my partial tree change, but it would have looked so lame after her showstopper I tried to juice it a little with glamour."

"That's understandable," Griffen said, soothingly. "It's only natural to try to make a good impression. I really don't think it's such a big thing. To tell the truth, I didn't even know that shape-shifting was one of the abilities you change-lings have."

"It isn't, really." Tammy grimaced. "A few of us can, but it's not part of the standard package. That was part of the game plan. You aren't alone in not knowing what we can or can't do, even though for most of them it's because they really don't care. We're supposed to be secretive and evasive about our powers, then show off some that people don't expect . . . like the shape-shifting. It's supposed to make people take us more seriously, or at least pique their curiosity."

"Well, it worked for me," Griffen said, putting a reassuring hand on her shoulder. "I, for one, am extremely curious about you."

The changeling suddenly brightened as if someone had turned on a lightbulb inside her.

"Really?" she said. "You don't know how much that means to me, Mr. . . . I mean, Griffen."

She put a hand over his and pressed down hard, effectively pinning his hand in place.

"I mean, I've always wanted to meet a dragon, but since that first day . . . you're nothing like what I expected."

Every alarm in Griffen's head was going off.

He had meant that he was curious about the changelings, but Tammy was obviously taking it personally. Moreover, her response was so enthusiastic there was no way he could see of correcting the impression without it sounding like a blunt rejection of her. Of course, he wasn't all that disinterested in her.

"Um . . . Tammy . . ." he said.

"Oh, I know," she interrupted. "I don't expect you to feel the same way. Still, curiosity's not a bad place to start."

Still holding his hand, she shifted it from her shoulder to the middle of her chest.

Griffen was suddenly aware that there wasn't a damn thing under that T-shirt except Tammy.

At that pivotal moment, Tail came into the bar with two of the other shape-shifters. Tammy saw him and let go of Griffen's hand, recoiling as if she had been struck.

Too late.

Tail spotted them and approached their table with a huge smirk on his face.

"Well, now we know what it takes to get our moderator to spend time with you," he declared in his gravelly voice. "Just phony up a demonstration, and you get his undivided attention."

Griffen leaned back in his chair and stared levelly at the intruder.

"You know, Tail," he said, "as moderator, I try real hard not to let my personal likes and dislikes show or affect how I conduct the conclave. Some people make it harder than others. For example, I was just telling Tammy here that I thought that your interrupting and embarrassing her during her demonstration was totally uncalled for and made you look worse than it did her."

"Really?" Tail said, crossing his arms. "Well, I suppose it's as good a line as any to try to get into someone's pants. Is she gullible enough to believe you?"

Griffen waited several moments before answering.

"Tail," he said finally, "is there any particular reason you're trying to be offensive and pick a fight? I find it hard to believe this is your normal way of dealing with people."

"This is pretty much it," Tail said with a grin. "Of course, I get particularly ornery around phonies. Take you, for example. Everyone's walking soft round you because you're supposed to be a hot-shit dragon, but so far you haven't shown me much. I notice you didn't favor us with a shape-shifting demonstration."

"Like I said at the opening ceremonies, I was invited here as a moderator, not a participant or demonstrator," Griffen said, trying to keep a grip on his temper. "This whole conclave is supposed to be about the various groups that were invited in. Not an excuse to show off dragon powers."

"Isn't that convenient." The shape-shifter sneered. "Well, this isn't an official conclave gathering. Any reason why you can't give us a little private demo of what you can do?"

Griffen glanced pointedly around the bar.

"Several reasons," he said. "The first is there's a conclave rule against showing our powers in public, which I figure I'm bound to follow. This also happens to be the town I live in, which gives me an extra reason to keep a low profile. And finally, I don't use my powers unless it's necessary, and I don't do sideshows."

"You know, McCandles, you remind me of a good old boy back home," Tail said. "He keeps sayin' he doesn't want to fight 'cause he's afraid of hurtin' someone. The fact that he doesn't really know how to fight and is really afraid of gettin' hurt himself doesn't have anything to do with it."

Griffen pursed his lips, then leaned forward, putting both his hands on the table.

"Tell me something, Tail," he said. "When one of the loup garou changes, exactly how hard are those claws he grows?"

"Hard enough to rip up most any critter you know of." Tail smiled. "Why do you ask?"

"Just wondered," Griffen said, smiling back as he leaned back in his chair.

Tail looked at him for a minute.

"I don't get it," he said, finally. "What was that supposed to do?"

"Take a close look at the table," Griffen said, giving a slight nod with his head.

Tail bent over and examined the cocktail table, his companions peering over his shoulder and Tammy craning her neck to see.

There were now ten holes in the Formica surface of the table, placed in two half circles where Griffen had rested his hands. The holes went all the way though the table and were wide enough they could see the floor through them.

"A word to the wise, Tail," Griffen said softly. "Don't fuck with me or any other dragon. When we get mad . . . even if we just get annoyed . . . we play for keeps. Now, I believe the door is that way."

He turned his head and blew a smoke ring in the direction of the door.

The shape-shifters left without saying anything else.

Thirty-nine

Griffen was irritated. It took him some time to realize just why, but as the conclave wore on, he found his mood steadily declining. Not so much during the meetings and demonstrations, but after. During times and periods that should have been social.

He realized that the clique mentality of it all was what was getting to him. With little exception, like stayed with like. Each of the groups fractured into smaller groups, and little clusters wandered around the French Quarter, never mingling. Even if two different groups found the same bar, they would sit at opposite sides.

Only at conclave-sponsored events did any serious degree of mingling take place. The first that Griffen attended was a sponsored breakfast at Café Du Monde. He suspected that even then, most just showed up because someone else was picking up the bill. He had only shown up to make sure it wasn't him.

Even then, it tended to be the lesser members of the various groups who showed up. The speakers and leaders seemed to avoid each other at all times. This was what was getting on Griffen's nerves, considering that the whole function of this mess was, supposedly, to create understanding between groups. The hypocrisy was driving him crazy.

So he was pleasantly surprised to stumble upon a few of the major players sitting around a low table in the hotel lobby.

He was further surprised by the cards in their hands and the piles of chips on the table.

A bit nervously he eyed the drinks as well, knowing that most bars clamped down on any gambling, but technically they were in the lobby. Someone must have been running drink orders to the bar. Either no one cared that they were playing cards, or someone had used their powers to keep the game from being bothered. Griffen knew he was simply happier not asking which was true.

Besides, he would never miss out on an opportunity to watch the group interact. Kane, Tink, and Tail he had some experience with, not all of it pleasant. The animal-control woman from Wyoming, Margie, was also playing. Next to her was Lowell. Two shifters, a fairy, a vampire, and a shaman. Playing poker. Oh yeah, no way Griffen was going to miss this.

He leaned against the nearest wall watching the hand. There was a certain amount of the cutthroat camaraderie that went on around most informal games. A bit of banter and conversation, most of it attempts to distract or gauge the other players. Griffen realized he played less now, despite running a gambling ring, than he had in college. Which was too bad, since he loved to play. Just watching one hand, he felt he knew more about these people than he had picked up in a half dozen encounters.

He was seriously considering stepping up to the game when Tail looked up and caught his eye.

"Do somethin' for you, McCandles?" Tail asked.

"Just watching the game," Griffen said.

Tail snorted, a disgusted sound that matched his souring expression. The others at the table watched the two closely. By now, everyone had heard about the incident between them.

"Just watching, not playing?"

It didn't take a dragon, or a card shark, to figure out Tail's motivations. He had backed down from Griffen, or at least that was what the rumor mill had turned the bar incident into. This was a chance to try to gain some face or make Griffen lose some.

If it had just been Tail, it wouldn't have been a problem. Unfortunately, the loup garou Kane piped up in his mixed accent.

"'Eard me dis dragon he one serious cardplayer. Don' know I wan' him in dis here game."

Tail turned his attention to the garou. If anything, his expression grew worse, almost a sneer.

"Wouldn't worry about that. I don't think 'dis' dragon is about to lower himself and play with our sort."

The garou blinked as he considered that. His eyes narrowed a bit as he looked at Griffen.

"Dat changes tings some. You no play 'cause you too good for de game? Or de company?" Kane challenged.

For a moment, Griffen considered how to respond, knowing that a moment might be too long. Like at the poker table, any hesitation was a tell. Of weakness, of deceit, of anything. As fast on his feet as he was, he wasn't sure he had an answer that would satisfy both of the shifters.

Then again, there were more players in this game than three.

"Now, isn't that fascinating," Lowell said. " A garou agreeing with another type of shifter. I'm amazed one of you isn't trying to mark territory on the other's leg."

Tail glared, but Kane threw out a bark of laughter. Short, sharp, loud. "Bark" was definitely the word.

"Good point dere, vampy. Still, what is said can no be took back. You tink you betta den us or no, dragon?" Kane said.

"Honestly, how could I know? I haven't really gotten a chance to know any of you," Griffen said.

"Den sit down and play dem cards, boy! Dat de best way to know people."

"Yes, Mr. McCandles," Margie said, "Solve it all neatly

and sit. I for one would like some new blood at the table. These four have grown far too predictable."

Griffen surrendered to the inevitable and sat. Once already a comment had been made, offhandedly, about the animal-control specialist having excellent judgment. It did seem the best way to settle things. He also noticed that her stack of chips was higher than the others'.

Griffen acquired some chips, and the next hand was dealt. He kept one eye on the table, and one firmly on Tail. Griffen didn't know what Tail had expected from this conversation, but it was clear he wasn't happy. He glared at his cards and muttered in a voice just loud enough for the others to hear.

"Figures he would be coddled up to by the *human*."

Margie stiffened, and the rest of the players went still. Even Tink, whom Griffen thought of as fairly laid-back, had gone rigid. His eyes were wide, shocked. Kane was growling low in the back of his throat.

"That was uncalled for," Lowell said.

"Low. Real low," Kane said.

"It's not my fault if she wants to suck up to the dragon," Tail said.

Several of the others spoke at once, all angry.

"What business is it of yours?" from Kane.

"She wasn't sucking up to anyone," said Tink.

"How dare you imply—" started Margie.

"HOLD IT!"

Griffen hadn't moved a muscle, but his voice was hard and loud enough to cut through the rest. Everyone looked at him, and he slowly, carefully considered Tail.

"What do you mean 'human'?" Griffen asked.

The others looked about uncomfortably; it was Margie who answered.

"Those who are magic see those who simply do magic as less. Humans playing with things they don't understand," she said.

"But what you do, call it magic or not, it is natural to you, isn't it?" Griffen said.

"De hoodoos, animal control, dey borderline. You notice we don' got no vodoun or wicca at the table," Kane said.

"Spell slingers are seen as lesser. Only the truly powerful ones are respected enough to even be invited to a conclave such as this," Lowell said.

"So when Tail called her human, he was calling her second-class. One who didn't belong?" Griffen asked.

The others nodded. Griffen ran that over in his head several times, but it was a slippery concept. To give himself a bit more thinking room, he asked the obvious follow-up question.

"Then how do you all feel about normal, mundane humans?"

If anything, everyone seemed even more uncomfortable. Tail had lost most of his angry look and now seemed merely embarrassed. Griffen hoped he regretted his comments. Margie spoke first again, perhaps because of the accusation.

"Feelings are mixed of course. But definitely less. They are so limited, and so arrogant with it. Thinking they are so much, when they do so little. And so much of what they do is harmful to themselves and everyone else," she said.

"Ignorant and proud of it," Kane said.

"Blind," Tink said, his voice so sad that Griffen was sure he was dwelling on some specific memory.

"Individuals can be respected. Individuals are capable of great glory, love, miracles. But as a whole . . . sometimes . . ." Margie said.

"What?" asked Griffen.

"I hate them," she finished, and hung her head slightly.

Griffen cranked the turrets around and focused again on Tail. Griffen would have to consider what they had all said, but later. These were heavy concepts, but it was obvious that Tail had meant harm with his words. That had to be addressed now and not allowed to pass.

Besides, he had finally figured out what to say.

"You seem to have a bad habit of insulting women when I'm around. So are you jealous of me . . . or of them?"

"What are you implyin'?" Tail said, angry again.

"Nothing, nothing at all," Griffen said.

His tone was full of false innocence, and no one at the table missed it. Margie looked up again, and Kane sniggered. Before Tail could respond, Griffen continued.

"But you should know that it takes more than this to get under my skin. You are just making an ass of yourself in front of everyone. Good thing Jay is your speaker, or you might be reflecting on all the other shifters."

" 'Cept us," Kane said smugly.

"I—" Tail started.

"You are being an ass," Lowell said, though surprisingly gently.

Tail stopped and looked around the table. He looked at Margie. For the most part she had remained calm, stiff but collected. He took in a long, slow breath.

"I apologize," he said.

She nodded and looked back at her cards. Tail turned his attention back to Griffen.

"I'm used to being the biggest fish in the pond. Ain't no shifter never who outdid me. Then you come and do nothing and get fawned over. So in that way, maybe I was jealous. I guess a part of me was hopin' to draw you into a fight."

Griffen was surprised once again. Tail was being honest, open, and—for him—eloquent. If this kept up, Griffen might have to reevaluate his whole situation. On the basis of a card game.

"I can understand that. But, Tail, I haven't seen you do anything either, and I never challenged the respect you were shown."

"Well, damn. You're right. Guess you are better then me, without doin' a damn thing."

This time Griffen didn't need a moment's hesitation.

"Not better," Griffen said. "Just different."

The delayed hand was finally played. Then another. It would have become nothing more than another card game. Though one where some peace was made. Would have been.

If Tammy hadn't walked into the lobby.

She flounced in, scanning the room, about an hour after Griffen had sat down. He actually heard her before he saw her. She let out a tiny, girlish squeal when she saw him, and when he turned to look, she was already rushing his way.

"I've been looking everywhere for you, Grif—"

She stopped a few feet from the table, eyes fixing on Tail. He and the rest were watching her. Hard not to considering her enthusiastic entrance. Griffen caught a bit of tightness around Tail's eyes, a bit of anger that was being suppressed. But suppressed well.

"Don't worry, girl," Tail said gruffly. "Still don't like that you cheated, but it's been pointed out to me that I've been being an ass. So let's forget the whole thing and start over?"

"Come join the game, Tammy," Griffen offered, nodding to a chair that could be pulled over.

The others exchanged glances. Griffen realized the hesitation. They were still major players, and Tammy a follower. Still, a truce of sorts had been made, and no one seemed willing to break it by excluding her.

She made it unnecessary.

"Oh . . . poker. No, thanks, but would it be all right to watch?"

This time Griffen glanced about, checking reactions. He didn't want to upset things either, now that they were settling down. Everyone seemed to have no problem with that, having relaxed and refocused on their cards.

"Sure thing, Tammy. Glad to have you," he said.

And turned to her to smile.

Which, from the sudden light in her eyes, was a mistake.

She gave off another half squeal, and as Griffen turned back to the table, he felt her stand directly behind him. At first it wasn't distracting. Till she leaned over to look at his cards closer. Brushing his shoulder with her breast might have been an accident. Whispering into his ear was not.

"Wow, you are really . . . good," she said, in a tone that despite his best intentions made his temperature spike a bit.

"Thanks."

Griffen was an experienced player, thought of himself as very good. He wasn't one to let distractions change his expression, or mess up his game. He had played in harder, and hotter, situations before.

She bit his earlobe, and he almost dropped his cards.

"Uh, Tammy, a little space please?"

"Sure thing."

She leaned back, and laid her hands on his shoulders. He was too polite to suggest she move farther. Or perhaps take a chair.

Griffen watched his other players, and they watched him. For the most part they seemed . . . amused. Kane was practically leering. Margie had a smirk on her face. Lowell was looking a little too closely at his cards, in that way one did when he wanted to be obvious about *not* looking somewhere else. Even Tail had a glint in his eye that meant he was either enjoying Tammy's show or Griffen's discomfort.

Tink looked nervous. As if he would get blamed for the other changeling's behavior. Tammy started to idly run a finger through Griffen's hair.

So, Griffen thought to himself, *this is what a gangster with a moll on his arm must feel like.*

"So, Griffen," Tammy said as the game went on, "I really

like New Orleans. I was even thinking about moving here. Say . . . do you know where I might find a place to stay? Or, maybe have some place I could . . . sleep. For a while."

No, if gangsters felt like this, they would shoot all the molls. Tammy was as subtle as a brick.

"I'm not sure that would be such a good idea, Tammy," Griffen said.

Her hands tightened against him.

"What isn't a good idea?" she said.

The card game had all but stopped. This was far better entertainment.

"Uh . . . would you excuse us? Tammy, can I talk to you, privately?"

"You can talk to me now! What isn't a good idea? Moving, or being close to you? Don't you like me?!"

He wished he had moved her away from the table earlier, but it was such a sudden shift that it caught Griffen flat-footed. He had forgotten how damn mercurial the changelings could be. And that last question was almost shrieked, and there just wasn't any good answer to it.

Griffen, in the tradition of brave, i.e. stupid, men throughout history, tried to answer anyway.

"It's not that, Tammy, but I already basically have two girlfriends as it is, and—"

It was not the time to think on whether or not Fox Lisa or Mai would mind the changeling girl for a night. Besides, with Tammy, he doubted it would ever be just "one night."

"Two! Two?! Well, then what's one more?"

"Tammy, relax, let me explain."

"Explain . . . I thought you wanted . . . I thought we had . . . YOU BASTARD!"

Tammy slapped him, and it hurt. It actually hurt as if he had been hit with a baseball bat. He looked down and saw that her hand was the color of wood. Though there was a slight crack in it, and tears streaming down her face.

"Ow!" she said, whirled, and ran away.

Griffen instinctively started to rise and follow.

"Stop."

Griffen looked over at Tink, who was shaking his head.

"I've seen her like this before. If you follow her, it will mean you love her, and you will never be rid of her."

"I didn't mean to . . ." Griffen said.

"I know. Nothing you did, or said, would have happened with a sane, normal girl. But our Tammy—she's something special, even for a changeling," Tink said.

He shook his head and stood.

"Cash me out, will you? I can follow her at a distance, and if she catches me . . . Well, it wouldn't be the first time. Trust me, Griffen, you don't want to follow, I learned that one the hard way," Tink said.

Tink collected what was left of his stake and strolled out into the night. Griffen watched him go, knowing Tink was right but his instincts telling him what a brute and fool he had been.

"Relax, McCandles. That truly was not your fault. That one is unbalanced," Lowell said.

"No one could have done better at that point. You made the right choices," Margie said.

"Yeah, we spread it round. You in da clear. She just crazy." Kane nodded vigorously.

Somehow that didn't comfort Griffen. He could only imagine what the rumor mill would make of this one.

And he certainly wasn't in the mood to play cards anymore.

Forty

Flynn knew there was someone in his room.

He had been out for an evening stroll, reviewing in his own head where things stood. Griffen seemed sufficiently distraught, the pressure of the conclave blending nicely with the pressures he had been heaping on. All that was needed was one last plan, one last push. Something from within the conclave itself perhaps. Flynn already had a seed of an idea, and the walk had been just the thing he needed for it to blossom.

Then, a few feet from his door, he knew someone was inside, waiting for him. Flynn wasn't sure which of his senses had provided the information, nor did he care. The first thing a dragon learned, a proper dragon, was to trust the gestalt of data that showed more of the world than any single sense. It was a trick that the young McCandles seemed to have grasped only barely, but then Flynn knew he wasn't a proper dragon. Not yet.

Flynn paused for only a moment before opening the door. The matter was rather straightforward. If whoever lay in wait was in his class, they already knew he was in the hall. If they weren't, there was no threat, and he might as well find out who'd had the stupidity to break into his room.

Of course, he hadn't considered the possibility of someone in a class all their own. He regretted opening the door as soon as he saw Lizzy, sprawled on her stomach on his bed, flipping channels on his TV.

"A hundred channels, and the funniest thing on is the news," Lizzy said, not bothering to look up at him.

"Perhaps you should go to a movie?" Flynn suggested.

"Hey, that's a great idea!"

Lizzy bounced off the bed and was reaching for a tattered leather coat that had been draped on a nearby chair. Her hand stopped a few inches from it, and she turned back to Flynn.

"Say, that was almost clever. You are almost as good at glamour as little Nathaniel."

Well, it had been worth a try, Flynn thought. Out loud he simply said, "Better, more subtle. But you are . . . difficult."

"You'd be amazed how often I am told so. Hey, do you get pay-per-view in this joint?"

With that she was back on the bed, remote in hand. Flynn sighed inwardly and pulled out another chair, sitting with his back to one corner of the room. He watched her aimlessly flip through movie listings, feet kicking in the air like a child. The problem with dealing with Lizzy was he was never sure how much was insanity and how much an act. Mostly the first as far as he could tell. He had a much better time sparring with a professional like Mai.

With his expressions carefully schooled, he bided his time, trying to figure out what Lizzy wanted. He was still getting over the shock of finding her here of all places. Had his attention really been so focused on McCandles that a powder keg like her could go unnoticed? Or had she just arrived?

"Long see no time, or is it the other way around?" Lizzy said.

"Look, Lizzy, I told you before. I won't help you start an 'acting' career without permission from your mother. I am not stepping sideways on her for you."

"And anyone else who told me no like that would be dead before they finished."

"Which you tried last time, so skip it," Flynn said.

Flynn didn't mention that they had both been lucky to walk away from that. He wasn't used to such a . . . physical confrontation. Most dragons considered themselves more elegant than that.

"Mumsy still thinks that the limelight would be too much for her delicate daughter. She says it's just better all around if Lizzy stays home," Lizzy said.

"Safer anyway," said Flynn.

"Exactly. Besides she wants to get her hooks in you herself. She says you go to all the best parties."

"Ahem . . . so then what can I help you with?"

Lizzy sat on the edge of the bed and looked at him for the first time. Flynn found himself fascinated by the broken eyes and the confusing mix of emotions that played across her face. Anger, fear, doubt. And random sparks of happiness that gave her a smile so cold Flynn found his heartbeat increasing slightly.

"I came to kill Valerie McCandles."

"I won't even help you get out of your mother's house. You think I'd help you kill someone?"

"Who says I need your help to kill anyone? Lizzy could kill the pope if she wanted to. Not a bad idea that, not bad, but I certainly don't need some pampered *agent* to help me with a kill! Not me, not Lizzy."

"Then what . . ."

"Because it's all gone *wrong*!" Lizzy screamed.

Flynn was on his feet a second after Lizzy, but she already had him by the shoulders. Her fingers were hard and sharp, as if the bones themselves were hidden blades. Shorter than him by a good head and a half, she still lifted him a foot off the ground.

"Don't you see? I took the shot, and now I don't know if I

can take another! I never expected this, not this. I just wanted her out of the family, didn't want Nathaniel happy. Not *him*. And now if Mother finds out about her and me and it and I just don't know what she'll do."

Flynn reached out, touch gentle but firm, and put his fingertips on the pulse of Lizzy's neck and against one wrist. For a moment Lizzy rubbed her head down against his hand like a cat, shattered eyes fading to softer, gentler colors.

With the connection made, Flynn flooded her with glamour.

"Put. Me. Down."

Lizzy screamed, and it couldn't have been as loud as it seemed in that moment. No one came beating down the door. No one came to rescue her.

Flynn caught a brief glimpse of himself through her eyes, glamour wrapped around him and making him seem glorious and terrible. A pillar of shining light, of burning fire, perfect pristine water. Images mixed and cascading, and each beating down on her senses, coupled with merciless reflections of her pitiful, mad little self. His self-image and her worst fears, all feeding off each other and building.

Flynn smiled cruelly; it had been years since he'd had an opportunity to be so blunt. To really cut loose. As much as he prided himself on his smooth touch, it was occasionally satisfying to smash down like a sledgehammer. It was as if he were showing her a glimpse into the Devil's own mirror, with him playing the part of both mirror and monster.

Lizzy fell to her knees, and the connection broke. Flynn needed almost intimate contact to maintain that level of power, and it always seemed to have a price. He purposefully didn't look down at Lizzy as she trembled and sobbed on the hotel carpet. A dragon's glamour was often a two-way street, and he didn't want to know what would be reflected back at him.

"Now try again," Flynn said. "You attacked Valerie Mc-Candles, and she is still alive. Is the sister really that tough?"

Lizzy shook her head, but didn't look up at Flynn again. Tears stained the carpet.

"Yes . . . no . . . she's tough, but stupid. I could have taken her."

"Then why didn't you?"

"I . . . I don't know if I should. Don't know if I want to. It all changed, in an eyeblink it changed."

"How did it change, Lizzy?"

Now Lizzy looked up, and from her cold glare Flynn knew the last traces of his glamour on her had faded. Pity, too, it was the kind of trick that was only easy once, before the mind had built up defenses for it. Still . . . this was only Lizzy.

"Wouldn't you like to know," she spat.

Flynn shrugged.

"Yes, I would. I am honestly curious. But at least tell me why you came to me."

"Not sure I know anymore, after that. Ah, yes, wanted advice I did. Can't go to family, family mustn't know, not till I'm done here and back home. Can't go to locals, locals are the McCandleses, and their pets. But knew you were in town. Saw you, tracked you."

Lizzy threw back her head and laughed, and Flynn felt mixed irritation and admiration. Irritation that she had known his whereabouts, and he hadn't even gotten a call from his network of contacts about hers. Admiration that, well, he had never seen someone pick themselves up so fast after a blow like that. That laugh, as it flitted through the scales like an insane hummingbird, was also filled with her strength coming back to her.

Sure enough, she got to her feet and planted her hands on her hips, glaring at him and showing no sign that anything had just occurred. Idly, he wondered if she remembered.

"And what are you doing here? I ask to me. Want the Mc-Candles boy, and completely ignored the sister. Misogynistic bastard. No wonder Mummy dearest runs circles around you old-school male dragons.

"Pot, kettle, black, my dear. You don't want to kill Valerie anymore; that is fine. But you can still make her suffer. Turn your attentions to her brother."

"Pot, kettle, polka dot!" Lizzy said triumphantly.

"I have no idea how to reply to that," Flynn said.

"Good. I have no interest in the boy-child, or your prophecy, and don't think I don't know about that. Lizzy will do what Lizzy wants to do."

"But you don't know what you want to do."

"I'll figure it out and hang about a bit in the meantime. Maybe I'll find a use for you after all."

Lizzy stepped to him, reaching a hand out, and even though he saw the claws, he didn't allow himself to react. Any reaction would just provoke her. She drew her hand across his cheek, down his neck, fingers sliding past the collar of his shirt to his chest.

Claws leaving a set of deep lines over his heart.

"Don't think for a second I don't owe you for that glamour, Earl," Lizzy purred and tightened her grip.

Flynn felt the scrape of claw on bone, and still he didn't move. She pouted some and stepped back, and the wound closed nearly instantly under Flynn's concentration. He had always been better at healing than at glamour, but damn did that girl have some wicked claws.

She wiped her fingers delicately on his bedspread and stalked out the door.

Flynn let his guard down, slumping into a chair as adrenaline he didn't know he had been pumping left his system. Unsteadily, he poured himself a tumbler of bourbon and sipped at it gently.

Despite the danger, and irritation, Lizzy had actually been right. Up till now, he had been a fool to focus solely on Griffen. Griffen's strength seemed to be largely those around him, and Flynn had thought that he could strip that best by influencing the boy directly. When it would be so much easier to target one of them.

But not his sister. She was not an easy target, not if she sent Lizzy running. That was something he would have to look into. Someone at the conclave perhaps?

Pieces were starting to fall together, but his train of thought wasn't quite as true as usual. He kept getting distracted by details.

And Lizzy was hanging around, and George, and there was Mai. This was getting far too complicated. Griffen was already on a collision course. Flynn had given him enough pushes, enough pressure, enough distractions, that it wouldn't take much more.

In fact, Flynn didn't really need to be here anymore at all.

Flynn pulled out his matched suitcases and began carefully packing, hands still just a bit shaky from alcohol and fear. It was time he got back into his own environment. This conclave was nearly done. Griffen would either falter completely or hang on by his fingernails. Either way, he would be ready when Flynn decided just what he wanted with him. The next step, if he bothered with one, would be the last, and it could be handled by proxy.

After all, what else are lackeys for?

Forty-one

All in all, the conclave progressed quite well. To be sure, there were some raised voices and occasional ruffled feathers, but nothing out of the ordinary when people of differing opinions gathered for discussion. If anything, it was tamer than most bar gatherings to watch an NFL game.

It came as no surprise, then, when things went bad. It was a surprise to Griffen, but not to any of the attendees. To them, it was only a matter of time before something blew up. The only question was when and over what.

What was noteworthy, and therefore discussed long after the conclave disbanded, was the aftermath.

It all started innocently enough. Someone suggested a scavenger hunt, and the bulk of the attendees thought it was a fun idea. Griffen was hesitant, but finally agreed with the consensus, only on the condition that no laws would be broken by any of the teams taking part. He had taken part in some scavenger hunts back in college, and knew firsthand how raucous they could become if hard-and-fast rules were not established from the outset.

That evening, players were divided into two-person teams, and, following yet another suggestion, each team was made up of individuals from different groups. This was both to promote conversation between the attendees and to ensure that the use of their various powers would be kept to a minimum.

One such team was composed of Lowell, the main spokesman for the vampires, and a young shape-shifter named Gustov. Early on, they agreed that they were severely handicapped in the competition as neither of them was local, nor had either of them been to New Orleans before. Even though the list of items to be sought was not particularly difficult, without much knowledge of the French Quarter they didn't even know where to start looking for half the items they were supposed to be seeking. As such, they decided they would not seriously pursue the quest but rather use it as an excuse to explore the Quarter a bit in the allotted time.

One item they chose to look for was an old LP record. For that, they wandered down Decatur Street toward the French Market in hopes of finding something in one of the small "retro" shops in that area. Unfortunately, they discovered that most of those shops had closed early, so they made their way leisurely back toward Jackson Square.

There were many interesting shops to catch their attention as they window-shopped their way along, and were both pleasantly surprised to find each other's company both relaxing and pleasant.

As they approached the Square, however, Lowell noticed that Gustov seemed increasingly uncomfortable, constantly glancing ahead and obviously distracted in his conversation.

The reason for this soon became clear.

As they drew abreast of the line of mule-drawn carriages waiting for fares in front of the cathedral, the animals became noticeably restless, shifting their feet and tossing their heads. Their drivers, chatting in the shade, broke off their conversations to attend to the mules, glancing around to try to figure out what was upsetting them.

Realizing what was happening, Lowell gazed at the animals, then made a small, barely noticeable gesture with his right hand.

The mules immediately calmed down, their ears coming forward and their fidgeting ceasing.

Gustov gave his teammate a small, embarrassed smile.

"Thanks," he said.

"Think nothing of it," Lowell said with a shrug. "Is that sort of thing much of a problem for you?"

"Not usually," Gustov said. "I live in a city, and there aren't many domestic animals around. I don't go to the zoo very often, though."

They walked a few more steps in silence.

"Do you think you could teach me how to do that?" the shape-shifter said at last. "Calm animals down, I mean. I can think of times when it could come in real handy."

"I really don't know," Lowell said. "I'm not sure how much of it is a learned skill and how much is an inherited ability."

He glanced around.

"Tell you what," he said. "Let's give it a try and see what happens."

With that, he led the way across the street and up the ramp beside the Jackson Brewery to the Moonwalk. Pausing, he peered up and down the sidewalk that ran along the Mississippi River to the Aquarium of the Americas and the River-walk shopping center. The walk was well lit by mock gaslight streetlamps, but there were still patches and stretches of near dark.

"There should be . . . Ah! There."

The vampire pointed at a rat that was snuffling around the litter at the base of a trash can.

"Now what you do is stare at it for a few moments to fix the image in your mind, then envision what you want it to do . . . like this."

He stared at the rat, then made a gesture. The rat left off its foraging, advanced several feet toward them, then stopped, sitting up on its haunches.

"That's neat," Gustov said.

"Now you try it." Lowell nodded, stepping back a pace.

The shape-shifter took a deep breath and stared at the rat. Several moments went past. The beast seemed to lose interest in them, sniffing the night air as if trying to locate a new food source.

"It doesn't seem to be working," Gustov admitted at last.

"Oh well," Lowell said. "Maybe it is hereditary. Then again, maybe you just need to practice a bit."

"What was that gesture you made?" the shape-shifter said.

"Gesture?"

"Yes. A little wave with your hand," Gustov said. "You did it just now, and before when you were calming the mules."

"Oh, that." The vampire shrugged. "It's just a way to focus your energies. You let the suggestion build, then release the instruction with a gesture. Watch."

He stared at the rat again, then gestured.

The rat stood up on its hind legs and waved its forelegs as if it were dancing.

Gustov threw back his head and laughed out loud.

"What are you doin'?"

The two men looked around.

A couple was approaching them. Apparently one of the scavenger-hunt teams from the conclave. The woman was one of the changelings, the leggy coltish one they called Tammy. The man was the tall skinny black man who was one of the hosting locals.

"Oh. Hi . . . Slim, is it?" Lowell said. "I was just showing Gustov here some of the basics of influencing animals."

"Uh-huh," Slim said. "Looks like a bit beyond the basics. You've got that animal doin' stuff it don't do normally. Mind letting it go?"

"Oh. Certainly."

Lowell gestured again, and the rat dropped back to all fours and shook itself.

"Sorry," the vampire said. "I didn't mean any harm. Friend of yours?"

There was an ill-muffled snort of laughter from the shape-shifter.

"We've worked together before," Slim said, stiffly. "More like an associate. I try to treat the animals I deal with on a level of respect. I guess that's one of the differences between you and me."

"Hey. Lighten up, Slim," Lowell said. "It's not like I set him up to swim the Mississippi."

"No. You just had him dancin' around like some street-trash hustler. That ain't somethin' he'd do normally," Slim growled, turning away.

"What? It's beneath his dignity?" The vampire laughed. "C'mon. It's just a rat."

"Yeah?" Slim said, returning to the fray. "And you're a vampire. How'd you like it if someone got into your head and had you dancin' around just for show."

"Slim," Tammy said, warningly, putting a hand on his arm.

"Like there's anyone at this conclave who could get that much control over me . . . or any other vampire," Lowell shot back.

"Hey, guys," Gustov said, stepping between them. "Don't you think you're overreacting a little?"

"And you stay out of this," Slim said, turning on the shape-shifter. "If I want advice, it sure won't be from the likes of you. What? Has he got a mind hold on you, too? I thought you were further up the food chain than that."

"What are you doing?" Lowell said, looking at the change-ling.

Tammy looked up from her cell phone.

"I'm calling Mr. McCandles," she said. "This whole thing is getting out of hand."

"Whistling up the dragon to bail you out of trouble?" the vampire sneered. "Well, he isn't strong enough to stop me if I really wanted to get into it with Animal Man here. Oh, put that thing away. We aren't . . ."

He started to reach for Tammy's phone, but Slim knocked his hand away.

"I don't care how bad you think you are," he snarled. "You don't touch her while she's with me. Leastwise, not unless she wants you to."

"And you don't lay hands on me!" Lowell hissed. "Better men than you have learned to regret taking such liberties."

Again, Gustov stepped between them.

"Gentlemen," he said. "There's no call for . . ."

"And I told you before to back off, Fido," Slim said. "Around here, a man fights his own battles once he starts 'em."

The shape-shifter struck a stance.

"That's twice you've insulted me, Slim," he snarled. "Both times I was trying to help. But if you . . ."

"What's going on here?"

Griffen McCandles appeared out of the darkness, striding toward them.

There was a frozen moment, as everyone held his pose in tableau like a bunch of guilty children when the front door opens. Then everyone started talking at once.

"We were just . . ."

"The man threatened to . . ."

"Started to go off on me over . . ."

Griffen held up his hand, and they lapsed into silence.

"Let's try this one at a time," he said. "Lowell?"

"Gustov asked me a question regarding basic animal-control skill," the vampire said. "We came up here, away from the tourist traffic, so I could give him a minor demonstration. Slim here came along and took exception to what I was doing. Something about offending the dignity of a rat. It went downhill from there."

"I see," Griffen said. "Slim? Anything to add?"

"He was makin' it stand up on its hind legs and dance," Slim said with a scowl. "To me, that's abusin' the power."

Griffen remembered how offended Slim had gotten when it was suggested that he use his animal-control skills in his street act.

"Did you say that to him?" he said.

"No. I just asked him to stop," the street entertainer said. "Don't figure it's my place to try to tell someone else how to use their abilities."

"That was it, then?" Griffen said. "A disagreement over how one's powers are to be used? I thought that was the kind of thing that was supposed to be talked out at this conclave."

"It got a bit heated, Mr. McCandles," Tammy put in. "There was some name-calling and muscle flexing. All in all, I'd say it was just a misunderstanding that got a little out of hand."

"Very well," Griffen said. "We'll leave it at that. I think a round of apologies is in order, and after that we can all forget it."

"I ain't apologizin' to him after what he said," Slim said stubbornly.

"All right," Griffen said, turning to the other two. "Lowell, Gustov, on behalf of the conclave, let me apologize for any offense offered you tonight. We know that there are a lot of old grudges and biases here, and we're all trying to work past them."

"Thank you, Mr. McCandles," the vampire said. "I, too, must apologize for my comments. They were said in the heat of the moment when I felt I was being challenged."

"And thank you, Lowell," Griffen said with a slight bow. "Now, if we're all . . . Slim?"

Slim was ten yards away, striding off down the Moonwalk with his shoulders in an angry set.

Apparently not everyone was ready to forgive and forget.

Forty-two

Griffen was sitting at one of the back tables in the Irish pub. While he normally sat at the bar so he could chat with the other regulars or the bartender, tonight he opted for solitude, and the others respected it. Sipping his usual Irish whiskey in larger-than-usual gulps, he brooded about the altercation with Slim.

Of all people to cause an altercation at the conclave, he would never have figured Slim. If anything, the street entertainer was the one who had served as Griffen's advisor about what to expect and how to handle it. For him to be the one to pick a fight with attendees from not one, but two other groups went beyond surprising.

Once again Griffen ran through what had been said and done once he arrived on the scene, but still he was at a loss to find a better way he could have played it. The situation had simply degenerated too far by then, and all he could do was attempt damage control.

"Hey, lover!"

Startled, he glanced up as Mai plopped down on an empty chair at the table, drink in hand. It said something about how focused he was that he had not even noticed that she had come in.

"Oh. Hi, Mai," he said, forcing a smile.

"Are you okay?" she asked, leaning forward to peer at him. "You look a little down."

"Just a bit tired is all," Griffen said. "This conclave thing has been running me ragged."

"Well, I sure haven't seen much of you," Mai said, leaning back. "I was just a little worried about you, is all. Thought you might be upset over your go-round with Slim."

Griffen stared at her.

"How in the world did you hear about that?" he managed at last.

"Well, I could just say 'It's the Quarter,' which it is." She grinned. "Truth to tell, though, some of the fey kids are holed up at a bar up the street and were talking about it. Your sister is working the bar and overheard a lot of it. Since she doesn't get off for a while, she gave me a call and asked me to look you up."

"Oh, that's just great." Griffen grimaced. "I was hoping the whole thing would just blow over. Instead, the word is spreading."

"Hope for the best, but plan for the worst," Mai recited smugly. "If it blows over, fine. You'd better be thinking about what you're going to do or say, though, if it doesn't."

"What can I say?" Griffen said, shrugging helplessly. "I know Slim has a thing about abusing the power to control animals, but he really seems to have overreacted this time."

"From what I hear, that was only part of it," Mai said, sipping at her drink.

"What do you mean?"

"I mean I don't think you got the whole story when they gave you the recap," Mai said, leaning forward and lowering her voice. "The animal-control thing is where it started, but it escalated into a pissing contest over whose powers were stronger and who could control who. Specifically, it really heated up when the question came up if you were powerful enough to control a vampire."

Griffen covered his eyes, then massaged his forehead.

"This just keeps getting better," he said.

"You haven't heard the best part," Mai said with a grimace. "The real subject of conversation is what you're going to do about it. It seems everyone is expecting you to come down on Slim."

"What?"

"Well, he is one of the locals." Mai shrugged. "And he not only got into it with a couple of the other attendees, he specifically defied and embarrassed you in front of witnesses. Some are thinking that you're going to have him bounced from the conclave. Other are saying that, since you're a dragon, you're going to come down hard on him just to make an example of what could happen if anyone crosses you."

Griffen slammed his glass down on the table.

"That tears it," he growled. "What am I supposed to do now?"

"I really don't know, lover," Mai said with a sigh. "I just figured I should pass along the info you didn't have. You're in a tough enough spot without people holding back on you."

Griffen favored her with a long stare.

"That sounds a little funny coming from you," he said.

"What's that supposed to mean?" Mai said, cocking her head to one side. "Has Val talked to you?"

"You never bothered to mention that you knew Flynn," Griffen said, straight-faced. "I had to hear it from him. He seemed to think you had told me all about him."

"I know a lot of people." Mai shrugged. "It didn't seem very important, particularly with you getting ready for the conclave. Besides, you seemed totally taken with him."

"From what he said, I got the impression that you two aren't very fond of each other," Griffen said. "Would you care to elaborate on that?"

"I'd say he's a snake, but it would be insulting to snakes," Mai said, playing with her drink. "I know he's been giving you advice, and that doesn't sound like the Flynn I know. He doesn't do favors. The only one Flynn is interested in is Flynn.

If he's being nice to you, you can bet there's something in it for him."

"You mean he might have a hidden agenda?" Griffen said with a smile. "If not, then he'll be the first dragon I've met who doesn't."

"Well, speak of the devil," Mai said, jerking her head toward the far door.

Griffen looked around. Flynn had just entered the bar. He gave a quick wave at Griffen, then stopped at the bar to order a drink.

"That does it for me," Mai said, finishing her drink and rising. "I'm sure he'll have all sorts of ideas about how you should handle things, but I don't have the stomach to listen to it. I'd probably get into it with him, and you don't need more problems right now. Just be sure to count your fingers if he shakes hands."

"Hello, Mai," Flynn said, stepping up to the table. "You're looking beautiful, as always."

Mai smiled prettily at him.

"Bite me, Flynn," she said. "Later, lover."

The whole bar watched her leave.

"I hope I didn't interrupt anything," Flynn said, easing into a vacant chair.

"It's not you," Griffen said. "Well, not entirely you. I'm not very good company tonight."

"Oh? Problems at the conclave?"

Griffen reflected for a moment on Mai's warning but decided that Flynn was too good a resource to waste. At the very least, he could listen to the older dragon's advice and not follow it.

Leaning back in his chair, he gave Flynn a quick summary of the problem with Slim.

"The way I see it, you've got a tempest in a teapot there," Flynn said with a shrug. "It will only get to be a big thing if you let it. Just downplay it, and it will go away."

"And how am I supposed to do that?" Griffen said.

Flynn leaned forward, putting his elbows on the table.

"Just get word to Slim that you want to talk to him. Then have a quiet sit-down and talk it all out. If anyone else asks, just say that it's between you and Slim."

"I guess that's as good a plan as any," Griffen said with a thoughtful nod. "At least it beats anything that I've been able to come up with."

He finished his drink and got to his feet, carrying his empty with him.

"And there's no time like the present, right? Catch you later, Flynn. And thanks!"

Flynn waved good-bye and watched him until he was out the door. Then he turned his attention to his own drink with a slight smile.

So far, he hadn't been completely satisfied with his success at dealing with the McCandles boy. While the kid was listening to him and asking for advice, he wasn't always following it. That meant that a lot of the carefully laid traps that Flynn hoped would weaken the support he was gathering weren't working.

This Slim incident might just do the trick, however. It reminded the other conclave attendees that Griffen was a dragon and had them on edge wondering how he would react.

Now all it would take was for something to happen to Slim.

Forty-three

Even though it was still several nights before Halloween, the conclave had an evening when no events or gatherings were scheduled. This was done specifically so the attendees could enjoy the Quarter during its pre-Halloween warm-up.

Halloween in the French Quarter was never just a one-night affair. Starting about a week before, various bars would host costume parties with cash or bar-bill prizes for the best entries. If one really had a hot costume, it was possible to hit different competitions on different nights, sometimes on the same night, and score several prizes on the same outfit. Of course, very few actually attempted this.

New Orleans was a town that liked to dress up. Between Mardi Gras and various theme parties, nearly everyone had an extensive wardrobe of masks, costumes, and costume pieces one could mix and match to come up with new outfits. For many, it was a source of pride not to wear the same outfit twice . . . or, at least, not twice in the same season. As such, if someone was hitting two different parties in one night, the usual procedure was to duck back to one's apartment or van and change into a totally different costume before hitting the next party.

All this meant that on any given night prior to Halloween, there would be individuals and groups roaming the streets and bars of the Quarter in costumes ranging from the clever to the borderline obscene. It was a field day for photographers and exhibitionists alike, and everyone had a good time.

Even tourists who weren't expecting such a display would get caught up in the fun, buying inexpensive feather masks and boas to join in the festivities. It was often referred to as a Mardi Gras for locals.

Griffen, however, took advantage of the opportunity to retreat back to his own apartment for a quiet night alone. Even though the conclave, for the most part, was running smoothly, he found it was still wearing on his nerves.

He refused several invitations to dinner or for bar-crawling on the vague excuse of "got to take care of something" and made his escape. On his way home he considered calling Mai or Fox Lisa for company but decided against it. Simply put, he realized he was just "peopled out," and wanted to be by himself. As a final, defiant gesture, he turned off his cell phone. Let them struggle through for one night without him. Tonight was going to be just for him.

Kicking back in the quiet of his apartment, he ran through the assortment of DVDs he had available. With the approach of Halloween, he had stocked up on an array of horror movies. Somehow, though, after what he had been going though at the conclave, the thought of watching a werewolf or vampire movie just didn't ring his chimes. Finally, as a sort of compromise, he settled on *Young Frankenstein* and settled back to watch.

It was classic Mel Brooks, and silly to the extreme. He had seen it dozens of times before, however, and as the story unfolded, he found his mind wandering.

Slim had not attended any of the conclave events that day. What was more, when Griffen stopped on the way home to ask some of the various street entertainers if they had seen him, no one was able to give him any specific information. It seemed Slim was making himself scarce for the moment. At some point, Griffen would have to decide if he was going to take time off from the conclave to run him down and clear the air, or if he should simply wait until the event was over and things had calmed down.

Then there was Tammy. She was still alternating between glaring daggers at him and looking like a kicked puppy every time their paths crossed. Despite Tink's reassurances that this was just Tammy being Tammy, Griffen still felt he should apologize or at least say something to her but was at a loss to know how or what. Then, too, there was the chance that if he was successful in dealing with her, she would take it as encouragement and decide to stay on in the French Quarter. He tried to envision his normal routine with Tammy bouncing in and out of it. His mind flatly rejected the image.

Heaving a sigh, he tried to focus on the movie.

A loud knocking on his door made him sit bolt upright, and he realized he had dozed off. Blinking, he tried to focus his eyes and mind as the knocking continued.

"All right. Coming," he called, moving to the door.

Valerie burst into the apartment as soon as he opened the door.

"Your cell phone is off," she said accusingly, as she looked around the apartment. "I thought I heard you moving around up here earlier. Are you alone?"

"Hello, Val. Good to see you, too," he said, sarcastically. "And, yes, I'm alone. Why?"

"Hold on to yourself, Big Brother," she said, grimly. "I've got some news, and it ain't good."

He started to make a wisecrack, but looked at her face and abandoned the thought.

"Okay. What is it?" he said.

"Slim is dead," she said. "Somebody killed him."

"What?!?"

"But that's not the bad news." Val sighed.

"It isn't?" He blinked. "Then what is? Or shouldn't I ask?"

"Word is going around that you did it . . . or had it done," she said. "That's why I wanted to know if you were alone. It would be nice if you had someone to alibi your whereabouts and actions tonight."

"But how could anybody think that?" he said, genuinely stunned.

"Well, let's see. Word is that you've been flexing your muscles at the conclave. 'Don't get me annoyed. I play for keeps.' Sound familiar?" Valerie said, looking at him hard. "It's also common knowledge that you and Slim went sideways to each other the other night. Then you take off from the conclave tonight, saying there's something you have to take care of, and then are asking around on the street about where Slim is. You tell me what that sounds like."

"This just keeps getting better," Griffen said, putting a hand over his face. "What's next? A visit from the cops?"

"I wouldn't worry about that," his sister said, sweetly. "Nobody's saying anything to the cops. Everybody at the conclave and on the street is afraid of you. They think you'll go after them next if they cross you."

Forty-four

If one wants information about a crime, instead of reading about it in the newspapers, it's better to go directly to a cop. Lucky for Griffen, Harrison's suspension had ended, and he was back on duty. He'd be the ideal source.

Griffen considered calling Harrison on his cell phone but decided against it. Doing that would call too much attention to himself and his interest in the case. This would be particularly bad if he was, indeed, a suspect. Instead, Griffen did what all good predators do. He staked out a water hole.

He knew Padre, the bartender at Yo Mama's Bar and Grill, where Harrison often went to indulge in their hamburgers or have a few beers. That let him drop in casually and, if Harrison was not there, to hang out for a bit chatting with Padre without it being obvious that he was looking for the detective.

As might be expected, much of the conversation in the bar centered around Slim's death. Everyone knew everyone else in the Quarter, if only on sight or to nod to in passing. While New Orleans had a bad reputation for murders, that was mostly in the outlying areas and usually involved the drug gangs fighting it out over territory and supply lines. A murder in the Quarter itself, particularly one involving a local, was rare, and therefore prime conversation material.

No one seemed to have much detailed information other than that Slim had been found on the Moonwalk, the stretch of pedestrian sidewalk that ran along the Mississippi from the French Quarter to the Aquarium of the Americas. There were a few tasteless jokes about someone really not liking street entertainers, but no real facts. Everyone seemed to like Slim, at least in hindsight, and no one had any ideas about who would have wanted to kill him.

Griffen was about to give up on his mission, at least for the night, when Harrison walked in.

The burly plainclothes detective always had the vague look of a biker to him, but tonight he was looking exceptionally haggard and unshaven.

Griffen waved him over, mentally rehearsing various ways to bring up the subject of Slim's death. He needn't have bothered.

"What a night," the detective growled, sliding into the booth and waving for a beer. "As if the Halloween craziness wasn't enough, we've got to deal with a dead street entertainer . . . without scaring the tourists, of course."

"Yeah. I heard about Slim," Griffen said, waving to add a drink for himself to the beer Padre was bringing over. "What happened there, anyway?"

"Still trying to figure it out," the detective said. "As far as we know, Slim was clean. No dealing or hustling, didn't drink all that much, no history of brawling. A couple of women he was dating casually, but no live-in girlfriend to get jealous or mad at him. He just worked hard at earning a living as a street entertainer, and that seemed to take up most of his time. Hell, McCandles, you knew him. He was about as harmless and inoffensive as they come."

Griffen thought briefly about Slim's temper when it came to animal control, but kept it to himself.

"How was he killed?" he asked instead.

"Stabbed through the heart," Harrison said. "No signs of a struggle or fight. Like someone he knew and trusted walked up and nailed him."

"Or someone he wouldn't suspect," Griffen said, thoughtfully. "Street entertainers work up close. It might have been someone who he thought was going to give him a tip."

"Maybe." The detective frowned. "Even there, the problem is still motive. Tourists and college kids come down here to get drunk and sometimes get into a fight in the process. They don't usually walk around killing street entertainers."

"Even if they did, a knife is kind of up close and personal," Griffen said. "You'd think they'd use a gun or something . . . except, maybe, for the noise."

"That's the real kicker," Harrison said, leaning in close. "It wasn't a knife."

"It wasn't?" Griffen said. "Then what was he stabbed with?"

"According to the coroner, something wooden," the detective said. "Maybe I'm letting the whole Halloween thing get to me, but it's like someone put a wooden stake into his heart."

Griffen gaped at him.

"A wooden stake? But that doesn't make any sense," he managed. "Slim did an Uncle Sam mime routine. Nothing to do with vampires. If someone went wacko and decided to hunt vampires, you'd think they'd go after a goth or something."

"Yeah, I know," Harrison said. "What's more, whoever did it took the weapon with them . . . or threw it in the river. The way I understand the stake in the heart thing is that you're supposed to leave the stake in. If you take it out, the vampire comes back to life."

Griffen shook his head.

"Beats the hell out of me," he said. "I'm glad it's your problem and not mine."

"Actually, I was hoping you might give me a hand," Harrison said with a wolfish smile. "You live here in the Quarter and know a lot of these weird groups. I'd appreciate it if you kept your ears open and let me know if you hear anything they aren't telling the cops . . . which is almost anything."

"I can do that." Griffen shrugged. "But outside of the wooden-stake thing, you don't have any leads at all?"

"Just one," Harrison said. "I've heard there's some kind of weird occult meeting in town and that Slim was somehow involved with it. Even heard he got into it with someone there. I'm going to try to run that down and see if there's any connection."

Griffen's stomach tightened. He definitely hadn't needed to hear that.

"I suppose it's a place to start," he said, just to say something.

"It makes as much sense as any other theory I've got," the detective said, standing up and tossing some money on the table for his beer. "I'll have to move fast, though. They'll probably be leaving town at the end of the weekend."

Griffen's mind was racing as he waved good-bye. Harrison would be moving fast, so he would have to move faster. Somehow, he had to get to the bottom of this mess before the detective discovered his own involvement with the conclave and started asking some uncomfortable questions about why he had withheld that particular tidbit of information.

Forty-five

Griffen was heading up St. Peter toward Bourbon Street when he was hoo-rawed.

"Yo! Grifter! Wait up!"

Turning, he saw Jerome jogging toward him. He waited until his friend caught up with him and slowed to a stop.

"What's up, Jer?" he said. "I'm kind of in a hurry here."

"Just a second while I catch my breath," Jerome said, breathing hard. "I've been lookin' for you all night. You know your cell phone's turned off? Anyway, man, you got problems."

"You heard, huh?" Griffen said, rolling his eyes.

"About Slim? Sure did," Jerome said. "Do you know it's goin' around that you're the one who hit him? Either that, or that you ordered it done?"

Griffen heaved a sigh.

"Yeah. Val told me. It gets worse. I just talked to Harrison. He's gotten wind of the conclave and is going to be checking it out."

Briefly, he filled Jerome in on what Harrison had told him, including the fact that, so far, the detective did not know that Griffen was involved with the conclave.

"Shit," Jerome said, shaking his head. "So now what are we gonna do?"

"'We'?" Griffen said, raising his eyebrows. "I don't see where any of this affects our gambling operation, Jer. I got myself into this mess. I figure I've got to find my own way back out."

"Hold on there, Grifter," Jerome said, drawing himself erect. "I know we haven't always seen eye to eye on this whole conclave thing, but you're still the main dragon down here. What affects you affects all of us, starting with me. There's no way I'm gonna stand around with my hands in my pockets while all this is goin' down. So let's put our heads together and try to figure this thing out."

"Thanks, Jerome," Griffen said. "I really appreciate that."

"So, like I said before, what are we gonna do?"

"Well, I hadn't been thinking in terms of we," Griffen said. "I was going to head over to the conclave and let them know what's going on . . . including the fact that Harrison's going to be nosing around. I'm thinking of suggesting that they cancel the scheduled meetings tomorrow. There's not that much slated, anyway. Mostly, people are going to be gearing up for the masquerade ball."

"I'm not sure that's such a hot idea," Jerome said carefully. "If Harrison spots you there, there's gonna be hell to pay."

"Well, I am sure it's not a hot idea"—Griffen grimaced—"but it can't be helped. I've got to let them know what's coming down the pike at them, and there's no other way. At first I thought of sending them a note, but then I realized it's not something I want to put down on paper."

"You got that right," Jerome said with a brief grin. "You know, don't you, that a lot of them will already be thinking that you're at the bottom of the trouble with Slim."

"Yeah, I know," Griffen said. "What I'm going to do is flat out tell them that I had nothing to do with it. There's no way to prove that right now, so they'll just have to either believe me or not. It's still early, so I'm going to try to catch some of the attendees in the hotel lobby bar, then check a few of the other clubs they've been hanging at. I'll leave it to the ones I catch to spread the word to the others."

Jerome looked around.

"Like you said, it's still early. Let's talk this out a little over a drink before you stick your neck out. I think there's a bar around here somewhere."

That got a laugh out of Griffen. One was never far from a bar in the French Quarter.

They stepped into one of the quieter bars available and ordered a round, carefully choosing seats well away from the other customers and the bartender.

"So, what have you got on your mind?" Griffen asked, settling in and taking a sip from his drink. "And can you keep it short? I really have to get over to the conclave."

"That's what I what to talk about," Jerome said. "You're so wrapped up in that conclave you aren't thinking."

"C'mon, Jer. I thought we were past that."

"I'm not talking about business," Jerome said, shaking his head. "I'm talkin' about what's goin' on now. Something smells about the whole deal."

"What do you mean?" Griffen said, cocking his head to one side.

"That's what I'm talkin' 'bout," Jerome pressed. "You got so much shit goin' on, you don't have time to think. Well, take a few minutes here and think. You think it's a coincidence, Slim getting killed so soon after you went head-to-head with him? While you're in the middle of tryin' to moderate that conclave?"

"Well, what else could it be?" Griffen said.

"It could be that someone's tryin' to set you up," Jerome said, pointedly. "If it isn't a frame for a murder rap, then at the very least someone's out to embarrass you big-time."

"I think you're stretching a bit to think that," Griffen said, skeptically.

"Well, I think you're stretchin' if you don't think that," Jerome shot back. "Look, all I'm sayin' is to think about it and watch your back. If I'm wrong and it is all just coincidence, there's no harm done. But if I'm right, and you keep trying to wave it all off as coincidence, you could really get blindsided."

Griffen started to speak, then hesitated. Taking another sip from his drink, he stared at the wall for a long minute.

"All right," he said at last. "I'll consider it seriously. My first question would be who would want to set me up? I'm getting along well with everyone at the conclave . . . well, nearly everyone."

"All it takes is one," Jerome warned. "Besides, it doesn't necessarily have to be someone from the conclave. You're not only a dragon, you're the head dragon in this area. That makes you a target. Every time you take a breath, you're gonna upset somebody . . . and they're going to keep coming after you until you stop breathing. Get used to it."

"Do you have anyone specifically in mind?" Griffen said.

"Haven't gotten that far," Jerome admitted. "Didn't you and Val go sideways to a couple of Melinda's boys a while back?"

"Yeah, but we haven't seen or heard from them since," Griffen said, then hesitated. "Did I mention to you that George is back in town?"

"The one who tried to kill you a couple months ago?" Jerome said, sitting up straight. "He's in town, and you didn't let us know?"

"I think it was more that he was testing me than trying to kill me," Griffen said. "And as far as him being in town, he says he's just here on vacation. As a matter of fact, he's Valerie's date for the masquerade."

"Uh-huh," Jerome said. "You've got a known supernatural hit man in town, someone from the conclave turns up dead, and you think it's a coincidence?"

"He only acts when someone is paying him," Griffen

pointed out. "Which would still leave us looking for someone with a motive. Heck, I'd be more likely to suspect Flynn
than George."

"Flynn? West Coast big-time dragon Flynn? He's in
town?"

"Yeah. I met him a couple of weeks ago, and he's been giving me advice on how to run the conclave," Griffen said.
"Why? Do you know him?"

"Never met him, but I've heard he's a major power player,"
Jerome said. "He's not one I'd figure to be giving out free
advice."

"Sounds like you've been talking to Mai," Griffen said
with a laugh.

"Heard about him long time before I met Mai," Jerome
said. "If she doesn't trust him, I'd say she's with the majority.
Anybody else in town you haven't told me about?"

"That's it. But I take your point." Griffen finished his drink.
"I'll go pass the word on to the conclave. You see if you can
round up Val and Mai and meet me back at my place. Maybe
between us we can sort this thing out."

"Half a good plan," Jerome said. "If you don't mind, I
think I'll tag along while you pass the word, then we'll find
the women. The more I think about it, the more it occurs to
me that you should have someone covering your back for a
while."

"**Hey**, Mai. C'mon in. I was just about to call you."

Valerie stepped back from her apartment door to let her
friend in.

"Griffen just buzzed me to let me know he was calling a
war council," Mai said, entering the apartment and flopping
down on the sofa. "I thought it might be a good idea if we
talked first."

"I was thinking the same thing," Val said. "Do you think there's anything to the idea that he's being set up?"

"I really don't know . . . but there's always the possibility," Mai said. "One thing I am sure of is that it's time we put a few more cards on the table."

"You mean . . ."

"I mean we've got to tell him about Lizzy," Mai said. "If we're going to sort this mess out, he's got to have all the pieces. That means letting him know who the players in town are."

"You think she's behind the setup . . . if there is one?" Val asked with a frown.

"Not really," Mai admitted. "But as crazy as she is, we can't rule her out completely."

"Big Brother is going to freak," Valerie said, shaking her head. "From what he said when he called, Jerome is already giving him grief about not sharing the information that Flynn and George are in town. When he finds out that we've been holding out on him as well, he's going to blow his stack."

"Can't be helped." Mai sighed. "Now he needs to know. We'll just have to tell him that we thought it would distract him from the conclave and decided to handle it ourselves."

"He's going to love that," Val said with a grimace. "What about the other thing?"

"Which other thing?" Mai said.

Val pulled herself up to her full height and patted her stomach.

The two women looked at each other for a long moment, then as one shook their heads.

"I don't think so. Not now," Valerie said. "Lizzy is my problem. So is this." She touched her belly.

"One crisis at a time," Mai agreed.

Forty-six

Even though it was late, the hotel lobby bar was still open. During its stay, the conclave had spent enough time and money in the bar to convince the management to schedule extra help to keep it open as long as they had customers, and tonight looked to be a banner ring.

Griffen had come and gone, and now a goodly percentage of the attendees had gravitated to the bar both to absorb and discuss the news he had brought.

"I don't like it," Tail declared, glaring into his drink.

"The whole situation abounds with things not to like," Margie said, cocking her head at him. "Which thing in particular don't you like, Tail?"

Surprisingly enough, of all the tactics the organizers had scheduled in an effort to get the various groups at the conclave to interact, the one that seemed to have been the most effective was the unscheduled poker game. Since that game, the participants had tended to hang and drink together, preferring each other's company to that of their own specific group.

"I don't like the idea of the cops poking around the conclave," Tail said with a grimace.

"I'll wager we've all had to deal with the cops at one time or another." Margie shrugged. "No reason this time around should be any different."

"Lot o' differences." Kane spoke up. "For one ting, dere are a lot of us dat have gathered in this here place. Too many maybe. Means de little tings dat make us different and we could normally cover on our own get blown up, dey get exaggerated. How many here you trust to not slip up, keep traps shut 'bout every little ting?"

"There's also the minor detail that we've got a body that is being tied directly to us," Lowell put in. "I myself don't like the bit about him being staked through the heart."

"See? I'm not the only one who's worried," Tail said triumphantly.

"I'm not saying that there's nothing to worry about," Margie said, raising her hands defensively. "I just think we'd be better off spending our time getting our stories straight instead of just sitting around and fretting. For example, what are we going to say about Slim and Griffen? That's the main reason they're coming around, isn't it?"

"I think I can handle that, since I was there," Lowell said. "I'll just tell them the truth. That there were some harsh words tossed back and forth, but nothing beyond that. Nothing to kill anyone over. What's more, McCandles didn't even show up until it was almost over. If anything, there was more bad blood between me and Slim than between Slim and McCandles."

"Bad blood. Good one dat, vamp," Kane said with a wink. "Not sure you should say such a thing to a cop now. Wit how Slim was killed and all."

"Why not?" Lowell said. "They don't know I'm a vampire. To them, I'm just another attendee of a weird convention. All of us are."

"So you sayin' we cover for him?" Kane said.

"I'm not covering for him. I'm just going to tell them what happened," Lowell said. "Besides, I don't think he did it."

"Because he said so?" Margie said.

"Because I don't see where he'd have any reason to," Lowell

corrected. "If anything, quite the opposite. He's been knocking himself out trying to run this conclave. Why would he do anything to disrupt it or to draw unwanted attention to it?"

"I'll have to go along with that," Tail agreed. "He rubs me the wrong way, but he's also doing right by us. We all expect certain things from dragons; Griffen has turned at least some of my ideas around."

"That's certainly true for us changelings," Tink said. "He always has time to talk with us and make us feel welcome. This whole thing with Slim, it's almost as if whoever did it wanted Griffen to look bad."

A silence fell over the group as they looked at each other.

"Why? Seems a powerful strong way to wrong someone," Kane said softly.

"Someone already said it." Tail frowned. "To mess up the conclave."

"Maybe by setting up one of the groups, like, say, us vampires, to appear to be disruptive influences, if not killers," said Lowell. "By the way, Tail, we really didn't send you that cake from the Three Dog Bakery."

"I think the real question," Margie said, "is not 'why?' but 'who?' Who would want to see the conclave fail at Griffen's expense?"

"What about a dragon?" Tail said, darkly.

"What is it wit you 'n' dragons? You got a serious mad on for a reason?" Kane grimaced.

"No. Wait a minute," Lowell said. "Tail might have a point there."

"How do you figure that?" Tink asked.

"Think about it," the vampire said. "Remember all the things we've heard about dragons, and how ruthless and power-hungry they are. This is the first time we've had a dragon at one of our conclaves, and we all like, or at least respect, McCandles. That's got to have some kind of impact on other dragons. They may see it as degrading."

"Or as an opportunity to do Griffen some dirt," Tink said. "Anything that happened could get blamed on his being involved with the conclave."

"Slow down here. Let's not get carried away," Margie said. "All of this is just speculation. We don't know that Slim's death was anything except random violence. We sure can't point the finger at any one person or group without some kind of proof."

"Well, there's nothing stopping us from doing a little investigating on our own," Lowell said.

"Reality check?" Margie said, raising her hand. "Exactly what do yo think we can do that the regular police can't?"

"Lots of things." The vampire smiled. "How about it, Tail? Is there anything you or yours could do to help track down the killer?"

"Not de way it work, Batman," the shape-shifter growled. "We're not bloodhounds. Even if'n we were, got any idea how many damn tourists passed by de scene of de crime by now? Worse'n a needle in a haystack, dat job."

"We might be able to help with that," Tink said. "One of the things we changelings are good at is finding things."

"And that helps us how?" Margie said, raising an eyebrow.

"Well, one of us . . . Tammy, you remember her . . . is particularly good at detecting supernaturals. If she could locate some that aren't involved with the conclave, and one of them turned out to have a grudge against Griffen, we just might have found our killer."

"That's pretty thin," Lowell said. "And we've only got, what, maybe thirty-six hours to do it in? Besides, from what I recall of that little scene at the poker game, I'm not sure Tammy will be all that eager to do a favor for McCandles."

"You don't know Tammy," Tink said. "She's probably cooled

down by now. Besides, it will give her a chance to gain his thanks, if not admiration."

"And if it doesn't work, we're no worse off than before," Tail pointed out. "Let's do it."

Forty-seven

Griffen wasn't sure what to expect from the conclave the morning after Slim's death. He had made calls to the various speakers and leaders the night before, after talking with his own inner circle, Jerome, Val, and Mai. He had almost called Mose, but the old dragon's distant attitude lately made Griffen hesitate. The advice from the others would have to be enough.

The conclave was already winding down. Today the scheduling was light, and tomorrow there wasn't anything serious at all before the big masquerade ball. It seemed they were used to everyone wanting to have time to rest up before the real party. Griffen had been assured that the speakers could handle most of the workload that day if he needed to deal with more important matters.

Which was exactly the problem. Griffen wasn't sure where his priorities should be. The loss of Slim had him mixed up emotionally, but he had been engaged as moderator. A moderator who didn't know which meetings during the "light" day were actually important. The weight of the tragedy and the weight of his inexperience were combining into something truly crushing.

So he was going in a bit early, to gauge everyone's reactions and feelings after having a night for the news to make the rounds and settle into everyone's mind. Then he would decide how best to use his energies. He tried not to think about what Slim would want him to do. Slim, who had been one of his biggest supporters as moderator until the unfortunate incident with Lowell.

As Griffen walked into the hotel lobby, he saw he wasn't the only one getting an early start. He wasn't sure which surprised him more, Harrison sitting in one of the low chairs in the lobby or the two uniformed police standing some distance behind. The last thing Griffen would have expected from the scruffy vice detective was obvious flaunting of what he was, but the uniforms didn't seem to have any other purpose.

Harrison was leaning in toward a young woman, someone associated with Gada and the magic types if Griffen remembered right. Harrison was talking low, but the girl kept glancing around nervously, afraid of who might see her and what they might think. Of course her back was to the door, so that she could see the two uniformed officers, and Harrison could see anyone who came in.

He looked up at Griffen, and the lines of his face deepened as he scowled. A few more words to the girl, and she craned her head back, eyes wide and startled. She muttered something back and quickly rose and scurried out of the lobby.

Harrison stood, and the two uniforms stepped up to flank him.

"This needs to be in private," Harrison said.

He turned and didn't bother looking back. Griffen hesitated only a moment before following him, the two uniforms falling in behind him. Harrison went into one of the conference rooms set up for the conclave itself. Once Griffen had entered as well, the door was closed by one of the officers, leaving the two men alone.

"Detective Harrison, I ju—"

Harrison grabbed Griffen by his shirt, cutting him off. Griffen was surprised by the strength of the man who jerked him around and slammed him facedown onto the conference table in the center of the room. Griffen had to concentrate hard to keep down his body's ever-growing reactions to danger. The last thing he needed was for Harrison to see scales.

By the time he was sure he wasn't going to slip, he felt the metal of a handcuff bite into his wrist.

"Griffen McCandles, you have the right to remain silent. Something you seem to be very good at, you little shit."

"Detective."

"Shut up! You held out on me. I thought we were square, McCandles. You seemed to get the rules. You do not jerk me around."

Griffen let his other arm be pulled back, hands securely cuffed behind his back. He didn't know if he could actually break a pair of handcuffs, but he was willing to give it a try.

"Not only do I find you know exactly what Slim has been involved in, because of you being the frickin' ringleader here, but I hear you and he been going sideways at each other. And I have no less than three local street performers willing to witness that you were looking for him before he was killed. You know how badly you got to screw up in this town for people to talk to the *police*?"

"I didn't kill Slim," Griffen said.

"You are the number-one suspect, and you are going in for obstruction and withholding. And I should break your teeth in. You are never getting another favor out of me or any of my boys, McCandles."

"Why is this even your case? I thought you were vice."

"I know the vic, I know the suspect, and it's my beat. It may not be my case, but they will understand me wanting to get at you first."

"With all the jurisdictional nonsense I hear in this town? I find that very hard to believe," Griffen said.

Harrison grunted, and Griffen was hauled back again. A heavy hand pushed him down into a chair, which wrenched his wrists. Idly, Griffen wondered if a dragon claw could pick a lock, if he knew how to control his shape changing that well . . . or knew how to pick a lock.

Harrison moved into the chair at the opposite end of the table. There were no bright lights in Griffen's eyes, no two-way mirror along one wall, but he knew an interrogation scene when he saw one. Except Harrison was definitely bad cop, with no good cop in sight.

"So maybe I called in a favor," Harrison said. "Just so I could hear it from you, why you lied to me, or why you killed Slim."

"I didn't lie . . . I just decided to wait till a better opportunity to talk to you. And I didn't—"

"Kill Slim," Harrison interrupted. "Yeah, and you know, I almost believe that. So tell me, what is this collection of whack jobs you've got going on, and what's your connection?"

"Honestly, I didn't help organize it. I just got asked to come in as a neutral party. Kind of keep the peace. That's the only reason me and Slim had a problem. He was causing a little trouble, and I had a word with him, it wasn't any more than that."

"Well, that can be an awful lot. And you didn't tell me who these people are."

Griffen looked at him levelly.

"You really don't want to know, Detective. Trust me."

Harrison looked back.

"The last thing I am going to do right now is trust you . . . but I might agree with you on that."

Harrison stood and walked over to Griffen. A few moments later the handcuffs were back in his pocket.

"There is no evidence, no sign of you on the body. No murder weapon. And witnesses who talked to me . . . might not be so willing to talk to whoever gets the case. But, Mc-Candles, this is your mess, and you got a group of people, suspects, who are skipping town in a couple of days."

Harrison opened the door. The uniforms were gone. Griffen wondered if they had been there just for him.

"You have till the end of your little convention here to get me some answers I can use. Or I am dragging you, and every last one of them, in on whatever charges I can cook up. And then I find out . . . everything."

The door closed behind him, and Griffen sat in the chair, rubbing his wrists and trying to figure out if he was more or less confused than he'd been earlier thas morning. A soft knock came from the door, which opened a crack. Jay poked his head in tentatively.

"We are ready to start the first meeting, if you are done with the room, Griffen," he said

"Sure, sure," Griffen said absently.

"Are you busy, or will you be sitting in?" Jay asked.

"I, uh . . . I'll sit in."

Jay nodded approvingly. He opened the door fully and in walked several of the conclave members. Griffen barely paid attention as they all found their seats, clumped into their cliques and groups.

The changelings gathered close to him, and after a few more distracted seconds, Griffen realized they were looking at him. Especially Robin and Hobb, their eyes wide and eager.

"Yes?" Griffen asked.

"Well, uh, we wanted to know, since you are still leading the meetings," Robin began, hesitantly.

"Are we still going to have our pre-Halloween ghost tour?" Hobb asked.

"Pleeeease," several of the changelings said at once, eager as puppies.

Griffen found himself smiling.

It was all about priorities.

Forty-eight

No matter what type of tourist you are, the Quarter has something for you.

Beautiful scenery for the shutterbugs, endless stores of all ranges of quality for the shopaholics, bars and clubs for the party animals, exotic and local cuisine for the gourmands, museums and galleries for the hoi polloi. Even clowns making balloon animals for the children. Though if you really want to experience the Quarter, it's always best to leave the kiddies at home.

For the most part Griffen had sampled all the various facets of the tourist-milking machine that is the French Quarter. He reveled in the low and the high. He even occasionally poked his head in the countless T-shirt shops to see if there was anything clever. Except for the tours. For all his months there, he hadn't been on a single tour. It just wasn't something that the locals tended to do, and it wasn't something that had any particular draw for him.

That was before he found himself made a moderator. With everything that was going on at the conclave, Griffen felt driven to try to keep things together. He was holding the bag, but that didn't mean he was going to choose the easy route and drop it.

One of the activities that had been planned was a group excursion with the Haunted History Tour. Again, Griffen knew very little about the tours themselves though he had seen them around. Groups of fifteen to thirty tourists would gather around a storyteller as he spoke of the Quarter's sordid past. Most of it was made-up; if one listened to rumor, it was invented on the spot. A really bored tour guide could be the worst, or best, thing that a tourist might encounter.

One of Estella's people had offered to give the tour, but Griffen politely declined. Not only did he want the conclave members to have a "normal" Quarter experience, he was hoping that most of them would keep their eccentricities in check with a normal tour guide.

Hoping, not expecting.

This was actually the most mingling he had seen among the various groups in the conclave. It was hard to form little cliques when you were all clustering around a single storyteller. Also, it was mostly followers, not leaders. Drake, Robin, and Hobb were there, but not Tink. Several of the voodoo practitioners had attended, but Estella was busy. Even Lowell was absent, though a few of his vampires lurked at the edges.

The garou were absent entirely, as were the higher shapeshifters. True to his word, Tail had invited the female shifter from the demonstration to dinner. Griffen had suggested the Desire Oyster Bar, and had a discreet word with Amos, one of the waiters there. He had convinced Amos not only to let him pick up the tab, but to be sure *not* to tell that he had done it. A small miracle in itself. As far as the couple were concerned, it was on the house.

Of the animal-control people, only Johansson had attended. Griffen gave him an uncomfortable glance when he saw the man approaching the gathering tour group. Johansson saw the look and walked up to Griffen directly.

"I want you to know," he said without preamble, "Margie and me, we don't blame you. This was his town, and he should have known the risks better than anyone."

With that he turned away from Griffen and joined the
tour group. Griffen let him; after all, what more could be
said?

As the tour actually got started, Griffen more or less tuned
out the guide. History really wasn't his passion. Yet another
reason he had avoided the tours in the past. He wasn't really
paying attention till after their first stop, when one of the
changelings spoke up.

"What do you mean we don't get to go inside?" Drake said.

"I'm sorry, sir," the tour guide said, "but all the sites on
today's tour are, of course, private residences. We don't have
permission—"

"You mean we are just going to stand on the sidewalk and
listen to you talk?" cut in someone else.

"Well, one of our stops is Jean Lafayette's Blacksmith
Shop, one of the oldest taverns in the Quarter. It is said that
many of the pirates who used to run with Lafayette still come
back to have one last drink at their old . . . haunt."

"A bar . . . go figure."

" 'Haunt'? Is that the best you can come up with?"

"A piece of eight says he will use the line 'dead drunk'
before the night is over."

The tour guide's jaw tightened noticeably, and Griffen almost stepped in. However, he also knew that tourists, any
tourists, put the locals through worse. For now, he would just
hang in the background, and pay a little bit more attention.

The tour moved on, and after a few more stops and unim-
pressive narratives, the guide obviously decided it was time to
spice things up a bit. He glanced a bit nervously at the changelings. Probably, Griffen figured, wondering who in the group
were their parents.

"Now, this was the château of a famous marquis in the late
eighteenth century. In the tradition of the Marquis De Sade,
this perverse nobleman entertained members of the French

aristocracy by beating and tormenting servants and local wayfarers. It is said—"

"Said by who?"

Griffen stifled a laugh.

"Tha . . . What?" the guide said.

"Said by who?"

"Yes, you keep using that line, but never quote a source."

That last was from one of the vampires, who was beginning to sidle up to the guide as he became more and more
distraught. Nothing like an easy meal.

"Not to mention completely glossing over your facts. You
didn't mention the marquis's name, the actual year, or even
what 'aristocrats' he was entertaining," Johansson said.

"And 'wayfarers'? Come on, man," Drake said.

The tour guide pressed on, showing much admirable de-
termination.

"*It is said* that you can still hear the moans of pain from
his victims."

Then a woman Griffen had not yet seen at the conclave
stepped forward.

"See, now you are way off. The marquis's château was three
blocks from here. This was an old brothel. And believe me,
it's not moans of pain you are hearing."

The tour guide threw his hands up.

"Moving on!" he said as he walked down the street.

The others all seemed to share a glance before following him. Only Griffen paused, some instinct in him telling
him to watch the woman who'd spoken. She turned to him
and winked, before turning transparent. The specter walked
toward the building in question as she faded away.

When he caught up to the group, they were standing behind Saint Peter's Cathedral. He was just in time to hear a

line so tired and clichéd, he was shocked that he hadn't heard it earlier.

"And if you listen closely, you will hear them," the guide said to wrap up whatever tale he had been spinning.

Almost as one, the entire group turned and cocked their heads. Listening.

They waited, and waited, and the guide started to fidget.

"Nnoooo . . ." one said carefully, "can't hear a thing."

"There are going to be ghosts on this ghost tour, right?" Griffen laughed.

"Maybe if we had a goat."

That came from one of the voodoo practitioners. Griffen was almost sure he was kidding.

"Hey, isn't Jackson Square on the other side of that church?" Robin asked.

Again, there was a pause, and almost as one the group surged past the guide, down Pirate Alley, and into the Square. Griffen smiled and, as he passed the befuddled guide, clapped him on the shoulder and tipped him a twenty. It did Griffen much good to see some of the conclave actually unified for a change.

Now, Griffen wasn't obligated to keep an eye on everyone, even in his own mind. That night he was more playing host than anything else. Still, most of the ex–tour members were congregating around the various tarot readers. There were over half a dozen tables set up, spaced well apart, and each was promptly filled by one of his attendees. Griffen strolled from table to table listening not too discreetly.

Some were good.

"Give me your hand," a reader said to Johansson.

"Be gentle," he said with an easy smile.

"Hmm . . . very compassionate. A gentle touch . . . especially with children? No, animals. You have much skill with animals. Have you ever thought about show business?"

Some were bad.

"The cards say you will marry but never have children. You will excel in business but never own one. You need to learn to communicate more with people."

Drake smiled at the reader across from him. His smile did not match his young features.

"I've already had three kids, no wives, and my youngest is about your age. Don't get me started on the businesses."

And some . . . well, "ugly" just didn't describe it.

"This . . . this is impossible. No one can have this many life lines . . . and they keep changing! Don't you ever stay the same?"

"Well . . . hold on. Let me try."

The young shifter looked down at her hand and focused. The reader's eyes crossed as the lines on her hand truly changed, the many wrinkles merging into one deep line, almost in the exact center of her hand.

"Is that better?" she asked innocently.

"That . . . that . . . that'll be twenty dollars if you please."

"Sure thing."

Griffen's attention was drawn to Robin and Hobb. They were actually standing behind one of the vampires, who was getting his cards read. The reader, an elderly man with an exaggerated lisp and a pink cowboy hat, was having some difficulties.

"Death card . . . again," the reader said.

All the cards on the table were death cards. Five of them in all.

"Is that some kind of trick deck?" the vampire said, scowling.

"No . . . no . . . someone must be playing a trick on me. The readers are competitive here . . . Let me try another deck."

Neither noticed Hobb elbow Robin in her ribs soundly. Griffen could just make out her comment as she giggled and elbowed him back.

"What? James Bond did it . . . kinda."

"Say, that gives me an idea."

Hobb leaned closer and whispered in her ear. She giggled.

"Ah, that's better," the reader said as he laid out the cards, "the Lovers."

"That woman on the card . . ." said the vampire.

"Yes?"

"That's my mother!"

Griffen was already hauling the two changelings away by their collars. He could hear the reader try to apologize fifteen feet away.

He was about to lay into them when again his instincts hit him in the pit of his stomach. He looked around and saw a very sedate shifter sitting at a table Griffen hadn't noticed before. The woman reading his cards had a shawl over her head, her face hidden. The shifter got up, walked right past Griffen, and left the Square. His face was troubled.

Griffen, forgetting the changeling couple for a moment, walked toward the now-vacant seat. The reader lifted her head, a faint smile playing across her lips then fading just as quickly.

"Hello, Rose," Griffen said.

"Read your cards, young man?" she said.

She didn't acknowledge his greeting, not even with her eyes.

"Look, I . . ."

"Sit, I can't say much right now, but I can read your cards." Griffen sat.

Rose nodded and began to shuffle an old battered deck. She blew on it before handing it to him. The cards felt oily and thick, more like fabric than paper. She had him cut the cards, then hand them back.

She laid out seven cards in a line. Griffen had never had his cards read, but from what he had seen, most readers used an intricate pattern, a cross or a horseshoe or even a star. She merely laid a line.

"Turn over the first card," she said.

The first card was Death.

Griffen looked up and around suspiciously.

"No, it isn't the changelings this time. You know what is on your mind, and what is causing you the most grief. This is the card of the now."

"Is Slim—"

"I may only read the cards. Turn over the next two."

The Five of Wands, the Seven of Wands, both reversed.

"You are conflicted inside, and at the same time spreading yourself too thin. These two cards together are disaster. Continue to try and do everything when you don't know what you even want, and you will only rip yourself up inside," Rose said.

"So what else is new? But how can I—"

"Flip the next two."

Griffen did. They were the Hermit reversed and the Seven of Swords.

"My, you do like conflicting pairings," Rose said. "The Hermit reversed, you can't do everything on your own, you have to accept the help of those who offer it. But the Seven of Swords, you can't trust many of those around you. They are poised to stab you in the back. You must be very careful to know your true allies."

Griffen reached toward the last two cards.

Rose reached out and rapped his knuckles with something long and hard. He didn't see what exactly before it disappeared again. It was covered with beads and a few hanging feathers, and it stung.

"I didn't tell you to turn over the cards," she said with a smile.

"I thought ghosts couldn't hurt you unless you let them," Griffen groused.

"You chose to sit down, didn't you?" she said, smiling more. "Turn over the cards."

The Princess of Swords and the Princess of Cups, both reversed.

"Women, it always does seem to come down to that. One unbalanced of the mind, one frustrated of the heart. Neither is a solution card, so these are the end of this road, but not a full answer. You will be left wanting."

"I repeat, so what else is new?"

"Nothing," Rose said, and she stood.

Griffen took that as a cue and stood as well. She smiled and reached out, as if to brush her fingers over his cheek. Only they passed through with only a bare whisper of sensation. She had seemed perfectly solid before.

"Good luck, Griffen. I will probably see you before the end of all this. Oh, and would you tell those adorable little changelings something for me?"

"Sure. What?"

"That their child will be fey."

With that, she and her table were gone. No one seemed to notice but him, but then no one had noticed them arrive. Griffen stood there and, with a frustrated sigh, rolled his eyes.

"Oh, sure, how am I supposed to work that into a conversation?!"

He was almost sure he could hear Rose's laughter on the wind.

Forty-nine

All good ideas get screwed up in committee.

There were multiple reasons the conclave utilized speakers for each of the groups, and those representatives were not chosen at random. Simply put, some of the members of the conclave weren't the sharpest. Not to mention well behaved.

Rumor already ran rampant among the lesser members attending. They debated back and forth constantly. Was Griffen guilty? Innocent? What would the speakers do either way? What should be done about the police? Most of those attending were concerned, and afraid. A few, though, found this to be the most exciting conclave ever, and were constantly playing devil's advocate to keep the conversation flowing.

Within hours of the impromptu decision to investigate the murder independent of the police, everyone knew. No one quite knew how the rumor leaked so fast, though a few of the vampires were likely candidates. They had been stirring up the discussion and sitting back with happy smiles as the emotions flared.

However, Tail, whether he knew it or not, was part of what made it worse. He had, in effect, spoken for the shifters on how they could, or would, help such an investigation. It was a small thing, but he had gone over Jay's head. Jay, the chosen representative. Any other time, it would have been no problem. But when things are unstable, a bubble of vacuum

in the power structure, no matter how small, can be a cata-
lyst.

Griffen didn't know any of this. All he knew was he had
been called in, again. And once again, he had to leave his
home and rush over to deal with conclave matters. At four in
the morning, because some young shifter had decked one of
the garou.

Griffen nodded to the desk clerk, who looked dead on his
feet and barely managed to wave. Then he braced himself
and walked down to one of the conference rooms. Whether
it was the hour, or some weeding had been done before he
got there, he was happy to see that there were only about a
dozen people in the room. Jay, Tink, Tail, and Kane were
seated. He almost missed Tammy, who sort of huddled in
one corner away from everyone. Standing at opposite ends of
the room were a group of shifters and all of Kane's garou.
One of the garou, Kevin from the demonstration, had tissue
stuffed up a nose that looked as if it had recently been broken. Griffen couldn't tell at a glance who his opponent had
been.

Small group or not, they all started talking at once as he
came in. Except Tammy, who merely glared sullenly at him.
It was loud enough, and he had enough lack of sleep that he
almost shouted back, but figured it would only make his
head throb more. Griffen waved them all silent.

Basking in the silence for a moment, he tried to decide
who to ask for information. It wasn't easy, tempers being what
they were. Griffen was too tired to want to deal with any more
unintended insults. He turned to the wounded garou, Kevin.

"What happened?" Griffen said.

"Got hit," Kevin said.

Griffen fought the impulse to throttle the life out of
him.

"A little more detail please," Griffen said.

"Well, we was talking about the investigation. And he said we couldn't do it. Said we needed some fairy to bail us out."

Griffen blinked and tried to rub some of the sleep from his eyes.

"What investigation?"

Kevin looked at him as if he were crazy.

"Us findin' out who killed Slim, of course," he said.

"I done tol' you, ain't gonna be done dat way," Kane said.

"You mean it's true!? You trust the fairies instead of your pack?" Kevin said, shocked.

"No, it ain't like dat, boy . . ." Kane said.

One of the shifters, whom Griffen didn't know, spoke up.

"How come Tail is talking for us now? Why is he stepping on Jay's toes and keeping us out of things?"

"I only said that we aren't trackers like that," Tail said.

"Which we?!" another shifter demanded.

"Packless riffraff," one of the garou muttered.

Several people started to talk at once, along the lines of traditional prefight rituals such as "What did you say?" A few of the garou and shifters took a step forward. Nails were starting to grow into claws.

"Hold it!" Griffen shouted.

He brought his fist down on the table, then had to recover as it went through the oak and he nearly lost his balance. He stood, trying to regain his control, watching his own claws fade away.

When he spoke again, it was dangerously soft.

"Tink, what are they talking about?"

Tink looked uncomfortable, and his eyes kept flicking to the damaged table.

"Well, it was maybe suggested that we do some investigating without the police knowing. See if we can't find out what really happened. There was some question as to whether any shifter could do any good, and I suggested maybe Tammy could try to help."

Griffen glanced at Tammy, but she seemed to have no comment to make. She crossed her arms over her small breasts and looked away from him.

"And no one thought about checking with me before sending packs of vigilantes through my town?" Griffen demanded.

"It wasn't like that. We weren't going to hunt that way. The rumors just sort of blew things up," Tail said.

"We won't be cut out," the young shifter said.

"No one is cutting anyone out, this isn't a game," Tail said.

"You don't speak for us, old man."

Tail bared his teeth in an expression that no one would confuse with a smile. Griffen hadn't seen anything like them before; they were all pointed and jagged, almost like a shark's.

Jay put a restraining hand on his shoulder.

"I do speak for you, at least at this conclave," Jay said.

The other shifter backed down, but the garou stepped up.

"We don't need a fairy to hunt for us."

Some people, Griffen thought, have little survival instinct. Still, he was curious. After his talks with Harrison, he needed some help. He thought he would toss the idea around a bit.

"Really? You can find and track a scent, in a well-traveled public place, without knowing anything but it will cross Slim's and maybe have a little blood spoor on it?" Griffen asked.

"Well . . . we could try," said the garou.

"Werewolves. We can do it," said one of the shifters.

"Oh? What's your specialty?" Griffen said.

"Uh . . . I mean 'we' as a group."

"You think like a group now? Things must have changed drastically this afternoon. Evolution at work, I suppose. Still, I'm curious. Always trying to learn, that's me. What type of shifting do you do?" Griffen said.

"I can change my density," the shifter said, and hung his head, his cheeks flushing red.

"That counts as shape-shifting, does it?"

Griffen realized he was feeling more than a little nasty and indulging the feeling too much. He moved on.

"Still, that doesn't seem to be a lot of help in a murder investigation," Griffen observed.

There were a few moments of awkward silence. Another shifter, Gustov, the one who had demonstrated with Kevin, spoke softly.

"Mr. McCandles, sir. If they want to help, can you . . . no, will you really stop them?"

Griffen stopped his knee-jerk reaction. Not only was he already getting a bad reputation, but that had been the most polite voice so far in the meeting. Griffen wanted to say it sounded like it would cause more trouble than it could possibly solve, but that would anger pretty much everyone. He was really beginning to hate politics.

He looked at the major players and saw reactions similar to his own thinking. None of them knew of a way out of this other than an iron fist. And the sad thing was, whatever the motivations behind it, these were people talking about helping Griffen. In their own backasswards way, they were trying to do good.

"If, and I mean if, I say go ahead with this nonsense, there will be some very clear rules. No public shifting or visible powers. No hassling locals or tourists. No more infighting. And if, God forbid, any of you encounter the police, you will be polite, helpful, fully responsive, and not have this come crashing down on everyone's head."

He looked at the shifters, who were nodding and trying to look harmless. The garou were doing likewise and failing miserably. Griffen sighed and went on.

"Since I know you won't work together well, two groups. Garou and other shifters. No more than four in each group, so you pick your best. Everyone else will carry on as if the conclave were normal, get ready for the party, not butt in. Do you all agree to these rules?"

There was a scattered chorus of affirmative answers. Griffen spoke directly to the leaders next.

"Please tell me, do any of you have a better idea?"

No affirmative answers this time. Tink spoke up, again tentatively.

"I still think Tammy should help one of the groups; if they can find any trail at all, she can help focus on it," Tink said.

"I already said I don't want anything to do with this . . . disgusting murder business," Tammy said, blanching noticeably.

Griffen sighed, and at the risk of her fixating on him again tried to move things along.

"Tammy, please? Let's make this as painless for everyone as possible," Griffen said.

She hesitated long enough, eyes blinking rapidly and looking around the room in a near panic. Every instinct Griffen had said that she would say no.

"Oh, fine! I'll go with the garou."

Apparently his instincts hadn't quite figured out changelings yet.

Almost at once the loudmouth garou spoke up.

"We don't ne—"

"Only a damned fool turns down a fair deal, ya hear? I got any fools in my pack?" Kane stepped in.

"No," Kevin said.

"Den you be nice to da little lady here. You listen what she say. Less you ready to challenge me for my spot?"

The garou shook his head and looked away. Kane looked at Griffen and nodded.

"All right, if everyone could leave except the speakers and

Tail. Go decide who gets into the groups. And I will say this once, I think I have been fair as moderator. Anyone who breaks these rules, answers to me," Griffen said.

The others nodded and filtered out. Tammy was the last to go, and threw one last disgusted look at Griffen before slamming the door. He shook his head and sat tiredly in one of the seats.

"Did anyone else see how to put a lid on that once they got the dumb idea?" Griffen asked.

The others all shook their heads.

"I'm honestly amazed you managed that much. It was far better than I could have managed," Jay said.

"I real sorry it came to dis, but you did good as anyone in your shoes," Kane said.

"This mess wasn't my fault, and it's pushing it to say it was under my duty as moderator. Tink excepted, if it hadn't been for the garou and shifters classifying themselves as separate, I could have left this to you bunch to handle," Griffen said.

"True, and we will watch over the bunch to make sure they abide by your rules and cause no more trouble than the Quarter is used to from nosy tourists," Jay assured him.

The others nodded agreement.

"Well, I think this particular bunch of shifters are more talk then anything else, no offense, Tail and Jay. And just maybe the garou and Tammy working together will actually do some good," Griffen said.

"I think dey just might, Grif," Kane said.

"Yes, and I don't think you have anything to worry about from Tammy. She seems to have cooled off," Tink said.

Griffen sighed, and after a few more minutes found himself on the way back to his apartment. He didn't feel much better for solving the crisis. In fact, he was pretty much where he had been a few hours ago. The slim hope that they might find something, weighed against the possible trouble they represented, just wasn't worth it.

And, just to prove that Fate really did have it in for him tonight, when he made it home he was far too wound up to sleep.

Fifty

It was the night of the masquerade ball, and Griffen simply wasn't in a party mood.

He sat alone in his apartment, fully aware that he was supposed to have been at the ball ten minutes before, helping with the final setup. Griffen had insisted that he should help, even though Estella had assured him everything was covered. That was all before Slim's death.

Griffen had given his word, as unnecessary as it might have been, and now had broken it. Such a small thing. As if anyone really cared whether or not he helped hang a few streamers or carried a punch bowl. Yet he couldn't help thinking about it. If only because it kept him from thinking of heavier issues.

No one had heard anything about the garou since they had taken off that afternoon. It seemed impossible that a pack of wolves on two legs could stomp around such a small area as the Quarter without anyone noticing, but that was exactly what they were doing. Either Griffen had underestimated them, or Tammy was helping with more than just tracking. The changelings were supposed to be good at hiding.

The other shifters had all been seen. They had been poking around the Riverwalk and the Irish pub, and had been wandering around the Canal Place shopping center last he had heard. They seemed harmless, and Griffen doubted they would be any help at all.

Harrison also had apparently dropped off the radar, but then that was normal for the detective. Griffen knew the deadline Harrison had given him was almost up, but didn't know what to do. Their next talk would most likely be happening in a police-station interrogation room.

All in all, Griffen felt helpless. What did he know of murder investigations? Less than he knew about running a conclave, and look at the mess he'd made of that. He couldn't even bring himself to attend the last event.

So he sat. Wearing a well-cut suit that he had last worn to a funeral. He didn't even have a mask. Ridiculous; every other shop in New Orleans had masks. From Chinese knockoffs to local-made pieces so elaborate they were a form of art. Griffen hadn't even bothered looking for one.

There was a knock at his door.

Griffen turned, about to tell whoever it was to leave. His words died as the door opened. As did his thoughts. His brain shut down for a few minutes. Proving that, dragon or not, he was still male.

Mai stood in the doorway, dressed like Griffen had never seen before. The basic style was an oriental dress. An embroidered collar at her throat gave way to an oval cut from the fabric, showing off some of her . . . assets. Slits up to the hip revealed legs Griffen knew weren't as long as they now seemed. What made the effect more startling was that the dress, skintight and hugging every curve it didn't expose, seemed to be made of black, iridescent snakeskin. Scales glistened in sharp contrast with her skin, highlights rippling and shifting with every breath.

A slim matching mask somehow emphasized her eyes, making them seem to smolder. Her hair was piled into an elaborate shape with long, sharp chopsticks protruding, and her nails were nearly three inches long.

Dragon Lady.

Those two words were the first coherent thoughts Griffen

had after her entrance. From the way her eyes darkened and her lips twitched, Griffen knew she had caught his reaction and enjoyed it. He mentally shook himself and got to his feet.

"You were supposed to pick me up," Mai said.

Her voice matched her outfit. Dark, entrancing, dangerous. Griffen had to drop into his poker face. He had never seen her slip into a role like this, and the combined effect was . . . powerful.

"I was?" he asked, honestly puzzled.

"Yes, but you didn't know it," Mai said. "You didn't give any thought at all to bringing a date to the dance, did you?"

Griffen would have smacked himself if he hadn't already stepped up his self-control. Of all the stupid things, and it didn't even occur to him. Of course he had been busy. He didn't have a clue what sort of messages he would have sent showing up to the masquerade ball alone.

He shrugged it off with a laugh. It sounded only a little forced.

"I didn't even remember to get a mask," he said.

"I thought not, lover."

Mai bit her bottom lip, eyes lighting up with what Griffen could only interpret as mischief. Her hand moved slowly, drawing Griffen's eye with it, as she reached through the hole in her dress. Those long, sharp nails actually left the faintest of lines across her skin as they dove beneath the neckline. He was unsurprised, but greatly disappointed, when her fingers came back out. They held a masculine version of her own mask in dark, glittering snakeskin.

Someday, Griffen thought, I'm going to have to worry about just how well she can push my buttons.

"I, uh . . . I don't remember inviting you," Griffen said.

"You would have if you thought of it. I assure you."

"Look, Mai, I'm not even sure I'm . . ."

"Going. I know, lover."

Mai smiled, then laughed. It was a full, throaty laugh. Suddenly, without any perceptible change in posture or attitude, she became her old self. Or at least, the one Griffen knew. Her tone and attitude were back to normal, excited, energetic, playful.

"Oh, that was fun. You are such an easy mark sometimes, Griffen. And the party is going to be fun, too. You have no idea how much I'm looking forward to this!"

Griffen felt his cheeks flush. Easy mark, was he? He was getting ready to tell her to leave when she stepped forward. Dragon Lady attitude or not, she wore that dress well, and he found himself trying to track the play of light along the scales.

"Fun? I can't see how it can be anything but a complete bomb."

"Because you have no idea what to expect. Believe me, you have no idea how rare mixed parties of this scale are. I've only been to two before, and those were much smaller. I think the only reason this fool conclave got started was to have an excuse for the ball at the end of it."

Mai moved up to him, close enough to press against him but stopping just shy of that. She stood up on her tiptoes, half-draping her arms around his neck as she slid the mask onto his face. She leaned her face up, lips close to his, whispering as she tied the mask.

"A little death isn't going to get in the way of that. In fact, if there is any place to go to forget such things, it is there. It's not your dark apartment, all alone except for your brooding."

Despite himself, the flirting was lifting Griffen's spirits.

"You are just saying that because they won't let you in without me," he said.

"They are awfully nervous about party-crashing dragons. Besides it's more fun to crash on the arm of the one man no one is going to argue with. Like going to a film premiere with the director."

She closed the last half inch of distance and kissed him. The scales of the dress felt warm and almost alive under his hands. Her teeth pulled lightly at the bottom of his lip.

"Please?" she said, not quite letting him go.

"Welllll . . ." he said, drawing it out as much as he could.

It was amazing how quick one's mood could change. With the right motivation.

"Besides, aren't you dying to see if your little sister actually shows up with the dragon hunter?" Mai said. "Enemies dancing together in polite society, making small talk in a potentially hostile environment. Won't it be fun to see them watch one another's backs?"

"Somehow I knew you would know about that. And you're right, damn it."

Valerie had been worried about something; maybe George stepped on people's feet literally as well as figuratively.

Mai grinned and slipped out of Griffen's grip. For a moment, she looked like a child who had just gotten the present she wanted. She even took a little spin before taking one of Griffen's hands in both of hers.

"Come on, then. If we leave now, we can be almost perfectly fashionably late," Mai said.

Griffen let himself be drawn out the door, mostly because it was the first chance he had gotten to see the back of her dress. From the back of the collar down, laces crisscrossed over an exposed spine almost to her tailbone. Definitely not a traditional oriental element.

He half realized that he was beginning to look forward to the night.

The other half of him thought that getting his hopes up was probably very unwise.

Fifty-one

Griffen walked into the Conclave Masquerade, and was overwhelmed.

Before his eyes could register details, they were filled with a barrage of colors. As soon as he walked through the doors and into the massive ballroom, he could only stop and stare. Mai, attached at his elbow, picked up on his hesitation immediately. She shifted her posture, framing herself against the backlighting from the doors. A part of him realized what she was doing, that she was making it appear that the two were just pausing, making a more dramatic entrance. That part was thankful, the rest was just taking everything in.

First of all, it was hardly like walking into a ballroom at all. Oh, the features were there: grand chandeliers that looked expensive and impossible to clean, architecturally useless columns along the walls, a sea of marble that made up the dance floor. That was where the similarity stopped, though.

It was like stepping into a forest glade. An unnatural, moonlit forest from someone's dreams. Fog covered the ground, ankle thick, except for the dance floor. It didn't move right, didn't seem to follow the light breezes in the room. Instead, it rolled in shallow waves and thin tendrils that seemed to explore. Moving of their own volition. Every once in a while a small snake of fog would move across the dance floor, almost seeming to twist to avoid the dancers.

Tables rose like stones in the fog. Tablecloths of soft gray and green covered them, looking like moss and rocks. The tables were small, big enough only for three or four people, an obvious attempt to break up the cliques and groups that kept forming all throughout the conclave. The only exceptions were two long tables, one covered in dishes of food and a small wet bar, and the other against the far wall, set so that those sitting at it could see the whole room. Nameplates sat at each place, and Griffen bet that his name would be on one.

The walls had been decorated, changed, with twisting cords or material that might have been rope or might have been live vines. If vines came in pale purples and blues and the occasional scintillating gold. Trees seemed to grow out of the walls, trees of metal and crystal and glass that still somehow seemed alive. The light filtered through the various materials and sent hundreds of small reflections glittering over the walls and fog.

And the light itself came not just from the candles or the chandeliers. Balls of colored light, greens, blues, purples, seemed to dance in midair. These constantly moving orbs cast little in the way of true illumination but enhanced and changed the colors of everything around them. Griffen had no idea what made them, just as he could see no obvious source for the fog, but the combined effect was breathtaking . . . magical.

And all that before he started tracking the individual people.

Griffen was beginning to feel self-conscious, and decidedly underdressed. Some of the people in the crowd made Mai look almost drab. Costuming ranged from simple masks to elaborate, from modern horror to Victorian drag.

A woman Griffen hadn't noticed before was dressed in a Carmen Miranda outfit, except that a straw stuck out of the pineapple hat. As he watched, she took off her hat, took a sip from the straw, and replaced it. She was chatting with a man

in a cloak so large and black that Griffen couldn't see his
hands, much less his face. Nearby, three people dressed as trees
talked, looking like the Forest of No Return at a cocktail
party. Griffen idly wondered if Tammy would be using her
shifting as a part of her costume, but doubted it after the rib-
bing she'd gotten.

Someone dressed up as a twelve-foot robot clomped
through the fog toward the buffet table, and was followed by
a woman dressed as a mechanic with a five-foot-long wrench.
Three people dressed as Abe Lincoln, at least one of them
female, sat together at one of the tables, engaged in a three-
way thumb war. And, of course, a classic at any Halloween
party, no matter how elaborate, one person standing near the
wall, wearing a sheet with holes cut out for the eyes.

For the most part, he couldn't tell who was who or, more
important, what. Which meant that no one was bothering to
group themselves together but mingled freely. Laughter
mixed with music and talk. Griffen smiled and stepped forward, Mai falling into step with him perfectly. The doors
shut behind him.

Perhaps it was the change in his attitude, or maybe the
observational skills that were part of being a dragon. As he
moved into the room proper, he began to see small details
that, anywhere else, he might dismiss as fantastic costuming.
Here he realized what he was seeing: the supernatural, letting its proverbial hair down.

A werewolf, more impressive than any he had seen on the
silver screen, sat at one of the tables, its tail wagging in time
with the music. A demon and angel danced together on the
floor, and though their wings were fake, each was dancing
about three inches above the fog. One of the first people
Griffen actually recognized was one of the "lesser" shifters,
who was dressed as a simple jester in red and yellow. Only his
hands were on fire. No, his hands *were* fire, and he kept arcing
it back and forth between them like a Slinky.

Griffen saw Tail, dressed in full samurai gear except for the face mask. His face was normal, but over a dozen foxtails hung behind him, constantly moving. He chatted with the woman from the shape-shifting demonstration, and from the way she smiled, the relationship was building quickly. She wore an elaborate butterfly mask, high heels, and butterflies. Dozens of them, providing her little more coverage than most bikinis. They flapped gently, and every once in a while one would take off and fly to a different location on her body.

Griffen suspected the butterflies were her, just as the tails were, well, Tail's. No one really seemed to be paying attention to any of this. It was just part of the atmosphere, accepted, normal. Griffen imagined for a moment what his life might have been like if he had known about dragons since he was a child. He could see just how much he would value a night like this.

He was finally realizing just why there was a traditional conclave at all.

Mai smiled at his side.

"Happy Halloween, lover," Mai said.

"First time I've ever really appreciated the holiday," Griffen said.

"Told you, Griffen. This was something not to miss," she said.

"You were right, though I would never have known what I was missing."

"Oh, you would have, eventually. You aren't dumb, lover. Just a little slow sometimes."

Griffen would have objected to that more if she hadn't chosen that moment to pinch him. She moved away before he could retaliate.

"I'm going for punch, and if it isn't already spiked, it will be shortly. You, go, mingle." She paused, glancing around. "Knowing you, I suggest you follow the bouncing ball."

Griffen followed her glance. Sure enough, one of the lights

was hovering a few feet away, bouncing up and down like an eager puppy. He looked back at Mai, only to see her retreating back, and watched that for a bit before turning back to the relatively less distracting magic ball.

As he approached, the orb slowed down its movement, hanging listless and still when he was right next to it. Out of the corner of his eye, he caught the movement of another starting to dance. Again, as he moved toward it, it slowed. Griffen shook his head, not quite believing it, but as the next ball started to dance, he gave up doubt and simply followed.

It wasn't long before he saw the source. Four lights hovered around a group consisting of a zombie and three characters from *Alice in Wonderland*. The zombie, thankfully, looked like a costume, though a movie-quality one. Alice, the Mad Hatter, and the March Hare chatted animatedly with it. The lights hovered around Alice, and as Griffen approached, one floated off to join the others throughout the room, and another one slowly coalesced to take its place.

It was only when he was right next to the group that he realized who Alice was.

"Tink!?" Griffen said.

Tink turned, petticoats ruffling. His face was perfectly straight.

"What, you thought you'd have this many fairies in New Orleans without at least one ending up in drag?" Tink said.

His straight face lasted for another few seconds, before he burst out laughing. The others in the group broke out with him, and Griffen joined them. It felt good to laugh.

On closer inspection, Hobb was playing the March Hare and Robin made a very fetching Mad Hatter. Griffen almost did a double take with the zombie, though. It was Estella, right out of a Romero movie except for a small bag and voodoo doll hanging from her neck.

"You are supposed to dress as something you are not, yes? It was either this, or dress up as a witch," Estella said.

Griffen hadn't put her down for that much of a sense of humor.

She smiled, showing yellowed and blackened teeth, and waved her hand at the ballroom.

"I told you you didn't have to worry. But are you all right? We almost sent someone for you when you were late," she said.

"No need. Someone beat you to the punch," Griffen said.

"No kidding. That was quite an entrance," Tink said.

"She'd beat anyone to the punch. Did you see that dress!" Hobb said.

Robin elbowed him in the ribs, in a playful sort of way.

"What do you think of the party, Griffen?" Robin said.

Griffen took time for one last look around, gathering his thoughts.

"Amazing," he said finally. "I've never seen anything like it."

Estella beamed.

"I told you not to underestimate those other than dragons. Still, you have not shown much of a dragon's attitude during this meeting, even counting various . . . incidents. You have been a fair moderator," Estella said.

Griffen didn't think so but wasn't going to spoil the mood.

"The lights are your doing, Tink?" Griffen asked.

"Yes, we call them will-o'-the-wisps. Very handy little buggers, and not just for mood lighting," Tink said.

"Sure beats pagers and cell phones," Griffen agreed. "But what if someone . . . not with the conclave sees them? What if some average person blunders in?"

Estella laughed.

"Mr. McCandles, who do you think is serving the food and drinks?"

Startled, Griffen realized he had been seeing people in service industry black-and-whites all along but had been too distracted by the fantastic to notice. Now he looked around and saw a few waitstaff walking around with trays of drinks or food, and one behind the buffet table. They each wore a slim black mask around their eyes.

"Relax," Estella said. "They, or anyone else who 'blunders in,' are unlikely to notice anything too unusual. Not only is this New Orleans, but the wiccan and I have worked up a little something together that will fog up their perceptions a bit. Anyone without something magic in their blood will remember nothing more than an elaborate party in the morning."

"Most people who are drawn to this town seem to have some magic in their blood," Tink said.

"Not enough, and so what? Even if they noticed or remembered more, what trouble could it cause?" Estella said.

"On the large scale . . . or the personal scale?" Griffen said.

His tone was a bit strangled, distracted, and the others looked where he was looking. At one of the waitresses, a tray of champagne in her hand, walking toward them. The black mask didn't hide the fire in her eyes, or in her hair.

"Hello, Griffen," Fox Lisa said.

Griffen knew, or at least had been told, that Fox Lisa had a little bit of dragon blood. He didn't know what that meant but had assumed that little to no actual abilities came with such a small amount. He now suspected he was totally wrong.

At the tone of her voice, his four companions all realized they had other places to be and left the two alone. Robin even took Lisa's tray for her, earning her a slight smile and freeing up Fox Lisa's hands.

"So this is what you have been busy with lately," Fox Lisa said, not asked.

Griffen realized at that moment how little he had seen of his occasional lover recently and how much of that had been his own fault. He hadn't given much thought to it until he heard the dry ice that was her tone.

"It's more complicated than it looks," Griffen said.

"I'll say."

She glared, but not at him. Out of the corner of his eyes he saw that one of Tink's will-o'-the-wisps was hovering nearby. Under her scrutiny, the white light was tinged pink and, with an embarrassed-sounding pop, disappeared. Fox Lisa stared at where it had been, and for a moment Griffen thought it would be too much for her. She shrugged it off with a visible effort and turned her attention back to him.

"Moving on, you have a hell of a lot of explaining to do. That just got added to the list."

"And what else is on the list?"

Griffen hadn't seen Mai coming, but she was suddenly behind Fox Lisa, an arm sliding around her waist and long fingernails tapping against her hip. She had slipped back into full Dragon Lady mode.

Fox Lisa actually had to swallow before she spoke.

"Mai, why am I not surprised to find you here?" she said.

"Because you know I turn up at the most . . . interesting . . . places," Mai purred.

Griffen was going to have to look into voice control. Fox Lisa actually shivered, and Griffen now knew she wasn't wearing a bra.

She rallied, though, and stepped away from Mai, turning so she could face them both. She stared at Mai's dress, almost exactly as she had at the will-o'-the-wisp's disappearance, and again her mind almost—but didn't—froze up and snapped.

"Explanations, owed by both of you," Fox Lisa said, then shivered again and moistened her lips. "But . . . later. I . . . I'm working."

"Later, then," Mai said.

She stepped up to Griffen, arm around his waist now but

eyes on Fox Lisa. There was a moment of tension, and Lisa turned and walked off.

Then stopped a few feet away, changed directions, and walked directly toward a large werewolf in torn blue shorts. She grabbed his tail, and before he could react, yanked hard. He yelped, a very realistic and pained sound. Fox Lisa glared at him, and he ducked his head, ears lying flat. She nodded to herself and stomped off.

Most people around them watched her leave and ignored Kane cursing and rubbing his tail.

"That," Mai said dropping her act and sounding full of admiration, "is one tough broad."

"And the two of you have arranged a very tough spot for me later," Griffen said.

"Yes, we did. And a fun spot if you play your cards right. That one is too smart to be kept in the dark anyway," Mai said.

Mai grinned and slipped her arm from his waist to his elbow.

"Come on, you. For this stay in your execution, you owe me a dance!" she said.

Griffen had been dreading this long before Mai ever showed up at his door. He knew about as much about dancing as he did about public speaking. With less practice.

He couldn't decide whether or not this particular dance floor made things better or worse. The dancing seemed to be as eclectic as the costuming. There was a couple waltzing. At least a dozen people going through an elaborate dance that would have fit in at a medieval court. Several people club dancing, including two more of the changelings, Nix and Drake. Apparently, the changelings had decided to dress in a theme: Drake was the Cheshire Cat, and Nix, with the help of a mask on the back of her head, was playing both Tweedledum and Tweedledee, depending on which way she was facing. And Griffen would have put her down for the Mock Turtle.

There was even someone dressed as a knight in full armor, doing what Griffen could only interpret as a very clanky version of the Charleston. And it all seemed to blend together. As surreal as it all was, it all blended together, the music acting as a melting pot. Partners would switch back and forth, those bothering with partners, and seamlessly step into a new style. Griffen didn't have a clue what to try himself.

Mai made the decision for him, by pressing so tightly against him he was sure she didn't have anything under the dress but herself. She started to sway to the music, leading with her body language more than anything else, and he followed. She rested her head against his shoulder, and he felt the soft touch of her lips against the side of his neck.

He began to let himself relax, flowing into the music, the atmosphere, the peculiar magic. Nothing in his life had really prepared him for an evening like this. Especially not the conclave; he would never have imagined the different groups blending together like this. For one night, just for Halloween, it seemed as if the supernatural attendees had found some happiness.

He hadn't had many rewards for this fairly thankless job but was beginning to think this evening might make up for it.

Then the doors burst open violently, shattering the music, and his illusions.

Everybody stopped and stared, and Griffen recognized the pull of powerful glamour. Dragon-style glamour, not whatever the changelings used. It pulled every eye in the room toward the figure of a small woman, dragging the bodies of three unconscious garou by their ankles. She held all three in one hand and, without so much as a grunt of effort, heaved them through the air to land with a thud on the dance floor.

Griffen noticed three things simultaneously. One, that every one of the garou was bruised, bloodied, and probably broken. Two, they were the ones Kane had set out to hunt for Slim's killer.

Three, the small woman had the maddest eyes he had ever seen. Both angry mad and crazy mad. They were like looking into the windows of a building and realizing only after you've seen inside that it was an asylum.

A split second after those observations, he heard a stifled gasp. He saw a brief glimpse of Val, and wondered how he had missed her till now. More important, he wanted to know why she was glaring at the small woman with more anger then he had seen from his sister in a long time.

"All right!" Lizzy screamed, voice cracking through different scales. "Who is the poor dead son of a whore who sent these puppy dogs after me!?"

Things clicked into place. He half turned toward Val, without taking his eyes off the newcomer for a moment.

"Who is that?" Griffen asked.

The tightening of Val's lips and the narrowing of her eyes were answer enough. Griffen knew his sister, knew that beneath the mask of anger was a good deal of fear. He'd ask questions later.

For once, Griffen didn't hesitate. He had taken this job, and whatever this was, he would deal with it. A surge of anger built, fueled by his sister's. He went with his instincts, stepped forward, and said the first thing that came to mind.

"I can handle this."

Fifty-two

Lizzy's laughter filled the ballroom, and all around people flinched. Griffen himself felt a heavy, cold weight in his stomach as the laugh filled his ears. No syllable matched, as if it were a dozen different laughs all fighting to burst free. It wasn't even the raw anger underneath that made it so terrible. Worse than that, something in it pulled at those hearing it, something infectious.

Madness that wanted to spread.

Griffen kept his reactions off his face and took another step forward. The laughter snapped off as Lizzy's eyes narrowed watching him.

"Handle this? You mean handle me! Darling, sweet baby boy, you couldn't handle me—well, not and survive anyway. Though the actual handling could be fun, to come think of it. Hey, I know! Let's ditch this place and go find out; I can always butcher your sister and friends later."

The last traces of fear evaporated under Griffen's anger. His fists clenched, and he felt his skin start to harden into scales. Lizzy smiled, a beaming grin of a happy child. Griffen realized she liked seeing him react, liked pushing his buttons. And realized just as quickly that he couldn't afford the luxury. He got his face under control, though under his skin he could feel the itch of the scales ready to manifest.

Lizzy's smile faded to a small pout as Griffen pulled himself together. She started to stalk in a wide circle around him, broken eyes riveted to him. People moved out of her way, clearing the floor space surrounding them. Though he noticed she circled away from Valerie, putting him between the two. As if reading his thoughts, her eyes flicked over his shoulder to his sister, then back to him. A new smile, sly and cruel, worked across her lips.

"So . . . Griffen McCandles. I've watched you, you know. Not much; you didn't look like much fun, but it was amusing. Watching you scurry about as I sorted things out in my head. Watching you walk with your 'friend' Mai, my my Mai, wasn't she a surprise. I sorted things out . . . things out of sort . . ."

Lizzy's eyes started to glaze, just for a moment, as her train of thought derailed. Griffen couldn't help but tense, almost leaped on her in that instant of distraction, but hesitated, trying to think through all the angles. She snapped back into focus and shouted, loud enough to shake the chandeliers, *"Don't think it, baby boy!"*

More people flinched, a few of the shifters actually falling to their knees clutching their ears. Griffen could practically feel Val's glare from behind him and could just make out a rustle of clothes he thought was her moving closer. Lizzy kept shouting, quieter now but just as emphatic, hands sawing through the air as she gestured, spittle flying from her lips unnoticed as she raved.

"Baby! Hatchling! Both of you are just sooo. Young! And stupid! And you still cause me all these headaches, all this confusion! I should have killed you both, blown up your house, blown up your city, never gotten close enough to have to think!"

She paused, going calm and suddenly serious, rubbing two fingers to her temple.

"It's problems like this that really make me wonder if I am . . . a little off . . . after all."

Griffen stared, without any clue of what to do. Someone that crazy, that confused, and she only wondered if she were a little off? And he had no question that she was very dangerous. Any direct fight, and who knew what damage it would cause. But how could you reason with someone like this? Or even talk them down?

Val made the decision for him.

"I really don't think 'a little' covers it, Lizzy, dear," Val said.

She stepped toward them both, and a little to Griffen's side, though he didn't dare take his eyes off Lizzy to look at her. Looking out of the corner of his eye, he could tell she was angry.

Valerie had come to the party as something out of the Greek pantheon. White dress, not quite a toga, embroidered with gold on the hem and neckline. A wreath of flowers and vines was in her hair. She looked more the part now as she stepped toward the threat of Lizzy. She was a good four inches taller than usual, and so tense she almost trembled.

Yet her voice was calm, quiet. Mocking, yes, but none of the warlike anger he usually expected from his sister in this kind of situation.

"Oh? What would you say, heifer?" Lizzy snapped, angry again.

"I'd say 'crazy,' but then I would have to spend the rest of my life going around to asylums and apologizing to the inmates for the comparison. I think we need a new word for the level of insane you are."

"Ooooh! It's trying to be funny! Everyone, the wonder cow is trying to be witty! Isn't that just great?!"

No one around responded, but Lizzy didn't seem to expect them to. Griffen recognized that look in her eye; they were just . . . backdrop. Unimportant, not worth noticing, and probably disposable.

"That's right, keep with the size jokes. Not all of us need

magic to look skinny. Or is it just bulimia?" Val said, her mocking tone now mixed with pity.

Lizzy's face contorted in rage, and for just a split second Griffen saw more than the package she presented. The bones that pressed against her skin seemed wrong, and for just a moment all her teeth seemed pointed. Then that second was gone, and she merely looked pissed.

"You know, now that I see you up close, not much of a resemblance between you two. Brother and sister? Naw . . . no chance. Mama must have been doin' the mailman."

A man emerged from the crowd, dressed as Zorro, complete with sword. Val looked at him sharply, and that drew Lizzy's attention to him. When he spoke, Griffen just barely recognized his voice.

"You really shouldn't confuse the McCandleses with your own family, young lady," George said.

"Wha . . . who are you? Who is this?! Why is he talking to Lizzy?" Lizzy shouted, head jerking back and forth between him, Griffen, and Valerie.

More important than "who," why *is he speaking?* Griffen thought. His mind was still in crisis mode, trying to make sense of what was in front of him, trying to find a plan. And at that instant he doubted that George would involve himself in this fight without reason, or a plan of his own. Looking at Lizzy, a lightning-bolt idea flared in Griffen's mind.

Distraction.

"Did you want something . . . Lizzy is it? Come here for some reason?" Griffen said in his calmest, most reasonable voice.

He hoped she didn't notice the approving glimmer in George's eye.

"Or did you just come for the party? Is one of these gentleman on the floor your date?" George said.

And moved a little more, so that Lizzy was now almost directly between him and Griffen, with Val somewhere off to the side. Lizzy tried to divide her attention between the three, actually shifting her feet a little uncertainly.

Val also glanced at George and Griffen, and an expression of understanding crossed her face, quickly followed by an expression Griffen hoped never to see again. Valerie suddenly looked like a cat with a new mouse.

But it wasn't Val who threw in the next volley; to Griffen's surprise, Tink appeared almost directly behind Lizzy.

"They stocked some really good wine, can I get you a glass?" he said, beaming with friendly innocence.

She whirled at him, fingers suddenly tipped with long claws. It was a surprised, automatic action, and he easily dodged, but it left her back to both Val and Griffen, who took another step toward her. She turned back almost at once but didn't seem to notice they were closer.

"No wine! No party! I want . . . Shit, what I want is . . . I mean," she stammered.

And all across the room others caught on.

Kane moved toward the fallen loup garou, now several feet away from Lizzy, but she tracked him anyway. He waved her off, kneeling by a garou and pressing an ear to his chest.

"I jus' gonna check on my boys, you no mind me none, miss. We settle up just whenever you ready," he said.

"I was just trying to offer wine," Tink said, his voice making it clear that he was enjoying this, "or maybe you'd rather a canapé?"

All around the room, conversations started up again, loudly. Not many, but enough to turn the ballroom into a swirl of echoes and voices. All eyes stayed on Lizzy, but those quick enough to see what was going on and what was being tried spoke up.

Of all the things Griffen had expected from those attending the conclave, he would never have imagined to see bravery.

And teamwork.

Estella was the next to push her way forward, looking over Lizzy as disapprovingly as one could while dressed as a zombie.

"You really should have dressed better, my dear. This is a formal occasion," she said.

"That's right, do you have an invite?" George asked.

"Do you?!" several near George said to him at once, then almost as one turned to each other and repeated the question. "Do you?!"

The conversation grew; somewhere, someone turned up the music. Every time Lizzy opened her mouth to respond to someone, another would speak up and cut her off. She jerked her attention around the room, mouth half-open and eyes bulging.

"I really must insist as moderator I know your business here, before we get back to festivities," Griffen said.

"I'm sure we could find a nice clown mask for you," Val said. "Or maybe something in red and white; you can go as a very short barber's pole."

"Oh, I have a spare mask," a random voice called from the crowd.

"Oh, I know what you want! Steak tartare," Tink said triumphantly.

"All my boys, dey is just fine, but you gonna owe them an apology. Maybe a dance?" Kane spoke up.

The fog swirled over the ground, Tink's will-o'-the-wisps danced brightly, voices surged in volume like a wave as people made demands on Lizzy. As surreal as the setting and the moment seemed to Griffen, he could only imagine the weight of it on a madwoman.

Lizzy snapped.

"Make the voices stop!"

The volume of the scream, and the force of glamour that rolled off her in her anger subdued the room. Something shattered high above, and Griffen realized it was some of the crystals from the chandeliers. Shards rained down, but few paid any attention. Lizzy was rocking back and forth, arms wrapped about herself tightly. And Griffen was shocked to see that a shard score across her cheek, leaving a line of blood. Those that hit him bounced.

Val spoke in the silence, and her tone was cold and filled with what Griffen could only think of as hate.

"I just figured it out, Lizzy, why me and Nathaniel bother you so. You must just be jealous," Val said.

"Jealous?" Lizzy said.

Her voice was so small and lost that Griffen regretted the whole thing. He looked to Val, and through her anger he saw something similar. She had words she had been about to say, and no longer could stomach saying them.

George must have seen it, too, for he spoke up. Griffen later convinced himself that whatever Val had been thinking, it had been nothing so cruel.

"No worries," George said. "I'm sure the twisted sicko prefers his sister in bed to anyone else."

It hung in the air, and Val glared at her "date" for the evening but picked up the line.

"I suppose so. You're safe . . . Elizabeth," Val said.

Fifty-three

Lizzy launched herself at Valerie, and whatever she was now, it wasn't human. Limbs too long, fingers too long, too many joints everywhere. She moved so fast Griffen couldn't see much more except for pale, iridescent scales and long fangs. He moved into the rush, intent on getting to her before she could get to his sister, his body already shifting.

And jerked to the side as something heavy hit him at the base of his neck and shoulder, sending him crashing to the floor.

Valerie, nearly twice as tall as she was usually, met Lizzy's rush. She spared Griffen only one glance before twisting and throwing Lizzy through the air with her own momentum. Lizzy landed on the buffet table, turning it into a shower of splinters and hors d'oeuvres. Valerie, facing Lizzy as she quickly rose, braced herself.

"Thanks, Big Brother, but I told you. This is my fight," Valerie said.

Only then did he realize that she had hit him.

Lizzy moved just as fast as before, but low to the ground, hitting Valerie around the knees and lifting her into the air. Valerie brought her elbows down on Lizzy's back and struggled to kick free. Lizzy seemed to be growing as well, and as the two titans struggled, Griffen got his first look at her.

Long limbs, long neck. Face human but alien at the same time. Just a hint of reptile in the shape of it, and glittering scales reflecting the colorful lights of what had been a party till her entrance.

She looked nothing like any dragon Griffen had ever imagined, despite a long tail and short, sharp-looking wings. Val in the toga that now rode her enlarged form like a miniskirt looked like a titan as the monster Lizzy grabbed her, wrapped around her. Odd details registered as they struggled, the tail split into two toward the end, and her hair was no longer hair but long tendrils of scaly material that seemed razor-sharp.

The hair stabbed at Valerie's belly, and he listened to his sister scream.

Griffen got to his feet and almost fell again. Dizziness threatened to blacken his vision. The base of the neck isn't a good spot for permanent damage, not with a fist, but for short-term disorientation it was very effective. He still couldn't believe she had hit him, but he was too worried to be angry.

Valerie grabbed Lizzy by that odd, living hair and her jaw and twisted. There was a snap, and Lizzy went limp.

Valerie backed away, hands going to her belly, eyes wide as Lizzy's limp form started to shrink back in on itself. Going human again.

"Don't stop!" George called out from the crowd.

Lizzy's head jerked up, and the whole room could hear the crackle of bone as she threw it back and laughed, and kept on shrinking.

Val shouted in anger as she realized what was happening, and dove for Lizzy, but by the time she had reacted, the other woman was so small that the fog that still covered the floor now covered her. Val missed a grab and somehow tripped. The ten-foot-tall woman fell, sending another table flying and fog boiling up like a slow-motion explosion.

There was no sign of Lizzy.

George was next to Griffen in a moment and putting a steadying arm under his arm.

"Griffen, she can't stop. You must help her. This is beyond her!" George said.

"You egged this on!" Griffen accused.

"I had to, it was the only way. You or Valerie, a broken neck would stop you. Not this one. You have to hit her and hit her until she is unable to repair anything at all."

Griffen snarled, waving his hand.

"She's gone now!"

"No, she's not. Not her. She won't stop now till everyone here is dead."

"Too right!" Lizzy shouted.

She appeared behind Val, and unless she could teleport, she had to have gone from a few inches to her full height in an eyeblink. She swung both hands like a hammer and slammed them into Valerie's shoulder. Val yelled and turned, only to get the upswing of both fists under her chin. This time Val sailed through the air and landed in the crowd.

And Lizzy, laughing her mad laugh, took two steps to the nearest person, broke his arm, and threw him at Valerie just as she was getting her feet back.

"Thanks for the idea, El Zero. You are all dead. You were all dead the day you decided to bother me!"

Up till now, the group hadn't panicked. Griffen hadn't noticed that while his sister was in a fight for her life, but now it struck him all at once. Any other group of people would have been screaming at the fist sign of violence, running around like sheep. The conclave members had kept their heads till now, if only because the sight of two dragons battling head to head had most too shocked to move.

Now everyone was in motion.

Few panicked as most would, screaming or running about, though there were some.

Several, like Kane and Tail, stepped toward the fray. But braced as they were, something in their posture told Griffen they intended to go down fighting but knew they were going down.

The changelings exchanged a glance, and vanished.

Among the screams and shouts, Griffen could hear chanting. The vodoun and other human practitioners casting . . . something. He didn't know and didn't care what.

He was pushing through the people roughly, heedless of any damage he might do, intent on getting to Lizzy.

Val scrambled to her feet, but he knew he would reach Lizzy first this time.

But someone was already there, Lowell, and two other vampires. Whether they had just been close, or had come close to act, they leaned toward Lizzy, and Griffen could *see* them drinking her energy. A swirl of air, a press of heat, a taste of madness spread from her to them, and the strength of it had her down on one knee, shaking.

"Vampires . . . Dragons hanging out with . . . vampires?!" Lizzy said.

"Didn't do your homework, did you? Ahhh . . . such despairing madness," Lowell said, and for the first time he looked dangerous.

His eyes were a dark, smoky red. No other physical changes showed, but his shadow seemed to boil, as alive and moving as the fog on the floor.

Lizzy snarled and picked up a piece of debris from the fight, a table leg. She lunged forward and slammed it into Lowell's chest. Lowell vanished.

The vampires' connection with her snapped almost audibly, but Val was there by now, and rammed into Lizzy. She hit her hard and fast, sending her back to her knees, then to the floor. She straddled Lizzy and struck down with all her weight behind her fist.

And Lizzy moved as if her bones were liquid. Val's fist cracked the marble floor, and Lizzy kicked her knees out from under her. There was a brief struggle, and their positions were reversed.

Lizzy straddled Val from behind and took Val's head in her hands.

And Griffen yanked her off by her throat. His hand was a claw, his arm covered in thick scales. He could feel his tail thrashing behind him. Lizzy's feet dangled high above the ground, kicking.

It had worked on George, but George wasn't a dragon. Lizzy pried Griffen's fingers free with strength that should have been impossible. She held his wrist in her hands, put a foot to his chest, and kicked, sending him tripping over his sister and flying through the air herself.

She landed gracefully several feet away and actually bowed.

"Oh, this is fun! None of you can stop me, no one can ever stop me! Screw it all, this is too much fun to stop! First one to die loses!"

Lizzy laughed, and for just a moment Griffen felt despair. It actually looked as if even he and Val couldn't stop this lunatic dragon.

Then again, it wasn't just Val and him.

"I can stop you."

Lizzy turned, and so did everyone else. There was no one there, just a vague disturbance of the air. Then Hobb stood there, dropping whatever glamour the fey used to hide. Robin appeared as well, several feet behind him, fear plain on her face.

"You?! *You?!* How do you think you can stop Lizzy?"

"With this," Hobb said.

He held up a small pocketknife.

Griffen expected her to laugh, she should have laughed. Instead, she looked insulted. Claws grew again at the ends of her fingers, and Griffen knew with a certainty the changeling had just committed suicide.

"With that, you would take a dragon with a letter opener? You are too stupid to live," said Lizzy.

"Well, you would know all about that," Hobb said.

He flicked open the blade, a plain, straight blade. He closed his eyes for a moment and drew the blade against his knuckles.

Blood welled over his fingers, and he clenched his hand into a fist.

Lizzy looked uncertain; she seemed fascinated by the dripping blood.

"What's that for?"

"This."

Hobb stepped forward, his face resolute and grim, and slammed his fist as hard as he could into her mouth. She didn't move, didn't bother blocking, just let him hit her.

It didn't even move her head back, didn't even split her lip. All the blood on her face was his. She ran a finger over her lips and sucked idly at the crimson smear.

"Well, that was cute, now if you don't mind I'd like to kill you and get on with my—"

Lizzy took a dizzy step backward and almost fell over.

"What did you—" she started to say, and almost fell again.

"Ms. Valerie, I would hit her now. I don't know how long it will last with a dragon." Hobb called out, stepping away from the staggering Lizzy.

Val didn't question, she approached cautiously, just in case it was another act. She stopped as George called out to her.

"Start big, work up from there."

He drew his sword, and it was obviously not a costume foil. He tossed it to her, and she plucked it from the air, staring at the still-dizzy dragon. Griffen wondered what good a sword was.

"Kill . . . must . . . kill," Lizzy sputtered.

"Must I?" Val said.

She shoved the blade through Lizzy's right eye.

Lizzy screamed and ripped the sword from Val's hand, throwing it away. She struck out again, clumsily, and Val blocked it easily. Her next hit sent Lizzy to the ground, and this time Valerie didn't hesitate, didn't stop. At first it was still a fight, then just a beating, all of Val's rage and frustration given a way to vent itself.

The crowd had gone still when Hobb had acted and went silent now. No one knew what to say.

Griffen saw a tear on his sister's cheek, and even in the quiet only his acute hearing heard her whisper, "I suppose I must."

Griffen saw her dig her hands around Lizzy's throat. The other dragon was barely conscious, and blood flowed from more than just the ruined eye. Val started to squeeze.

"Val, stop, don't do it!"

Val didn't stop, but tears still flowed over her face.

"She won't stop, Griffen. You have seen it. What other way?!"

"We will find one. You don't have to be . . . like her."

"I have to protect . . . everyone," Val said.

"Actually . . . that's more my job description."

Griffen usually was tough to surprise, but the shocks he had received in the last few minutes had burned out his resistance. He stood with his mouth hanging. He knew that voice, and of all the people he did not expect tonight, this one was more surprising than Lizzy.

He was dressed as a ghost, if you can call a sheet with holes in it a costume. Everyone was pretty much looking puzzled at him, no one but Griffen and maybe Mai or Val recognizing just the voice. Few even recognized him when he pulled the sheet off, though most stiffened when they saw the revolver in his hand.

Detective Harrison looked happier than Griffen could remember seeing him ever before. A vice detective must always enjoy coming out from undercover.

"Ms. Valerie, most of what I've seen tonight has been self-defense. You don't want to make my life hell by having to drag a pretty lady like you in for murder, do you?" Harrison said.

Val stared as openly as Griffen. Harrison idly waved with the revolver. Despite how little that must have meant to her just then, Griffen was relieved when his sister released Lizzy's throat and stood up.

Lizzy smiled, her sunny smile, ruined by several broken teeth.

"Din' wan kill you anyway . . ." she said hoarsely, blood bubbling from her lips. "Like . . . to be . . .'untie Lizzy."

With that, she smiled brighter, and her remaining eye rolled up into her head. She passed out, though she kept breathing, ragged and slow.

Griffen filed what she'd said away for later.

"Detective Harrison—" Griffen started.

"Shove it, McCandles. You have a hell of a lot of explaining to do."

Harrison looked around the room, and for a second his eyes seemed haunted. Even before the fight, he had to have seen many things that night, too many things.

"Would this even hurt you?" Harrison asked, pointing his piece at Griffen.

"Are we going to find out?" Griffen said.

The two locked eyes, and for a long moment it looked as if the answer was yes. Griffen saw several people shifting behind Harrison. They had helped him with a dragon; they wouldn't hesitate over a human cop.

Harrison shook his head and put the piece in his holster.

"No. I've got my murderer. You are off the hook on the Slim case."

"What makes you think she is the murderer?" Griffen said, confused.

People started all around the room. Apparently, everyone had pretty much come to the same conclusion as Harrison. Lizzy was obviously insane, and violent, and a whole lot of other things that would make her suspect number one in any murder investigation.

But Griffen hadn't once thought to connect her to Slim, and now wasn't sure why.

He looked around the damage of the room. The broken furniture. The wounded guests. Lizzy's own trashed and bloodied body. The loup garou she had dragged in.

"What do you mean? Of course she's a murderer!"

"Probably . . ." Griffen said distractedly.

He was still running on adrenaline, but now he wasn't consumed with his fear and anger. He was thinking clearly, thinking fast. The loup garou . . .

"A murderer probably. But what makes you think she's *your* murderer?" Griffen asked.

"Look, McCandles, if you are jerking me around again . . ."

Griffen tuned out the detective for a moment. A body. The search parties. Lizzy.

A wooden stake.

"Tammy," Griffen said quietly.

"What?" Val asked, still standing over Lizzy, still on guard.

"Tammy isn't here . . . She was hunting with the garou. Why wouldn't she be with them?"

"Maybe Lizzy killed . . ." Val said.

The doors to the ballroom burst open for the second time tonight. Déjà vu washed over most of those sensitive to such things. This time the shifters dragged in a woman, instead of the other way around. The lesser shifters, dragging an enraged Tammy.

Fifty-four

"**If** one more person pops out of nowhere, I'm testing whether this gun does any good or not," Harrison growled.

Griffen was too busy watching the young shifters drag a struggling Tammy into the ballroom. Someone toward the back of the crowd had the intelligence to shut the doors behind them, but Griffen was too focused to quite notice who. Tammy's otherwise-pretty face was twisted ugly with fury, tears of frustration on her cheeks. She cursed with shocking skill as her captors pulled her toward Griffen.

Her eyes locked onto Griffen's, and she spat at him. It didn't have the distance to score.

"Tell your scum-sucking lackeys to let me go!" she shrieked.

Griffen ignored her, not bothering even to argue the term "lackeys." He turned back to Harrison, whose eyes were a little too wide, and jaw a little too clenched.

"You were saying, Detective. Why do you think Lizzy here killed Slim?"

"Are you kidding me, McCandles? I don't know who this is or what is going on now, but I just watched 'Lizzy' there stake a guy!"

Griffen's heart sank and twisted, stomach turning. In the middle of action, he had been so concerned for his sister that he had tucked Lowell's death into the back of his mind. Now it all hit him in a rush, Lizzy slamming a piece of table into his chest. Griffen turned to look for the body, bracing himself and holding as firmly as possible to his outwardly calm face.

And lost it completely when he heard Lowell's voice from the crowd.

"But Slim was not a vampire," Lowell said.

Griffen, and most of the crowd, stared in shock at Lowell. He was lounging at one of the still-standing tables, sipping a drink, and with a good six inches of wood protruding from his chest. The other vampires sat with him, looking relaxed. There was a certain gleam in their eyes, a lazy smile on their faces that one gets after a very good meal or a good time in bed.

Once he had the room's attention, Lowell put down his drink and drew the impromptu stake out of his heart. He winced slightly, and laid it on the table. Oddly, no blood flowed from the wound, but the stake was covered in it.

"You people and your analogies and superstitions," he said, taking another sip from his drink. "Sure the shock of impact can break a deep feed, but shove a half a foot of anything into me anywhere, and you'll get the same reaction. It would take a hell of a lot more than a bit of wood to do in a vampire, especially after a meal like that!"

Griffen couldn't help but smile, relief filling him. All this time he had heard that a vampire fed off emotion and energy, and hadn't once bothered to think of what benefits they got in return. He looked back at Harrison, and the smile faded as quickly as it had formed.

Harrison had his piece back in his hand, though pointing safely at the floor. His left eye had begun to tick.

"Vampire?" Harrison asked softly.

"Yes," Griffen said, as plainly and as gently as possible. Like a man talking to someone standing on a window ledge and wearing very slippery shoes.

"He is a . . ."

"Yes."

"And are you?"

"No."

"Then what . . ."

Harrison's eyes clouded over for a moment. Griffen suspected he was thinking back to one of their early conversations. And, of course, Griffen had shifted at least once in the fight, maybe more. He was always a little hazy on just how much he shifted, and not once had he had a convenient mirror to tell him exactly what he looked like.

Hopefully nothing like Lizzy.

"Dragon."

Harrison shook his head hard, yanking himself back to the present. His eyes were back in focus. Cop eyes, cold, acute, guarded. The left one still twitched a bit around the edges, but he was picking up steam again.

"Right, dragon. Got it," Harrison said. "I can deal with that . . . later. What I can't quite get my head around is that you are trying to tell me that, despite having a violent lunatic knocked out practically at my feet, I'm looking for another psycho running around my goddamned town, shoving stakes into people's hearts!?"

Griffen nodded, the adrenaline rush fading fully now. A wave of sadness filled him, followed by an almost crushing press of exhaustion. Griffen turned toward Tammy, who had gone still in the shifters' grips.

"One who didn't leave a murder weapon. Or throw it in the river, because it wasn't a weapon exactly. She did it by hand . . . or at least limb," Griffen said.

"And it took the big bad dragon this long to figure it out," Tammy said.

The arrogance and smugness in her voice was just as ugly as her fury. Griffen took a step forward, and took a tight hold on himself. It wasn't his way to hit a woman, much less one someone else was holding. But the temptation was there.

"Why, Tammy? What did Slim ever do to you?" Griffen said.

"Nothing, nothing at all. It wasn't about *him*. It was about you! Making you hurt because you hurt me, and making you look like the shit you are in front of these idiots who worship you because you are a dragon."

Tink stepped out of the crowd and up to Tammy. The changeling spokesman had been gentle, coolheaded, serene throughout the entire conclave. One of the biggest helps, in many small ways, to Griffen in his role of moderator.

When he struck the back of his hand across Tammy's jaw, it was a cold, calculated gesture. The sound of it reverberated through the ballroom, and when he spoke, his anger was as cold and harsh as a blizzard.

"You little hypocrite! If he wasn't a dragon, you wouldn't have given him a second glance. You killed a man who had given you no cause, out of spite?" Tink said.

"Tail or the other shifters would have been too hard, they might have healed. Slim was . . . vulnerable. Human. And one of the scale bag's biggest supporters," Tammy said.

She shrugged as best she could with two other men holding her arms.

"It sounded like a good idea at the time," she added. She looked at Harrison, then at Griffen. "The human police will never prove anything. And Griffen won't do anything, not to me. Will you?"

She pursed her lips and took a half step, hips cocked and small breasts pressed against her shirt. Her voice dropped several registers, still sounding girlish but also husky and wanton. The whole act disgusted Griffen.

"I would never have imagined you so cruel, so manipulative, Tammy. Your bubbly, enthusiastic self is one hell of an act," Griffen said.

"Oh, but it's not an act; neither is this. I'm fey, I change with the winds."

Tink nodded and sighed.

"That is an aspect of all changelings, but Tammy more than most. I expected the winds to blow her despair away, not to push her into . . . this," Tink said.

Which made a disturbing sense to Griffen. He had seen the mutability of the changeling moods, and it was only one step past that to personality. And the shifts would be all the more dangerous than, say, the mood swings of someone like Lizzy. Where Lizzy was obviously broken, the changelings were just responding to what was natural to them. Making them subtle, deadly.

Griffen felt himself feeling in a very small way grateful that things hadn't been much, much worse.

"And when I asked you to help the investigation?" Griffen asked.

"The nerve! Asking me to help you, when you didn't want me, want to help me."

A tear welled up in the corner of Tammy's eye and she bit into her bottom lip.

"I did help you, Tammy," Griffen said.

"Humph. Not enough! So I scried about for a big, nasty-looking power that looked unconnected to the conclave, and led the garou to it. Figured while they were getting the tar beat out of them, I could skip town."

Griffen nodded, having figured out that much. What he couldn't figure out was how the other shifters had caught her. The only possibility seemed to be . . .

"You were following the garou, figuring that they were better trackers after all but that you might be able to beat them back to me with any information they found?" Griffen said to the lesser shifters.

There were some embarrassed glances about, and one of those who wasn't holding Tammy at the time nodded. In other circumstances, Griffen might have smiled at how the young man blushed.

"Not all of us, just one, me, keeping tabs on them. I saw Tammy break away from them as they went into a building, and a few seconds later the sound of fighting. I called the others and decided to follow Tammy. When she caught us, she tried to shove her fingers through my skull, and that kind of clinched the whole thing for us."

Griffen looked through the crowd for Jay, Tail, and Kane. The various representatives of the shifters gave embarrassed looks and shrugs back. Silently, he agreed with them; there were other things that took precedence just now.

"You are all missing something very important," Harrison said.

The crowd turned its attention to him, and, one-handed, he drew a cigarette and lit it, taking a long drag. The other hand still held his firearm, but it was almost as if he had forgotten it was there.

"I don't know what you all are, or why you are all here. But I know perps and murderers. I can buy this kid doing something like this, but not thinking it up. You said, 'sounded like a good idea at the time,' but you said it oddly. So I have to ask—who did you hear it from?"

Griffen played back the conversation in his head. Harrison was right. Tammy's tone had tightened just a bit, her eyes glancing away for just a moment. She hadn't come up with the scheme. Someone had played her like a violin.

At the moment she just glared at the cop and clenched her jaw. It was clear she wasn't going to answer.

Tink, who no one seemed to pay attention to till he moved, slapped her again.

"Answer," he said, and this time Griffen could practically feel a chill breeze off his words.

"He's wrong; it was my idea!"

"Bullshit. Maybe your impulse, but you never have been one for planning," Tink said.

"It was just a guy in a bar, pointed out I couldn't take

Griffen, or Tail, or anyone else I was really mad at. Suggested who I might get at."

"What guy?" Griffen said.

"Why should I help you?!" Tammy spat, and struggled again in the shifters' hands.

Tink raised his hand, and Tammy subsided.

"It was just a guy, tall, dark hair. No smell of serious power on him. Said he worked for a dragon. Someone who didn't want your life to be all roses. Never said more," Tammy said.

It was Valerie who spoke up next, a handful of words that expressed all the frustration Griffen was suddenly feeling.

"Well, *that* doesn't narrow it down much," she said.

Griffen agreed, the list was long in his head. Stoner he hadn't heard anything from in a while. Flynn he had begun to mistrust. It was the kind of indirect move that could be the style of Melinda, or even George if Tammy had been wrong about the dragon part.

For that matter, where had Mai gone to when Lizzy appeared?

And now he had no idea what to do. Tammy was half-right when she said he wouldn't punish her. He didn't really know how.

Harrison was pulling a pair of handcuffs out.

"Right, that's enough for here. I will get more out of her behind bars. Will these hold her?"

"Links of iron? Oh yes. But you aren't taking her with you," Tink said.

And with those simple words the tension level in the room skyrocketed once more. The fairy, still dressed like Alice just out of the looking glass, squared off with the detective, his sheet of a costume lying forgotten on the floor somewhere.

"She is under arrest," Harrison said.

"Oh? You think you will get her to sign a confession? Think you can prove anything she has said? Hell, if you have a wire on you, I'll bet you your pension it's fried and with nothing usable on it," Tink said.

"You are just going to let a murderer go free?" Harrison shouted.

"No, we will take her, and punish her. She was our responsibility; it is a matter of honor that one of ours who violated this conclave be dealt with by our hand," Tink said.

Griffen spoke up, feeling the weight of his responsibilities.

"And just what 'punishment' do you have in mind, Tink?"

"Death would seem appropriate, or the stripping of her glamour. Or we could just force her form into something else. Does this hotel need a new potted plant?" Tink asked.

"I'm not sure I can let you do that. Another murder won't erase the first, and I am responsible for this conclave and any decisions of this magnitude," Griffen said.

"Decisions between the groups perhaps; this is between us changelings."

"It's vigilantism, and I won't tolerate it," Harrison said, outshouting the other two.

George moved, and something about the swirl of his cape drew eyes all around the room. He bent next to Lizzy, glancing sidelong at Val, and picked up his fallen sword. The room watched as he wiped it off on a table napkin and slid it into its sheath.

"Murderer aside, may I ask just what you plan to report about all this?" George asked.

"That's evidence, and self-defense for the brawl. I don't think anyone needs to see jail time for it. But don't push me. You were a chief agitator, and, at very least, I could drag you in for aiding and abetting."

George smiled.

"No, you can't."

He turned, took Val's hand, and kissed it. She was too tired and shocked to pull it away. "Thank you for a lovely night." He stood and vanished.

"Show-off," Valerie muttered.

Harrison stared at where he had been and turned back to Tink and Tammy. Griffen could tell some of his resolve had been eaten away.

"She has to go in. This must be settled by due process," Harrison said.

"Due process, yes, but not yours. This is outside your law," Tink said.

"No, nothing is outside the law."

Griffen fought down a clever remark, but it was a funny thing to hear from a vice detective. The room was beginning to fill with life again, people milling about. This was good and fascinating entertainment, but things were relaxing, with the immediate danger well past.

There was a soft sigh behind him, one he recognized. He spoke softly, under his breath, as the two argued.

"What took you so long, Rose?" he said.

"Wrong kind of magic flaring up, things have only just settled down enough for my sort," she said.

"Did you know how much of a mess you were pulling me into?"

"Would you be happier if I said yes or no? I only wanted what's best for the conclave," Rose said.

"And what's best, out of this mess?"

Griffen waved his hand at the two men still arguing. Tammy had slumped in her captors' grips, defeated. Tears running down her face. The shifters holding her kept looking about, not sure what to do next.

"I am glad you asked, but you won't like the answer."

Rose cleared her throat loudly enough to draw attention. A few of the voodoo practitioners gasped, including Estella. Rose walked through the crowd, careful not to brush against anyone, though most people moved back out of her way, even those who didn't know who she was.

Estella's voice was strangled.

"Rose?"

"Shh, I know you have questions, but you do fine without my answers. Besides, I promised your mother I would let you go your own way," Rose said, and walked past the high priestess.

Tink was staring at Rose, something in his posture telling Griffen the changeling knew damn well what this was, if not who. Harrison likewise stood captivated, though Griffen wasn't sure why.

"Long time, no see, David," Rose said with a sly smile, looking at Harrison.

Griffen was tired of being shocked that night, but he was once more. He had never once caught Harrison's full name.

"Rose . . ." Harrison said, and his voice had the unmistakable tones of someone talking to an old love.

She smiled and turned away from him, stepping up to Tammy.

"I'm afraid that you will be coming with me, my dear. It is best for everyone," Rose said.

She leaned in, and brushed her lips against Tammy's forehead. The fey girl's eyes widened, then closed, and her breath went out in a long sigh.

Then she slumped, a deadweight in the shifters' hands.

Harrison's hands trembled as he pointed his gun at Rose. Griffen stood rigid, no question in his mind what Rose had just done. He was appalled and relieved and terrified all at once, and hated having to be in this position.

"What did you do?" Harrison said.

"What I had to," Rose said.

"Don't make me . . ."

"What? Shoot me? Oh, David, I am so glad to see you haven't lost your sense of humor."

Rose moved into him, and the gun passed through her body as if it weren't there. She smiled, and brushed a barely tangible hand over Harrison's cheek. For just a moment, Griffen could see a vague, coltish outline standing behind Rose. Tammy's wide eyes looked at him, even though he could see right through her.

Then both ghosts vanished, and the shifters lowered the body to the floor.

There was a long silence.

"McCandles," Harrison said.

"Yes, Detective?"

"I just remembered something."

"What would that be, Detective?" Griffen asked.

"I'm a fucking vice cop. None of this shit is my problem."

With that, Harrison holstered his pistol and looked around the room.

"Far as I'm concerned, I was never here. I suggest you find the psycho Lizzy a nice, small clinic where they might not file police reports. You decide what to do about Tammy, but I'd call it in."

He paused to look down at the body, which looked like that of a coltish young woman in her early teens.

"Looks like heart failure. Natural, happens all the time," he said.

He glared momentarily at Griffen, in a clear message that said "but we will be talking about all of this, after I've had a few days, and probably a few drinks." Then he walked out of the ballroom.

Tink shook his head and muttered half to himself, half for Griffen.

"Good man, stubborn, but good. Don't worry. We won't have to put him on a spot. Her body will fade in three days."

Griffen blinked at him but didn't have room to doubt him.

Griffen looked around the room. The decorations had been trashed. There were signs of blood and debris from the fighting. Lowell was still sipping his drink, and the floor contained one corpse, four unconscious werewolves, and a still-bleeding dragon.

Kane spoke up, his accent thick.

"Well now, dat sure was one helluva party! Not no bad conclave either, when all is tol' and done."

Griffen did something he wouldn't have thought possible on a night like this.

He smiled.

Fifty-five

It was the night after the masked ball.

Valerie sat alone in the courtyard of the complex. She was always slightly amazed by being able to see so many stars from what was essentially the heart of a major city. The skies always seemed to glitter in the French Quarter if one looked past the neon of Bourbon Street.

It had been a long while since she had taken the time simply to enjoy that. Her job was hardly demanding; she could change a beer keg or unload boxes faster and better than any of the men at the bar. Still, it seemed when she got home there was always some major or minor crisis that drew everyone's attention. A part of her was grateful for that. After all, it distracted her from her own worries.

It was nice, though, to take a few minutes of solitude, with nobody else intruding on her thoughts. It didn't last as long as she liked. The gate opened and closed noisily, stirring her from her thoughts. Despite a bit of irritation at the interruption, there was a small smile on her face as she saw her brother approaching. Some company was always welcome.

"Hey, Big Brother, it's barely after midnight. What's the matter, you sick?"

"Just didn't feel like drinking. Shocking, isn't it?" Griffen said.

"Very. What's the matter? No female companionship to stroke your . . . ego?"

"Wasn't really what was getting to me. I've spent the day wrapping up the conclave. Most everyone's left town, or at least gone back to their own parts of it. Though I'm afraid to say a few will be back."

"Yeah, but some of them are okay. I think there is a good chance of Robin and Hobb coming down here to settle," Valerie said.

"I wouldn't know . . . None of the changelings wanted to see me today. Tink just left a voice mail on my phone. Thanking me for all my courtesy and assuring me none of this was my fault."

"Which you won't believe even if it's true," Val said.

"You know me so well, sister of mine."

Val smiled and stared up at the stars.

"Have all the chats you need to? Harrison, for example?"

"Tried that one; he gave me a very definite 'you don't call me, I will call you.' A lot to get his head around I suppose."

"Ya think? How about Fox Lisa? I half expected you and her to end up here tonight. You know, 'talking' things over." Val smirked.

"You couldn't be more wrong. Lisa is currently staying at Mai's."

"What?!"

"You heard right. It seems when Lizzy burst in, Mai took it upon herself to gather up the waitstaff and get them out the back. Clear out those who really didn't need to see dragons brawling. I'm amazed that no one else had the sense to think of it."

"For the most part everyone ignored the waiters all night—something about the fog . . . or a ward . . . or something," Val said.

"Yeah, and I'm glad Mai did remember. I don't trust whatever Estella and the rest had cooked up to deal with the image of warring dragons. But it still left her and a still-pissed Fox Lisa alone in an alleyway. And I have no idea yet what they have talked about," Griffen said.

"Mhmm, and whether it is good or bad, both will enjoy making you sweat it out. So they decided to camp out together. You do realize your love life is going to start becoming one of the Quarter's most popular spectator sports?"

"Maybe I should have Jerome start a new betting pool."

"He'd give you lousy odds. Sit down and shut up, Big Brother. Join me in a little stargazing."

Griffen did as he was told, pulling up a lawn chair and setting it next to Valerie's. He stared upward, watching a light cloud drift over a sliver of moon. It seemed to glow and sparkle as it obscured and revealed stars in its passing.

"So what does it look like to you?" Griffen said, looking for a shape in the cloud.

"Perfect timing," Valerie said.

It was such an odd comment that Griffen looked over at her. She knew that she was worrying him but couldn't help it. Even in the darkness, he could see the twin trails of tears that had begun to streak her face.

"Val!" Griffen sat up straight. "What's wrong?"

"Nothing . . . everything. No, nothing. I've just made a decision I should have made a while ago."

"And that would be?"

"To tell you something. Relax, Griffen. Lean back, look at the stars, or at least not at me."

Again, Griffen did as he was told, though this time it was obviously a lot harder. She watched the tension in him as he leaned back and looked upward. The night went silent, but for the soft sounds of Valerie crying. It wasn't sobs, it wasn't sniffles, just the gentle flow of emotion too long pent up. Griffen watched the cloud and waited.

"I'm sorry I held this back . . . You've just been so busy. So many things going on. Romance, the conclave, so much pressure, so much responsibility. I wanted to be strong for you, Big Brother."

"You are one of the strongest people I know, Valerie. Even though I'm still ticked that you could hide something like Lizzy from me, the reasons you did it for . . . Well, stupid as it was, strong and brave and self-sacrificing doesn't cover it. I've always admired that. Hell, I've always envied it, a little."

"That's because you're a dope."

"Well, of course."

Griffen's eyes flickered to his sister. She smiled a bit, so he did, too, then looked back up.

"I'm pregnant."

Griffen opened his mouth and closed it, as if he couldn't find the words. When he finally managed to find his voice, it was strained. Valerie couldn't sort through whatever mixed emotions filled that voice and doubted he could either.

"So that's what Lizzy meant. How long?"

"I've known for over a month, but . . . It was Nathaniel. No one else possible."

Valerie watched him out of the corner of her eye, and to his credit he kept his eyes firmly on the clouds above. Again, his mouth and throat worked, as if he were tasting words before letting them out. Still looking up, he reached out, and managed to find her hand in the darkness.

She tightened her grip around his and silently hoped he didn't say the one thing she couldn't stand to hear just then. *Sorry.*

It was a long pause before he spoke.

"I want one thing perfectly clear," he said, "it is Uncle Griffen. Uncle Grifter sounds too much like a bad forties cartoon character."

Val laughed and dropped his hand. She reached out and affectionately smacked Griffen on the back of the head. Griffen somehow managed not to get knocked out of the chair.

"I can't believe you just said that," she said.

"Yeah, I'm pretty unbelievable."

Griffen took her hand again and looked over to her face.

"You know that it'll be all right. I'll be here for you. God, Val, I should have been here for you from the beginning, and you should have known that. Lizzy I can understand, kind of. But this . . ."

"I did know that, but you had to be here for a lot of other people, too. And I had to be here for you."

"Family comes first, Valerie . . . Or at least, you come first."

"And what about this?" She touched her hand lightly to her stomach. "Does this family come first?"

This time, he didn't pause for a moment.

"Yeah. If you have decided to keep it, then I'm Uncle Griffen. And if I kill his father, we won't tell him till his sixteenth birthday."

"I get dibs."

"We'll talk."

The two shared a glance, and Griffen gave back Valerie's hand. Then he reached out and smacked her on the back of the head.

"Hey! What was that for?" Valerie said

She smacked him back, on the shoulder. She didn't want to give him a concussion.

"For the 'this is my fight' routine when you are pregnant? Getting bashed around a ballroom is not motherly behavior," Griffen said.

"Like I had much choice?"

"Not knocking me out of the way and keeping me from the fight sounds like a pretty valid choice to me," he said.

Valerie sighed.

"Yeah, well, maybe next time," she said.

"Next time?!"

Valerie smiled at his shocked tone. She shrugged.

"Truth be told, I expected her to go for the stomach a lot more. Guess she really was conflicted over the whole mess."

"You expected it, and still jumped into the deep end without looking. You got lucky, sis, real lucky."

"Me and you both, brother. Luck seems to be keeping us afloat these days. Almost as much as skill. Must be in the blood."

"Dragons' luck? Would explain a few things," Griffen said.

The two lapsed into silence again. Valerie looked over at her brother, and saw the deep frown. He shook his head, a little too hard, and she watched him force the expression away. Though he couldn't completely hide the look of concern in his eyes.

"I just can't let it go. Why, Valerie? Why keep this much from me?"

"I thought I had to. Mai pointed out how much trouble you were in right then."

"You told Mai instead of me?" Griffen didn't try to hide his surprise.

"No, she figured it out and came to me. I would have probably told you if we hadn't talked. But she made a lot of sense."

"Did she now . . . ?"

Griffen looked back up at the clouds, eyes narrowing ever so slightly. His sister knew him well enough to know that he was suddenly very angry with Mai. The two stared up at the sky together. Val broke the silence first.

"A puppy dog with one club foot."

"What?" Griffen blinked, not sure where that came from.

"The cloud, stupid. It's a puppy with a club foot. Pay attention," Val said, grinning.

"You pay attention, it's clearly a duck with a hat."

"What kind of hat?"

"Cowboy hat."

"You're crazy, Big Brother. I think you are suffering from lack of alcohol."

"Yeah, probably. How about we go out together?"

"Why not, it's early. For this town."

"Yeah. It'll be nice not to have to worry about what supernatural nut I'll run into at my favorite watering hole," Griffen said.

The two stood, and Valerie grabbed Griffen and hugged him as tight as she could. He didn't comment as his back popped, just hugged her back fiercely. She let him go finally, smiling hugely, and turned toward the gate.

"But!" he called after her, "strictly nonalcoholic beverages for you!"

"Ah! He's nagging already! I knew no good deed went unpunished!"

The two laughed and headed out into the night.

Epilogue

It was a small clinic, tucked away far from the tourist areas of the Quarter. It was the kind of place that really didn't ask questions. Run by the kind of doctors who didn't care about their patients' pasts, but were just worried about making sure they had a future. Mose had surprised Griffen by telling him just how much their gambling organization contributed yearly to the clinic. It and several other shady groups in the city.

You never knew when you might need such a place.

One of Mose's people, or Griffen's people depending on how one counted, sat in the lobby. His instructions were plain: call up the line if anything happened, and don't interfere. He wasn't told any more than that, or any less.

A long, black car pulled up in front of the clinic. The type of car that never, ever got seen on this side of town. Not even passing through. Three men, built strong and solid, stepped out of the car. They all looked professional, dressed in suits cut just big enough to hide the bulge under each of their jackets. Yet they also seemed to have a family resemblance.

Next out of the car was a short, round woman who still seemed just as solid as the boys. Her face was fleshy and plain, but her eyes were sharp as a hawk's. Even out in the street, the man inside could tell that she was watching everything. This was someone he would never, ever play cards with, and that was how he made his living.

The four of them came into the clinic. They didn't stop to ask for directions. They didn't pay any attention to anyone but watched everyone just the same. The woman seemed to lead, even though two of the men stood in front of her and the third just behind.

They walked to the room Griffen's man had been told to watch. Didn't knock, didn't hesitate, just went on inside. He pulled out his cell, put out the call, and did not interfere. Orders were orders, and he was glad for these ones. He had thought it was the woman inside the room he had to worry about.

Inside, Lizzy lay on a hospital bed, and even in the dim light, she looked awful. Her face was a collection of bruises. Gauze was packed over one eye and wrapped around her head. Most of her was hidden by a blanket, but at least one leg was in a cast and an IV provided a constant drip of painkillers.

She stirred, seeming half-conscious, and her good eye rolled for a few moments before tracking, even the fractured colors in it appearing pale and sickly. When it caught sight of the woman standing just inside the doorway, it widened. Lizzy tried to sit up and groaned, falling back in bed.

Her voice was soft, quiet. A wounded-kitten voice.

"M-m-mmmother?" she stammered.

Melinda stepped up to the bed and picked up the chart hanging off the end of it. With one hand on the bed rail, she read it while her fingers tapped a slow rhythm. Her anger apparent only in the force of her drumming fingers, which were slowly denting the metal.

She put down the chart, and her voice was molten iron as she spoke two simple words that made her daughter flinch and try to curl in on herself.

"What. Happened?"

From *New York Times* Bestselling Author
ROBERT ASPRIN
and
JODY LYNN NYE

DRAGONS DEAL

As head dragon and owner of a successful gambling operation in New Orleans, Griffen McCandles has a lot on his plate. Especially since the Krewe of Fafnir—a society of dragons—has asked him to be the king of its Mardi Gras parade. Being the king is a huge honor, and despite the extra responsibilities, Griffen can't resist the krewe's offer to lead the biggest party of the year.

But not everyone is happy with Griffen's new leadership status. A group of powerful dragons is conspiring to bankrupt his business, from the inside out. And when a young dragon in Griffen's employ is murdered, it becomes clear that certain dragons will stop at nothing to dethrone the new king . . .